Embracing

The Zoe Eferhild Chronicles
E.C. Lawton

First Edition: December 2024

Names: Lawton, E.C., author.

Artist: Xenia

Title: Embracing, The Zoe Eferhild Chronicles, Book Three/ by E.C. Lawton

Description: First edition.

Audience: Ages 18 and up.

ISBNs: ebook: 979-8-9885648-6-7; paperback: 979-8-9885648-7-4; hardback: 979-8-9885648-8-1

Printed in the United States of America.

Contents

To those struggling to embrace all that you are.
I hope you find your courage to love all of you.
You are all stars in the darkness.
All of my love,
-E.C. Lawton

This story contains material that may be uncomfortable for readers. This work is intended for readers eighteen and older. While Zoe's story is one of hope and designed to empower those struggling with mental wellness, reader discretion is advised.
Content Warning: allusions and references to suicide; sexual assault (non-specific or graphic- flashbacks); self-harm scars; recovery from alcohol abuse; drug abuse; domestic violence; death of a family member; Post Traumatic Stress Disorder (PTSD); depression; anxiety; violence.

Quick Reference Guide

<u>Kingdom of Canis</u>

King Aldrich

Queen Farron

<u>Court of Vega</u>

Lord Astral Elvy

Lady Astral Zoe

Star Elemental Realm for Water

Realm of Lyra

Delmira—Second

Clodovea—Third

Blaz—Emissary to Canopus

Imelda—Emissary to Arcturus

Finnian—Emissary to Rigil

<u>Court of Algol</u>

Lord Astral Oleander

*Queen Hesperia

*Tiergan—Sublunary Leader

Star Elemental Realm for Spirit

Realm of Perseus

Zadie—Second to Oleander

Court of Rigil
Lord Astral Terran

Lady Astral Sierra

Star Elemental Realm for Ground

Realm of Centaurus

Court of Arcturus
Lord Astral Kai

Lady Astral Seraphina

Star Elemental Realm for Fire

Realm of Bootes

Court of Canopus
Lord Astral Abel

Lady Astral Aura

Star Elemental Realm for Air

Realm of Carina

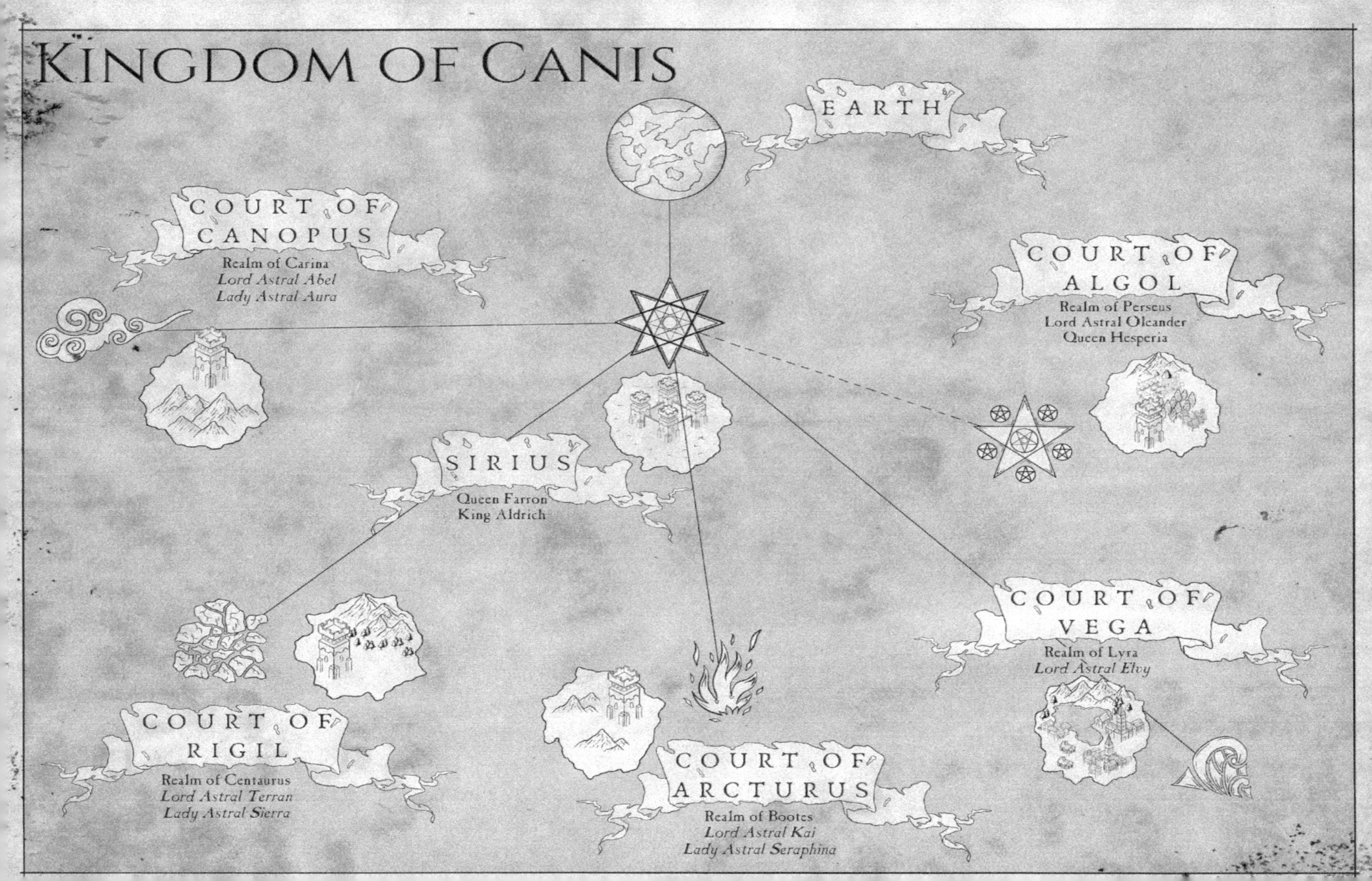

KINGDOM OF CANIS
EARTH
COURT OF CANOPUS
Realm of Carina
Lord Astral Abel
Lady Astral Aura
COURT OF ALGOL
Realm of Perseus
Lord Astral Oleander
Queen Hesperia
SIRIUS
Queen Farron
King Aldrich
COURT OF VEGA
Realm of Lyra
Lord Astral Elvy
COURT OF RIGIL
Realm of Centaurus
Lord Astral Terran
Lady Astral Sierra
COURT OF ARCTURUS
Realm of Bootes
Lord Astral Kai
Lady Astral Seraphina

1

Prologue

THE ARCHER

Born in sorrow. Forged in fury. Created in desperation.

That was the fate of my first daughter.

I'd become the thing I hated most in my haste to make my father and celestial—Algol—pay for the torment he had ordered of the mortals of Earth and the immortals of the star courts.

I'd created a well of darkness within her. The shadows I'd felt in her conception had fueled her very spirit. Starlight seemed to recoil away from the shadows that constantly surrounded her, clinging to her as if they loved her.

A love I did not want to feel.

And I hated myself for it.

Or maybe what I hated most was knowing that I had done *this*. I corrupted her. Maybe I loathed the fact that a secret part of me knew I would always love her.

I felt her presence with no need to turn from the palace window where I watched my child—my creation—kill the bioluminescent plants that were interwoven into the gardens. She smirked as the flowers wilted to nothing, and my stomach turned sour at the evil I bore witness to.

"What am I supposed to do, Nova?" I whispered in defeat. "The future is unclear."

Nova placed a gentle, tattooed hand on my shoulder. An oddly affectionate gesture for her. I didn't want to turn to see the never-ending cosmos in her eyes, staring back at me with pity and *knowing*.

"I didn't listen to you," I admitted.

"No," she agreed. "Hesperia will not bring peace to the realms."

"I thought I knew better than my father," I said, not sure of who I was trying to convince in this moment. "That I could be better. Do better."

My voice broke on the last word. Tears welled in my eyes, but I refused to give in to the grief I felt. There was no greater failure than me.

"She's cruel. So hollow," I said, distraught. I clenched my teeth together, trying to bring myself to do what must be done, but I would likely fail this, too.

"Her fate is not yet sealed, Archer," Nova whispered, eyes glazing over in search of a future that had yet to pass.

"I have seen enough, Nova. If I don't stop her now… she will bring chaos—death—to the star realms."

Nova held her hand up to silence me, and my heart beat loud enough that I was sure she could hear it.

"The blade strapped across your back will not accomplish what you seek tonight. What is set in motion is set in motion. Hesperia now has a role to play."

I slid my hands through my hair and let my right hand rest on the hilt of my sword. This could all be over in seconds. I just had to bring myself to do it.

"I must do this," I whispered, pulling out of Nova's grip, and she let me go.

"And what of the venom in your pocket?" she called, and I stilled, sweat pooling at my back and neck.

"It holds the punishment I deserve after such an act," I said, voice strained. "To murder my own child… I deserve nothing less."

Nova crashed through the mental shields of my mind and flooded my vision with the future that would come to pass if it was ended before the right moment. Darkness eclipsed Sirius entirely. The starlight—the hope—disappeared from the Kingdom of Canis and spread like a poison throughout the universe.

I crashed to my knees, a broken male. My chest tightened with a pain that even the most experienced healer could not aid. My hands would forever be stained red, and it would be my burden to bear.

"No, Archer," Nova said, crouching next to me with elegant grace. Her translucent skin glistened under the light of the cosmos. "She will burn. For you. With you. The light that lives within her is the only source powerful enough to vanquish the darkness of Hesperia."

I mustered up enough courage to look into Nova's cosmic eyes, and she continued.

"If you end your existence, the star realms will forever suffer. There will be no one to mend what has been broken by the celestials. And if you kill Hesperia, your spirit will be so stained that no child of yours could be worthy of the fate of Realm-Healer."

"How do I create such a child?" I whispered in desperation.

Nova shook her head, smiling softly as I gripped her hand in mine. She didn't flinch.

"Then what? What do I need to do to move forward?"

She raised an eyebrow curiously, as if the answer were obvious. I suppose it was.

"Love, Archer," she answered and rose from her knees, holding out her hand to help me up. "A child with the heart of a wild mortal girl will heal the star realms. And she is the only hope we have against Hesperia… and the corruption of the celestials."

"How do I find her?" I asked, frame trembling.

"Follow the stars, of course. They'll lead you home."

2

The Mask I Wear

ZOE

I'd never noticed how loudly clocks ticked with each second that passed before now.

One fleeting moment gone. Nothing more than a sound that documented the passing of time.

Except that one seemingly insignificant noise felt like a weighted eternity without my flame—Elvy—by my side.

Twenty-one seconds. Twenty-one ticks of the clock were all it'd taken my deranged sister to steal him from me. The word *sister* tasted foul across my tongue, even though I kept silent as I beat the living hell out of a punching bag.

My knuckles bled and screamed in pain, and I welcomed it. I refused healings, wanting to feel something real. I needed some kind of evidence that I was alive, which was an equally difficult burden to bear in knowing that I was safe—relatively speaking, anyway.

But Elvy was not. My sister controlled his shadows. A sister I had no idea existed until the very recent past. Though I still could not work out why she loathed me so much, and our shared father—The Archer—had gone radio silent since the bombshell news threw my world upside down. Why I expected anything different, I don't know.

I screamed, letting my rage fuel my adrenaline.

I slept because my body demanded it. If it were up to my mind, sleep would mean nothing to me.

"Zo?" a familiar voice called, pulling me from the storm of shadows around me. I no longer kept my darkness at bay. My shadows knew me intimately and answered to me like a yearning lover. If I had learned to embrace them sooner, Elvy would still be safely by my side. But I'd failed.

I would not do so again.

I turned to face Blaz, and I noticed the subtle flinch at the sight of my black eyes. He quickly hid his discomfort and crossed his arms pointedly.

"You're going to be late," he said. Blaz had recently moved into the role of the commander of the Shadowed Legion of the Court of Vega. It was a role Elvy usually held as Lord Astral, and I had too much on my plate to take it over myself. Not to mention, Blaz outweighed me in war strategy by many centuries.

Delmira—mine and Elvy's second—had recently been the commander while a few of us had been searching the star courts for The Archer's bow. She'd done nothing but a great job, but even she was spread thin.

Now that we had the bow, we also had a whole host of new issues to address. I was tired of meetings and playing politics. However, I would do whatever was required of me to protect my flame and fulfill my fate.

"Is it bad to say that I don't care?" I asked as Jelly, my bonded simargl, bounded through the door, wagging her tail. Jelly was in her more tame form of a border collie with angel-soft wings, but her looks were quite deceptive. A snarling beast of a wolf with fatal fire magic lurked within her. I wore her brand proudly across my chest.

"You know I hate these things, too," he said, joining me in scratching Jelly's upturned belly. My heart seemed to thaw, warming some at the love my guardian held for me. It wouldn't last, though. It never did. And if I were being truly honest with myself, I didn't want it to. My heart was an empty hearth without its flame, and the bonds that tied me to Elvy grieved him with each passing second.

"I can do this," I coached myself.

"Have you decided what you're going to tell them?" he asked, cupping the back of his neck anxiously.

"No," I said honestly. "I don't know what the right thing is anymore. I'm hoping my *sight* will tell me something."

My *sight* and I weren't on the best of terms. I was a little pissed that my magic had failed to *see* Elvy being taken from me, but deep down, I knew that thought was illogical. I'd had the sense of foreboding for a long while before he'd been taken, but we'd had to go through with the mission. It hadn't been optional, and we'd paid the consequences.

"Let me take care of that," Blaz said, motioning towards the blood coating my knuckles, but I stopped him. The thought of anyone other than Elvy healing me repulsed me, as unreasonable as the thought was.

"I need it, Blaz," I whispered, welcoming the sting of pain. "I deserve it."

The truth tasted bitter, and my heart ached, knowing my flame was suffering at Hesperia's hands. My sister was a dead female walking. I felt like all the work I'd done in therapy with Emma had been for nothing, but I knew deep within me that wasn't true. Emma's death was another piece of evidence that Hesperia deserved nothing less than death.

"No, you don't," he said, bumping his shoulder next to mine. "Just like you don't need those," he added, turning my chin towards him, exposing my shadowed eyes.

"It's who I am, Blaz."

"No, Zoe. It's a part of you. Only a part."

I wanted to snap, but it would prove futile against the goodness that Blaz saw in me. I turned towards the mirror, taking in the reflection of the female in front of me. Dark purple circles lay beneath my eyes. My typically shiny brown-silver hair seemed a little duller. I'd lost some weight, but my muscles were still strong from the excessive training I'd forced my body through.

The immortal mark that resembled an eight-pointed star with four cardinal points glowed blue and black as I embraced my truest form. My semi-translucent wings sprouted from my back with blues, blacks, and whites embedded in the feathers. I tilted my shoulders so I could see the map of the stars across my shoulder blades, partially hidden by the black tank top I wore.

Blaz had a nearly identical one across his bare chest, but the stars for Algol and Vega were larger on mine and the constellation of The Archer rested above the map of the Kingdom of Canis. I traced the invisible scar that had once marked the night that I'd tried to end my existence while I'd still been human.

I'd never felt that level of sorrow after witnessing my sister murdered in front of me until Elvy had been seized from me, too.

Now the scar was gone. It'd healed completely after I'd found all the pieces of The Archer's bow. I didn't know whether to be grateful or pissed off about it. The rage and grief coiled in my gut again, and I closed my eyes, trying to find my center.

Elvy's steady heart, and the call of the ocean, had become my gravity. While I couldn't hear him anymore, I focused on my favorite memories of him—of us. I let his warmth and safety flood my soul. He was mine. And I was his.

When I opened my eyes again, brilliant green irises greeted me, but I didn't tuck the shadows away. They lingered around my frame, comforting me, and I embraced them.

"I'll become who I must to win this war, Blaz," I said, voice strong.

"And I'll be right here by your side," he vowed. "The Luminaries all will."

The Luminaries were the Vega's inner court members. Delmira—our second. Clodovea—our third. Imelda was Clodovea's partner and the emissary to the Court of Arcturus—fire realm. Finnian was not only Delmira's twin but also the emissary to the Court of Rigil—the realm for ground. Blaz, who had something going on with Delmira, though the stars only knew what that entailed, was the emissary to the Court of Canopus—the realm of air.

The Vega court was the star elemental realm for water, and there was a fifth and final star court, Algol—the spirit realm. Up until my Emergence as an immortal, Algol had been separated from the Kingdom of Canis when Hesperia had severed the tethers. We hadn't announced who the emissary for the spirit realm would be, but it wasn't like we'd had time, as we'd been searching the star courts for the lost bow of my father.

And fighting Hesperia along the way.

I was about to face representatives from all the star courts on what our next move should be against her, and I didn't have the slightest clue because we were all at a serious disadvantage.

She had control over Elvy.

And Elvy had unmatched death magic that could mist away thousands of immortals with a nod of his head.

My heart sank. How was I supposed to win this battle? How was I supposed to protect him and save the realms, too?

"Come on, Zo," Blaz said, holding out his hand to lead me away from the gym. He ever so subtly sent healing magic to my open wounds, and I decided against chastising him for it.

Jelly followed dutifully beside us as we moved through the hallways of the ocean-side manor, made up of glittering moonstone. Accents of gold and midnight blue were delicately placed, bringing warmth to the white of the stone.

Jelly's soft wings gently nudged me, letting me know she was with me. My sweet little dragon.

"We'll get him back," she whispered through our bond, sending her angel-like voice through my mind. The determination in her voice was a vow bound by the stars themselves.

"I know," I murmured back through our guardian bond.

Blaz paused outside of mine and Elvy's bedroom.

"Should I come get you before the Astrals arrive?"

I shook my head. "No, I'll see you there."

He bowed slightly, and Jelly followed me into the bedroom that felt lifeless without Elvy. It was the one place I could break down in peace, and I let my mask crumble. The pain that shot through every atom of my body nearly caused me to collapse to the floor, but I held resolute.

"What I wouldn't give to be able to heal this?" I muttered, then thought better of it. The pain reminded me that I was alive. And if I were alive, then I still had breath in my lungs to do the impossible.

The impossible was something I was well acquainted with. I'd Emerged as Zoe Eferhild, Realm-Healer—Emerging of Legends. I'd threatened the life of Algol, and I'd brought my sister back to life. Saving my flame would be my fate if I had anything to say about it, and I most certainly did.

My thoughts briefly moved to Freyja—my sister. She was off in the realm of Nova in her own Emerging trials. I had no doubt that she would Emerge as an immortal. There was no soul more worthy. The cosmos shone down through the skylight in this never-ending realm of night, and I sent my strength to my sister.

A knock sounded at the door, startling me from my thoughts. I wiped the tear that had escaped and opened the door to find Octavia standing before me with a cup of coffee.

"Something told me you needed this," she said, handing me the one thing I loved, whether I was mortal or immortal. I was pretty sure my blood was at least fifty percent caffeine.

"Thank you," I said, taking it graciously. "You truly make the best around here."

"I haven't seen you much in the library," she said pointedly, and a twinge of guilt passed through me. Octavia was one of the Keepers in the library, and she'd been an incredible friend to me in my transition to becoming an Emerging immortal. But there was too much of Elvy in the library. Though there was too much of him everywhere, really.

"I'm sorry, Octavia," I said. "It's just…" I paused, not knowing what to say.

"You don't have to explain," she said quickly. "Just wanted to remind you that you have a place there. And an ear if needed."

"I appreciate that," I said, voice stiffer than I'd meant.

"I have something for you," she said, pulling out a fraying tome from her satchel. I raised my eyebrow curiously. "From Finnian."

"Oh," I said, taking the fragile book from her.

"Just a little light reading?" she asked, a little too curiously, though I could not blame her. It was odd.

"He's helping me with something," I said, brushing it off.

She gave a small, sad smile that she tried to hide, and I pretended not to see it.

"Please send for me if either of you needs help finding anything," she said, turning away.

"Thank you," I said, shutting the door behind me and sliding down until I sat on the floor. The blue-green flame of the fireplace crackled a soothing song, and I tried to embrace it.

It hadn't taken me long to figure out what Finnian and Zadie were trying to achieve under the direction of Oleander when they'd returned to Vega. Whether it was Finn's pity or loyalty that led him to tell me, I wasn't sure.

Jelly laid her head on my lap, and I welcomed the pressure and sensation, grounding me to this moment.

I let my shadows fall, and they caressed me softly as they called for vengeance for our bond—our mate.

And I would answer them.

3

Emerging

FREYJA

I'd never seen so many stars, and that was saying something, having lived in the star court of Algol for several months with Ander.

Living was a generous word. I'd technically been dead for most of it, but Zoe had bargained for my life. It'd been no surprise that she'd come out the victor with the odds against her.

And now I was here in the star realms to prove my worth as an Emerging. She'd gotten me here, and it was up to me to see this through.

I would not fail.

"Freyja," a female called from the shore.

I was currently panting for dear life on my back, having just made it to the sandy beach. The warm water washed against me, taking the sand with it. I gingerly sat up to find a female covered in dark tattoos of a language I had no hope of knowing against pale white skin. Her eyes struck fear into me as the cosmos swirled within them.

"You must be Nova," I whispered.

"Yes, child," she said, waving a hand, and I was instantly dry. "Come, follow me."

I had no choice but to obey and trailed behind her gliding form.

There wasn't much to my surroundings other than a glowing gargantuan palace before me and some cliffs off in the distance. The island had little else, and I wondered how long I'd be here.

"That is entirely up to you," Nova said, reading my thoughts, or perhaps my future. I didn't think she'd take too kindly to being questioned.

"When do we start?" I asked, ready to take on the trials and get back to my family.

"Patience, Emerging," she said, leading me to a massive dining table filled to the brim with a variety of colorful foods. I couldn't place them all, but my stomach wasn't opposed to trying them. "Eat. Rest. Then the trials will begin."

"I don't suppose we could speed them along?" I asked, knowing I was walking on thin ice.

"That is entirely up to you," she said again, turning her head in my direction. "Do not worry about those in the star courts. You have your own battle to face, child. It is important that you remain present."

The viper in me wanted to snap, but I didn't have a death wish, so I nodded.

"Alright," I said, taking a bite of fruit. I immediately fell into bliss and began eating more, noticing how hungry I truly was.

"Do you have any questions?" she asked, watching me stuff my face. She ate nothing.

"How many trials?"

"Three," she confirmed. "Each trial will be built on the other. Should you fail, your mortal death will be completed. There are no more second chances."

"I won't need any," I said firmly.

Nova said nothing, which didn't exactly fill me with hope, but I was in control of my fate. Not her.

She smiled.

"And I'll Emerge as an immortal of Algol?" I asked.

"Should you succeed, yes, child."

I took another bite of a purple exotic fruit that left a bitter aftertaste, but was somehow delicious. When Zoe had first brought me back to my mortal flesh, my senses had been overwhelming, and I fully embraced them now, having gone years without feeling, tasting, or *experiencing* anything.

"What's Algol's problem, anyway?" I asked, licking my fingers after getting some type of berry sauce on them in my haste to try a bite of literally everything offered.

She raised an eyebrow at my boldness.

"The celestials are… emotional beings. Jealously is dangerous to creatures so powerful."

I rolled my eyes. "Sounds like an excuse."

"Where there is evil, there is also an insurmountable ability to be good. Some beings choose wrong."

"Will they ever choose right?" I asked, sighing in satisfaction at my full stomach.

"It is not for mortals to know."

"Ah, but I don't plan to stay mortal, Nova," I answered.

"I see you and your sister share the same ability to annoy those far beyond your own comprehension," she replied, dodging the question.

I smiled, not disagreeing. My sister and I had never been afraid of anything. Not until the night that was the catalyst for getting us all here in the first place.

Nova's eyes softened, and I stiffened, slipping my mask of strength on. I desired no one's pity.

"Come, Freyja. It's time for you to rest," she said, standing and motioning for me to follow her down a hall made of solid white marble. I rubbed my arms to keep the cool breeze off me, but it was instantly warmer at the thought.

"Should you need anything in my realm, you need only think it," she said, opening a door to her left.

It was cozy, with a large, seemingly fluffy bed and a balcony leading out to the ocean.

"Is this the same room my sister was in?" I asked, longing for some attachment to home.

"Yes, Emerging."

I wanted to ask her more questions, but turned to find her gone. I explored the room, opening drawers and doors to find a bathroom and a closet. A dress made of shimmering fabric that transitioned to turquoise towards the bottom made my heart still. I recognized this dress as Zoe's from the last night of her humanity. Somehow it had ended up here in the realm of Nova, and I pulled it into my arms, breathing in the fabric, hoping to smell something familiar and comforting.

Zoe's scent still lingered in the folds, and a tear escaped my eye. She was here with me. Always.

"I'm going to make us proud, Zo. Just hang in there until I get back," I whispered to no one.

I gingerly placed the dress back in its place and stripped off my own clothes to hop into the bath. The water was the perfect temperature, and I let the sensation relax my tensed muscles. My thoughts drifted to Ander, wondering what he was up to in Algol and if he was safe. I already missed the endless blue of his eyes, and the way my body seemed to be so in tune with him.

I quickly washed my body, leaving my hair alone in its double braid.

As I lay down in the most comfortable bed I could wish for, I pushed out my hopes into the universe and to those I was fighting to get back to… Ander, Zo, Jelly, Tiergan—even Zadie.

"I'll see you soon," I murmured as my mind succumbed to fatigue, promptly wandering to the world of dreams.

***

I was so anxious I could barely eat a bite of the breakfast that had magically appeared by my bedside, but I forced down bite after bite, knowing I would need my strength. Mindlessly, I rubbed my thumb across the calluses beneath the base of my fingers, grateful that I was prepared for anything. Ander had helped me remember my courage and find new spirit to build on. I had been pissed at him through a lot of it, but I'd known it was what I'd needed. To feel strong. He'd known that, too.

A knock sounded at the door, drawing me from my memories of Ander training me mercilessly… and the rewards afterwards. God, I could not wait to get back to him.

"It is time, Emerging," Nova called, opening the door.

I smoothed down my black mesh shirt and utility pants. Time to meet my fate.

I stood from the bed and followed Nova through the palace and up the grounds to the cliffs I'd seen when I'd arrived here last night. The rocky terrain leading up to the plateau was difficult to navigate, but once we reached the top, the rocks turned to voluminous grass with twinkling blue plants scattered throughout.

"Your first trial begins now, Freyja," she said, as if that explained everything.

"What do I do?" I asked.

"Into the stars, Emerging," she said, disappearing right before me.

I whirled around, straining my eyes painfully, trying to find my challenger, but no attack came.

My heartbeat slowed, and I put my hands on my hips in thought. Into the stars. I gazed into the brilliantly lit night sky that was so vivid I had no problem seeing long distances. The ocean reflected beneath the surface, mirroring the sky above exactly.

"Well, going up isn't an option," I said, pulling off my black combat boots and slipping my pants off right after. I silently thanked myself for going for full-coverage underwear.

I placed the balls of my feet at the edge of the cliff, feeling the pressure against the stone as I calculated my leap. I'd never feared heights, but even I had to admit this was a little intimidating with little clue what was down there.

"To hell with it," I said, filling my core with every bit of resolve that I could. Once I jumped, there was no going back. "Here goes nothing."

For my sister, who stood in the same position in an oath to bring me back.

For Ander.

For myself.

I leapt.

4

Beneath the Stars
CLODOVEA

Falling for Imelda had been as easy as breathing.

But neither of us had been quick to trust each other in the beginning… and in the middle, too.

And with both of us being born immortals, time was once a luxury we could afford to indulge in until we were both good and ready.

Time was an uncertain foe now. There were no promises that we would both make it to tomorrow's rising moon.

Imelda brushed my cheek softly, instantly calming the worry that had threatened to take me from this moment.

"You haven't eaten much," she said, holding a large golden berry against my lips, and I bit into it gently, holding her honey eyes in mine.

"Delicious," I said, licking the sweet nectar from my lips.

Imelda brushed her lips against mine, tasting for herself.

"I love you, you know," I said, pulling her closer, and her laugh sent a thrill through me.

"I do know," she answered, leaning back. "Eat… then maybe you can have dessert."

She bit down on her lip with intention, and I shoved the rest of the berry in my mouth eagerly.

"Slow down, Clove!" she yelled, but there was amusement in her tone.

It really was a beautiful night, and she made it all the more stunning. We were having a picnic in a hidden garden in one of the forests in Musterion—a newly revealed city that had been lost to the immortals of Vega until Finnian and Imelda had found it while I'd been with Zoe searching for the bow.

I wouldn't know we were beneath the surface of the ocean right now with how tall the evergreen trees stood around us. Just above the treetops, the top of the terrarium-like dome shimmered beneath the cosmos reflected in the water.

"Do you think someone from Rigil created this garden?" Imelda asked, gently brushing her delicate fingers across the petal of a glowing blue flower. All the plants surrounding us glowed every color of the rainbow, but blues and greens seemed to dominate the most.

"I wouldn't be surprised. This city was created when the star courts all lived in harmony."

"It's beautiful magic," she mumbled, taking another bite of fruit.

"Maybe it was created by lovers to escape everyone else," I said, crawling towards her with a different kind of hunger in my eyes.

She didn't pull away this time, laying down on her back, and my long braids provided a curtain around our faces.

Imelda turned her neck in offering, and I slowly trailed kisses down to the base of her collar, biting her gently, sending a shiver through us both.

We both wore our midnight blue leathers, and I unzipped her top slowly while helping her remove the sports bra underneath.

She lay back down laughing, and I kissed her greedily.

My worries faded to nothing when I was with her. In all the realms, she was the one soul I could never live without.

I relished the gasp she let out as she gripped her hand into my hair, coaxing me to give her more. There was nothing I wouldn't give to this female I loved more than my own life.

"Bridge your hips," I said, sitting up, and she didn't question me.

I pulled the rest of her Shadowed uniform off, tossing it to the side.

"Stunning," I said, letting my gaze roam over her soft curves.

She sat up, pulling on the zipper of my leathers, and I stood, slipping them all the way off.

"Come here," she beckoned, motioning me back into position over her.

I swirled my tongue down the sensitive parts of her, demanding pleasure from her. I trailed my fingers down her muscled abdomen and used my fingers to elicit her bliss.

"Greedy, little thing," I murmured, moving my lips lower, tasting just how much she was enjoying me—enjoying us.

"More," she said, and I lifted my other hand to explore her body, creating as much friction as I could for her, savoring the way she felt as I sent her into euphoria. I helped her extend her pulses of pleasure as I ached painfully for her.

It only took mere seconds for me to rip off the rest of my clothes, and her eyes darkened at my exposed skin.

Imelda pushed me into the ground, using her fingers and mouth to bring out the elation writhing inside my body.

"Imelda," I said, close to coming apart for her already.

"Let me help you forget," she whispered against my skin, sending a ripple of desire through me. I moved against her as I braced for her to unleash me.

She dragged her finger down my body, sending her water magic to the most sensitive parts of me, cooling the water to almost freezing, and I cried out in pleasure.

I found my release with her, as sweat drenched us both.

I pulled her into my arms, cradling her against me as she tangled her limbs in mine.

"I love you, Clove," she whispered, as we both stared into the glowing treetops. "Do you think we should move to Musterion when all of this is over?"

I didn't like thinking about the future anymore. Nothing was guaranteed, and I didn't like breaking promises, be it by my death or not. But she needed reassurance in this moment, and I would give that to her.

"I'd love that," I said, pulling her closer while stroking her hair.

I smiled with a secret I'd successfully kept hidden from her. I'd finally found the perfect ring for her after wanting to make her my wife for years, but she deserved the best of everything. Now, I just had to find the right way to ask her, and I had no idea when that was supposed to be.

We'd talked about getting married a few times over the time we'd spent together, but it hadn't felt necessary. Now I wanted to be connected to her in every way that a soul could bond.

"I've missed this," she said, snuggling in closer somehow. I felt like she would meld to my flesh if she adjusted anymore. "Just being in your presence. Feeling your skin on mine. We've been apart for too long recently."

"I know," I said, stroking her arm aimlessly. "I wish it were different."

"No, you don't," she said as a matter of fact, and she wasn't entirely wrong. My duty to Elvy and Zoe—and my court—was important to me. I didn't know that it was more important than her, though.

"I can love our positions in the Luminaries and not like that it takes us away from each other. They aren't mutually exclusive."

"You're right," she agreed.

I sighed, knowing our moment alone was coming to a close.

"We need to start making our way to the surface. The Astrals will be arriving soon."

Imelda groaned, hiding her face.

"What is Zoe going to do? We can't betray Elvy," she said, and I agreed with her.

"I trust her to make the right call," I answered, and I meant it. "She loves Elvy more than any of us, and she still has a duty to the immortals of Vega and the entire Kingdom of Canis. All we can do is present a united front and support the decision she makes. No matter what."

Imelda sat up, nodding her head in agreement. "She has had our backs. And we'll have hers. If anyone can find a way out of this, she will."

"Come on, let's get dressed," I said, handing Imelda her clothes.

"Let's go support our Lady Astral," she echoed.

5

Something Wicked
DELMIRA

With Blaz taking the Shadowed Legion over after the mission to find the bow concluded, my mental load lessened slightly. Emphasis on the word slightly. Zoe had thrown herself into the running of Vega after Elvy had been captured, but I was still taking care of most things. I couldn't expect her to do it alone, nor did I want her to.

Until we got Elvy back, she had our band of misfits, we called the Luminaries, and I was the alpha of the pack. I didn't care if Blaz had been around longer… I was the Astral's second for a reason.

Being the second had become my identity in a way. I wasn't sure how to be anyone else, and that was a thought I wasn't ready for. The pressures of leading Vega in their absence had gotten to me in ways I wasn't sure I'd ever recover from. I swallowed my thoughts. No matter what I may want or need, I'd sworn an oath. I had a duty to serve and protect. I would not break it.

I returned my focus to the present, taking stock of what needed to be done. Blaz had gone to check on Zoe, and I was trying to find my twin brother, Finnian. He had been avoiding me for the past few days, and I planned to find out why.

I centered myself, trying to locate his mind using the vibrations of the psychic field to which he and I were so linked. For once, I really wished our powers were reversed, so I could figure out what the hell was going on with him.

Controlling emotions was a neat trick, but reading thoughts? Now, that was something special.

This also meant he always knew when I was coming. Even with my shields up, we were just too attuned to each other's minds to ever fully block out the other.

"Got him," I said to no one.

My mood soured a little when I realized where he was. The Hall of Memories. The creepiest place in the entire universe. How anyone could stand the silence for longer than a few minutes was beyond my understanding.

If Finn thought he could hide in there, he was sorely mistaken. I'd pick a fight anytime and anywhere.

The city streets of Vega had lost their life with almost all of our immortals in Musterion, where we could keep them safe from Hesperia, though if we lost I suspected it wouldn't matter where they were hiding. She'd ensure that we are all obliterated to stardust.

I stood outside the moonstone hall that had taken a liking to my brother. There was something sentient about this place that I feared would go to bat for Finn if it felt like he was in danger, but I wasn't scared enough that I wouldn't go in there.

"I'm going to find out what you're up to," I said, taking a step towards the entrance, but the door slammed open, revealing my brother.

"Delm?" he asked. "What are you doing out here?"

"Where's Zadie?" I asked, knowing the red-headed female had been hanging with Finn for the past few days.

"She's gone back to Algol for now. Oleander will be arriving in her place for the war summit."

"What were you two doing?" I asked, trying to keep the demand from my tone. Blaz has been trying to help me be a little softer on my deliveries, but I'd never been a quick student of societal pleasantries.

"What any consenting couple does in times of war," he answered, folding his arms across his chest. A sign that he was lying.

"You can't lie to me, Finn," I said. "You consider the Hall of Memories sacred."

So much for my soft response, but he laughed, stepping towards me with hands raised.

"Since when do you keep secrets from me?" I asked seriously

It had always been Finn and me against the world, whether we were mortal or immortal. We didn't keep secrets from each other.

"Delmira, don't make me lie to you," he said, pressing his lips together.

I searched his eyes, looking for an inkling of what was going through his mind that he couldn't trust me with. He revealed nothing, a master of masking his feelings when he needed to. He and I were both excellent at that.

"Just tell me you're not in trouble," I begged, ready to battle for him if I needed to.

"I'm not in trouble," he promised, but there was something off about it.

"You're not alone in it?" I asked, grasping for something to calm my nerves.

"No, I'm not alone," he agreed, and I knew in my gut that Zadie knew about it. I didn't trust her with a ten-foot pole, but my brother did, and I respected his judgement… most of the time.

"Does Zoe know?" I asked.

"You think I would act without her orders?" he mused, and I read his emotions clearly. Zoe was aware of whatever they were doing. I wasn't sure how I felt about that.

"Just promise me you'll tell me if it gets too much."

"Should the time come that I must act, you will be the first to know, Delm," he swore, and I believed him. "But let's hope for everyone's sake it doesn't come to that."

"Twelve strikes?" I asked, referencing a code we'd used as mortals. If we ever got separated, we had made a pact to go to the top of the bell tower and wait until the last stroke of midnight. If one of us didn't show up, we were in trouble. The worst kind.

Ever so subtly, Finn nodded, and my heart sank. Twelve strikes meant he was preparing for the worst, and there was nothing I could do to stop him. I wasn't sure I wanted to if things were this hopeless.

I wrapped myself in his arms, and he embraced me back fiercely.

"I believe in you, even if you are my annoying little brother," I murmured, trying to find some kind of humor to latch onto.

"By ninety seconds, Delm," he said, and I knew he rolled his eyes.

I pulled back, hands on my hips.

"And don't you forget it," I said, punching his shoulder.

A wave of ease flooded us, and he rolled his shoulders, relaxing the tension stored there. My magic had its uses.

"Walk together?" I asked.

"Sure, I was getting ready to head that way when you arrived," he said, waving his magic over the door, sealing it shut. I raised an eyebrow at him, but said nothing.

We walked in comfortable silence towards the manor as the cosmos shone down brilliantly. The moon had a bluish tint to it tonight, and I prayed that indicated Vega's favor, that things would go well for Zoe tonight. She was facing an impossible choice. One I didn't know the right answer to.

"Any idea what Zoe's going to tell the other Astrals?" he asked.

"No," I admitted. "But no matter what she says or doesn't say, I'm going to be on her side."

"As will we all," he agreed. "Zoe will not stand alone in this."

"What would you do if you were her?" I asked as we drew nearer to the moonstone home.

"I think I'd tried to be as honest as possible," he admitted. "Though I know it's ironic to hear that coming from my lips."

I shook my head, disagreeing.

"It's not. You are a convicted male, Finn. Whatever your reasons for your silence, I know they are just."

A beam of swirling purple light opened just ahead, which was the transport zone the Astrals were supposed to be using tonight.

"Looks like they're arriving," I said, picking up my pace. "Evander will be there, waiting."

Evander was one of Elvy's favored captains, and my time leading the Shadowed Legion had made me realize why.

"Time to see just how loyal the Astrals are to our lady," Finnian said, matching my quickened stride.

6

Silence or Violence

ELVY

My knees seemed to shatter as they collided with the rocky surface, but I was too drained to be certain.

A bitter laugh took amusement in my pain.

My stomach recoiled as Hesperia drew closer to me. Her sickly, thin black hair was pulled back, which usually meant she was here to do more damage to my broken body, though it had been healed many times over at this point.

The chains holding my arms above my head lowered, and it took every ounce of my mental resolve not to give her the satisfaction of crying out. My shoulders rolled into their sockets painfully, and I found that I didn't have the strength to lift them. There was no physical part of me that could defend her in this state.

All I had was my silence.

And the knowledge that my flame was safe.

"Oh, Elvy, why must you put us through all this unnecessary roughness?" she purred, gripping my chin tightly so that my dark eyes met hers.

I didn't think it was possible, but even my shadows hated the female that stood before me.

Whenever they were no longer under her control, they marked her for a swift but painful death. I would cheer them on as the light disappeared from her eyes.

I smiled at the thought as dried blood pulled on my lip, which had been sliced open hundreds of times with Hesperia's shadow blade.

"Do you find me amusing, Elvy?" she asked.

Only your death, I thought to myself.

I talked a lot to myself in this burning, dark hell. I prayed my mind made it out of here intact.

Zoe hadn't stopped trying to reach me through our flame and bonds in the shadows. My shadows screamed in defiance, wanting to answer her call, but they couldn't. I wouldn't allow them to give what Hesperia desired most—my starlight.

I wanted nothing more than to feel Zoe's energy save me from this place, but I couldn't risk her. I wouldn't.

"Don't you want to know why I've let you down?" she asked, gazing into my eyes, trying to see beyond them.

I feared her answer.

"My shadows have told me something rather interesting, Elvykins."

She trailed a nail down my bicep, drawing blood as she smiled wide enough to show all her teeth.

My heart pounded, wondering what fresh hell she was about to put the star realms through.

"The shadows tell me that the Astrals are convening in your beloved court," she said, as if this was the news she had been waiting for. "It seems Zoe intends to lead the charge against me, and we can't have that."

My desert-dry throat felt like it was closing with the horror washing through me. I had to keep Hesperia away from Zoe. At all costs.

If Zoe died by my hands… I would follow her into the afterlife shortly after.

I hated myself for the words that were about to come from my lips, and I'd take it up with my maker when it was my time to return to the stars.

"Water," I mumbled, voice cracking, showing her just how weak I was.

Her eyes widened in shock. I hadn't spoken since she'd drug me to this place, but I couldn't let her go to Vega.

Surprisingly, she called for water from one of her minions. All of them were here by choice now. She was using every bit of her magic to keep my shadows under control. It was costing her, too. She would break eventually, and I'd make my move.

The water slowly trickled down my swollen throat, letting the power of water refuel my magic in the process. Drinking too much would probably make me sick with how dehydrated I was, and it took everything I had not to chug every ounce she offered.

"Are we ready to cooperate?" she asked, eyes dancing with glee.

I had to stifle the knee-jerk reaction to bare my teeth at her.

My breathing labored, and speaking felt foreign after so much silence.

"You know where the Astrals will be?" I asked.

"I do," she nodded. "And then I can get my father's bow from that difficult sister of mine."

A low growl rumbled in my chest.

"Come now, Elvy. I thought we were becoming friends."

I still needed to figure out what the hell she wanted with that bow. Whatever it was, it was nothing good.

"You're missing the bigger prize," I whispered, voice hoarse. The guilt I felt raked through me, but I'd made my decision. I'd protect Zoe first. Always. In every moment in time. She came first.

"Oh?" she asked, eyebrow raised in genuine curiosity.

"The other courts will be vulnerable."

Her body froze—stilling at what I'd suggested. It was a gamble to let her know we knew she needed star seeds from every court.

"Why would that matter?" she taunted, but I saw the calculation in her eyes. She'd let her hatred for my flame blind her to the obvious opportunity in front of her.

"Arcturus is without protection. You know this," I said, urging her through the thought.

"They have dragons," she argued, but she was taking the bait.

She was so quick to believe me that I had to assume she *wanted* to believe me. Loneliness made mortals and immortals alike stupid.

"What's dragon's breath against shadows?" I asked, swallowing down the shame I felt.

I secretly hoped the simargls had restored the fire realm to its former glory, but I had no way of knowing this. I felt like they had better odds against Hesperia than Rigil—the star court for ground.

Maybe I'd get lucky and a dragon would burn her alive.

I had no idea what Zoe had told the other Astrals about me, but I hoped she had warned them of the very real danger I posed to them. I wouldn't try to stop them if they tried to kill me.

"Tonight is your lucky night," she said, making her choice. "You're going on a little field trip with yours truly."

I gulped another sip of water. My arms cried out at the movement, and her eyes noticed the wince I couldn't hide.

For once, I hoped she left me in this state. My magic would burn out quickly with how weak I was, which hopefully meant I would deal less damage.

"Guards!" she yelled, and two males approached us. "Get him cleaned up and healed. I need him ready for realm travel as soon as possible."

Oh *no*.

"This will take time, my queen. His weave of magic is greatly damaged," he said, seeming to stare right through my skin and into the heart of my star's power source that resided within me. There were very few immortals that I knew of who wielded that kind of power.

"Just get it done," she spat, then walked out of the cavern that had become my personal prison.

The one who could see my magic leaned forward, black eyes piercing through me. His bald head gleamed in the moonlight. A permanent snarl was etched across his face.

"This is going to hurt," he said, smiling cruelly. "But no worries. We fixed up that Air Astral just fine. We'll have you fully operational in no time."

I bit my lip as he began the excruciatingly cruel torture of forcing my body and magic to weave back together again.

7

Throne of Vulnerability
ZOE

Outwardly, I was fine.

My curls had been braided down the length of my back, and my tanned skin glowed with the moisturizers I'd slathered on every surface after I'd finally mustered up the courage to take a shower.

My leathers fit me perfectly, and my knives were sheathed in their designated places.

I pushed a secret button in our bedroom, revealing The Archer's bow in one solid piece. Finnian had been right about how to put it together. The limbs were from the fire realm, and the bow grip was found in the ground elemental star court. We'd found the string in the Court of Canopus—air.

Underneath the bow was the arrow I'd found during my first visit to Algol. I'd snuck it out before Hesperia had the chance to finish me off. It hadn't felt right to leave that tool of destruction with her, even though it seemed to be worthless now. Any magic it had once held was long gone, destroying my hope that it would be the key to making the bow work in tethering the realms back together. It was as useless and void as I felt now, which made me wonder why The Archer had sent me after it in the first place.

My stomach dived into a free fall as a flashback of Elvy being taken from me flooded my mind. Jelly was instantly beside me, rubbing her soft wings against my body, trying to regulate me. I let her cool snout shock my system against the palm of my hand.

"I'm safe, brain. Reliving that moment won't help us right now," I said, coaching myself.

My water elemental magic had been the key to sealing the pieces together. That left me—the archer—as the fifth and final element of spirit.

Now, I wielded the power to restore the Kingdom of Canis together, as my father had intended, though I didn't know how to use it yet. This would allow the immortals of all star courts to serve multiple stars and keep all the magic they were born with. They wouldn't have to choose who to love or which parts of themselves to keep over the other.

And this all started with the jealousy of the celestial Algol. They hated that the Vega Astral line possessed users from both Vega and Algol, as if the immortals were personally responsible for this.

My shadows longed to see their death, but at the moment, that wasn't possible for several reasons. One, if Algol died, so did I, since their life force was tied to my own. Secondly, I wasn't sure if their death was the right answer to actually solving my problems without creating new ones. Thirdly, I knew that killing myself would kill Algol, but I didn't know how to kill them without untethering us, and untethering us was vital to keeping the immortals of Algol alive. Killing an immortal was hard. A celestial? Quite impossible.

Hesperia had come as close as one could when she'd severed Algol's bonds to the Kingdom of Canis. Even then, the celestial hadn't died. At least, not before I'd saved them. I suppose they would have passed after several more centuries.

I pushed the button again, locking the bow away.

It was useless to me until my father—The Archer—decided to get back to me about how to use the blasted thing. What good was a bow without arrows that could actually do something?

Jelly whimpered, forcing me to pay attention to her and not my disdain for my father.

"I know, my good girl," I said, scratching her ears, and she wagged her tail.

"Something doesn't feel right," she said, pawing at me, and I tried to soothe her.

"We'll be on our guard when the Astrals get here, but we must move forward with the meeting, even though I still have no idea what the right thing to do is."

Jelly nuzzled her head against mine, and I took a few deep breaths.

"Ever forward," I mumbled, standing up from where I'd sat on the ottoman at the foot of our bed.

I left mine and Elvy's bedroom, and the painful memories it held as I made my way down the hall to Aura's room.

She answered quickly after the first knock.

Her belly had swelled more, showing the precious life she carried in her womb. One she had gone to great lengths to protect.

"Hey Aura," I smiled.

"I wasn't sure if you'd come by tonight with the summit," she said, dressed in more formal attire, since she would attend the war council as the Lady Astral of Canopus.

"If you need more time to get ready instead, I can make up for it tomorrow. Whatever is best."

"Oh no, now is fine," she said, motioning for us to come in, and she locked the door behind her.

I sat in my usual chair in the small living space just before the room where her actual bed was.

"Are you sure you're feeling up to this?" she asked seriously. "We'll need you on your best game in a bit."

"I wouldn't offer my help tonight if I did not have the magic to spare," I promised, holding out my hand.

She placed the silver bracelet, interlaced with moonstone, in my hand, and I felt that the magic was almost empty, which indicated she'd been struggling recently.

"Nightmares?" I asked, closing my eyes to feel the well of my healing magic within me, so I could infuse her bracelet with specific magic that was geared more towards spiritual and emotional healing than physical.

"Yes," she admitted. "I've had them most nights this week. Not sure why. I'm so tired of that male plaguing my mind."

"We could up the treatment if needed," I suggested. "Until you're feeling a little better."

The bracelet was now fully charged with my magic, and I handed it back to her.

"I couldn't ask that of you," she said, eyes avoidant.

"Aura," I said gently. "I know you're used to having to please others before yourself, but I meant it when I said I would not offer my help if I could not fulfill it. It's not your job to worry about me. Let me take care of you."

I couldn't help Elvy right now, but I could help her. So I would.

"Alright," she said, nodding her head and holding out her hand for me to clasp.

"If your nightmares have been about something specific, release it to me," I instructed. "The memory will still be yours, but let me take the disturbance you experience from it away."

We both gathered our breaths as she sent the memory flooding into my mind. I now saw what she experienced through her eyes as I embraced her pain.

★★★

"Why do you make me do this, Aura?" Abel yelled, gripping my upper arm so tightly I knew it would leave a bruise. "If you would just listen, I wouldn't get so angry."

I'd learned that silence was my best friend in these moments. There was no realm in which he would take accountability for himself. I was always the one in the wrong in his eyes. Defending myself would get me into more trouble.

"Answer me!" he demanded.

"I—I'll do better," I said, voice shaking.

"You've said that so many times before, Aura. How am I supposed to believe what you say? You are a liar."

I winced, fear evident in my eyes. He was out for blood tonight.

"I think you need to be punished to learn this lesson," he said, eyes going manic.

Any reasoning had left his brain. He had been looking for a reason to lay his hands on me. My mistake? I'd agreed to help one of our subjects with transportation to the city center because she did not have wings to fly, and Abel refused to build bridges to connect our floating cities together.

He gripped me tighter with one hand and reached for the belt hanging in his wardrobe.

"Not a word," he said. "Or I'll give you something to cry about."

There was no fighting him once he got like this, and I fought him the only way I could—with my mind.

I thought of the adventures I used to go on with my mother to find our rarest birds. It had always been so thrilling when we found giant beasts of birds thought to be long extinct. It was our job to protect them as Lady Astrals. My mother had taught me that, and I'd never shared the knowledge with anyone.

Smack.

I knew the belt was hitting me, but he couldn't reach me here with my mother and the birds.

"Fly high, little bird," my mother whispered as she held me against her chest.

★★★

I let Aura's memory become my own, allowing the pain that her body and heart experienced in that moment transform into healing through my magic. I took just enough to give her power over the memory instead of the other way around.

The tears that escaped my eyes were all for her, and the grief I felt at the suffering she'd experienced for far too long.

I opened my eyes to find her drying her tears and moving a strand of hair behind her ear, catching on the soft feather that she always wore.

"Little bird?" I asked, still holding her hand until she was good and ready to let go.

"I was my mother's little bird," she said, smiling fondly at a distant memory.

"My father calls me little bear," I offered as she let go of my hand, and my chest recoiled, thinking of my absent father.

"Not a fan of Papa Eferhild?" she asked, rubbing her pregnant belly soothingly, as if to protect her baby from the memories buried within her.

"It's not that," I disagreed, leaning back in my chair to get more comfortable. I didn't know what it was about Aura, but she put my mind at ease with her own kind of special magic, and I welcomed it. "I think my father is ultimately trying to protect me from a fate he fears will come to pass, but what he doesn't realize is that I'm ready to face it head-on."

"Maybe you should tell him that," she suggested sincerely.

"Believe me, if I ever get the chance, I will. Unfortunately, I haven't been able to reach him."

"Maybe there's a good reason."

"Maybe, but right now it's hard to move forward when there's still missing pieces, and I have a meeting room full of Lord and Lady Astrals waiting on me to announce the next movements against Hesperia."

"The Court of Vega has only shown me kindness," she said, leaning closer. "And you have selflessly and tirelessly worked to hone your magic to help me—a complete stranger. You will do what is right."

A belief I wasn't sure I held because at the end of the night, it was him. Always him, I would put first.

That didn't mean I couldn't find a way to protect my court as well. I just had to find the answer, and time was yet again not on my side.

"I'll leave you to finish getting ready, Aura. I'll see you soon," I said, nodding.

"You're never alone, Zoe. Remember that," she called as I shut the door behind me.

I didn't care if all the other Astrals were waiting for me. Something told me it wasn't my time to meet them, and I trusted that, letting the song of my magic lead me where I must follow.

8

Violet is Violent

DELMIRA

I'd left Finnian and Evander to handle the arriving Astrals while I went to find Blaz.

"Delm!" Imelda called from behind me, just outside the manor's entrance. Clodovea was trailing behind her, and they both wore devilish grins.

"You're really rocking the just had sex hair," I said, pointing to her wilder than normal curls.

"Oh hell," she said, combing her fingers through her hair, and Clodovea helped her with a smirk playing on her lips.

"I think you have time to freshen up. I'm about to head to my room to do the same," I said, laughing, and it felt good to let loose that feeling.

"Who has arrived?" Clove asked.

"Lady Astral Sierra," I answered. "Lord Astral Terran from Rigil has stayed behind in their realm for safety measures. I feel like most will."

"Not good," Imelda said, crossing her arms. "They know it's bad then."

"Wait until they find out just how bad," I said, losing my optimism with every word. "The others will be arriving soon."

"I hope it's Seraphina, not Kai," Imelda said grimly, but we didn't have much control over hope, so I didn't comment. Both of them were on my watch list until further notice.

"I'll see you two in there," I said, bounding through the manor on the way to my room, hoping Blaz was in there.

He hadn't exactly moved into my room, but he slept in there more than in his own. I simply refused to sleep in his room. It was clean and everything, but it felt like a military-issued dorm room with zero personality. Plus, he tried to freeze me out with unnecessarily frigid temperatures.

The door scanned my immortal mark, granting me access, and I came face to face with Blaz. My heart melted, but my mouth didn't know how to say that.

"You look like hell," I said as Blaz stripped his training leathers from his annoyingly beautiful olive skin.

"Then why are you drooling, Delm?" he taunted, always ready to meet my banter with ease.

"I am not."

"You are," he said, placing his massive hands on the smallest part of my waist.

I was.

He was completely naked, and my eyes trailed over him in appreciation for the training that had crafted the specimen before me.

"Maybe *hell* was a little too harsh," I said, leaning on my tiptoes to plant a kiss against his lips.

Blaz swept his tongue against mine, and a low moan escaped me.

"Take a shower with me," he said, pulling me with him as I leaped into his arms, wrapping my legs around his waist.

"I really shouldn't. My hair is already done for the summit," I said, but my heart wasn't in the statement.

"Don't get your hair wet. Got it," he said, setting me on the counter and stripping me out of my clothes with expert hands.

He stepped away from me to turn the shower on, and I took the opportunity to check him out. I mean, those glutes were mouth-watering.

Before my brain could catch up to my feet, I stood behind him and slapped his backside, making him yelp.

"Delmira," he said, chuckling.

"What can I say? You have a *slapable* butt."

He tossed me over his shoulder, dragging me into the hot shower, but he was careful not to get my hair wet.

"It's funny you mention that, Delm. I personally think yours is the perfect shape for my hand," he said, squeezing my right cheek as water fell against my skin.

My core instantly heated as he continued to tease and knead my curves.

Even with his butt now in perfect view as I dangled over his shoulder, I could barely concentrate on anything as his hand moved up and down my legs and swirled around my backside.

I whimpered in anticipation—in need.

"You like when I worship you, don't you, Delm?" he asked, gently popping my backside, but I wanted more.

"Yes," I said, biting my lip, internally begging him.

He circled my cheek again and reared his hand back, slapping me firmly. I clenched my legs together, enjoying every second of it.

Blaz continued this tortuous cycle that had me begging for more every time he trailed his fingers down the sensitive spot just beneath the cheek. On his way up this time, he slipped two fingers into my apex to find me soaking with pleasure. It didn't take him but a few strokes of his fingers for me to find my release, and I grasped his waist for dear life.

I was really drooling this time.

"Oh Delm, what am I going to do with you?" he asked.

"More of that, hopefully," I said breathlessly, and he twisted me right side up, kissing me softly.

"You're everything that I need, and more than I had ever dreamed for myself," he mumbled, pushing me against the warm wall of the shower.

I didn't possess the words to answer, but I knew I wanted to make him feel good. I took him into my hands and began pumping.

"Delm," he growled, biting down on my neck, and I welcomed the sensation.

I bent down, lining him up with my center, and he shifted in, filling me completely.

We both let out groans as our bodies began moving in perfect tandem. The way he made me feel... I'd never felt this with anyone—mortal or immortal. It terrified the hell out of me, but I wasn't running.

He used one hand to hold me up, and the other found pleasure in other parts of my body, causing me to cry out as I wrapped my arms around his shoulders.

He trailed his fingers down my torso until he found my clit, and he began circling at a tortuously exquisite rhythm to find my elation.

"Come with me," I begged, meeting his movements with fervor. My core braced as I felt the buildup of my bliss coming.

Blaz grunted, slamming into me a final time, filling me with his pleasure as I rode him through the waves of my own bliss.

He nuzzled my neck, and I felt his smile against my skin.

"I think I may just be falling for you, Delm," he murmured, and I held him close, still too afraid to say the words confirming I felt the same.

He planted a soft kiss against my lips and didn't press me to say anything I wasn't ready to.

Pulling himself from me, he stood me up gently and grabbed a loofah and soap.

"What are you doing?" I asked as the loofah lathered easily with the lavender body wash.

"I'm taking care of you," he said, as if it were obvious, and I supposed it was.

Blaz washed me thoroughly, careful not to get my hair wet, then cleaned himself up. I'd never felt so pampered.

I started to step out of the shower and reach for a towel, but Blaz pulled my hand back.

"Will you just let me do this?" he asked, laughing, and grabbed the towel before I could. He gently dried me off, then himself, and carried me into the bedroom.

"This is ridiculous," I said, embarrassed by all the attention.

"It's how I show I care," he answered, placing me on the bed.

"Are you going to dress me, too?" I asked, brow raised.

"I will if you want me to," he said, looking around my wardrobe as if he was really going to do it.

I stood up from the warmth of my fuzzy towel and grabbed my own clothes this time.

"I got it," I answered, and Blaz smirked as he found his own clean leathers that he kept in my room.

We dressed quickly, having spent a little too much time in the shower. Both of us did a final check of our weapons before we headed out the door to the potentially most important war summit of our lives.

9

Oceans Away

ZOE

I stumbled to the private beach of our manor with Jelly following beside me silently.

I had a longing for the one thing that had always brought me peace before I'd met my flame.

The ocean roared tonight, such a juxtaposition from its usual tranquility. It's as if the ocean knew Elvy had been taken from it, too.

I embraced its wrath, and let the sounds of its grief bring me comfort. The sound confirmed that this was all real, but I wasn't safe.

"I'll bring him back to us," I vowed to the ocean and the stars. It felt like this was all on my shoulders, but I knew I had a family that would ride with me into the depths of hell.

Closing my eyes, I listened for a wave off in the distance and focused on its energy as it eventually crashed onto the shoreline. Yes, this was my reality, but I did not accept it.

I threw up a shield around me as an extra precaution as I let my rambling flow freely. Maybe Elvy could hear it through our flame, but part of me felt guilty about that, too. I checked the pathway that led to him in my mind, but it was sealed tightly shut on his end. I didn't possess the strength to tear it down.

"How do I go into that room and tell them your secret without putting you at risk, Elvy?" I whispered into the cosmos.

"You could have let her take me," I said, angry, though I knew the thought was irrational. He had to protect me in that moment. His shadows—his flame—demanded it. More than that… his love needed to protect me.

The Archer's constellation twinkled brightly in the sky, and a new wave of violence rushed through me.

"I hate you," I said, flipping him the bird.

My fury had been forged, and any who crossed me now should fear for their very lives. I was a life-bringer no more.

The ocean crashed against the rocky shore, as if rallying me to war.

"Zoe?" a voice called from behind me, just as Jelly let loose a low growl in warning. My tensed body relaxed some, recognizing his voice.

I dissipated the shield and motioned for him to sit next to me.

"Glad you could make it, Oleander," I said.

He bumped my shoulder as he sat down, and I recoiled some. I hated that he knew of Elvy's secret. It made him a liability. Dangerous. I shook my head of the thoughts.

Jelly laid her head in my lap, and I stroked her wings gently.

"He's our friend," Jelly said in her sweet voice.

"I know," I reassured her. The shadows didn't always like to play nice.

She leaned her head into my open palm, grounding me to this moment.

"Everyone's waiting," he said gently. "And they can keep waiting if you need them to."

"I still don't know what the right thing is," I admitted.

"Maybe that's your problem. You're trying to do the *right* thing. Doing what's right is subjective."

I perked an eyebrow at him, turning to find his blue eyes staring into mine.

"Do the thing that you can live with when this is all over. You're the only one who can decide what that is."

"But we don't know if there will be a time when this is all over," I argued.

"Then it won't matter either way," he said. "You're waiting for your father to tell you what to do next, and that's crap, Zo. He's not the one that has to live with what must be done. You are. So do it."

I'd never been one to enjoy tough-love speeches, especially when they were directed at me, but he was right about one thing. I'd come out to this beach in hopes that my father might show up at the last minute to tell me what to do.

"Maybe this is some sort of test," I said, still stroking Jelly's soft fur. "To what choice I make."

"Perhaps," he agreed. "Perhaps not."

I pressed my lips together in concentration. I had a crazy idea that was going to either work or fail epically, and Vega would be the one to suffer the most should we fall short of victory.

"I guess we'll find out," I said, standing from my spot on the beach and wiping the sand off my backside.

"I've got your back," he said seriously. "Whether I agree with you or not."

"I know it must have been difficult to leave Freyja's side to be here," I said, placing a hand gently on his bicep.

"Zadie will watch over her should she wake while I'm gone, but I can't imagine she will this soon."

"No, I don't think so," I agreed. "Given the length of time she's been gone, she may still be in the first trial."

"She'll make it back to us."

"I have no doubt in her," I agreed.

"To the summit?"

I nodded. "Time to face the music. Let's hope the songs of fate are singing loudly tonight."

I strode forward with Jelly on my right and Oleander on my left. I still wasn't sure exactly what I was going to say when the moment came, but I prayed my *sight* would lead me true.

10

Ignorance Isn't Bliss
FREYJA

An orb of light was in my sights as I pushed through the water around me.

I was like a moth to a flame, drawn to this glowing ball of light in the depths of the ocean. There was no turning back now. I didn't have enough breath to make it to the surface if this was not the answer.

My lungs burned in need as I collapsed my hands around the starlight.

The pain instantly released, but I was no longer in the ocean or the star realms? *Realms*? Why had I said that? Wait, where was I?

My consciousness took in my surroundings, and I recognized my bedroom immediately.

This wasn't right. I haven't lived here for ages. Pictures covered every available wall surface from places I'd been, and places I wanted to go desperately. Castles had recently piqued my interest, and I stood from my bed, gazing at a familiar onyx castle that I couldn't quite remember why it felt like I'd been there before. I was positive I'd never been.

A knock sounded at the door, drawing me from my thoughts.

"Freyja?" my sister asked.

"Zoe?" I asked, still a little confused, but the fog was slowly fading away. I was home, but I had the sense of having lived this day before.

"Are you ready?" she asked, looking me over with a worry line forming between her eyes.

I glanced down at my clothes, and I was wearing jean shorts and a white blouse. Perfect for this ridiculous humidity.

"Yes," I answered, grabbing a crossbody purse from my nightstand.

"Then let's go thrifting!" Zoe said excitedly, worry gone from her, which put me a little more at ease.

Zoe led me through our familiar home right off the beach in Saint Andrews, Florida.

"Where are you girls off to?" my mother called after us just before we reached the front door.

My heart stilled in grief, and I couldn't figure out why.

"Freyja and I are going to a few thrift stores down the main road," she said, smiling brightly.

"You two be careful," my father said, standing and poking his head out of his office.

My heartbeat picked up, and my eyes fluttered, and I couldn't figure out why.

"Are you sure you're well, dear?" my mom asked, cupping one of my cheeks in her hand, and for some reason a tear escaped my eye.

"Freyja, what's wrong?" Zoe asked, voice full of concern. My father—Grant—strode forward with worry in his eyes.

"What's going on, Viv?" he asked, as they surrounded me with so much love, I felt like my world was shattering around me.

"I'm sorry," I said, wiping the tears from my eyes. "I think I just missed you all."

That seemed to set all of them at ease.

My mother laughed easily. "You're right. We need to spend more family time together."

"I'm sorry I've been so busy lately with the business," my dad said with guilt in his voice.

"No, I know you're busy. It's okay," I said, trying to reassure them with my overreaction.

"We don't have to go, Freyja," Zoe said seriously. "We can just have a night in."

"No, no. We don't need to change our plans just because I'm being hormonal," I brushed off.

Zoe moved to argue, but I stopped her.

"Family dinner tomorrow," I said. "Promise."

My parents both nodded their agreement, but I could tell Zoe was still concerned.

"Come on, Zoe," I said, pulling her out the door.

"Love you!" both of my parents called in unison, and we sent them kisses as we made our way down to the first thrift store a few blocks away.

There was a nagging feeling I couldn't shake. Something wasn't right, but I couldn't quite put my finger on it.

"I'm so excited about the next trip," Zoe said, hooking her arms through mine as we walked down the busy main street with our eyes on our favorite discount store. We could almost always count on scoring something cool from there.

"Me too," I said, though I couldn't recall where we were going. "Where's that again?"

Zoe roared with laughter. "Did you hit your head last night or something?"

"I don't think so, but I do feel a little funny," I said, laughing half-heartedly.

Zoe stopped our pursuit, causing me to look into her eyes.

"You okay, Freyja? Seriously. We can go back. Have a day in. We can binge *Supernatural* for the billionth time."

I paused, taking in my body. Everything felt fine other than this weird gut feeling like something bad was going to happen.

I shook it off.

"All good, Zoe," I said, pulling her through the threshold of the thrift store. "London. We're going to London."

"Yes, we are," she agreed. "The way I am ready for Nando's and curry."

"Seriously," I said, mouth watering at the thought.

We split up to cover more ground, and I headed over to the men's jackets to hopefully find some gems. Zoe wasn't too far away, but her back was turned to me. I sifted through some decent jackets, but nothing caught my eye until I came across a vintage denim jacket and a leather jacket side by side.

"Score," I said, pulling them from the rack.

My stomach twisted, as if it were trying to speak to me, and I stilled. Our late grandmother had always said to trust our instincts, and that God didn't make women dumb. My gut was telling me I was being watched.

I whirled around to find a man in a dark baseball cap seemingly browsing in the row diagonal to mine.

I had no reason to suspect he was doing anything except shopping, but the hairs on the back of my neck stood up. Red flag alert.

I wasn't afraid to make a scene if it came down to it. I hurried over to Zoe with fear in my eyes.

"What's going on?" she asked, instantly picking up on my anxiety.

"That man over there," I said, pointing behind me. Zoe's eyes followed where I pointed, and she frowned.

"Freyja, there's no one over there."

"What?" I asked, turning back to where I'd just seen him, but he was gone.

"Can I help you with anything?" a kind woman came up to us with a name tag that read Rachel.

"Has anyone else been in here in the last fifteen minutes?" I asked, eyes still gazing around, trying to find the man.

"I don't think so," she said. "It's been pretty slow today. Most people are at the beach."

She was right. Most of the crowds had been heading to the ocean or beverage stands. It was the tourist season.

"We're good, I think," Zoe said. "I think we want these, though."

She grabbed the jackets from my hands and pulled me to the register to check out. Once we were outside, my sister pulled me to the side.

"Freyja, you're worrying me. Should we just go home?"

"I'm sorry, Zo. I'm just frazzled today," I admitted, still feeling a little uneasy.

"Then let's just spend the night in and watch *Dirty Dancing* if you're not wanting Dean and Sam eye candy."

I took a few deep breaths, laughing at myself.

"You know I'm a John girl," I said, letting myself relax. "Let's go get margs and tacos like we planned."

"Where did you get that fake ID again?" she asked.

"I can't reveal my sources," I said.

Zoe was just as wild as me, but breaking the law was simply not her thing. Not that she hadn't underage drunk because she absolutely had, but she hadn't tried to be so blatant about it.

"Alright, alright," she conceded as we headed into the bar with the best frozen margaritas around.

We ordered our drinks and food and sat down in the outside patio.

"See, no issues," I said happily.

"Yeah, yeah," she said, rolling her eyes. "What did we end up buying, anyway?"

I pulled out the two jackets and tossed her the denim one.

"That one is for you," I said confidently and pulled on the leather one myself. "Fits like a dream."

She followed suit and pulled hers on. With the sun setting and the breeze picking up slightly, the jackets were actually comfortable in this weather.

Before long, our sustenance arrived, and as I devoured the shrimp tacos and margarita, my nerves began to relax.

I was having fun, and I didn't want this feeling to end.

"Let's go dancing," I suggested as I finished my second margarita, thankful we only had to walk a few blocks to be home.

"You know I can't dance," she said, smiling. "But… as long as you're ready to scar your eyes some more, we can go."

"Yes!"

We paid our bill, and I was enjoying the buzz, but as I went to leave, the same man I'd seen with a ball cap on was sitting at the bar.

I knew I wasn't crazy now. He's right there.

"That's him, Zo," I whispered. "The man at the bar with a ball cap. He was in the thrift store."

She turned to follow my gaze.

"Okay, I see him," she agreed, but she didn't look concerned. "Do you still feel weird about it? We can go dancing another night if you want."

I studied him, and he seemed normal enough. Maybe he was just out enjoying his night like we were, though this was more of a local hangout. I recognized several faces around the bar, but I'd never seen him before.

I shook the feeling away again.

"No, it's fine," I said. "Let's go dancing!"

11

War Summit

ZOE

I sat at the head of the table in the secure conference room on top of the manor.

Oleander sat to my left, and Delmira was to my right. Clodovea, Imelda, Finnian, and Blaz sat behind me against the wall. Jelly lay at my feet, ears on alert. We all wore our fighting leathers, as did all the other Astrals.

I imagined we were an intimidating, united front. Each of the star courts had sent one of their Astrals instead of both. Neither the King nor the Queen had responded to my invitation with their borders to Sirius sealed tightly shut. I wanted to be angry with them for not providing more aid, but I understood their reasoning all the same. It didn't mean I had to like it or agree with them. I'd fight them another night on the pointlessness of their actions despite their good intentions.

I couldn't afford to close the borders to Vega. One, it wouldn't be effective. Hesperia could find her way through them, and two, I was about to offer the very opposite.

Sierra's gaze pierced through mine, and I felt like she had a bit of intuition magic about her. I wouldn't be surprised if she had Algol in her bloodline somewhere before the severing of the tethers.

Seraphina from the Court of Arcturus sat across from Sierra. I was somewhat thankful that Kai had been the one to stay behind, as I wasn't up for his doubt today. I needed them to go with me on this, and it was going to be a big ask of trust from them. Even my stubborn self recognized that.

Aura sat at the other end of the table as the sole representative of the Court of Canopus. We hoped to reconnect her with her court when it was safe to do so. I hated to think of the suffering her immortals were going through at the hands of Hesperia, who had taken up residence there after we'd taken back control of Algol.

"Thank you for traveling to the Court of Vega. I know that itself was a lot to ask of each of you with the threat of Hesperia lurking around," I began, and I felt the weight of each of their eyes on mine.

"Tell us what you need, Zoe Eferhild," Sierra said with knowing in her eyes. She had always been quick to trust me, and it appeared she still felt the same way now.

"I'm afraid we are waiting for one more representative to arrive," I said, just as Evander escorted my favorite mustached male into the room—Tiergan. The Sublunary rebel leader.

Oleander's crooked grin greeted him, and Aura smiled brightly.

The other Astrals seemed a little tense at his arrival, but they weren't reaching for their weapons, and I decided that was a good sign.

"Tiergan," I said, motioning him towards the empty seat next to Aura. "I'm glad you could make it."

"Of course," he said gruffly. "I've been waiting for this moment my entire life."

"Seraphina, Sierra, this is Tiergan. The leader of the Sublunary and ally to our cause."

"We can trust him?" Seraphina asked, and I wanted to lash out against the suspicion. I trusted him much more than I trusted her and Kai.

"We can," I said, voice not allowing for contradictions. "And we need all the help we can get."

"I'm pleased to meet you. I am Sierra," she said, smiling politely, and he returned the gesture.

"It has been much too long since I have visited the beautiful Court of Rigil."

"You will be very welcome," she answered.

Seraphina didn't offer him quite that much grace, but she did introduce herself. "I'm Seraphina of Arcturus."

Tiergan bowed in acknowledgment. "I am sure we will work well together."

"Now then," I said, gesturing for everyone to stop gawking at the rebel leader, but Seraphina interrupted me.

"The Court of Arcturus sends its allegiance and grief at the loss of the Lord Astral Elvy," Seraphina offered, bowing slightly to Jelly.

"He's not lost to us yet," I said, voice steady even though I felt like breaking at the mention of his name.

"You are quite right," Sierra said, and Aura nodded her agreement.

"I have a proposal," I said, swallowing. "And I ask that you keep an open mind and know that I have the entirety of the star realms at heart."

"Does this have to do with Elvy?" Sierra asked. "And why you asked us to move our shields to the front lines?"

"Yes," I said, nodding. "It does."

"Go on," Aura said encouragingly. Oleander pressed his lips together, bracing for the impact of what I was about to say.

"We know Hesperia needs a seed of your star's power source for a ritual she wants to do that would make her a vessel for all five elements. I still haven't figured out what she plans to do with that kind of power, but in the end, it won't matter because I will kill her before she can enact her intention."

"Bold assumption," Seraphina muttered, but I didn't address it because it was a very bold wish.

"And what's the proposal?" Sierra asked.

"I'm asking you to let her take it, but don't let her realize that you are giving it so willingly, if at all possible," I said, voice calm.

"That goes against everything we stand for," Seraphina argued. "We're still trying to make things right as it is."

"Believe it or not, I promise you this is a step in the direction of making the realms right again."

"Why shouldn't we fight?" Sierra asked, eyes analyzing different outcomes in her mind.

"Because you won't stand a chance against my husband," I said seriously, saying every word with as much intention as I could muster. "It will be a slaughter."

"No one is that powerful," Seraphina said, but I could tell she read the truth in my words.

"I assure you that you all will die if you stand against him."

"What kind of power does he possess?" Sierra asked, seeming to be a little hurt that Elvy had never shared that with them despite their closeness.

"That's beside the point," Oleander drawled. "Zoe speaks the truth. You are signing your own death if you don't listen to her. And you will not hold her or Elvy responsible if you don't heed her now."

Sierra turned her head in thought, taking in his words.

"And you trust her?" Seraphina asked, but her gaze was on Jelly, who gave a curt nod.

"There are very few scenarios that will result in us winning against Hesperia. Perhaps only one," Oleander said, pausing for effect. "And I believe Zoe will be the one to lead us through it."

"Or die trying," I agreed.

"But you won't tell us why Elvy is dangerous?" Sierra asked, not letting that part drop.

I trusted Sierra. I leaned into my gift, trying to understand if it was safe to speak the truth—to trust. A part of me believed that to trust others, sometimes… you simply have to trust them and let them show you they are worthy of it. I swallowed, back pooling with sweat.

"Death, Sierra. Death is his gift. I will not answer any questions about it. If you listen to me, Hesperia will have no reason to act against you. Keep your immortals safe behind your shields. Allow Hesperia to take the star seed."

There was an unsteady pause from them all, but there were no calls for pitchforks or any rash decisions. They either had faith in me, or they did not understand the gravity of Elvy's power.

"What about you?" Aura asked, moving the conversation away from my flame.

"She already has what she needs from Canopus and Algol. Once she has retrieved the star seeds from Arcturus and Rigil, she will have no choice but to invade Vega," I said, turning from their waiting eyes to the night sky. "Vega is where we will make our last stand. Once and for all. She will die, or she will prevail as the victor. Either way, it'll happen on my terms in my court."

Delmira spoke for the first time, but her eyes had been studying the other Astrals the entire time.

"We ask that you stand with the Court of Vega. When the time comes."

"What about your immortals?" Sierra asked with genuine concern. "You are putting them at great risk to bring war to their doorstep."

Musterion was once a shared place, and I hoped that it could be again.

"My Luminaries found a hidden city, and they have all been evacuated there. This place is full of relics of the past that show evidence that the star courts were very much intertwined once, and I hope to restore that again. I can protect them when she comes. I am only sorry I do not have room for all."

It broke a part of me to tell them of Musterion, even though it wasn't much, but I needed them to understand that I'd thought this through. I was asking them to trust me. I had to trust them.

"Okay," Sierra said, bowing. "The Court of Rigil will fight with you... and we will let Hesperia take what she seeks."

"The Elvy that is your friend is not in control right now, Sierra," I said seriously. "He will have no choice but to kill you if you stand against him."

"I understand," she said seriously.

"The Court of Arcturus will stand with you," Seraphina agreed. "Our dragons will be ready."

I bowed my thanks, and the tension in my shoulders relaxed some.

"There are many Shadowed loyal to me," Aura said, voice tight. "I know where to find them in Canopus."

"It's too dangerous," Tiergan intervened, but she raised her hand. He didn't argue with her.

"Hesperia does not know my court nor the way of wind. The Court of Canopus will stand with Vega. We have just as much right to fight with you."

"I only ask that you take some Shadowed or Sublunary with you," I suggested.

"They will only get in my way," she argued, and I wanted to be on her side.

"It's your choice, Aura, but you are the only leader of Canopus that is still alive and pure of heart. Your immortals cannot afford to lose you."

Aura nodded, and I hoped that meant she conceded, or I feared Tiergan would have an absolute fit.

"Alright. A select few can come with me," she said, and Tiergan relaxed back in his chair.

I cleared my throat, bringing the attention back to myself.

"I will do all that I can to return the seeds Hesperia takes. I'm not sure what happens to them once the star's essence has been absorbed, but we know it makes her physically weaker to consume that much energy. In theory, by the time she reaches Vega, she will be at her weakest physically. I fear that she will be at her strongest magically, though. However, it's our best time to strike. If we kill her flesh, it won't matter the strength of her magic."

"Have you worked out how to end her permanently?" Oleander asked, and I shook my head.

"Not yet. I don't want there to be any margin for error when it comes to her."

"No, there will be no room for mistakes," Oleander agreed. "We will only get one shot. We have to make it count."

"So, we will," I agreed.

I turned to look at the Astrals that were choosing to trust me. Choosing to believe in me, gratitude and fear swelled within my heart. While I was not alone in this war, when the moment came to attack, it would be my hands that stained red with the blood of my eldest sister. My sister, who refused to be saved.

Seraphina suddenly cried out, standing from her seat, and the beat of her dragon's wings descended upon us.

"Seraphina?" I asked, rushing to her side. "What is it?"

Before she could get the words out, a flash of Elvy's face and his dark eyes flooded through my mind, and I recognized the court of Arcturus all too well.

"Can your dragon tell Kai to stand down?" I asked, as we both raced towards her waiting black dragon, who let out a war cry of his own.

"We're trying to get through, but something is blocking us!" she shouted, leaping onto the seat of her dragon.

I unfurled my wings with the rest of the Astrals, and my Luminaries were hot on my tail. Jelly had shifted to her true simargl form.

I nodded towards the other Astrals. "Go, protect your immortals."

Sierra disappeared into the shadows, not needing to be told twice. Tiergan stood with Aura, not letting her out of his sight. Smart male. She'd probably ditch him in an instant.

"I must go to him," I said, just loud enough that it wasn't a whisper. "Elvy is with her."

"It's too dangerous," Oleander disagreed.

"I will not let his fate be death nor the fire court's," I spat.

My eyes shifted to black, and I embraced the shadows.

"You can come with me or you can get the hell out of my way," I said.

"I'm coming with you," Blaz said, and Imelda stepped forward with him.

I nodded. "Time's up. We must go. Delmira, you know the drill."

She bowed, and Finnian and Clodovea followed her retreating form.

"Last chance, Oleander," I said, as Seraphina's dragon disappeared into the cosmic portal.

He unfurled his massive black wings.

"Of course, love."

And then we were flying to meet my mate and my fate head-on.

12

Innocent

FREYJA

Zoe and I were both coated in sweat, dancing the night away.

The DJ was on point tonight, and the crowd could feel it as our bodies swayed to the rhythm of the beat. Zoe and I both had ditched the alcohol for water an hour ago, and my buzz was fading.

But my soul was on fire as I danced away the worry I'd felt earlier.

"I can't wait to hit up the nightclubs in London!" I shouted in Zo's ear, and she gave me a thumbs up, smiling widely.

This wasn't her scene naturally, but I could tell she was enjoying herself. The first dance club we'd gone to had been entirely lame, and even I'd felt awkward swaying my body. I'd convinced her to give this new place a shot, and her body was loosening up here.

A couple of guys had tried to dance with us, but we shooed them away, just wanting to be sisters tonight, high on life.

I forgot about the man in the baseball cap, and I dismissed the negative feelings that came along with him.

I'd traveled to foreign countries and far scarier cities than the little innocent town of Saint Andrews. I had nothing to worry about. There was no safer place than right here at home.

Eventually, we decided we'd had enough dancing, and it was well past midnight at this point. I could have kept going, but I knew Zo was tired and she had work tomorrow afternoon with June at the rescue.

The cool, crisp breeze of the ocean air hit us as we exited the club, and the stars were shining brightly tonight.

"That was fun," I said, smiling. "Thank you for going out with me tonight."

"Of course," she said, hooking her arm through mine again. "I know I prefer mountains over the city life, but you know food is the way to my heart."

"But not dancing?" I asked, laughing.

"You buttered me up with this amazing jacket and tacos. You knew what you were doing the whole time," she accused, and there was some truth there.

"Maybe," I agreed. "But you love me, anyway."

"Yeah, yeah. I do love you, Freyja."

As we rounded the corner to take the back way home, my heart sunk straight into my stomach.

Hiding in the shadows to our right was the man in the baseball cap.

And he wasn't alone.

Zoe saw them, too.

On instinct, she pushed me behind her, and I was completely frozen. At least one of us still had a functioning brain to move into action.

"Well, well, well. What do we have here?" the man stepped forward. Four more moved behind him. We were totally screwed if they tried anything.

Zoe didn't hesitate. "Back the hell up. We aren't interested."

"You don't know that, darlin'. You don't know what kind of fun we can have together."

They laughed, and my heart pumped faster.

Zoe shielded her body with mine as best as she could. An aura of death radiated around her.

"This one is a fighter," one of the men groaned. "I love it when they fight."

It all happened too quickly. We both screamed for help as loudly as possible, but with the music from the clubs, no one could hear us.

And neither of us was strong enough to fight that many at once.

Death didn't come quick enough for me, and I felt the heat of my tears run down my cheek as I died.

***

I sat in a brilliantly white witness stand, just like I'd seen in all the trashy court dramas.

Nova sat in the seat of the judge. Zoe sat in the prosecutor's seat.

"What's going on?" I asked, turning to Zoe, but she just sneered at me.

"A trial of the soul," Nova said, and the memories came flooding back to me. I was still in the first trial of the Emerging, and Nova had made me relive the night I'd died.

"How could you do that to me?" I spat, stopping myself from calling her something terrible.

"I don't decide these things, child. You do."

There was sadness in her voice. Sorrow even.

"Zo, what is going on? Why are you here?"

My sister still wouldn't look at me, and my heart broke into shattered pieces. She blamed me. For what happened that night, and she was here to punish me for it.

"Court is convened," Nova said, waving her hands. "Let the prosecution begin."

Zoe raised from her seat silently and walked towards me on the stand. There was only darkness in her eyes. My actions had snuffed out all of her light. Because of me, she would live with this torment for the rest of her days.

"You saw the man in the ball cap two times before the *incident*?" she asked, like the word tasted foul in her mouth. "The man that was obviously tracking us. You saw him twice and still continued on?"

I couldn't believe my sister was saying this to me. The sister who loved and protected me above all else.

Shame flooded through me. This was all my fault.

"I did." I hung my head in shame. "I didn't trust my gut."

"And now look at us," she taunted. "You dead. And me living every day in a tortured state, scared to death of my own shadow. All because you didn't speak up."

Tears pricked my eyes, but I embraced the guilt. Let it pour down on me.

"Did I not ask you at least three separate times to go home?" she asked, voice harsh, and the tone cut me to my core.

She had. Zoe had all but begged for us to go home several times. I hadn't listened. I'd failed her.

"You did," I agreed, and my eyes clouded with tears.

"I hate you," she said, voice low as her gaze pierced through me. "I can never forgive your silence."

The tears flowed easily now down my cheeks, and my heart wept painfully.

"The world is better without you in it," she said again, twisting the proverbial knife deeper into my gut.

"The prosecution rests," Zoe said, sitting back down on her chair, glaring at me. I wish she'd go back to ignoring me.

"And the defense?" Nova asked, raising a brow at me.

I had nothing to defend. I was guilty. Everything Zoe had said was true.

"Am I guilty?" I asked, voice breaking through the sobs.

"It is not I who decides such things, child," Nova said softly, and I was suddenly placed in the judge's seat with Nova sitting where I had just been.

"Decide," Nova commanded, and there was so much grief in her eyes for a future I may never see.

I took a few deep breaths, focusing on the beating of my heart until it slowed enough to not feel like it was bursting from my chest.

"Get it together, Freyja," I mumbled to myself. This was a trial in more ways than one. What I felt was real, but this wasn't reality. Zoe was not here. My sister loved me. There was a heap of evidence to prove that.

I turned to look at Zoe and blinked rapidly, trying to see through the illusion—the trial.

"You're not real," I said sadly and a little bit relieved to know my sister didn't hate me. The stars could never take that bond away from us. She'd literally threatened her own life and that of a celestial to save me in some twisted act of love that would have ended every life bonded to Algol. She loved me in her own crazy way.

Zoe smiled, and she turned into a mirror image of me.

Understanding was beginning to flood through me. Understanding of what this trial was testing.

"It's me," I whispered. "I decide my fate here. I choose whether I am guilty or innocent."

Nova said nothing, but turned her head in curiosity, eyes glazing over as a different future crossed her path.

"Bad people do bad things," I said. "What we wore, what we drank, and what we failed to see did not make those vile men hurt us. They did so because they are evil. Because they wanted to."

I swallowed, hugging my arms, showing myself the love I should have always offered myself around that moment. I forgave the parts of me that had held onto the guilt—the shame for not stopping it. For not going home, the chances we could have. I let the shame leak from my soul and out into the cosmos, rid of it once and for all.

Because bad people do bad things.

And I am good.

"I am innocent," I said, voice strong.

Nova smiled. "So be it."

She snapped her fingers, and I was jolted to awareness at the bottom of the ocean, still clinging onto the orb of life. The star propelled me to the surface of the water far faster than I could have done on my own.

I swam the rest of the way to the beach, somehow feeling lighter than I had when I'd gone down.

"You let go of a guilt that was not yours," Nova said, helping me up. "Rise stronger, Freyja."

And I did.

Everything about me felt freer. More alive.

"How long has it been?" I asked.

"One week," she answered, and I breathed a sigh of relief, fearing it had been much longer.

"Is everyone still alive?" I asked, though I wasn't sure she'd answer the question.

"Your loved ones are still fighting for control of the star realms," she nodded.

"Are they winning?" I asked hopefully.

"That remains to be seen," she said, as I followed behind her to my quarters. "Zoe's plan is a strong one, though it leaves zero room for error."

"So you're saying there's a chance," I said, and she said nothing, neither confirming nor denying my enthusiasm.

"Rest, Freyja. You have done well. I should hate to see you fail the next trial."

"I should hate that, too," I agreed, stifling a yawn.

"I will collect you when it is time. Be well," she said, shutting the door.

"One trial down, Ander and Zo. Two more to go and I'm coming home," I whispered.

I stripped off my clothes and hopped in the shower to scrub the saltwater from my hair, though having grown up in the ocean, I knew it never really left me.

Something about completing that first trial had made that night almost seem distant, less disturbing. It was still there, sure. It hadn't erased my memories, but… it wasn't debilitating for me anymore, either.

It's like I'd taken the right kind of ownership for it.

And I was grateful for that.

I finished in the shower, turning my mind to happier thoughts. There was no sense in trying to figure out the second trial. I wouldn't have a clue where to start. I just had to trust myself to make it through and make the right choices.

"I'm coming home," I whispered into the cosmos. "Just stay alive until I get there."

I closed my eyes, letting sleep embrace me in a sweet melody as I drifted off into a deep slumber.

13

Not Her

ELVY

We descended upon the fire realm like a dark mist of fury and shadows.

There would be no mercy. No survivors if the immortals of Arcturus did not submit to Hesperia's will. Even then, Hesperia may not leave without smiting some souls from existence.

I didn't regret my decision to keep Hesperia as far away from Zoe as possible. To hell with the consequences.

The only solace I found was in the sweat drenching Hesperia.

She was erratic and unhinged on so many levels after consuming the star seeds from Algol and Canopus. I hadn't seen her do it, but the guards were moronic. It wasn't hard to overhear their whispers and see the sign of chaos and mania coming from Hesperia.

While it seemed to be making her weaker, it also meant that she was more unpredictable. Reality looked very different for her.

My feet landed uncomfortably along hardened lava rock, not far from just outside the city center's borders.

The smell of sulfur wafted through the air, and my stomach turned sour as I remembered my time here with Zoe.

When she'd earned the trust of Skoll and Tala—the alpha simargls—was yet another moment that I fell more in love with her.

She was my gravity, my sun, my moon, my… moment for as long as there was breath in my lungs and maybe even past then. I would find her in the next life. She was wife—my flame—and I was hers. The revenge of a mad female could not shatter or break our foundation.

"Come," Hesperia purred in my direction, crooking her pointer finger at me.

Every molecule in my body desired to resist her… to turn her flesh into mist. I knew Zoe wanted to claim her death, but my shadows had different ideas. They wanted to end her existence in payment for what she had done and planned to do, even though I still had no clue what her end goal really was.

"Such a good boy," she said, smiling widely, and my flame wanted to melt it off her face.

I managed a low growl as my dark eyes stayed locked on her.

"Charge up, dear. We need you ready to dazzle us with your magic should the Astrals put up a fight or if they simply annoy me."

My nostrils flared in disgust at how callously she talked about ending an entire realm's life.

My heart ached for the dragons who would do anything to protect their riders. Even they did not stand a chance against my death magic once it was unleashed.

Please don't let them fight.

But I knew that was not the way of dragon riders. They were born in bloodlust, destined to fight for their realm—for their star.

Just this once. Stand down.

I didn't know who I prayed to. Maybe it was the celestial himself to come down and save his immortals. Maybe it was God. I just knew they couldn't end. Not like this.

My attention jerked to the sky as a portal opened up through one of the transport zones, and Seraphina, with her massive black dragon, crossed the threshold, sword drawn.

Not good.

My heart simultaneously broke and cried out at who I saw behind her.

Zoe soared through the cosmos like an avenging angel of death. My flame had come for me. I was both angry with her and thankful to catch a glimpse of the one who loves me—despite it all.

Jelly had shifted fully into her flaming simargl form to her right, and Blaz was to her left. Imelda was right behind them.

I'd never been so happy to see Oleander flying behind them with a look of death in his eyes.

If I had any tears to give, they would flow freely down my cheeks. I stifled the screams threatening to break through and schooled my face into a cool facade.

Zoe's eyes fell to mine, and she was screaming at me to let her in, but I kept the door shut, refusing to risk her. It was too dangerous to expose her to the grip Hesperia had on me. We didn't know what would happen, and the unknown was unsafe.

Kai and his brown dragon met Seraphina's as they landed about a hundred yards away from Hesperia's shadowed.

My eyes took in everything, searching for answers I wasn't sure I wanted.

I briefly saw Imelda send a message through an iris, and I hoped it was not for reinforcements. Too many immortals were at risk as it was. And one soul was the most important to me in the entire universe.

Of course, she'd come for me. I would have done the same.

My magic felt the shields surrounding those from Arcturus. They would hold against me for all of five minutes before I would be forced to shatter them.

Hesperia stood beside me, fuming, breaking her usual insane glee at the ensuing violence.

I caught Oleander's eyes, and he turned his head in curiosity, trying to read the playing field. I used the opportunity to feed him the one desire I had if Hesperia tried to use me. Death. My death. My facial expression never changed. I couldn't afford to give anything away, and Oleander made no indication that he saw what I wanted him to do—what my intent was if Hesperia tried to use me.

I glanced back over at my flame, wishing on the stars themselves to come down and swoop her away from this.

But she'd kill them for it and would march right back here.

To this moment.

Zoe turned to face Hesperia, expression ruthless, yet giving nothing away.

My girl had a plan.

I just hoped my magic didn't screw it up.

Hesperia's eyes were wild beside me, and her body convulsed as if she were doing her best to control herself. Maybe she'd burn out if we were lucky.

That fear had always lived within Zoe.

My flame.

What was she doing here?

"Move aside, sister," Hesperia said, pitching her voice across the field. "They have something that I need."

"No," Zoe said simply, clenching her jaw.

What game are you playing at, flame? You know what she will make me do. I wanted to tell her those words through our bond, but I wouldn't risk it until there was no other choice. She knew the danger. Had to know.

"Have you brought me the bow?" Hesperia asked, gliding closer to the shields and pausing just outside them.

"No," Zoe said, not elaborating. She wasn't here to play.

"Then I guess I'll just have to have more fun with Elvy," she said, slicing a sharp nail down my left bicep. It was enough to draw blood, but I didn't allow my body to flinch. What was a little scratch compared to what I've been through?

Zoe's face held no expression, but internally I knew her flame and shadows seethed for blood.

Her eyes were already shifted to her beautiful black darkness, and her shadows embraced her lovingly. Mine begged to join their bond. It was almost painful how badly I ached—we ached—for her.

Hesperia's grip on them was too strong, but I had a feeling she would not be able to hold me the more star seeds she consumed. It was only a matter of time, and I just had to survive until then.

"Look at you," Hesperia said, black hair sticking to the sweat on her neck. "Embracing who you truly are."

"It's not too late," Zoe said, voice just high enough for us to hear, as if it was sent by the wind across the field. "You don't have to do this."

"You know nothing!" she screeched, hurting my ears. "Do you know what it's like to have your father think of you as an abomination? One that he sought to kill?"

Zoe said nothing.

"Of course you don't," Hesperia sneered. "Because you're the second daughter. The perfect child. The chosen one."

"There is nothing perfect about me," Zoe said, stepping forward. "I cannot change what our father did or didn't do to you. But he's not the one calling the shots right now. You are. And you are choosing wrong."

Hesperia's eyes narrowed in madness. She didn't like how reasonable Zoe sounded.

"What is set in motion is set in motion," Hesperia said, letting her bloodlust for vengeance fill her to the brim. There was no reasoning or negotiating with her.

"So be it," Zoe said, unsheathing two blades from across her chest.

If I weren't so terrified for her, I'd be in awe of her beauty—her justice.

"I think it's time for you to die. What fun it will be to deliver your dead body to our father. Do you think he'd be proud of me then?"

How deep did her daddy issues go? Either way, it was affecting what was *mine*.

"Come here, Elvy," Hesperia ordered, and I had no choice but to come to her like a whipped puppy.

Zoe gave nothing away, but her dark gaze locked on mine. She seemed to scream at me to just trust her.

I did. Without question. I just hoped it went the way she wanted.

I noticed Oleander subtly leaking his magic into the shield of Arcturus. He was the strongest shield I knew outside of Zoe. My role suddenly got a little more difficult.

Kai and Seraphina mounted their dragons, and their beasts roared, ready to fight if that's what it came to. Though they would all die by my hand—my magic.

"Showtime, handsome," she said, pulling on the strings of my magic, forcing my will to bend to her whims.

My death magic came in waves against the shield, but it did not break through.

There was a foreign magic here… not Oleander and not the fire magic of Arcturus. This was different… yet familiar.

Hesperia's wicked smile ebbed into one of confusion. She whirled her head around, trying to find the source of what we all felt.

It was warm, loving—a protection that could not be broken.

Howls echoed across the field, and Hesperia lost her grip on my magic as she startled at the unexpected sounds.

Simargls. Fully shifted—fire wielding—simargls stood in front of the dragons.

Skoll and Tala were at the front with flaming crowns floating above their heads. Jelly and Zoe were at their side.

Whatever magic that protected the simargl grove was now protecting all immortals behind their line.

"Impossible," Hesperia whispered, eyes widening in shock.

"Your eyes do not deceive you," Zoe said, taking a vial from Imelda, who had disappeared from the front lines when she arrived. "Take this and go."

Zoe threw the vial in the middle of the field, and Hesperia seemed to salivate for its contents. A star seed. It must be.

I wanted to ask why in the universe she would give Hesperia what she wanted, but Zoe's eyes asked me to trust her again, so I would. I had no choice but to do just that.

"The next time you come into our realm, your head will no longer be attached to your body," Seraphina promised. "It will be posted outside our walls as a warning to all who dare threaten the fire realm."

Hesperia collected the vial and headed back in our direction.

"Go before my dragon burns you alive," Kai agreed.

My eyes were locked on Zoe's, trying to remember every part of her beautiful face. The darkness—everything. My perfect equal in every way. My girl.

Her eyes shifted to the beautiful green flames that had enamored me to her from the moment I'd first seen her on that beach in that stupid volleyball tournament. I was hers right then and there.

"I love you," she mouthed.

I let the feeling embrace me—warm me—at my very core, where nothing but coldness had taken residence under the torture of Hesperia.

Before I could even try to respond, Hesperia was dragging us through the transport zone and away from my flame.

I couldn't look back, but I felt her eyes on me.

I'm coming back to you, Zoe Eferhild. Just seeing her had reignited some hope within me. She was the word herself—hope. Realm-healer. Emerging of Legends. She would save us all. Save us from ourselves.

My starlight.

14

The things I didn't say
CLODOVEA

"I melda and Delmira are both going to kill you once they find out you came with me," Aura whispered under her breath for the third time.

"I think they will be forgiving as long as we don't die, okay?" I said, and Tiergan chuckled gruffly.

"In and out. Just like we planned," he said, and four of his Shadowed Sublunary were behind him.

"With Hesperia distracted in Arcturus, this should be easy. We don't even need to go to the city center. It's on a different island."

"How do you know they'll be there?" I asked, eyes scanning for threats. Imelda really would bring me back to life just to kill me again if I didn't make it back from this mission. It was one thing when we knew the other one was on an order, but to dip out without telling anyone—not even Delmira—that was against every protocol.

"Because those who knew about the abuse made a plan with me if things ever got bad. I'd say this is bad, right? Plus, it's a place my mother showed me a long time ago. Vega is not the only realm with secrets."

"Point taken," I said.

"Yes, Aura," Tiergan answered. "This would qualify as bad."

"They'll be there," she said. "And if they aren't, then they are dead."

"Then I hope they are there, Aura," I said sincerely.

She'd added a second, smaller feather to her hair. A blue one. I wondered if that had anything to do with the baby, but it felt rude to ask, so I didn't.

"Why didn't you just tell Delmira?"

"Because she would have said no," I said, gripping the hilt of my longsword. "And I would have defied her. Better to ask for forgiveness than permission."

Tiergan laughed again, smirking. "You are not so unlike the rebels, Clodovea."

"Perhaps not," I agreed.

We all perched on the ledge of a cliff as the other Sublunary held back.

"You see that glow down there? Through the waterfall?" Aura asked.

I followed her finger, trying to find what she was talking about.

"No," I said, shaking my head.

"Good," she said. "You're not supposed to. Follow me."

Aura unfurled her wings and leaped towards the valley, gliding as close to the water as she could get without actually hitting it, and we all followed suit.

From the looks of it, there was only a very solid rock wall behind the roaring waterfall, and I had half a mind to turn around before we went splat against it, but I swallowed down my fear, dashing through the spray to go right through the illusion.

"Oh hell," I said, shaking the cold water from my face. "Warning next time, Aura."

She laughed, landing easily on her feet and holding her belly.

"Come on. We're close," she said, guiding us through the confusing passageways. No way was I getting out of here without her help.

Tiergan brushed shoulders with me, and my muscles loosened from their tense state.

I hadn't exactly bonded with the male, but he'd shared his story about Janus with the rest of us. My heart ached for him in ways I couldn't explain. To lose a love like that… I didn't know how he still had breath in his lungs.

"What troubles you?" he asked quietly.

"Who says anything is bothering me?" I asked.

"I can just tell," he said, shrugging, as if that was an acceptable answer.

"I'd feel selfish talking with you about it since my partner is alive and well," I admitted. "What do I have to complain about? My existential crisis is insignificant."

"This isn't a battle of who has had it worse," Tiergan said pointedly. "I'm just saying I'm here if you want to talk. That's all."

His sincerity was unmistakable, and I prayed the stars would have good things in store for him in the future.

"Thank you, Tiergan."

He smiled and turned to other matters as we continued following Aura, who led us deeper into the winding caverns. If she listened to us, she didn't give herself away. She seemed lost in her own thoughts, guided by magic to lead her to those who were loyal to her.

"Where do you think she's bringing us?" he asked.

"Not sure, but the air pressure has changed. Can you feel it?" I asked, opening my mouth to clear it out. We'd been on a steady incline since going through the falls.

"Indeed, but the air feels… fresher the more we move up."

"The way of wind," Aura muttered, slowing down her pace to match ours. "It's been so long since I've been here."

She paused abruptly in front of a white stone door that was part of the rock wall.

"How long?" he asked, placing a gentle hand on her shoulder.

"Long enough," she sighed. "I had to protect them. From him. We tried to fight back as silently and efficiently as possible. Bringing people to our cause against him. Now that Abel is gone, they have a new enemy."

"How many immortals are hidden here?" I asked, heart beating stronger somehow.

"The last time the numbers reached me, we were five hundred strong, but I expect more now. Abel became more volatile in recent years. It wasn't safe to communicate with the immortals here anymore."

"My dear Aura… were you forming your own rebellion?" Tiergan asked, eyes twinkling with raw adoration.

"I always liked you," she said, smiling. "Yes. These are the best of my immortals. They will fight for us."

"With us," I said.

Aura nodded and rubbed her swollen belly.

"What are we waiting for?" I asked, not impatiently.

Aura embraced the bracelet around her wrist and closed her eyes, sighing in small relief.

"The male I love is behind this door," she whispered, like a secret. "He doesn't know about…," she trailed off, looking down at the little life in her womb.

Tiergan and I both stepped closer, placing a hand on each of her shoulders.

"We'll help you tell him if you want," I offered, and a tear rolled down her cheeks.

"I'm sure he will just be glad you're alive. Do they know what's happened?"

She shook her head.

"I sealed them in. For their own protection. The last thing I saw when I closed this door was the broken look of betrayal on his face. But I did it for him. To keep him safe."

"I know," I said, folding her into my arms.

"He knows," Tiergan added, embracing us both, and I let him.

"What if he hates me?" she asked, voice breaking, and my heart threatened to shatter into pieces.

"Don't let fear stop you from flying," Tiergan said.

"We are with you. Every step of the way," I vowed.

I wiped the final tears from her eyes and leaned my forehead against hers. "You are worth loving. You and this child."

"And I will snap his spine in half if he is unworthy," Tiergan added, and I nodded my agreement, all too happy to promise violence.

"He is a good male. That's why I'm so afraid, I think. To embrace someone who truly loves me in all the ways I should have been by my husband."

I laced my fingers through hers.

"Fate is ready to greet you, Aura. Let's not keep him waiting."

She nodded her head and placed her mark against the air sigil carved into the door.

I shielded my eyes from the sudden brightness coming from the door as we all stepped through together to pluck the string of fate once more.

15

Not Him

ZOE

Not him.

That's all I could think as I watched her take him away from me again.

It took every ounce of reason I possessed not to fly after him, but the songs of fate knew better. It was not time for me to claim what was mine. Going after him now would only result in one or both of us dying.

"Zoe?" Oleander asked, placing a gentle hand on my shoulder.

Jelly circled me, whimpering softly.

"I'm here, Oleander," I said, staring at the empty shadows from which my flame had just disappeared.

The black tendrils still swirled around me, and they mourned for their bonded, and I wanted to wail with them.

"We will get him back," he said firmly, nudging me to turn towards him, but I didn't want to turn around. If I did, then my failure would be real.

"I'm going to kill her," I said, voice low—an oath.

"I know," he said, pulling me into his arms, and I let my stiff muscles relax into him. "We're both going to reunite with those we love."

"You ever going to tell her that?" I asked, letting my eyes turn back to green flames.

"Freyja knows I love her," he countered, and I stepped back from him.

"Perhaps, but I'm sure she'd like to hear it."

"Maybe I wanted to give her a reason to come back to me," he said, voice cocky, but I saw through him. He sincerely feared their love—of being abandoned.

"My sister does not love easily," I said, bending down to scratch Jelly's ears. "But once you have her heart, she's yours."

"Feeling sentimental, are we, love?"

I held his gaze.

"If I lose love, I lose me."

Oleander's eyes softened at my vulnerability. He knew what I meant.

And he wasn't the only one who felt this overwhelming feeling of radical love. Clodovea and Imelda. Delmira and Blaz. Finn and Zadie. All choosing to love each other recklessly in a time when we didn't know if we'd see tomorrow's rising moon. In a time where we all might turn to stardust before we were meant to. A time when our life in the starlight was waning and flickering with every choice we made.

All we had was hope. Not in the future. But in right now. In this very moment.

Blaz and Imelda moved in closer to us. I was sure they saw the fight in my eyes.

"We're with you, Zo," Blaz said, clasping my hand in his.

"We will follow you anywhere," Imelda agreed. "To the end."

Oleander looked at me solemnly, but rolled his eyes. "I'm here, aren't I? Have been since day one."

"Oh, how the tides have changed since then," I said, rolling my shoulders, trying to release the strain that had grown there since seeing my husband—my flame—at the mercy of my sister.

Skoll and Tala trotted up to us then, pulling me from the thoughts that whirled around in my mind. Their crown of flames had been extinguished, but their power still radiated around them.

Jelly bowed slightly to the alphas, and Oleander and I followed suit.

"You came," I said, smiling softly.

"It is our duty to protect the life of Arcturus," Skoll said through my mind.

"And so we did," Tala said.

"I am grateful," I answered. "We all are."

"Your words when you left the grove were not forgotten, Zoe Eferhild," Skoll said. *"It had almost been too long since we'd sealed off our grace to the immortals here."*

"We have much to atone for," Tala added.

Kai and Seraphina came beside us and knelt before the alphas.

"If it's all the same to you, let's move forward together. Let us leave the past where it lies now," Kai said, and Seraphina nodded the sentiment.

"They're right," I agreed. "Forward is all we have."

Oleander gave me a wink, and the alphas bowed.

"So be it," Skoll agreed.

"Thank you for what you have done for the realm of Arcturus today," Seraphina said, rising with Kai. "I fear it will not be the end."

"That fear will ring true," Oleander said. "The simargl would be a great help in the final battle."

"We cannot ask that of them," I said hastily.

"Ask and it will be done," Skoll said. *"We may serve Arcturus, but we are united as one. If one realm falls, so shall Arcturus."*

"Call on us. We shall answer," Tala said.

"We will all answer you, Zoe. We swear it," Seraphina said, unsheathing her knife, ready to make a star vow.

"Enough blood has been paid," I said, shaking my head. "Keep your word, and you will be redeemed in the eyes of the Court of Vega."

Seraphina smiled, nodding.

"Thank you for coming," Kai said as their dragons landed behind them. "I can only imagine how difficult that must have been."

Oleander pulled me to his side before Kai could offer the words of sympathy for Elvy that were on the tip of his tongue. I didn't want to hear it, but I understood his sentiments and did not begrudge him for it.

"We'll be going back to Vega. We need to make sure Hesperia goes to Rigil next."

"We await your orders, Zoe," Seraphina said, mounting her dragon.

Blaz and Imelda joined us as Jelly circled around Oleander and me.

"See you soon," I called as I unfurled my wings to head back to Vega with my family by my side.

I smiled as greenery began flowing through the grounds below me, with the promise of life lingering in the air. A vow fulfilled by the simargls.

16

Lilac Existence

DELMIRA

"**W**here the hell is Clodovea?" I bellowed to no one in particular.

Imelda was going to end my lilac existence if Clodovea was off this realm.

"Calm down, Delm," Finnian muttered, running a hand through his hair, but I could sense the uneasiness from him, too. He knew he was just as screwed as I was. Clodovea would have little mercy for either of us.

"Do you think she went with Aura?" I asked, feeling uneasy about that possibility.

"I can't sense her anywhere here. She must have," he agreed.

"Why would she do that without telling me?"

"Would you have let her go?" he asked, brow raised.

"Hell no," I said, hands on my hips. "It's my job to keep you all alive. It's a hell of a lot harder to do that when you go into unsanctioned enemy territory."

My chest was tight as my heart raced. I wasn't sure if immortals could have heart attacks, but I felt pretty close to one.

"Then you have your answer," he said, shrugging as if it were no big deal.

My iris warmed at my side, and I whipped it out, praying it was Clodovea, but it was Evander.

"Lady Astral Zoe has returned with the others. They are heading your way," Evander's calm voice came over the iris.

I didn't bother responding to his report.

My heart raced at the anticipation of Blaz coming back unharmed, and with slight fear that Imelda was about to end my life, just as Blaz and I had fallen into a good rhythm.

"Of course not," Finn muttered.

"What?" I snapped and shook my head. "Sorry."

"Evander said Zoe, not The Astrals. They didn't get him back."

My heart broke all over again for Elvy. I hadn't really expected them to, but apparently I'd still hoped, if my disappointment was any evidence of that.

"Yet," I said, voice steady. "That wasn't the mission. We didn't expect him to return to us."

He nodded his agreement. "I know. I just hoped… somehow, you know?"

I did. I'd hold that hope in my heart until it burned me alive.

Moments later Zoe strode through the doors with Jelly, Oleander, Imelda, and Blaz following behind her.

Our Lady Astral's form was rigid. I feared if I put just the right pressure, her entire body would shatter. I could only imagine what seeing Elvy had done to her. Even the air around her was heavy—lethargic with grief and vengeance.

"Was the mission successful?" I asked.

"Hesperia got the star seed of Arcturus," Zoe said, voice eerily calm, but her eyes were not focused on me. They were somewhere else entirely.

I hesitated before asking the next question, but I needed to know. "Casualties?"

Zoe's green eyes finally found mine. "None."

"None?" Finn asked, saying what I felt—utter shock.

We'd expected at least some fatalities.

"The simargls from the grove," Imelda said. "They came. Their magic protected every life there."

"And Hesperia's growing weaker. Her body isn't meant to be a vessel for that many stars," Zoe said, smiling wickedly. "She's definitely consumed the star seeds from Algol and Canopus already. I could feel them within her. I don't think she'll be able to control Elvy much longer."

"Really?" Finn asked, voice vulnerable. "She's gaining more magic than any immortal alive, yet it is too weak to handle it. What a pity," he mused.

"If my *sight* is to be reliable, then yes," Zoe confirmed. "She's not even controlling the shadows anymore, except what is in Elvy. She can't control him and her followers at the same time, so feel free to kill any of her legion you come across. They are there of their own free will."

"When do we strike to get him back?" I asked, shifting my weight to the balls of my feet, ready to pounce with a single word from her.

"Rigil," she answered. "She'll consume the star seed from Arcturus before going there. Hesperia will be weakened enough that I think we can take him back."

"But we won't have the protection of the simargl," Oleander said, crossing his arms.

"I know," Zoe said. "We'll have to make a plan to take Elvy before he has a chance to use his magic. The shields won't hold him."

"And we can't use the simargl's power?" Imelda asked.

"No," Zoe shook her head. "The magic is from the grove itself. It cannot travel past Arcturus."

"Hell," I muttered. "That would have been useful."

"We'll figure out another way. We need to learn what we can about her plans."

"What, like a spy or something?" I asked.

Zoe smiled. "We already have who we need. We just need to wake them."

"My immortals are still in a coma," Oleander said. "Your last healing did not wake them."

"I know," Zoe said. "But I want to try something different this time. My treatment with Aura gave me an idea."

"If you can wake them up before we have to face Hesperia again… that would be invaluable intel," Finn said appreciatively.

"What do you want us to do in the meantime?" I asked as Blaz moved subtly closer to me.

"Is Sierra still here?" Zoe asked.

"She left when you all did to check on her realm, but she has since returned."

"Good. Blaz, help Clodovea and Sierra start work on a plan to get Elvy back in Rigil with minimal loss of life, yeah?"

I swallowed.

"Where is Clove?" Imelda asked, scanning the area for her.

I sighed, knowing this was coming.

"We think she's with Tiergan and Aura in Canopus," I said, voice steadier than I felt.

"*Think?*" she clarified.

"She left without clearance," I said.

"Why would she do that?" Imelda asked. "I'm going after her."

"That would not be wise," Blaz said, moving beside me. "You don't know where she is, and you could compromise her position if you left now."

Imelda's face was filled with worry, and my eyes softened. She just wanted to know she was safe.

"Aura knows her realm far better than Hesperia," Zoe said, placing a hand gently on her forearm. "They'll be in and out."

"Just like Elvy was in and out?" Imelda snapped back with instant regret in her eyes.

Zoe's jaw clenched, and Jelly let out a warning rumble.

"I'm so sorry," Imelda said, hand covering her mouth in embarrassment.

"Emotions are high right now," Oleander said, voice smooth. "Let's all take a step back. You need to get packed for Algol, Zo."

"We're good, Imelda," she said with a neutral tone. "Delm, Blaz, keep me updated while I'm gone."

I nodded. "Of course."

Oleander and Jelly followed her out of the room, and Imelda turned her gaze towards me.

"I can't believe I said that to her," she said, plopping down on the velvet teal couch.

"We've all said stupid things," I said, sitting down next to her.

"I mean, I say dumb stuff at least once a day," Blaz agreed, sitting on my other side.

Finn leaned against the rustic desk, crossing his arms.

"No agreement there, twin?" I asked, raising a brow.

"I'm empathetic, Imelda, though I can't relate personally," he said, smirking.

We all flipped him off, and he laughed, exposing all his teeth.

"I've got to get back into the archives," he said. "Shoot me a missive through the iris if you need anything or if there's been a development."

"Love you, too," I called after his retreating form.

"Love you, Delm," he answered, closing the door behind him.

Imelda kicked her boots off and moved to the fluffy gray rug on the floor to stretch out.

Blaz and I moved together on instinct, but we didn't touch. We hadn't exactly told everyone we were dating. Hell, we hadn't even called this dating. We didn't know what it was yet. I wouldn't say we were hiding it, but we were just taking our time in trying to figure each other out.

"So, when are you two going to come clean about screwing each other?" Imelda asked, eyes closed, but a smirk played on her lips.

"What are you talking about?" I asked, stiffening.

"Your sexual tension is suffocating," she said. "Plus, I totally saw you two doing it in the locker room."

"What the hell, Imelda!" I yelled, throwing a pillow at her, but she just laughed. Blaz roared with her, not embarrassed in the slightest. After all, he was a secure male.

"How long have you known?"

"A while," she shrugged. "No one cares, you know?"

"How many know?" I asked.

"Everyone?" she mused. "I'm not sure. It's kind of hard to miss."

I ran a hand through my hair.

Blaz pulled me next to him, placing a kiss on my head, and I swatted him away.

"Don't you get any ideas about public displays of affection," I said seriously, and his eyes twinkled with delight.

"Seriously, Delm. Everyone's cool with it. No matter what happens," she added. "Plus, I owe you like a century's worth of torment for all the crap you both gave me and Clove."

"Can I beg for your mercy?" Blaz asked, though it didn't sound like he really minded the teasing at all.

"Not a chance," she answered.

I hated feeling exposed. It made me feel vulnerable, like there was something for someone to exploit, but I trusted Imelda and the Luminaries. Most of all, I trusted Blaz to keep our private life between us.

"You good?" Blaz asked, expression serious. He knew me too well.

I nodded, not trusting my voice to convey that truth.

"We need to find Sierra," I said, rising from his embrace. "Want to come, Imelda?"

"Nah," she said, yawning. "I'm going to think of the ways Clodovea is going to make this little stunt of hers up to me."

"I'd hate to be on the receiving end of that smirk," Blaz said, standing next to me.

Imelda said nothing, but grinned wider.

"Meet for dinner?" I asked.

"See you then," she agreed, never opening her eyes.

Blaz laced my fingers through his and pulled me to the guest quarters to find Sierra.

"Are you actually good?" he asked, raising our interlocked fingers. "With this being more public than you thought?"

"I think so," I answered, not willing to give a blanket yes. "I'm really happy with how things are… I just don't want anything to ruin it, okay?"

"Okay," he said, kissing the back of my palm. "I told you I'd give you time. I meant it. Your pace, okay?"

I nodded, squeezing his hand, enjoying it. I'd analyze my fears another day.

We reached Sierra's door, and I pulled my hand away to knock.

She answered quickly and greeted us with a smile on her face. Her silver hair was braided down her back, with flowers interwoven throughout.

"We need your assistance," I said, trying to remind myself to be softer in my delivery. Ask, not demand. "Please?"

Yuck. The word made me want to punch something.

Blaz shot me a smirk that Sierra couldn't see.

"Oh?" she asked, inviting us into her space.

"The hell?" I whispered aloud without meaning to. She had completely transformed her guest quarters into a magical fairy forest with live plants and twinkling lights.

"Made yourself at home, huh?" Blaz chuckled, amused.

"I find that I am much more relaxed in this environment. Don't worry, I'll take it all down before leaving," she said, but I wasn't worried about that, really.

"No worries," I said, waving her off.

"Come sit," she said, gesturing to a moss-covered sofa, and I sat down on it, hoping my backside didn't get wet or something. I almost groaned in surprise at how comfortable it was. "What can I help the Court of Vega with?"

"You know Hesperia will be making her way to Rigil next if things go according to plan," I said, pausing for her to nod in confirmation.

"I do, yes. I've already informed Terran."

"Great," I said, moving along. "We plan to get Elvy back that night as well, and we would like your help with that."

"I believe Zoe made it quite clear that to go near him while he is being controlled would mean death."

I ran a hand through my hair again.

"Right," Blaz agreed. "We're not suggesting you do anything, and we'll handle all the dangerous stuff. We just want some insight on how to move through Rigil. What area should we lead her to? That sort of thing. We'll need to strike quickly before Elvy can release his magic."

Sierra sat back in her flower-covered throne of a chair and hummed in thought.

"Well, the answer is obvious," she said. "The tunnels."

Blaz's eyes lit up. "If we had a ground user with us, we could snatch him through the tunnels."

"But that wouldn't break the connection she has with him," Sierra argued, and she had a point. "That would leave my immortals vulnerable."

"What if we broke the link first?" I asked.

Sierra nodded, pursing her lips.

"That could work, but not a moment before."

Big ask, but I understood the why behind it.

"Alright," I agreed. "We'll figure that part out. Is there a specific place in Rigil we need to funnel her to?"

"No," she answered quickly. "Our underground system is vast. We'd be able to reach her from anywhere."

"Full on trench warfare," I mumbled.

"Except a lot deadlier," Blaz said.

"With greater risk," Sierra added.

Blaz and I both rose from our seats, and I was pleasantly surprised that the moss had not left any moisture on my backside.

"Thanks for the help," Blaz said.

"Will you be leaving soon?" I asked.

"I would have already left, but I was waiting for Clodovea."

I swallowed. "She's gone on a mission. Not sure when she'll be back."

Sierra's eyebrows furrowed as she sipped her tea.

"Very well, then. I'll be on my way back to Rigil as soon as I'm packed up."

"I'll send Evander to escort you back."

"No need," she said.

"I insist, Lady Astral. We need all the Astrals safe and accounted for," I answered.

"Alright," she consented.

We both bowed slightly and left through the door we'd come in through.

"Sparring?" he asked, and I was suddenly filled with the energy to break some bones.

"You're on."

17

Freedom on a Mountaintop

FREYJA

I followed Nova onto the island after eating breakfast.

My dreams had been filled with Oleander's blue eyes, and my body longed for him.

I shook the memories from my mind, needing to focus.

My feet ached, and the pack on my back was beginning to feel uncomfortable on my shoulders. I didn't think the island was this big. In fact, I was certain we should have circled the starlit island at least twice by now, but a mountain grew in the distance.

"What is this?" I asked, dumbfounded.

"The island reveals what it needs to reveal to each Emerging," Nova said, as if a mountain popping into existence made total sense. I suppose it did to her.

After what felt like hours of walking, we arrived at the base of the mountain, which revealed a snow cap at the top beneath the gleam of the moon. I silently cursed at my already throbbing feet.

Nova paused her walking at the foot of what partially resembled a trail, but I wouldn't call it well-maintained.

"Climb," Nova instructed.

"Climb?" I asked, swallowing hard. "How far?"

"To the summit," she said, as if it were just a regular night. "The pack has everything you need to be successful."

"Is there a time limit?"

"No," she answered. "But you can always end the trial if it seems too much."

"That would mean failing," I said, shaking my head. "Not an option."

"Remember that time moves differently here," she said in a surprisingly gentle tone.

"I had better move fast then," I said, tossing the pack on the ground.

I checked the bag for essentials. I was no expert mountaineer, but Zoe and I had summited our fair share of mountains as mortals. As long as there was some type of trail, I'd make it.

"How many feet?" I asked, sizing up my enemy.

"Fifteen thousand feet," she answered.

Great. Depending on the switchbacks and mileage, this could call for an overnight camp.

The pack consisted of a one-man tent, sleeping bag, food provisions, medical supplies, water, crampons, warmer layers, and hiking poles. No map. No compass. I prayed the trail was marked somewhat, or I was going to be screwed. Zoe and I were both bad at directions.

"What's this supposed to prove, anyway?" I asked, pulling on the pack and strapping it snugly against me.

"Give me that answer when you finish, child."

I nodded, taking a deep breath. One foot in front of the other. Nova was gone, which left me with only my thoughts for company.

The trail was rocky, and my shoes did little to support or prevent the rolling of my ankles. I also had no fancy watch to tell me how many calories I burned, so I needed to listen to my body on when to replenish, or I'd never make it up this mountain.

I wondered if this was amusing to the celestials. To make a mortal climb up this mountain when they could simply fly. If only I had wings, this would be over in mere minutes, but I didn't. Wishing for that would only make my pain worse, so I shook the longing from me and refocused on my surroundings.

So far, the rocky climb was well-marked, but it was by no means smooth. My heartbeat rose, and I did my best to take rests to allow it to come down. These switchbacks could be the death of me if I let them. And so far, this mountain was a steep ascent with few flat surfaces. This was both good and bad. It meant I would reach the top faster if I didn't stop too much. It would also be brutal on my body. As long as my mind didn't break, neither would my body.

I munched on some kind of granola as I sat on a rock, letting my body rest for a couple of minutes. The view was already stunning beneath the light of the cosmos. Nova's palace looked small from up here, and with how brightly the stars shone, it almost made the island look fake—like a painting. I swallowed the rough granola with a few gulps of water. Then, I quickly bandaged a spot on my right foot that was showing the telltale signs of a blister. I still had a way to go, and getting a blister was not on my to-do list.

I'd occasionally hear the breaking of a branch or the scurry of little feet, but I never saw the animals that were responsible for the sounds. I kept hoping to see one of them, as the stars only knew what kind of creatures lived on the island with Nova. This thought also struck fear into me, as I didn't have a weapon to fight bigfoot either if he was feeling hungry.

My skin was caked with the grime of my sweat, and my side burned with an ache I couldn't soften.

I was certain one more step was impossible.

But I took one more step.

And another.

My calves screamed, and my rests became longer.

With no watch to track the passing of time, and no sun to guide me, I had no idea how long I'd been hiking up this mountain.

But I kept going. I couldn't stop. The air cooled against my sweat-drenched skin, making my body convulse in shivers. This meant I'd reached a higher elevation.

Mercifully, I came across a flatter surface next to a straight drop down the mountain. It wasn't ideal, but I didn't know when I'd find a more suitable place to make camp for the night. My hands and forearms were sore from gripping the hiking poles so tightly.

My fingers fumbled as I tried to pitch the tent. Each task felt like an eternity, and I held in a scream as one of the tent poles pinched my finger. If one more thing went wrong, I was going to lose it.

I finally got it secured to the ground and tossed in some food, water, and the sleeping bag. It wasn't snowing at this elevation yet, but it was freezing cold. I'd have to wear the crampons tomorrow.

I stripped off my layers until I got to the base and forced myself to lie on top of the sleeping bag until I was no longer sweating. I munched on some more dried food, not really tasting much of anything. The food was only replenishing the calories I burned and nothing more. I gulped down more water, checking how much I had left. Enough. I had enough.

Curling up in my warm sleeping bag, I squeezed my hands between my thighs, trying to find some warmth and comfort. I let my thoughts drift to Ander… and the arms I craved to hold me. Stretching my ears, I tried to hear his voice, still connected to my body in the realm of Algol, but I heard nothing. I knew it was an irrational hope to hear him here, or Zoe, for that matter.

That last trial had nearly broken me, and I shuddered at the vehemence that had been in Zoe's expression, despite knowing it wasn't really her. I wondered if she'd found Elvy yet and if they were okay. I couldn't help but grieve for them, despite needing to focus on the trial before me.

Sighing, I closed my eyes as the soft putters of footsteps surrounded me, and I resolved to embrace death by bigfoot if he came. It wasn't long before the sounds of the mountain lulled me to sleep, and worries of tall tales were forgotten.

***

Stiff. My entire body was stiff as I rolled out of the sleeping bag.

"I shouldn't have stopped," I whispered, folding my body into a downward dog pose in a futile attempt to stretch out the tight rubber bands I had for muscles now. This was going to be rough.

I found a place outside the tent to take care of my business, and sorted out my layers for the day, opting to attach the crampons to my shoes already. By how cold it was, I anticipated hitting snow and ice sooner rather than later.

I ate my fill of food and drank more water, then packed up the minimal campsite while glaring at the top of the summit. Fortunately, it was a clear night, and my head turned as I caught the flash of something bright at the very top of the mountain. Starlight. It must be.

With one final stretch of my stiff muscles, I set out on the rocky terrain, grateful that I'd opted to wear the crampons as ice soon met my feet.

Even then, my feet threatened to slip from underneath me, and my hands gripped the poles for dear life. One slip down this mountain was going to hurt, if not kill me.

"Just a few more miles," I lied to myself, and I crawled along the steep incline on the hundredth switchback of this summit.

The gloves I wore did okay in protecting me from the elements, but my arm muscles were exhausted trying to keep me upright.

The orb of light grew brighter, and a hum of power filled the night air. I was getting closer. Had to be, right?

As I stepped onto a particularly difficult spot on the trail, my crampons failed to find purchase, and my right leg went sliding down the switchback, carrying me with it.

My heart hammered as the faces of those I loved flashed before my eyes. I didn't even have the strength to scream in terror as death zoomed towards me.

At the end of this switchback was death, so I dug my feet into the ice, as well as my poles, and gave all the strength I had left to stopping my tumble into darkness.

The screech of the ice filled my ears as my body came to a halt on the mountain.

Tears pricked my eyes and my lips quivered as I sat paralyzed in fear of what could have just happened.

Ander wouldn't have been there to catch me like he had at the rock wall. I would have ceased to exist.

I let out a wail of fear and anger as my whole body shook, despite feeling like a block of ice.

I was petrified to move another inch, and I also had no choice but to move.

I wanted to break.

Breaking wasn't a choice.

Fear wasn't welcomed here. Not now. Fear would get me killed.

I swallowed the lump in my throat and wiped the tears from my eyes.

"I am not alone," I said. "They are with me."

I thought of my mother first, letting her memory fill me with her love. Then I thought of my father, letting his memories fill me with strength. Then I moved to Ander and Zoe. My rocks. My anchors. The souls who could get me through any storm.

My story wouldn't end here.

I'd come too far.

I rose.

"One foot in front of the other," I whispered.

I took a step, finding purchase beneath me, and took another, ignoring the ache in every atom of my body.

With every step that felt uncertain, I kept going. Despite the fear of falling, the fear of failing was even worse. So, I wouldn't. I'd keep going.

I got through the difficult section, but I didn't breathe a sigh of relief. Not yet. Not until my hand touched that orb of light, signaling the end of this trial—of this moment.

Three more miles of hell, and I came to a halt at the miraculous sight.

Tears filled my eyes as the orb of light came into view.

The hunger. The thirst. The pain.

I was here despite all of that.

Stumbling my way to the orb, I paused, glancing out over the island and the sea of starlight. I breathed in its beauty, grateful for the breath in my lungs.

I embraced the starlight.

18

Feathers of Fury
CLODOVEA

This place reminded me of Musterion.

A sacred place hidden away by someone who loved their immortals more than their own life.

The light led us into a terrarium of sorts that seemed to be hidden by winding caverns up above, shielding this place from prying eyes. The rocks turned into grass the more we moved forward, and the cosmos shone brightly above us, which was the cause of the blinding glow when we'd opened the door.

The chatter of immortals of varying ages greeted our ears, and my braids blew in a breeze created by the enormous wind turbine in the center of the naturally hidden field.

Voices drew closer to us, and I was fairly certain that the only thing keeping Aura moving was the pull from Tiergan and me on either side of her arms. Each of us looped one arm around her.

"Aura—Lady Astral?" a petite female with blonde pixie hair asked, eyes growing wide.

Aura nodded shyly, and the female burst into tears at the sight of her.

"Oh, my stars!" she exclaimed, tossing the basket she'd been collecting mushrooms in to the side. "You're back!"

"I am," Aura responded, sounding a little more sure of herself.

A crowd was gathering as we paused a few feet away from the windmill.

There were shouts and whispers of *she's back* as far as my immortal ears could hear. Everyone seemed excited to have their Lady Astral returned, which I hoped was a good sign that things would go well.

"Aura?" a male asked, stepping closer than anyone else had dared to. His brown skin mirrored her own, but his hair was lighter than Aura's. His green eyes held love for the female I was keeping upright.

"Rai," she said, stepping towards the male, a little unsure of her footing.

His gaze moved slowly down to her hands that caressed her belly. He quickly looked back up, and the adoration in his eyes made me loosen my hands from the fists they'd become… just in case the male was stupid.

"Are you okay?" he asked.

That was all he asked. Rai didn't ask about Abel or the fate of the star realms. He just wanted to know that Aura was okay, and my body relaxed even more. Tiergan's gaze caught mine, and he subtly nodded, shifting his weight to loosen up as I had.

"That's a hard question to answer," she admitted, stepping closer to him.

The smell of smoke and fire drifted in the air, and I saw a few immortals working on creating a massive bonfire. A celebration of the return of Aura.

"Try," he said softly, moving a few more steps closer.

"I'm physically okay," she promised.

"I hear a *but* at the end of that sentence, whether you choose to speak it," Rai said, closing the distance between them.

"Rai," she breathed, and the love I heard in her voice made me want to avert my gaze at their reunion.

"How long do you have?" he asked, and I realized that he had no idea that Abel was dead.

"I'm here to stay," she said, grinning widely, but there were tears in her eyes.

"Stay?" he asked. "Does that mean…"

The air had gone silent with a pregnant pause.

"Abel is dead," she said, voice strong.

"Can it be?" Rai asked, looking towards both Tiergan and me.

"That sorry excuse of a male is gone. For good. He won't be coming back. Not again," I confirmed.

Rai raised his brow at the 'not again' part, but he was too busy whirling Aura around in his arms to inquire further.

"You must tell us everything," he said, and the crowd cheered loudly, scattering to make preparations for a feast.

I moved closer to Tiergan and sat with him on a log that was much more comfortable than it looked. The immortals here had created a lovely village in her absence. I left them to it until Aura called for us to join them. She greeted each immortal with a smile and hug as they beamed their well wishes for her. My heart softened further for all this female had done to protect this place.

"That female deserves some happiness," Tiergan said, eyes shining with delight.

"I couldn't agree more," I said seriously. "To think… it's been here all this time. They've been waiting for her. He has been waiting for her. The torment he must have felt at knowing what Abel was doing to her."

"These immortals would have gone to battle for her," Tiergan said, crossing his arms. "But she wouldn't let them."

"They would have died," I said, weighing the odds in my mind. "She knew that and would not risk them."

"I long for a day when we are allowed to love freely without the threat of death lingering over us in the shadows."

"I long for that, too," I whispered, pushing my braids behind me.

"Do you think you'll find it again?" I asked. "Love, I mean."

"I don't know if I will ever love anyone the way I loved Janus," he admitted. "What do you do after such a great love?"

I shook my head, not knowing the answer. I wouldn't know what to do if I lost Imelda. Loving again after her felt like an impossibility. That was a certainty.

"I'm glad Aura is getting this chance," I said.

"Me too. It makes an old male smile," he said, stroking his mustache in thought.

My spirit melted for him even more upon seeing his purity. How I had once hated the male rebel leader embarrassed me.

"Was it worth it? To denounce the stars?"

He shifted his foot on the grass beneath us.

"It was never a choice, Clodovea. My family knew what the stars had taken from us. I had the burden of knowing what the realms could be. What The Archer had helped create them to be—truly intertwined. Peace. Harmony. Balance. Freedom. All of those things. This division and hatred for nothing more than the magic in our veins… something we have no control over… I could not stand for it. I could not swear allegiance to a celestial that did not accept every part of me."

I paused, turning my head at the confession.

"More than Algol runs in your veins?" I asked, heart racing.

"Oh yes, Clove. And I would not choose one or the other, and I was not as powerful as the Astral line of Elvy or Zoe. So I had to denounce the stars entirely, and even then, they chose for me. Took my magic from Rigil. I'd never felt so empty."

My heart broke all over again.

"My condolences are not sufficient," I said, unsure of what to say.

"You're right about that," he said, laughing softly. "But I still have hope."

I was impressed with this male. To still have hope in the stars after all they'd taken from him.

"You hope that once Zoe reunites the realms, your magic will come back."

"Yes. I do hope for that," he admitted. "I believe in the stars. Despite it all. How could I not when they gift such beautiful magic? That doesn't mean I don't hold them accountable for the mistakes they've made. For letting their greed cloud their purpose. They have much to make up for in earning our trust back."

"But Janus?"

"The stars did not take him from me. Hesperia did that. And her due is coming."

"Zoe will make sure of that."

"Indeed, she will."

Aura's voice rang out through the crowd. Laughter. She was laughing at something Rai whispered in her ear. Both of them were barefoot, dancing around in the grass to music that came from somewhere I couldn't pinpoint.

Her gaze caught mine, and she motioned us over.

"Come join us. We're about to begin."

I turned to Tiergan.

"Begin what?"

"I feel like we are about to learn the way of wind," he said, standing from his seat and offering a hand to me, which I took gladly.

I looped my arm through his as we made our way to find a seat next to Aura, who beamed at us as we drew close.

Gone was the timid female I'd always known.

Aura embraced her true authentic self in this moment—amongst the immortals who loved her the most.

Tiergan and I both took plates of food from the blonde woman whom we'd met upon entering the hidden caverns.

I wasn't sure what it was. The food tasted good, and I wasn't a picky eater. I believed it was venison with a side of rice. Simple yet filling.

Aura sat across from us with Rai by her side.

"It's time that I tell you all my story," she said, taking a sip of some pink fruit drink.

She glanced at us, and I nodded my head in encouragement.

"With the way of the wind," the immortals around us answered, and goosebumps flooded the back of my neck.

Aura called on the power of the wind, and the air seemed to wait to collect her words to carry them off somewhere. Hues of blues, pinks, and oranges all whirled around her with the magic she possessed.

I shivered in awe at the magic she wielded, so unlike anything I'd seen before.

"I was once a little girl who loved her mother very much. And my mother taught me to love the birds of wind. The beasts that the rest of the world was too corrupt to know about."

The swirls of magic she possessed moved into images as she spoke, as if the way of wind was telling her story. All eyes were on the magic before them, but not Rai. Rai's eyes were only for Aura, and my heart warmed at the love I saw there.

"As long as I was with the birds, I was safe. Free. To be and love," Aura said, voice softer on the last word. "My mother taught me to respect the way of wind, for she is mighty and full of vengeance if disrespected. With love, the way of wind can give us power and prosperity. It is by our actions that we earn her favor or her wrath."

Aura paused, wincing slightly at her next words, and the images in the wind moved from her and her mother to her and a male I assumed to be Abel.

"As I grew, along came a vile male. Abel. But he was not always that way, or he hid it very well."

The once bright colors of the wind turned into something darker around the image of Abel, and the longer the story went, the more of Abel's shadows stole the light from Aura.

"It was much too late… for both my heart and other things… when I realized what he truly sought was power. And with my mother now passed, I was lost. But I was safe as long as I was with the birds." She paused for a moment before continuing. "I knew that he must never learn of them or the true powers in the way of wind. They were too beautiful for something as wicked as him."

There were quiet murmurs of agreement throughout the crowd, and my hand twitched as well, despite Abel being very much dead now.

"It's time you met them. The creatures of wind," she said, smiling and lifting her gaze up into the cosmos.

A thunder of air seemed to surround us as hundreds of…

"Are those phoenixes?" I whispered to Tiergan.

He nodded with a tear in his eyes and a hand over his mouth in wonder.

"And hippogriffs," he said.

Tiergan truly was a kind-hearted male, and I stepped closer to him, clasping his free hand.

What must have been the alphas of each descended close to Aura, and she walked up to them lovingly.

The phoenix was beautiful with bright orange, purple, and yellow feathers and was large enough for an immortal to mount into battle. The hippogriffs were just as large and were mostly gray, white, and black. The hippogriffs had the body of a horse, except that the two front legs were the talons of an eagle. Intelligent, but beady eyes of an eagle stared at me from a few heads taller than where I stood, seeming to study me.

I stood frozen next to Tiergan as I watched these two creatures lovingly embrace Aura as if she'd known them her whole life, and I supposed that was likely true.

Aura caught my eye and motioned us over. I followed behind Tiergan, a little hesitant to approach too quickly.

The phoenix and hippogriff turned their heads towards us curiously.

Aura motioned to the phoenix first, who seemed to almost be purring at being reunited with her. "This is Zephyra."

Tiergan and I both bowed in reverence to creatures we'd thought extinct or only myth. Zephyra nodded back and approached me first. I gently raised a hand, and Zephyra nuzzled her beak into my waiting palm, and I gasped at the gentleness.

"She likes you," Aura said, like a proud mother. "And this is Samir."

Tiergan and I both nodded to Samir, and the hippogriff bowed back to us.

He didn't approach either of us, but he didn't seem hostile either. His stance was to protect Aura, and I respected that.

Rai wrapped an arm around Aura, pulling her close to him, while Zephyra still stood next to me, and I couldn't help but stroke her feathers.

We gazed out into the field of starlight as the hippogriffs and phoenixes greeted the immortals here.

"We will fight with you," Aura said, voice strong—determined. "When Zoe is ready for the battle in Vega… we'll be there."

"She will be grateful. We will be grateful."

"It's time the Kingdom of Canis remembered how powerful the way of wind is," she said, tears in her eyes. "And how merciful we can be."

I laced my fingers through hers as Tiergan stood on my other side.

"Together," she said, nodding, savoring the win of the moment. "We will rise from the ashes."

19

The Realms Between Us
ZOE

Freyja's body was so still.

But her chest rose and fell, and her heartbeat was steady. She was alive. I had to remind myself of that.

It was eerie knowing this was what my body had looked like while I'd been fighting for my life in my own Emerging trials. One out of ten, I do not recommend.

I wiped a stray hair out of her face and threaded her hand into mine. My beautiful sister, whom I loved so much that I did idiotic crap to bring her back to me. I knew she'd do even more to make it back to us. I held onto that knowledge like a prayer.

"Is she okay, you think?" Oleander asked, kneeling next to me. Jelly nuzzled his free hand, demanding attention, and I laughed at his immediate willingness to give her what she wanted. Spoiled rotten.

"She's safe up there," I said, careful not to say too much. "Safer than with us right now."

"Any chance we'll be all done with Hesperia by the time she's back?"

I sighed.

"I doubt it, but that's a nice thought."

"I thought so," he said, grinning.

"Where's Zadie?" I asked.

"She's gone back to Finnian," he said, a little too casually.

"I see," I said, brows raised.

"You don't seem surprised?" he asked.

"I'm not," I admitted. "Finn has been in the Hall of Memories nonstop for a while."

"Do you know what they are doing?"

"Not entirely," I said, making sure my shields were up and strong.

"I don't actually know either. Figured the less that knew, the better."

"You're probably right," I agreed.

"As long as we are successful, then I imagine it won't really matter what they are up to," he said, and I tasted the truth on my tongue.

"Don't fail. Got it."

"You won't," he said seriously. "Come on. I'll show you to your room."

Jelly leaped up from her position by Freyja and wagged her tail enthusiastically at me. She was willing to do whatever I wanted.

"Just take me to the immortals," I argued.

"No. Go to sleep. Rest. Then you can play here all you want."

I crossed my arms, unmoving.

"Do not make me sling you over my shoulder and throw you in that room," he said, mirroring my stance, but Jelly gave him a playful growl, daring him to get through her. "I'm just looking out for your ward, Jelly."

She barked in response and quit displaying her canines ever so menacingly.

"I'm perfectly fine to do a little healing magic," I said, and I bit my lip to keep myself from yawning. He was right, and it made me irrationally angry.

"Bed. Now."

"You sound like Blaz, you mother hen," I said, calling Jelly to follow me. I could have sworn she barked a laugh at Oleander's expense.

"The audacity," he said, rolling his eyes.

He paused outside my door, waiting for us to go in.

"So little trust in me," I said, throwing open the door.

"Remind me what you did the last time you stayed the night here?"

"Yeah, yeah. Freyja didn't exactly try to persuade me not to," I countered.

"You two are trouble and give me high blood pressure."

"I promise. I'll stay here all night," I said, holding out my pinky with a look of sarcasm.

"I'll see you at morning moon," he said, shutting the door behind him.

After using the bathroom and brushing my teeth, I stripped off my traveling clothes, leaving myself in my underwear and oversized cotton blouse. I left my hair in its braid, as I called Jelly to my side. She twirled a few times in the bed to find the right spot. She may be a simargl now, but she was still just Jelly with the same habits of her border collie form.

"Good night, girl," I said, flipping the lights off and curling into the warmth of her.

She didn't answer, but nuzzled in closer.

I prayed for sleep to come quickly, begging my racing thoughts not to keep me awake tonight. I couldn't stand it. Despite my argument with Oleander, I knew that to be entirely true.

Mercifully, my eyes grew heavy and my tense muscles relaxed as I drifted off to sleep, thinking of my flame.

***

The smell of the ocean was familiar to my immortal senses. I knew this beach. I knew the pier was just over there to the east.

I was back in Saint Andrews, but I couldn't be. Because I was in the star realms. I was in Algol, which meant...

"Little bear," my father said from behind me.

I wasn't sure I wanted to turn around. The broken part of me wanted to pretend he didn't exist. If he didn't exist, then he couldn't hurt me. The other shard of my existence wanted to slap him across the face. Yet another part of me wanted to curl up in his arms and cry. How could all three of these things be true? And which one did I follow?

Swallowing down the conference room meeting going on in my brain, I took a deep breath. Logic. I would choose logic. I needed answers, and he was going to give them to me.

I turned around slowly to find a mirror of my green eyes in his own. He wore his usual casual clothes and wafts of liquorish came from him.

My heart broke all over again, and reason wanted to escape me. I wanted to let my emotions rule this moment. But then he might leave, tail between his legs, and I wouldn't get the answers that I needed.

"I have the bow," I said, voice stronger than I felt. "Now, what do you need from me?"

He winced at the harshness of my words, but I didn't care. I chose not to.

"I have these for you," he said, pulling out arrows that shone in the light of the moon. They were not unlike the arrow I already had in my possession. Maybe I kept it out of some kind of longing to be close to my father.

I took them from him. They were lighter than the metal they seemed to be. They wouldn't weigh me down.

"What was that first arrow for, anyway?" I asked.

"Allowing Hesperia to keep the arrow that had been used to shatter the bonds of the five elements was not something I could allow. A weapon of destruction could be in her possession no longer."

It was a decision I could get behind.

"Five arrows?" I asked. "Five realms?"

"To connect the magic of the realms back together."

"Can they kill Hesperia?"

"No," he said, moving closer, and I took a step back, not sure I wanted the distance to be closed between us. "I told you long ago where to look for that answer, little bear."

"I don't know what that means," I admitted, and I hated the thought of him having any advantage over me.

"You will. When the time comes," he promised, putting his hands in his pockets. This was the first time he had ever seemed so unsure around me. His movements, his expressions... everything seemed vulnerable. "I know what you're up to with Finnian. That course will only bring you grief, Zoe. Look to the beginning."

"I'm already in grief, Archer," I mumbled, not allowing him to persuade me otherwise.

"Why?" I asked finally. "Why did it take you so long to reach out to me? Knowing what I have been through with Elvy… learning Hesperia is my sister. And she has him. Why?"

Tears stung my eyes, but I would not let them fall. I refused to show just how hurt I was.

"Facing you… after knowing that this is ultimately my doing. My greed. My ambition. The only reason you are in this position is because of me. My carelessness. My refusal to listen to Nova—to reason."

His voice was on the verge of explosion. Not at me, but at himself. He ran a hand through his hair, taking a step closer to me. I allowed it, though I couldn't understand why.

"I think it is far past time to tell me the truth. Why does Hesperia hate me so much? What happened back then?"

He swallowed, averting his eyes out onto the ocean. "I suppose maybe it is. I came here tonight to do just that, but I admit that I do not want to, little bear. For fear of how you will see me after."

"I don't see you well right now, Archer," I said, voice low.

He nodded, accepting my truth.

"When my father made me undo the magic of the bonds between realms… something inside me broke. To hear the cries and torment of the immortals. Their grief shattered me, and I swore to avenge them. To make things right."

He sat down on the soft sand and motioned for me to sit next to him. I did, but didn't allow our shoulders to touch.

"I practiced the sight. I got as perfect as one can with something so imperfect, and I knew my offspring would heal what was broken. So, in my haste to have this vision come to fruition, I created the ideal child."

"Created?" I asked.

"Yes," he answered. "Created as I was with Algol. There was no mother or love in Hesperia's conception. She was born from the stars… a wicked thing. I sensed it in her the moment she breathed life."

"A baby can be evil?"

"You can't think of her as you, or your sister, Freyja, or those who are born in love. I tried to love her, Zoe. I tried to nurture her. Teach her a better way. None of it worked. She only got worse. So, I planned to do the unthinkable. Even killing a child as evil as she… it filled me with so much guilt and hatred towards myself. I wouldn't have lived after that. Hadn't planned to."

I swallowed, reaching out a hand on instinct, but dropped it before he noticed.

"What stopped you?" I asked.

"Nova," he answered. "She showed me another path. This time I listened. Despite knowing this path would break me, too."

My heartbeat raced as I tried to read between the lines of what he was saying.

"Because?"

"Because what should be my burden is now yours. And I find that hard to live with."

"So do I," I said, voice hard. "But we must. You don't get to hide away and quit when this gets hard. That's not the kind of daughter I am. I'd hate to think of my father as weak."

"I know. And I am sorry," he said, voice sincere. "When you call, I will be there. At the very end. Should your heart want me there."

"You're telling the truth," I stated. It wasn't a question. He meant what he said.

"I swear it," he promised. "I will be by your side at the right moment. When you need me most. As it is fated."

"But not before?"

"Not if it will change the course you are on," he answered.

"Will these arrows come with me through this dream?" I asked curiously.

"They will," he agreed. "To tether the realms back together… you'll need to attach a string of your essence to the arrow. It'll take practice to pull your essence out like that."

"Show me," I said.

He nodded, closing his eyes, and I followed suit.

"Find your ground," he said, voice soft. I found the farthest wave I could find and followed its crash to the shoreline. I repeated this process until my mind was nothing more than the power of the ocean.

"Picture an orb of starlight within you that is not only the power of your magic, but the source of who you are, who you were, and who you will be."

I did as instructed, picturing an orb of blues, blacks, and visualized all the emotions of my humanity and of my immortality. The love. The grief. Everything that was, is, and could be. I embraced them all, coaxing these moments into an orb of light.

"When you feel ready, take your hand and pinch the center of your chest as if you were pulling out a string of light."

I paused, visualizing this as best I could, and when I thought I had it, I opened my eyes to find… nothing. No string of light.

"It takes practice," he said again. "But I felt your magic stirring. You have the right idea. Once you're able to pull the string out, you'll attach it to the arrow and… shoot."

"At what?"

"Into their star, of course," he said. "You'll be able to see it when you're ready."

"No pressure," I said.

"You can do this."

"I can't. Not yet. Not until Hesperia is no longer a threat."

He bowed his head low, but nodded in agreement.

"I know she must be taken care of first."

"Do you know what her endgame is? What she really wants out of all this?"

"Death," he answered without hesitation.

"Whose?"

"Mine," he said simply. "And by default. Yours. To punish me before I die."

Something in my heart skipped at the thought of him being taken away from me. Despite the anger I had towards him. There was a part of me that loved him dearly, and the idea of him no longer existing didn't sit well with my soul.

"That won't happen," I said, not caring to look at the sight.

He held out his arms to me, and I allowed myself to embrace him. It felt too much like a goodbye. Like this might be the last time I ever get to hug my father.

"I love you, little bear."

I didn't say the words back, but I felt them in my heart as he sent me back to the world of peaceful dreams.

20

Colliding

DELMIRA

Blaz's too heavy arm encircled me as he slept soundly beside me.

The male radiated heat, which made me sweat almost uncomfortably, but I was too enraptured by him to move or care. I thrust the covers from my feet, trying to cool off some.

I wore a silk violet tank and shorts combo, and he was shirtless, per usual.

My eyes drifted to the rise and fall of his chest, and down lower to the ripple of his abs.

I wonder…

I should probably just let him sleep, but it was two in the morning and I was wide awake.

The sparring had helped calm and distract me, but the racing thoughts had turned into nightmares. I'd never been fond of the word *nightmares,* though I supposed that's what they were. I didn't care to go back to sleep just yet.

A cheshire grin crept along my face.

I slipped the covers down lower, exposing his snug briefs, and trailed kisses down his torso as I pushed my fingers past the waistband. Blaz was *heavy* when he was dead weight, but I maneuvered his briefs down, exposing his arousal.

"Delm?" he asked, sleep in his voice, but he quickly awakened when I bit his hip.

"Delmira," he said, voice lowering seductively. "What are you doing?"

"I need you," I said, my mouth hovering just over his desire.

He smirked, gripping my hair tightly. "Then, by all means, go ahead."

I did not need to be told twice.

As I invoked pleasure from Blaz with my hands and tongue, I glanced into his eyes, finding him watching me, full of lust and adoration.

Blaz relaxed both of his hands behind his head in a casual gesture, but I saw the tension. He was ready to spring on me, but he was letting me have the control I needed and wanted in this moment.

I savored every inch of him. The taste of him made my center ache with a need to have him inside me.

"Delm," he growled, shifting, and I moved off him, crooking a finger in his direction. "Finally."

He ripped my clothes off, shuddering.

"I need you," I whimpered, repeating myself, and he didn't hesitate in sinking inside me, filling every delicious inch of me.

He moved at a tortuous rhythm and bent down so that his hands had access to my sensitive body.

I bit my lip on the edge.

He lifted me up with one hand so that I was sitting on him, deepening his strokes. With the other hand, he reached over to the side table drawer, getting a vibrator. He never stopped moving as he expertly turned it on, smiling wickedly at me as he placed it against the most sensitive part of me.

I screamed out as my pleasure rocked through me. I gripped each of his shoulders so I could control the thrusts, and my nails dug into his skin. He didn't seem to mind as he moved the vibrator around again, and I felt another release building.

"Blaz," I said, gritting my teeth as he sent me over the edge again.

It took no time for Blaz to roar his release with me. We had both stopped shaking from the euphoria, and he circled me gently in his arms, wiping the hair from my face. He tenderly kissed my forehead and cradled my head in his hand.

"You okay?" he asked, voice low.

I nodded.

"Honesty?" he asked.

"I'm not sure," I admitted. "Just couldn't sleep. Lots of thoughts."

"Will you tell me if there's something I can help you with?" he asked seriously.

"I will," I promised, silencing his worries with a kiss. A yawn crept over my lips. "Maybe I just needed you."

He laughed, setting me down on the bed to go to the bathroom. He came back quickly to help me clean up, and my eyes grew heavier with fatigue.

"Sleep, Delm. I'll be right here," he promised, sliding in behind me, and I let him tangle himself in my limbs, knowing he needed that closeness just as much as I did.

I drifted off into a mercifully dreamless sleep.

★★★

Waking up in the arms of Blaz was a treat—one I wanted over and over again.

He nuzzled his nose into my neck, sending shivers all the way down to my toes, and I groaned as he tightened his arms around my torso.

"Do we have to get up?" I whined, not wanting to leave the luxury of his arms and my bed.

"I could think—" Blaz began, but was cut off by a pounding at the door.

"Open up!" Imelda shrieked through the door.

Blaz and I were still naked, and I didn't think Imelda would wait long enough before trying to barge in. I leaped out of bed, tossing Blaz his clothes and slipping into my casual sweats before ripping the door open with death in my eyes.

"What the hell, Imelda?"

The tears that threatened to burst from her eyes had me scanning the hallways for any sign of a threat, but finding none. I casually sent my gift into the air, giving Imelda a touch of calm. Not enough to make her a zombie, but enough to help her think through whatever was overwhelming her.

"What's going on?" Blaz asked, standing behind me, still shirtless, but at least he had black sweats on.

"It's Clove," she said, tears drying.

"Is she okay? What have you heard?"

"She's stuck in Canopus with Tiergan and Aura. She says they're safe."

Imelda collapsed into my arms, and I stiffened at the touch. I shifted her uncomfortably to one of the violet leather chairs in my room.

Too many emotions made me recoil. I'd like to blame it on my gift being overstimulated, but if I were being honest with myself… I just didn't like *feelings.*

"Do you know where in Canopus?" Blaz asked, assuming the role of general of the Shadowed Legion.

"No," Imelda said, voice steadier. "She said it was crucial she wasn't compromised, but she is waiting for us to send word when we leave for Rigil."

"Trust her," Blaz said, arms folded across his chest. "She knows what she's doing."

"I know," she admitted. "I just… I don't know."

"You're tired," I said, reaching out to offer a comforting gesture, but my hand dropped to the chair before touching her. "We all are."

"What if Hesperia finds her?"

"Then we'll face it," I promised. "But she won't find her."

"I feel so stupid," she said, laughing softly, and I had to physically restrain myself from rolling my eyes.

"It's not stupid to be afraid for someone you love," Blaz disagreed, and I felt his eyes on me. I didn't meet his gaze. Not here. Not now.

I was slowly becoming more vulnerable, but that was with Blaz. Only him.

"I'm still going to kill her when she gets back," she promised.

"And I'll help you," I said, easily agreeing. "I'm still pissed at her."

She laughed, but I allowed myself a brief smile.

"Have you told Zoe?" I asked.

"Yes," she admitted. "I sent the message on the iris."

"Good," I said, pulling her to her feet. "Let her do her job, and we'll do ours."

Imelda's resolve was fully back now. She'd just needed to break for a moment.

"You're right. Let's get our Lord Astral back," she said, brows narrowed.

21

Letting Go
CLODOVEA

"Want to try flying?" Aura asked, as Zephyra continued to stay close to me.

We'd been in the realm of Canopus for a few days, unable to leave with Hesperia's arrival back in this realm. I'd sent word to Imelda on our first day here through the iris, and she had been simultaneously angry and thrilled to hear my voice. I missed her.

"I've never done something like that before… unless I was flying, of course," I answered.

"Well, at least you have your wings if you fall," Tiergan chuckled beside her.

"Alright," I agreed. "Why not?"

"I think that will be my new philosophy in life. Why not?" Aura exploded with laughter. I'd never seen her so carefree, and I couldn't help but be joyous with her.

Rai's eyes twinkled with something like wonder at anything Aura did.

"You ready for a mounted flight, girl?" Aura asked Zephyra, and the phoenix bowed her head. I wasn't getting out of this.

Zephyra bent her neck down and turned her head at me expectantly. For a bird, her eyes were gentle and kind, unlike the beady, greedy eyes of seagulls.

"What do I do?" I asked, a little nervously.

"You'll sit right there, behind her neck in the center of her back, so you don't impede her wings."

Zephyra bent down further, and I leaped onto her soft wings and secured myself as best as I could using my inner leg strength and gripped on tight with my hands.

"Don't pull her feathers," Aura warned. "She'll not thank you for it,"

I loosened my grip on the feathers some, and nodded.

"Now what?" I asked.

"Ah!" I screamed a second later.

Before Aura could answer the question, Zephyra had taken off, and I was pretty certain I'd left my soul back on the ground.

"You literally fly all the time, Clove," I mumbled to myself, but it was different when I wasn't in control of the situation.

Aura flew beside me on Samir, and she had her hands spread wide with a brilliant grin on her face.

The sound of her laughter caught on the wind, and I decided to dig deep into my bravery.

I opened my hands to embrace the light of the moon, and laughter immediately erupted from the pit of my chest. The stars were immaculate tonight, with not a cloud in the sky. This was what living felt like after drowning in stress for so long.

I was going to ask Imelda to marry me. Soon.

Zephyra took a dive back to the ground, but I didn't jolt with fear. I leaned my body flat to decrease the resistance for her, and she let out a war cry of her own. She seemed to be enjoying stretching her wings. The phoenix landed with grace, and I thanked her for the experience.

"Jelly is going to be jealous," I said, letting Zephyra nuzzle me, and she looked at me curiously. I silently wondered if she could understand me the way the simargls could.

"Lady Aura!" the blonde woman shouted, racing through the crowd to meet Samir and Aura as she landed. Rai was, of course, right there waiting for them.

"What is it?" Aura asked, eyes searching for an unseen threat.

"There's been reports that Hesperia has sent scouts throughout Canopus, threatening the immortals to join her cause. It is not safe for you to leave here," the blonde woman urged.

"Is there a way to open this place up to those loyal to you, Aura?" I asked, and Tiergan nodded beside me.

"Too risky," the woman reiterated.

"How do you know she's sent scouts?" I asked logically. "You have been sealed in this protective domain for some years."

"The moment the seal was broken, parts of our magic returned to us that had been cut off by that protection. We also sent our very own scouts under Aura's orders."

I smiled at Aura as she embraced her role as the Lady Astral fully.

"We'll take in whoever we can. As safety allows," Aura decreed. "Can you tell Imelda what is happening, Clodovea?"

"I can," I said, though the thought of being apart from her when danger was near was not what I had in mind. I didn't want to add to her worry.

"We'll send her a message," Tiergan said, stepping in. "We need to get an update on their movements, anyway."

He was right about that.

"Imelda is going to lose it," I said.

"Maybe," he admitted, leading me somewhere more private to send the message. "But she already knows you are stuck here for a while. This changes little to nothing."

I pulled out the iris, allowing my immortal mark to charge the magic there.

"Hesperia is trying to recruit more immortals of Canopus to her side. We are going to open the borders to this sanctuary as safely as possible. Don't worry. I'm not going on anymore crazy missions," I added, blushing slightly with Tiergan's presence, but he had no judgement within him.

It didn't take long for the iris to warm with Imelda's response.

"I get it, and I'm still pissed. I love you." Her words were clipped with hurt, but love nonetheless.

I charge the iris again. "I love you, too. What's happening there?"

Her response was quick.

"We have a plan for getting Elvy back in Rigil."

My heart sank with relief. Thank the stars.

"What's the next move?" I responded.

Tiergan stepped in closer as the iris glowed again.

"Zoe is in Algol with Oleander. She's attempting to get information from the immortals Hesperia had under her control. When will you come home?"

I looked at Tiergan. "We could follow Hesperia when she leaves… and bring some friends along the way."

"We'll follow her discreetly when she moves on Rigil," I said through the magic of the iris. "We'll bring reinforcements."

The magic flowed through the realms, and her missive came back through.

"Save it for Vega. That's when we will need all of our allies."

I charged the magic for the last time. "Tiergan and I will still follow after and meet you in Rigil or Vega. Wherever Zoe needs us. See you soon."

Her words were simple. "Yes, you will."

"They must have a plan if they don't want to bring in the allies here," Tiergan noted.

"A good plan," I agreed.

"You're nervous," he observed.

"I don't like feeling trapped," I admitted.

"I know the feeling," he said, gently hugging me with one arm.

"I guess you do," I said, allowing him to comfort me.

"We had better go find Aura and tell her what's happening."

"And let Aura know we will be staying indefinitely until Rigil. Who knows when Hesperia will decide to leave?"

"We'll be ready," Tiergan promised, and I believed him.

Aura took the news well, but didn't like the idea of Tiergan and me going off on our own after Hesperia. She'd initially insisted that she would come with us. It took some convincing from Rai for her to accept that it wasn't the best decision right now, but that her help would be welcome in the final battle.

"Alright then," she said finally. "You both have a home here for as long as you need it."

"Thank you," I said, grateful to have a place to stay. "See you at the moon rise."

22

Unbroken

FREYJA

My physical ailments were gone.

My chapped lips were smooth again, and the muscles that had been shredded were repaired, leaving me feeling… whole.

I stood on the Cliffs of Three, staring out at the ocean, waiting. For *what,* I was not certain.

Nova glided towards me, and I turned to face her.

She paused when she reached me, her cosmic eyes studying me.

"I didn't break," I said, voice resolute.

"No, you did not, child," she said, smiling ever so slightly. That one movement filled my soul with pride, but we weren't finished yet.

I stood waiting for her, knowing this wasn't over until she declared it so.

"What did the stars test?" she asked, repeating my question back to me at the base of the mountain.

I'd mulled over that question. The obvious answer was my physical strength, but that didn't feel correct. My body may have tried to break on me a few times, but it had never truly failed me. The only thing that had kept me pushing onward and upward was my mental resolve, but it was deeper than even that. It was about what I had control over and letting go of what I couldn't control.

I didn't have control over the mountain. It was its own entity. I didn't have control over the icy conditions or the weather in general. All I had control over was myself. In the belief I had in myself to push on. The knowledge I possessed to keep myself as safe as possible in foreign terrain. I only had control in placing one foot in front of the other and hoping it was the right move. The rest... well, that hadn't been up to me.

"My acceptance of what I have control over and what I don't. To be right here. Not in the past or the future. To be present. To *own* that."

Nova smiled, and I took that as a good sign.

"Very good," she said, nodding in appreciation. "Come. Rest. Replenish."

I followed behind her, fearing the question that I needed to answer.

"How long was I up there, Nova?" I asked, hating the shake in my voice. "Are they still alive?"

"Yes, child. They still prevail and watch over your body still. Four days," Nova answered.

"Only four?" I asked in disbelief. I must have been moving faster than I'd thought.

"You moved with purpose," she said simply, and I grinned.

Only one more trial stood between me and my freedom. It couldn't get here fast enough.

Nova sat at the head of the table, and I loaded down my plate with sweet potatoes, chicken, and anything else that looked enticing to my nearly empty stomach. I ate my fill and gulped down the juices offered, finally satiated.

"I won't remember this place?" I asked.

"No, child. You aren't meant to remember this realm. Neither was your sister. So is the way of fate, who has the ultimate authority in the end."

"And tomorrow… tomorrow's it?" I asked.

"Yes," she agreed. "Your death or your Emergence."

"I feel oddly ready," I admitted, circling my thumb against my other palm.

"Then you shall prevail," she said, rising. "Go rest. I'll collect you with the rising moon."

I stood in front of her. "I'll see you soon."

"So you will," she agreed, and there was a sense of heaviness around her, and I resolved myself not to wonder about the possible futures she saw for me.

I traced the familiar path back to my suite, stripping off my clothes with ease the moment I crossed the threshold of my room. I would be thankful to the stars for granting the restoration of my body after the second trial. It made me feel more prepared for the coming test, knowing my body would not give out. It was the least they could do at this point.

Once the steam from the hot water filled the room, I got in the shower, letting the water wash away any lingering fatigue. I imagined Ander there next to me, washing my hair… touching my body and making me feel alive with every touch. I was so close to having the rest of forever with him, yet he felt eons away. It was as if he was within my viewpoint, but just outside of my reach—not unlike when I'd been part of the living dead.

He was my peace and the fire that could melt the ice around my heart when I shielded myself away not only from others but from myself.

Ander.

My body, my soul—every part of me—missed him. Somehow, I knew he felt the same. Fire and ice weren't really so different. Both could leave a bite. I smirked in the mirror, flattening my silk pajamas across my stomach, ready for some deep sleep.

I winced as the feeling of ice ran through every atom of my body, and my eyes fluttered open in confusion at what stood before me.

It was me, but not me.

I raised a hand to the Freyja before me, and her hand mirrored mine exactly.

"What the?" I asked, and the mirror Freyja did the same.

The image was clearly me, but she was more see-through. Like I had once been in death, and I shied away from the thought. Was I hallucinating, or was this reality? Or perhaps something altogether different?

"An astral projection?" I asked, and the Freyja in front of me mimicked me.

As I tried to touch her again, she flew back into me… somewhere, and I shuddered to think exactly *where* this thing was inside me. I rinsed my face, but the hot water felt much too hot. I quickly turned it down, trying to make sense of what I'd just seen.

"Could that be my magic… my *gift*?" I asked no one. "I can project? Or astral project anyway, which means…"

I quickly brushed my teeth and tossed my hair into a haphazard braid, too excited to care much about my appearance. I bounced onto the soft bed, closing my eyes in concentration.

I focused on Ander, the feel of him touching me the first time we'd given into our passion after I'd been brought back to life. I bit my lip, thinking of the way his tongue explored my body. The way I'd been so completely full of Ander and the sting of his teeth on my skin. I focused on the heat in my core and the sensation that had brought out my magic while in the shower.

I swallowed, knowing how much I still needed and wanted my Ander.

The chill ran through my bones again as a projection of myself materialized in front of me. She looked at me curiously, as I'm sure I looked at her with the same interest. She was me, and I was her.

"Can you find Ander?" I asked, but this time she didn't repeat my words, but paused in thought.

Before I could ask her anything else, she touched my forehead, and then I was seeing my body through her eyes.

I gazed into the mirror to see my own reflection, but there were two of me in the room.

I had no idea how to make this magic work, and I was risking a lot to go find Ander if I couldn't get back to this body. I ignored my worries and decided to live for this moment.

"To Ander," I said, and my projection began floating into space and time through the cosmos until I was descending to Ander's balcony attached to his room. It had been nearly effortless to find his onyx castle. He was like a beacon of light to me.

I didn't know my abilities or strength in this form, but I pushed on the door, finding it easy enough to open as my projection solidified.

A knife was at my throat before I stepped a foot inside across the threshold.

"Freyja?" he whispered in confusion, and my heart fluttered at the sound of his husky voice, still tired with sleep.

He dropped the knife and wrapped his arms around me, and I embraced him back.

"What are you doing out here?"

"I don't have long," I whispered against his neck, breathing in his scent.

"What do you mean?" he asked, fear in his sea-blue eyes.

"This isn't me. Well, not fully anyway," I said, smiling. "My magic manifested."

Oleander studied me closely, looking me up and down. I shifted my form again, dissipating into my projection. "Freyja, what the hell is going on?" There was fear in his eyes, and I moved to quickly reassure him that I was alive and well. Seeing me like this probably scared the hell out of him.

"I can project. Astral project," I said, smiling. "I guess my experience in the world of the dead allowed me to manipulate this kind of magic pretty easily."

"You feel like… you," he said, tucking a strand of hair behind my ear, and I shivered at the sensation.

"I'm still me," I promised, shifting back to something more solid.

He leaned in closer, brushing his lips against mine, as if testing, and I sucked in his bottom lip.

"I've missed you, Freyja," he murmured, and trailed kisses down my neck, and my chest ached with want.

"One more trial, and I'll be home," I said, as he traced his fingers underneath the hem of my shirt. They promised a night of pleasure.

One I knew I couldn't have. Not yet. I'd already spent too much time here.

I tugged his hair in my fingers, crushing his lips to mine.

It took both of our strengths to pull away from each other.

"I'll see you soon," I promised. "Send Zoe my love."

There were a thousand questions I wanted to ask, but couldn't. I saw the same in his eyes, but I knew I wouldn't be able to answer them without Nova smiting me from existence.

"I will," he said, still cradling my face with his rough palms. "Come back to me, sweetheart."

"Always," I said, giving him a kiss on the cheek, and I turned back to the cosmos.

"To Nova," I murmured, and my form was jetting off into the galaxies I had no prayer of navigating without this magic guiding me. The magic propelled me faster than a shooting star.

I arrived back at my still sleeping body with a smile on my face and swollen lips.

Stars, I loved that male.

Not entirely sure how to get back to my body, I did what felt natural and gripped my sleeping form's hand. I visualized myself exchanging consciousness, and my sleeping body jerked awake. I saw through my eyes again to find my astral form gone.

I grinned at the memories of Oleander, and curled back into a ball to await the moonrise, knowing that he was waiting for me on the other side.

23

Death Infusion

ZOE

The moon has drawn my attention more than usual lately.

I studied the soft glow, wondering what its light wanted me to know.

I leaned into my gift and felt… peace. Nothing more, nothing less. It was like an invisible protection. It was a sense of safety that I wish I could bottle up and send to the entirety of the star realms, but maybe this feeling meant the moon was on our side. Perhaps she too looked down at us in wonder, wanting to believe in the best of us. Maybe that was enough.

"How'd you sleep?" Oleander asked, leaning against the balcony's railing and pulling me from my rather philosophical thoughts.

My sister lay in her peaceful comatose state on a velvet red couch that was just through the open doors. She still fought, and I hoped she was progressing quickly, knowing she could very well still be in the first trial.

Jelly's wings were folded against her as she slept peacefully next to Freyja, and I was a little envious at the yips she was making in her sleep. It seemed to be something tranquil for her.

"The Archer came for a visit," I said, rubbing the sensitive spot around my eyebrow. A stress point from my mortal life that followed me into the immortal realm.

"Oh? And how do we feel about that, love?"

"Conflicted," I said, pulling the five arrows from my black leather satchel from beside me.

I handed one to Oleander, but he seemed hesitant to touch them.

"What are they?" he asked, eyeing them curiously.

"The way forward," I said, sighing.

They seemed to glow in the starlight, giving them an innocent air, but I knew it was a farce. So did Oleander, apparently.

"There's something off about those," he admitted. "I'll let you be the one to touch them, thanks."

"Oleander is scared of something," I said, chuckling. "Never thought I'd see the day."

I didn't bother to tell him about the magic it would require to make them work—to heal the realms.

"We're all scared of something, Zo," he said, a little too seriously for the mood I was in, but I met his eyes to find them softened with vulnerability. I wouldn't shame him for that.

"You're right about that," I agreed. "I just have to figure out how to make them tick."

He handed me a cup of coffee, and I took it greedily, making him laugh softly.

"You'll figure it out, oh mighty realm healer," he said, smirking.

"Best remember it, too," I said, taking a deep, luxurious swig of the black coffee.

I enjoyed the sound of his laughter. It made me feel alive, even for a moment. It simultaneously made my heart ache for my flame.

"I also had a visitor last night," he admitted a little sheepishly. My brows furrowed at him in question and a slight accusation. I wasn't above killing him if he betrayed my sister.

"Freyja," he said. "I thought it was a dream when I woke this morning, but I don't think it was. She came to me last night. As an astral projection. She's got one more trial."

My heart pumped faster as my eyes flickered towards my still sleeping sister.

"Such a show-off," I muttered. "Already through the first two trials? I'm impressed."

"This is good, right? She could be back with us any moment."

"She could," I agreed. "In the meantime, we have to get ready for what's coming," I said, staring at the mountains in the distance.

"Any word on Hesperia's movements?" he asked.

I winced, knowing that Elvy was suffering and there wasn't a thing I could do about it with him blocking the bond.

"No," I said, shaking my head. "Imelda gave me a report this morning on her last known movements. Clodovea will send word when she departs Canopus. We'll be moving some of the Shadowed Legion to Rigil. We'll be ready when she comes."

"Then it's just the final battle," he said, eyes narrowing on a future he couldn't read. Hell, I'd tried to *see* the outcome at least a hundred times myself, to no avail. Whether it was too many moving factors, decisions that hadn't been made yet, or the celestials blocking me… I knew this would be one fate that I'd be blind to until the very last moment.

"Hesperia's reign of terror ends in Vega," I vowed.

Oleander laid a hand over mine gently. I hadn't realized my nails drew blood in my palms.

I jerked my hand out of his, healing it quickly.

"You're not alone," he reminded, and I nodded.

"Take me to the immortals," I said, silencing his worried look. I needed the distraction of productivity.

He nodded and motioned for me to follow him. Jelly was still dead asleep next to Freyja, so I left her there to watch over my sister while I went to work. Oleander led me to the makeshift medical wing of his onyx castle. It didn't resemble a mortal hospital in the slightest. There were no tubes jutting out of various places, and there was no stench of bleach, which had always made me loathe hospitals. Each immortal lay on a regular bed and was encased in a shimmering membrane of… starlight. They looked at peace with the rise and fall of their chests, as if they were only sleeping, but I knew better.

I approached a male with short brown hair and sharp facial features. He looked familiar, but I couldn't quite place him.

"This is James," Oleander said, standing on the opposite side of the comatose immortal. "He and his brother were captains in the Shadowed Legion. I'd felt so utterly betrayed when they joined Hesperia… I should have known. It was so out of character for them."

I didn't offer condolences to him because I knew they would do nothing to assuage the guilt he felt. I'd been in his shoes too many times.

"I'll bring him back. And his brother, if you've found him?"

He shook his head. "I haven't seen Liam."

"We'll find him," I promised, assessing the male. "How do I touch him?"

"The membrane will adjust to accommodate you," he said, demonstrating with his own hand, which passed easily through the substance.

I nodded. "Whatever you do, Oleander, don't interrupt the process. No matter what you hear, what you see—any of it. It will be unpleasant."

"Alright, love," he conceded. "Go on."

I sat on the chair next to the bed and clutched the hand of James. Closing my eyes, I let my healing gift open to him, finding what was broken in him. Physically, my magic found nothing, but spiritually… emotionally, his soul screamed to me—wailed through me. A single tear trailed down my cheek, and I'd only just begun. My heart threatened to shatter at the soul-destroying agony this male laid silently in.

I found the black mass on his soul where Hesperia's shadows had controlled this male against his will. I caressed the damaged spirit gently—intentionally. This broken part of him was resistant at first, but the damage was too severe. He couldn't fight anymore after what she'd done to him.

I braced myself against the bed and stilled my spirit for what I was about to do.

"I've got you," I whispered, and I let his darkness flow through me. I allowed myself to absorb his terror, sorrow, shame—*all* of it.

Tears flowed down my face freely now as the onslaught of emotions enveloped me. The weight would crush me if I let it.

Flashes of images flooded my mind… it was no longer his hands that killed innocent lives, but my own.

Oleander spoke somewhere in the background, but I couldn't focus on him. I had to see this through. I would give this male back the life that had been stolen from him.

On and on it went. I drowned in the well of trauma and tragedy. The evil she had forced this male to do. My hands slaughtered innocents whose only crime was not to bow down to a tyrant queen.

I didn't lean into my hatred of Hesperia. It would not serve me now. This wasn't about her. It was about James, and he would get my undivided attention now.

Painfully slow, his soul began to glow again in the starlight of the cosmos. Gone was the blackness of despair.

My magic attacked the darkness within me, destroying every atom that was not my own.

I screamed out as the last of the embers faded to nothing—like ash floating away after an explosion.

The male gasped out a breath, and I opened my eyes to find kind, brown eyes staring back at me.

The membrane encasing him dissolved around him, and I stood weakly before him—magic expended in this moment.

"James?" I asked, voice soft, but not cracking.

"You… you brought me back," he said, voice unsure, and he glanced at Oleander.

"You can trust her," he said, flicking his eyes back to me.

James broke, wrapping his arms around my waist, sobbing into my leathers. I said nothing as I stroked my fingers through his hair in an effort to cool his trembling body.

"Is it really over?" he asked.

"Your pain is," I said, continuing to soothe him as he clung to me.

"Where's my brother? Where's Liam?"

I didn't have the strength to tell him. I was barely able to keep myself standing right now.

"We don't know," Oleander said, moving to my side, eyes anxious. He saw through my resolve—knew how weak I truly was now.

James looked into my eyes again, and my heart stilled.

I suddenly realized why he had looked so familiar.

My eyes darkened, and I took a step back.

I knew exactly where Liam was.

I'd killed him.

He'd been the one to warn me that Hesperia was watching. He'd been one of the three my shadows had shredded to ribbons that day I'd hunted some fleeing members of Hesperia's legion in Vega.

My eyes darkened with shadows, wanting to burst to the surface.

"Zoe?" Oleander asked, hands outstretched as if to appease a bear.

And that's what I was.

A vicious bear with no mercy.

I said nothing as I ripped open the nearest window and took flight.

I didn't know where I was going, but for now, I just needed to run. Run far away from what I'd done.

24

One final trial
FREYJA

One final trial stood between me and my family—Oleander and Zoe.

One more test, and I would be with them for the rest of our immortality.

And if we lost this war, then I would be with them until the very end. I just needed to get through this.

"What are we testing today, Nova?" I asked, following her to the Cliffs of Three. "Charm? Wit?"

"You shall see, child of the cosmos," she said, smirking at my banter.

I'd expected nothing less from her, but a little tip would have been nice. A girl could dream. I briefly wondered if she knew about my little escapade last night, but I figured outing myself by asking wouldn't be my smartest option.

"Should you succeed, you will be transported back to your body with your very spirit transformed into an immortal. Should you fail, peace be with you."

"I knew you liked me," I said, winking. Apparently I'd lost my mind; however, Nova offered a small laugh.

"Good luck, Emerging."

I gave Nova a final salute before diving into the cosmic water, headed for the ball of light that would send me toward my fate.

The moment my hands gripped around the glowing orb, I was transported to unfamiliar territory.

My body plopped down on the hard moonstone surface, and the stars shone brighter than I'd ever seen. I was positive that if I reached out my hand, I'd be able to pluck one from the sky.

I'd never been to the surface of the moon and knew little to nothing about it, but I'd imagine it'd feel something like this.

There were no mountains that I could see, only the stars interweaving complex galaxies filled to the brim with hues of blues, purples, and oranges. Our creator was such an artist.

I took in my surroundings, trying to figure out my next move on this seemingly deserted planet. What was I supposed to do? Run around aimlessly? That seemed like a good way to waste precious energy.

Two monumental thuds that shook the stone beneath me sounded behind me, and I whirled around to come face to face with… beings. My mind flooded with faded memories of the celestial Vega that I was certain I only remembered now because they allowed me to.

Vega stood before me with whirls of gold and blue and features made up of the elements of water, forming a plain face—neither male nor female. A darker figure made up of shadows and mist stood beside Vega.

"You must be Algol," I said, crossing my arms in front of them.

"Must I?" they asked, waving a hand, and a large moonstone table and chairs formed next to us. "Let's get more comfortable."

I wasn't going to argue… yet. I took a seat, wincing at the coolness of the stone, even through my long-sleeved shirt and pants. Not to mention, stone chairs were simply not comfortable.

Vega and Algol both took their respective seats, and I waited for them to begin. I wasn't sure if it would be a twenty questions scenario, so I would wait for them to tell me.

"Your sister went through much trouble so that you could sit here across from us," Algol began, and their tone of voice indicated how they thought of my sister. It wasn't great, which filled me with pride. It took something special to have a celestial hate you, even though my sister quite literally saved their life.

"We don't give up," I said, choosing not to go down the rabbit hole Algol would like me to.

"Your sister continues to be difficult," Algol said, pressing further.

"Well, she did save your life. A little difficulty should be inconsequential," I said, then changed gears at the sneer across their face. "Is this trial about me or about my sister?" I asked, defiant as always.

"We have reason to believe she is on the path of considering something that will be truly unforgivable," Algol answered vaguely.

"I'm sorry, she is not a puppet you can manipulate to your whims."

Vega said nothing and let Algol continue. This couldn't be good.

"Even if she plans to knowingly sacrifice your life?" Algol asked.

"She wouldn't," I said, voice certain. I had nothing but faith in my sister.

"Let us show you," they said, and Algol waved another hand across the moonstone table, which now displayed their memories like a holographic video.

Finnian, Zoe, and Zadie were in a stark white room with books and tomes all around. They were huddled over a decrepit-looking scroll, voices raised in frustration.

"I have no idea if this will even work!" Finnian yelled, slamming his palms on the table. Zoe didn't so much as wince.

"It's more than we had."

"You realize what this means?" Finn asked, directing his question to Zadie.

"I'm ready to die, Finn. If it means saving the rest of the realms."

"Your sister, Zo. Your sister will die, too, if we get any step of this wrong," Finn said, seeming to urge Zoe to see reason.

My heart stilled. I stopped breathing. She would never hurt me…

"That's only if we fail," she said, eyes heavy with shame. "Shouldn't we at least try? If it means saving everyone else?"

The memory disappeared, and the table turned to moonstone once again.

"What was that?" I asked, voice shakier than I wanted.

"Zoe choosing her mate above you," Algol sneered.

"But what was she trying to do?" I asked, refusing to believe what seemed so black and white. I trusted Zoe, and I knew she would make the right choice. She wouldn't… she couldn't… It would be highly illogical for her to end my existence after everything she'd done to ensure I had a future. This didn't add up, no matter how Algol or Vega tried to spin it.

"A power even higher than us forbids us to speak it now," Vega answered, speaking for the first time. They did not seem so sure to hate my sister, unlike Algol who seemed more than willing. Perhaps being separated from their sibling stars warped them beyond repair.

"Why show me half-truths? They are nothing but lies."

"I showed you a memory that will come to pass. It is certain," Algol said, and I believed they were telling the truth.

"What's the test?" I asked. "Give me my trial."

I had no control over what my sister did. Only in my actions. Had the second trial not taught me that?

"This is the test, child," Vega said gently.

"What? I have to believe my sister will willingly kill me? Not going to happen."

"No," Vega disagreed.

"I want you to stop her," Algol said.

"How will I do that when my memory of these trials will be gone? And what if she shouldn't be stopped? What then? What if what she is doing will save us?"

"I will leave you with an extra gift of… intuition. Not *sight*. You only need to stop her should she go through with her plan."

"You want me to turn against my sister? The one who saved your life and still keeps you alive, by the way?" I asked, growing more frustrated.

"You just saw your sister agree to your death, yet you question me?" Algol asked.

"Of course I do because that is not what I saw at all."

Vega seemed pleased by this. Algol, not so much.

"You have a role to play in this, Freyja. Make sure you choose wisely. Consider *all* the outcomes," Vega said. "There will come a time when Zoe will learn something. Your task is to make the selfless call. The right call."

Algol looked at Vega curiously, and I knew the confusion was mirrored in my own expression.

"I have and will continue to do just that," I said, agreeing to that at the very least. "If Zoe has lost her marbles, I'll protect her from herself. That's my best offer."

"Then so be it," Algol said, holding out the orb of swirling darkness. They seemed to understand I would not simply vow to stop Zoe, who was quite the unstoppable force once she decided on something. "Embrace your Emerging."

I rose from the unforgiving stone chair and clutched the orb of darkness in my hands.

The orb was cool to the touch and warm all at the same time.

My sister was on my side. That much I knew. I just needed to get the whole story. And I would. Even with my memories wiped from this place. I knew my sister better than anyone else. What she did, she did for the good of the many.

I plunged the orb into my very essence, embracing all that came with it as my spirit soared through the galaxies and back to my body.

25

Punishment

ELVY

I was back on the chains again, shoulders already out of their sockets.

It was definitely worse now that I'd been granted such a long reprieve from them, but Hesperia was pissed that she'd failed to shed a drop of blood. My body would do all the bleeding until her bloodlust was satisfied. Stars only knew if I'd have any left by the time her madness was full for a while.

Given her response at the outcome of Arcturus, I doubted she'd let Rigil go so freely.

I shook the thought from my head, not allowing myself to think of Terran or Sierra. My two closest allies and friends outside of the Luminaries, and it could be my hands that end their existence. They did not deserve that, and I would have to trust that my flame would protect them from me.

It'd killed me a thousand times over to see my flame—my starlight—and blessed my broken soul all at the same time. She'd been as beautiful as ever, and we'd said a thousand words between us without uttering a single syllable. She was pissed at me, but loved me through it anyway.

My head rolled back, too weak to hold it.

The moon greeted me through a crack in the cavern that was my prison. It must have changed position in the sky if I can see it now. The moon sent me comfort, and the scent of coffee wafted through the cell. Was the moon sending me my Zoe, who always smelled a little like coffee and the sea? I raised a brow towards the beacon of hope shining down on me, and I drew deep breaths as I continued to breathe in my bond.

I smiled, wincing at the pain that shot through my split lip.

The words we'd said repeatedly over our time together echoed through me.

For the heart of the new moon… and the life in the starlight.

One thing that would always remain true was the cycle of the moon—waxing and waning. The moon would remain ever sure. A new moon for new beginnings. The moment I'd laid eyes on Zoe that day on the beach… my life had finally begun after so many centuries of living in fear of who I was and the destruction that I could be. Ashamed. Deadened. Broken. But there she'd been—my starlight—ready to embrace all that I was without a seed of fear in her heart.

She *was* the life in all starlight as far as I was concerned. They certainly paled in comparison to her.

And I would become the darkness to make sure she glowed.

I would become death if that's what it took.

I did not look away as the groan of the door to my prison cell indicated someone had ventured in. Hesperia's scent was hard to miss as my stomach turned sour at the unpleasant smell of decay surrounding her very essence. I knew she would not leave here until the floor beneath me was stained with my blood, and I did not fear it. Not tonight. Hesperia had made the mistake of letting me lay eyes on Zoe. She had rejuvenated my spirit just enough for me to bear this torture a little longer.

"Elvy, Elvy, Elvy," she purred. "You failed today."

Silence. I said nothing as I stared into the heart of the new moon above me. And in this moment, I felt the moon stare back at me, as if it did have a heart that cried out in sorrow for me. A few drips splashed across my face, as if the moon mourned me from all the way up there. For the first time in this hellish dungeon, I didn't feel alone. Zoe was with me, though I continued to keep our flame sealed off for her own safety. Tonight, the moon protected us.

"Don't tell me you've lost your voice again," she said, slicing a nail through the thin flesh at my neck.

I didn't allow myself to wince. My heart. My mind. My soul. It was with the moon right now. She couldn't touch me. Not where it counted. She could only hurt my flesh, and my mind was far away from my body in this moment. I was sitting on Zoe's front porch in her beach bungalow, sipping coffee as she was curled up against my chest in the swing. No, Hesperia couldn't touch me here.

Hesperia's breath was erratic. Oh yes, she'd consumed the star seed from Arcturus. She was physically weak and growing weaker. I had doubts that she'd be strong enough to hold all five star seeds, despite the magic she stole from them.

Unfortunately, she was still strong enough to make me bleed.

My shadows swelled with the realization that they would not be caged by her for much longer.

So she would try to break me tonight in a different way.

But I was untouchable this night, and I gazed into the void of the moon, back to the front porch and my flame.

She sliced the knife from the middle of my chest to my navel.

I felt nothing as I stared back at the moon, filling my love with the power of my flame. I was careful not to access Zoe directly. Always protecting her. She'd never let me live it down, I knew. And I looked forward to it.

"You will bow before me," she snarled, and I smiled wider, which I knew would send her into a frenzy.

I would bow to no one except Zoe. Only her. Until there was no longer the sea breeze flowing through my lungs. And maybe even then.

"I will break you."

As long as there was breath in Zoe's lungs and a steady beat in her heart, I remained unbroken to all else.

My smile unnerved the queen.

Hesperia tore into my flesh.

But I felt nothing.

Nothing but the love of my flame, and the peace I'd been granted by the moon and stars tonight.

26

Secrets

ELVY

Something was incredibly wrong with my flame.

I'd fallen into unconsciousness after Hesperia had sliced through nearly every surface of my skin.

But Zoe's terror had woken me from my hazy slumber.

I blinked rapidly and found no one in the cell with me.

It was a risk.

One I had to take.

I sent a silent prayer to the moon for a few more moments of protection after what my body had endured last night. My flesh was still raw and bleeding from how deeply she'd cut me. Every movement was torture, but I had enough resolve to control this magic.

I gently opened the bond of our flame, throwing up every morsel of a shield I could to prevent any of my magic from being detected.

If the stars were on my side at all, Hesperia and her cronies would assume I'd be knocked out for several more hours yet. Every bone in my body ached, but none of that mattered. Only Zoe did.

"Zoe?" I asked gently through the bond.

"Elvy?" she asked, as if she were too scared to believe the truth.

"I felt your terror. It was all-consuming."

Silence.

"Let me help you," I coaxed. "Let me take this from you."

"It's not for you to take," she said, voice unsteady. She was spiraling and on the verge of breaking.

"Let me in," I said again.

"You haven't let me in," she argued.

"To protect you, Zo. Even now, it's a risk. But I had to know you were okay."

"I haven't known if you were okay this entire time, Elvy," she said, voice numb. "The only way I knew you were alive is the barrier for me to slam my fist into every time I tried to reach you never failed."

"And if I had let you in, she could've gotten to you through our bond."

"Then why risk it now?"

"Because I felt you breaking, Zoe Eferhild. I couldn't let you."

Sobs met me through the bond.

"I love you, my starlight," I said, wishing I could just hold her. "Let me take this from you. Whatever it is."

My shadows seemed to nod their agreement. They couldn't stand to hear our girl like this.

"What has she done to you?" she asked, and I felt the tears in her voice.

I traced a mental caress down our flame, offering what little touch of comfort I could. My entire soul throbbed to touch her again.

"She can't hurt me where it matters," I said, voice steady. "We don't have much time. Tell me what happened, Zo."

Her pause was long enough that I thought she was going to shut me out again, but her voice came through—vulnerable as ever.

"I saved a male today from the damage Hesperia had ravaged on his soul. I took everything from him. Absorbed it. Healed the darkness."

My mind stilled, fearing the worst.

"I never lost myself. I embraced who I had to become to perform that kind of magic. But then—"

Quiet tears met me then, and I sent her all the love I had for her through our minds, and my soul and shadows wanted to cry out at the sorrow I felt there.

"I realized I had killed his brother. My shadows shredded him when he was still under the control of Hesperia."

There was no apology on my lips, and I knew she would hate me for saying the words.

"Use that anger," I said. "Use that grief. Let it propel you toward justice."

"There's so much blood on my hands," she whispered, voice threatening to go numb, but I needed her to feel something. Even if it were rage.

"And there will be more," I said honestly. I knew my flame, and she was stronger than she realized. I would always be her safe harbor, but I would not let her believe she should be hidden in the shadows. She was starlight and darkness all at once—wickedly ethereal. And I loved all of her. I knew I spoke my next words for her just as much as I spoke them for myself. "We embrace who we are, Zoe Eferhild. All of us. The secret parts of us that revel in the euphoria of chaos and bloodlust. The soft side of us who would lay down our own lives to save those we loved… Both parts of us are true. The light and the dark. Grieve what was done and move forward. Always forward. Embrace all that you are, and the darkness can never eclipse the light within you."

"How can you be so sure?" she asked with a little more life in her voice.

"Just as I know the morning moon will rise, I know you will, too, starlight."

Another brief pause greeted me.

"I miss you," she said, voice strong now. Determined. "I'm going to get you back."

"I know," I said, sending my confidence in her through our bond.

"I'm still angry with you for blocking me out."

"I know that, too," I said, a little laughter in my voice. The first time I'd thought of laughing since Hesperia took control of my shadows.

Footsteps echoed through the chambers of my prison cell.

"Someone's coming. I have to go."

"I will see you soon," she promised, and I began blocking her out again, as painful as it was.

"For the heart of the new moon, Zoe."

"And the life in the starlight, Elvy," she responded, as I closed my bond off to her again.

I opened my eyes as Hesperia's sickly black eyes came into view.

"Elvy, Elvy, Elvy, what have you been doing?" she asked, eyes wild with the hysteria of consuming so much magic not meant for her.

I stared her down, seeing in her eyes that she wasn't sure what I'd been up to. That was enough.

"My legion felt a stir of magic coming from down here," she said, smiling a wicked grin. "And you know what they found?"

Silence. All I had was my silence.

"A shield," she said, slicing a blade through my barely healed skin across my chest. "What are you hiding?"

She clenched her fist, forcing my shadows to attack me from within. A new tactic. The air dripped with her desperation.

I refused to talk. Even as it felt like each atom in my body was both fire and ice at the same time.

My silence dared her to do her worst.

"You know, Elvy. You're beginning to outgrow your use," she said, sighing. "Such a pity to execute someone so handsome."

I recoiled at the sultry look in her eyes.

"If only you would forget about my weak little sister and see who the real prize is."

If I had anything in my stomach, I'd vomit at the thought, but some laughter did escape me. The image was simply too absurd. She couldn't be serious.

She moved the blade to my throat.

"If you won't join me, Elvy, then perhaps I should deliver your head on a platter to my dear little sister. I never gave you two a wedding present after all."

She wouldn't kill me. Not here. So, I laughed a little more, sounding more hysterical by the second. Maybe I was losing my mind down here.

"After I make you kill the immortals of Rigil, I'm going to kill you, and I'm going to make sure Zoe watches me take everything from her, just as she took everything from me."

Some fear went through me then, but I didn't let her see it. I wouldn't give her that satisfaction.

So I gave her my silence and rolled my head back to look at the moon again.

I heard the moon's cries as the cutting began once more.

27

Calm in the Eye

ZOE

I brushed my fingers down my cheek, wiping away the rest of my tears. I imagined Elvy's fingers caressing my face, and if I closed my eyes, I could have sworn I felt him next to me.

Hearing Elvy's voice again had energized me, and my entire being longed for him.

Flames weren't meant to be apart this long, and my shadows weren't exactly happy about it either.

The hair on the back of my neck stood up as I felt a presence behind me—not one I was familiar with. I turned with my hand on the hilt of one of my many blades. My brows furrowed in confusion as I took in the sight before me.

"Don't you recognize me?" the male asked, turning his head. His form reminded me of Freyja's before she'd been brought back to life. This male was in the in-between—a spirit.

I stepped closer to him, and his features solidified a bit more, bringing recognition to me.

"Liam," I said, wanting to look away immediately, but I refused to insult him.

"I was drawn here," he said. "You must have been thinking about me pretty loudly."

"I suppose I was," I admitted, voice shakier than I'd like. "I healed your brother, James."

Liam stepped closer, and his form flickered some. He didn't have as much control as Freyja did. New spirits probably wouldn't.

"Thank you for freeing him," he said, tears in his eyes. "I've been wishing for him to die, knowing what he was living with in his mind."

There was no shame in his voice. He meant what he'd said.

"I'm sorry, Liam. For what I did to you."

"You freed me, too," he said, smirking. "Though it would have been nice not to die."

"I wish I could give you that," I admitted.

"Maybe you'll find a way," he said, shrugging.

"I can't bring you back," I said, shaking my head.

"No, you can't," he agreed. "But that doesn't mean we can't be… useful." He smiled at something or someone behind him that I couldn't see.

"What are you thinking?" I asked, desiring to make things as right as I could for him.

"You have much to learn about the ways of the dead," he said, grin widening.

"Teach me," I pleaded, and he nodded.

★★★

I wasn't sure how long I'd worked with Liam, but I sealed the information in my mind, vowing to protect it with my life. Liam and all others who had been killed by Hesperia would have their vengeance. I'd promised him that I would not breathe a word of this to anyone, not even Oleander. I owed him that much.

Sighing, I stood from my hidden spot on a cliff not too far from Oleander's castle. I cracked my knuckles and spread my wings, taking off into the sky.

It didn't take long for me to reach Oleander's balcony, where he was already pacing, running a hand through his blonde hair. My heart sank with a heap of guilt at the little form following behind him.

Jelly leaped into my arms with a few choice words of her own for leaving her behind with Freyja without telling her what was going on. I offered her my apologies.

"My job is to protect you. I felt your pain, and could not find you," she accused through the bond of the simargl. Jelly gave me a chastising look for a creature so adorable.

"I know," I said, giving her ear scratches. "I'm sorry. It's no excuse, but I just needed space."

She nuzzled her snout against my body, and Oleander stood across from us with folded arms.

"You've been gone for hours. You good?" he asked, brows raised. "I very nearly went after you and left poor James alone."

I winced at the male's name and sighed. Hell, I was tired.

"I'm glad you didn't do that," I admitted, undoing the length of my braid.

"What happened back there, Zo?"

"I know what happened to Liam," I said, choosing to embrace this—own this—part of my story. With a deep breath and a dash of courage, I proceeded. "I killed him some time ago. He had been under Hesperia's control, and I hadn't been in alliance with my shadows at the time. They demanded his death, and I let them end him."

I took a deep breath.

"He was a good male. He fought against her until the very end. I just hadn't realized it in that moment. I'd been too blinded by my shadows and hatred."

Oleander pressed his lips into a thin line. I felt a smidge bad about keeping my interaction with Liam from Oleander, but it wasn't my secret to tell. The less that knew what was coming, the better.

"I'll tell him," I offered, ready to give more of myself again… because I was both the light and the dark. An avenging angel of death when I needed to be, and an angel of grace and healing when required.

"No," he said, shaking his head. "I'll take care of it. You need to rest."

"You're right. I do. My reserves are lower than I like. How many more besides James?"

"Only four others have survived," he said, as if it were his personal fault that they had been killed.

"We will do it in cycles, then. I'm going to have to rest for a few hours in between sessions, but I'll get it done," I promised.

He folded me into his arms, and my body stiffened at the initial contact. Slowly, the muscles relaxed, and I let myself feel comfortable with him.

"Thank you," he said, not saying a negative word about what I'd done to Liam. I hoped James offered me the same grace, and if he didn't, I'd face that, too.

Oleander pulled away, but held my gaze.

"Let's go rest with Freyja. There's a pot of coffee for you. I'll come with you."

I followed behind him and plopped onto the couch next to the one that held my sister. She was as beautiful as ever, with a peaceful look on her face.

I laced my fingers through hers and sent her all my love in the realm of Nova.

Oleander handed me a cup of piping hot coffee as Jelly made herself comfortable at my feet, tucking her wings in snugly.

"Who is with James now?" I asked.

"The healers from Vega," he said, crossing one leg over the other.

I nodded, making a mental note to thank them later.

"So what's the plan for Rigil?" he asked.

The questions and answers never stopped.

"I don't know yet," I answered honestly. "I have Blaz and Delm working on it. I'll check in with them soon."

"Any chance it will go as smoothly as Arcturus?"

"There's always hope," I said, taking a deep gulp of the coffee. "Is it likely, though? I'd say no. She's royally pissed and won't let us get away so easily."

"I guessed as much," he said, gaze sliding over to Freyja. "I feel like she's close."

I looked at my sister's peaceful form. "I hope so."

"She's going to be a beautiful immortal," he said, smirking.

"That she is," I agreed, taking the final swig, and Oleander filled the cup again. I nodded appreciatively.

"I need to get back to Vega soon. This is going to be a long twenty-four hours."

"I'll keep the coffee coming."

"Perfect," I said, feeling my wells of magic already brimming to the surface.

"Send Zadie home when you get back. I'll switch out with her when you go to Rigil."

"You should stay with Freyja. She could wake up any moment."

"But you need my shield against Elvy," he countered.

"Elvy would have gotten through your shields without the simargls," I said softly. It wasn't an insult, just a fact. It was unfortunate that the simargls could not extend their protection to the other realms in the same manner. "If we can't get Elvy back before she commands him to release his power, a shield is going to be useless."

"But what if you can't get him back?"

"You should know by now I always have a backup plan," I said, wiping the sweat from my palms. There were so many things that could go wrong with this. I didn't have the space to think about it right now. I had a couple of ideas about what we could do, but I needed to talk to Finn first to see how realistic it could be.

"Are you sure, Zoe?"

"Do you trust your second?" I asked seriously.

"Implicitly," he said, nodding.

"Then stay with Freyja. I'll feel better knowing you're here and that she's safe."

"As you wish, love."

I put down my third cup of coffee and stretched my arms above my head. I was ready for another round of healing torture.

"Take me to the next immortal," I said, standing, no longer able to delay the inevitable.

Jelly jumped up next to me, tail wagging in solidarity.

"Come on then, Realm-Healer," he said, leading me back to the medical wing.

One immortal at a time.

I'd heal them all. Not to atone for my sins.

But because I believed in a healed world—a better world.

Where we could live without the threat of despair—both immortals and mortals alike.

We would know peace and have the freedom to embrace every part of us we felt was too much for the rest of the world to see.

We would be safe enough to dream and know that these dreams were possible. The realms would know it as surely as they knew the moon would rise. We would all believe in the life of starlight again.

Before I reached the door of the next immortal, James called for me, pausing me in my tracks. My palms became clammy, but I would not run from him. Not this time.

"Zoe?" he asked, voice steadier than I expected after what he'd gone through.

I put on the mask of a warrior and drifted to his bedside.

"I'm glad to see you up," I said, smile tight. My soul braced for the crushing of his words—the accusation of evil. I shoved my hands into my pockets, afraid that the stain of red would be visible to him, even though the logical part of me knew the burgundy was only in my heart. Not to mention that Oleander hadn't had time to tell him the news about Liam. When I'd spoken with Liam, he had also made it clear that he did not want to see his brother. Not yet.

The words of loathing didn't come.

"I need to tell you something," he said, and the song of fate sounded her war cry. "Something you don't know about Hesperia yet."

I swallowed, bracing for impact.

"Go on," I said, swallowing down the fear that threatened to unleash from within me.

28

My Lady Astral
DELMIRA

"Is this really going to work?" Imelda asked, analyzing the playing field.

"With the intel Sierra gave us about Rigil… this could work," Blaz said, nodding appreciatively.

"Zoe will be arriving soon. We'll let her make the final call," I said, slumping back into my seat.

I didn't think any of us had worked this hard on a battle strategy before, but we had to be meticulous with this if we were going to get Elvy back without him killing everyone on Rigil. Sierra had left a while ago to get things started in her realm.

"We'll get him back," Blaz said, face set with determination.

"Clove will send word as soon as Aura's scouts report that Hesperia has left."

"We'll already be in Rigil by then," I said, then corrected myself. "You two will be, anyway. I'll be here with Finn."

"Do you know if Clodovea will come back to Vega or meet us in Rigil?" Blaz asked.

"She'll do whatever the Lady Astral deems," Imelda said.

The soft beating of wings echoed outside on the balcony just then, and Zoe and Jelly made their entrance into the secure meeting room on top of the manor.

We all stood in reverence to our lady, though Jelly bounced into Blaz, knocking him to the ground.

"Missed you, too, girl," he said, laughing.

"Please, sit," Zoe said, plopping down on the seat next to me.

She was exhausted, and the circles underneath her eyes suggested she had little rest in Algol.

"Were you successful?" I asked.

"Yes," she said, nodding. "I got more than I bargained for."

"Oh?" Imelda asked, crossing her legs and folding her arms.

"Yes," she said, eyes on a distant memory or maybe glazed over, trying to see a future that has not come to pass. "I healed them and learned what I needed to know."

I knew true fear when I saw it. Whatever she'd learned, she was scared, and if Zoe was scared, then we should be, too.

"What is it?" I asked.

Zoe shook her head. "I need to talk to Finn. Where is he?"

"He's in the Hall of Memories," I answered automatically. "With Zadie."

"I'll go find him," she said, rising again.

"Wait," I said, pulling her arm. "What's going on?"

"Are the preparations ready to go for Rigil?" she asked, dodging my question, which made me irrationally angry.

"Yes, of course," I said, laying out the plan for her. It was flawless. Well, as flawless as it could be, when considering free will and unpredictability.

"This is good," she said. "Excellent."

Zoe's eyes kept darting around the room, but she wasn't really here with us.

"Too many factors. Too many futures," she whispered, no longer focused on the battle strategy that would get her flame back, which I found to be peculiar at the very least.

"Zo, let us help you," Blaz said, snapping his fingers in front of her face.

Zoe barely registered it.

"No one can help this… except maybe Finn," she said thoughtfully. "I need you to trust me. I will tell you everything I know when the time is right. When I have an answer to give you… I don't want to give false hope. Prepare to leave for Rigil within the hour. We need to be ready."

She walked off with Jelly trotting behind her, leaving us all confused and on edge.

"What the hell did she learn in Algol?" I asked, fear icing over my heart.

"Nothing good. Not if she's like that," Blaz said, face full of concern.

"What do we do?" Imelda asked, hands on her hips.

"As she says," I said, locking away the plans securely. "We prepare for Elvy's extraction, just as we planned. This changes nothing."

"Nothing about Rigil, anyway."

"Go. Do what you need to do," I said, hating the betrayal I felt creeping in.

Imelda turned to attend to what she needed to, but Blaz caught my eye.

"Where are you going?"

"To find my brother. Something is going on that he isn't telling us," I whispered forcefully. "And now Zoe is hellbent on seeing him. I want to know what's going on."

"She said it was vital that we not know yet."

"Bull," I said, anger flooding me. "I'm her second. It's my job to protect her. Even from herself."

"Let me go with you," he said, blocking my way out.

"No," I hissed. "You're too large to be stealthy."

"I've found you like the large parts of me," he said, trying to lighten the mood, but I just punched him in the stomach. He grunted and side-stepped out of my way.

"You left yourself wide open!" I yelled.

"Fine," he said, "But don't do anything stupid."

"No promises," I said, racing out the door before he could stop me.

★★★

I prowled the empty streets of Vega, feeling like a traitor in my own home.

I'd never been more grateful to live in the realm of stars, allowing the night to cover my movements with little chance of exposure. Fortunately, there was a decent cloud covering the brightest of stars.

I made my way to the Hall of Memories and paused just before the entrance. I glanced Zoe entering, and I took a deep breath.

I hated this place with a passion, and now I'd have to hope the Hall of Memories would let me in.

"Please," I said as sincerely as I could muster to the gargantuan doors. "I know you have a thing with my brother."

I wanted to roll my eyes at how ridiculous this sounded.

"I care about him, too, okay? I'm trying to look after him. Please, let me in."

Silence greeted me. Fantastic. I guess I would have to beat my way in. It'd give my position away, but I didn't care at this point.

Before my fist made contact, the door groaned open, as if it still wasn't sure it was making the right choice by letting me in.

I didn't give it enough time to question itself before slipping into the darkness.

I threw a shield around me, muffling my footsteps as much as possible in the halls that seemed to echo the very breaths from my lungs. My shields weren't as good as Zoe's or Oleander's, but they'd do well enough. I sent out my magic ahead of me, letting the atmosphere around become calm and inconspicuous. Apart from Finn, Zoe, and Zadie, I doubted any other soul would be in the Hall of Memories, especially with most of our immortals hidden away in Musterion.

The bond with my twin didn't lead me astray as I crept closer to some of the inner catacombs, with the most ancient of tomes.

Voices drifted softly through the iron door before me, and it was much too risky for me to open without alerting them. I bit back the feeling of being a traitor to my Lady Astral, but at the same time, it was my job to protect her—even from herself.

A soft tap on my shoulder nearly made me piss myself, and I was even more surprised to find Octavia staring back at me.

I moved to silence her, but she held a finger to her lips, shushing me and motioned with the other hand for me to follow her. My brows furrowed in confusion, but I decided to follow her. I was caught either way.

She led me through the gloriously white halls, such a juxtaposition to the dusty conception of the history stored here. I was immediately suspicious of Octavia. Had she followed me here? Why? All questions I couldn't ask as she led me up some hidden stairs to a balcony that overlooked the meeting between my brother, Zoe, and Zadie.

Octavia crooked a finger to come closer, and she pointed through the glass that gave us a perfect view of the trio.

"They can't see or hear us," she said, voice louder than I'd expected.

"Are you sure?" I whispered.

"Quite," she assured. "I've been keeping tabs on them for a while."

"That doesn't seem to align with your job description, Keeper," I seethed.

"It wouldn't be to you," she agreed. "Or any ruthless brute. You think you have a monopoly on defending these realms, but you are mistaken."

My mouth dropped with an insult ready on my lips, but she silenced me again.

"The Keepers answer to the Astrals, yes. But our purpose is greater than watching over a collection of tomes and books. We are the history keepers, and we have an important role to play in not only preserving history, but in shaping the new future."

"Then why all the lost history from the actions of the celestials?"

"Even we are not immune to that kind of power. And we have no intention of it happening again," she said, peering down at their rapidly moving lips. "We learned what Hesperia planned to do in severing the tethers from Algol much too late. We can't let anything like that happen again. No matter who does it."

"I should slit your throat for keeping tabs on our lady," I said, voice going darker.

"I could say the same for you," she said, crossing her arms. "Besides, I'm not against our Lady Astral. I am always for her. She has been kinder to me than most immortals. She saw me when very few bothered to acknowledge my existence."

"Are you, like, into her or something?" I asked, confusion written all over my face.

"Could you blame me if I were?" she laughed softly. "But no. I have much respect and love for Elvy and Zoe. However, their choices directly influence all of us. We want to make sure they choose... wisely."

"Zoe would do anything for the star realms," I said, voice certain.

"Therein lies the problem, Delmira," she said.

"I will kill you without a second thought should you lay harm to her," I promised.

She didn't seem particularly bothered by that.

"What if it saves your brother, too?" she asked, brows raised. "Listen."

Octavia waved something over the glass, and their voices echoed to us as if we were standing right next to them.

Finnian spoke first.

"You don't know what you're asking me to do. The gravity of it," he said, voice far more distressed than I'd heard in a long time.

"Have you found a different solution? A better one? If you have, I beg you to tell me," Zoe said, eyes glancing at both Finn and Zadie.

Finn shook his head.

"I'll do it," Zadie said. "If it comes down to it. I will do it."

"Are you insane?" Finnian asked. "I won't let you. Either of you."

Finn ran a hand through his lilac hair, eyes flitting through countless scenarios I had no hope of figuring out for him. On instinct, my magic wanted to ease his worries, but I locked it down, not wanting to give away our position.

"It's a last resort. This plan won't even work unless Sirius helps us," Zoe said. "This plan will only be used if all else fails."

"We have no guarantee your little failsafe will work," Finn said. "We are risking too many lives if we get anything wrong. Your sister, Zoe."

What the hell was he talking about? What had Zoe gotten them into?

"I know what is at stake, Finnian. It'll work," Zoe promised, but there was uncertainty in her eyes. "But all of this will be a moot point if the stars are on my side for once."

Zoe took Finnian's hand, imploring him to look at her.

"I need you with me on this," she said. "I can trust no one else to see it through."

Finn sat down next to her.

"Lose one to save the rest," he said, voice hardened. The warrior that lived within, who was so rarely seen, was shining through his lilac eyes.

"That's what I'm asking," she said.

Slowly, Finn nodded, and Zoe breathed a sigh of relief.

"Swear it," she said, handing him a blade.

Finn and Zadie both sliced their palms—an oath written in blood.

"It will be done," they said in unison.

"But only at the last moment. Only when there is no other option," Finn said seriously.

"Only then," Zoe agreed. "Let's all pray it does not come to that moment."

They sat in silence, staring at each other, and I turned my attention back to Octavia, whose eyes analyzed the information.

"What the hell was that about?" I asked.

"I'm not sure," she admitted. "But it seems you need to confront your brother before he does something irreversibly stupid."

"The magic will kill him if he doesn't fulfill the oath," I whispered, chest filling with horror.

"Then you better make sure Zoe has no need to call in the oath," she said, hands on her hips.

Could this night get anymore screwed?

"But we don't even know what it is!" I snapped. "It may be something good."

"Then why wouldn't she tell you as her second?" she questioned, and I hated that she made sense.

"I'll speak to my brother," I said.

"That would be wise," Octavia said, pursing her lips, and I turned my focus back to my brother.

What have you got us into, Finn?

29

Resolute

ZOE

Making the blood oath with Finnian and Zadie had not settled my spirits, despite the hope that it would.

I had asked him the unaskable. I knew that. Knew that and had asked it of him anyway, but hopefully it wouldn't come down to that vow. Hopefully, I will figure out another way out of this hell.

I needed Elvy. My soul craved my bond, and if I could just know he was out of her grip, I could think clearly. I could figure out how to end all of this.

Even if it meant sacrificing something precious to me.

We'd landed in Rigil a day ago and despite the circumstances of our visit, Sierra and Terran had been nothing but welcoming.

I'd put on my mask of confidence, but internally, I was in turmoil over what I knew.

I couldn't reason with chaos, and that's all Hesperia craved. There would be no swaying her or making her see reason. That ship had sailed long ago.

Jelly whimpered by the wooden tub I soaked in. The water was so hot, my skin was reddened and irritated, but I welcomed it—anything that would get me out of my mind.

I dipped my head beneath the surface of the water, blowing out air through my nose.

One.

Two.

Three.

Four.

Five.

Six.

Seven.

Eight.

Nine.

Ten.

I resurfaced, breathing in fresh air, hoping it would bring me stillness, but the image the awakened immortal had given me proved too powerful. Hesperia's plan was far more devastating than I could have imagined any being capable of.

My father should have slaughtered her that night when she was a toddler. He should have had the guile to kill her. Daughter or not. The thought was cruel and cold, but I was past the point of caring.

I hadn't told anyone what I knew except Finnian and Zadie. The only reason I'd even told them was the need to have someone carry out what I couldn't if the time should come. It would be my burden to carry. They needed hope, and I would give it to them. I would play my part well in making them believe we had a good chance of winning.

In letting them have hope in the rising of the new moon and the love of the starlight.

I dipped my head beneath the surface again and repeated the counting process, but I increased the numbers until my lungs burned.

When that had settled my spirits some, I practiced pulling on the magic like my father had taught me. I focused on my being within, embracing all that I was and hoped to be. I opened my eyes to find a sparkling gold orb of light hovering above me, but before I could try to reach out and pinch a string off, the light flooded back inside me, causing me to shiver at the sensation.

Slowly, I got out of the water, stomach queasy with acid. I hadn't eaten since… I wasn't sure when the last time I'd eaten was. I wrapped myself in the soft green covers, wishing to hide away from the world.

I was lying to most everyone and disgusted with myself.

"You need to trust your friends," Jelly said through the magic of our brand.

"I do trust them," I said, lying naked beneath the covers.

"Then why do you lie?"

"Because I love them."

It was a pitiful answer, I knew, yet it was my truth. Knowing the answer would only cause them distress and sadness.

But more importantly… if they knew the truth of what she was planning, they'd lose the one thing that kept us going through all of this—hope.

I would continue to be their beacon of light, only breaking in the solitude of my isolation.

Finn knew the truth. Zadie, too. Finn had vomited when I told him.

There was nothing good that would come of me telling everyone else now.

A knock sounded at the door, and I groaned.

"Is it important?" I asked, voice much more level than I actually felt.

"Yes," Blaz said, pounding again.

"I'll be out in ten," I said. "Beat on that door again, and I swear on the stars I will send a knife through it."

Blaz laughed through the door, and I listened intently as his footsteps carried him away.

I slid off the bed, examining my body in the mirror.

I'd lost even more weight, but my muscles brimmed on the surface. My jawline seemed sharper and had lost its softness.

My rich brown hair had lost some of its shine.

Who was I convincing?

I brushed through the strands of my hair and added some oil that was already in the room. It smelled more earthy than floral, which I appreciated.

I massaged my dry face with some moisturizer, which brightened my skin and seemed to give me a bit of a false illumination. I worked some lotion into the rest of my body, trying to believe that this would make all the difference.

After that, I brushed my teeth and put some kind of lip balm on the desert that had become my lips.

I pulled on my fighting leathers, satisfied with the effort I had made.

"Let's go," I said, beckoning Jelly to follow me.

Blaz waited outside the door, eyeing me suspiciously, but said nothing.

"What's up?" I asked.

"Imelda received word from Clodovea. Hesperia is on the move."

"So soon?" I asked, brow raised. That was unexpected.

"Seems she's desperate."

"Good. Desperation breeds stupidity. How are we coming along with the preparations for our mission?"

"Nearly there," he said, seeming satisfied, and I trusted him to see it through. "We will be ready when she arrives."

"Is there an ETA?"

"Nothing concrete. She hasn't left Canopus yet. She's rallying her forces."

I touched the hilts of my blades on instinct, making sure they were all accounted for. My bow and regular arrows were stashed away in my room. I didn't see any point in bringing the magical ones with me, though I had brought the original arrow I'd found with me in Algol. It was sharp, so though it held no magic, it certainly could deal damage. Well, it could destroy anyone except Hesperia, who was immune to simple things such as weapons. I would bring the bow into battle with me, if nothing more than to distract Hesperia and have some semblance of closeness to my father.

After the revelation about James, I knew exactly why she wanted that bow, and it had nothing to do with her endgame at all. My *sight* had urged me to bring it with me from Vega, and I'd obeyed, curious as to what destiny had in store for me on this night.

Hopefully, my mate back.

Finnian joined us in the hallway, and Blaz gave him a slight nod.

"Remind me why we brought the scholar along on a battle mission?" Blaz asked.

"I'm right here, jerk," Finn said, shoving Blaz lightly.

Finn was indeed a scholar and our resident researcher, but muscles were hidden beneath all that as well.

Blaz knew that, and I saw through his joking. He was legitimately curious about the choice. I feel like it had something to do with how pissed Delmira had been when I informed her of the decision. Something had been off about the whole interaction with her, but I hadn't had time to get into it with her either.

"I need him," I said lightly. "He's the best strategist of all of us."

Lies.

Well, that bit was true, but that's not why I'd brought him.

Finn didn't meet my eye.

"And Zadie?" Blaz pressed.

"A representative of the Court of Algol," I said casually. "What's with the twenty questions?"

"I'm your general, Zoe. It's my job to know things."

"Well, now you know," I said, following him through the door to the meeting room in Rigil.

Imelda was already seated, as were Terran and Sierra.

Delmira had stayed behind in Vega with Evander and the entire Shadowed Legion. Clodovea and Tiergan were still with Aura hidden away somewhere in Canopus. That left Blaz, Imelda, and Finnian with me.

"Good evening," Sierra said, smiling towards me, and I greeted her with matched energy, though the effort was great.

I couldn't deny the beauty of this place, no matter the inner turmoil that resided within me. The walls were lined with vines, with twinkles of light interwoven delicately throughout, and the sound of the underground river sang a beautiful melody.

I took my seat to their right, and Blaz sat opposite me. Finn sat to my left, and Jelly curled up next to me, giving me a pointed look I chose to ignore.

"Did you rest all right?" Terran asked, and I nodded politely.

I'd slept terribly, but that had nothing to do with their accommodations. No need to tell them that.

"I hear your ground users have made quick work of the plan?" I asked.

"They have. The new tunnels are nearly complete," Sierra answered.

"And the star seed?" I asked.

"Ready," Sierra answered, producing a glass orb that contained a glowing star seed from Rigil.

"Are you sure this is the best way?" Terran asked.

I let my eyes glaze over, turning black as I leaned into my *sight*. I let my words speak freely as I told them what my gift saw should they refuse to give up the star seed or try to fight Hesperia and Elvy for it.

Death. Most of their realm would be lifeless and ravaged. Their beautiful magic would be lost to the whims of a tyrant. An oppressor I could not wait to kill. As soon as I figured out how to do that. And I would.

"I see," Sierra said, handing me the starlight. "I am entrusting this to you, Zoe Eferhild, Realm-Healer—Emerging of Legends."

I couldn't hide the wince at the word trust. I hid it just as quickly.

"This is the best way to save this realm," I promised, and that was the truth.

My burden. Not theirs. I would embrace that.

Imelda's iris lit up with the vivid colors of the rainbow, such a juxtaposition for the dark words that would come from it.

"Hesperia has left Canopus with Elvy," Clodovea's voice came over the iris.

I nodded, swallowing back the bile that wanted to come out.

Brave face, Zo.

"Tell Clove to head back to Vega."

"And Tiergan?" she asked.

"Tiergan will do what needs to be done."

Imelda nodded, relaying the message.

A Shadowed from Rigil entered the room.

"The tunnels are complete, Lord and Lady Astral," he said, bowing.

"Get the legion ready. She's coming," Terran said.

The Shadowed wasted no time in asking questions, making his exit swift.

"Blaz and Imelda, you will have two ground users with you should anything go… wrong," Sierra said, and I stood.

"The moment your hand touches him, transport him back to Vega," I said, tone leaving no room for argument.

"What about you?"

"Finnian and Jelly will be with me," I said. "Get him home. I'll meet you all there."

"He's not going to like it," he said.

"He'll like not laying waste to innocent immortals at the inclinations of Hesperia even more. Do as I ask."

Blaz and Imelda both nodded, but I felt their questions, nonetheless.

"I'll see you out there," I said, dragging Finn and Zadie with me to grab my bow. Jelly trailed behind us. She disliked the omissions towards Blaz the most.

"We should tell the others," Finn whispered. Fortunately, I'd thrown up a silencing shield around us already.

"What good would it do?" I asked.

He remained silent.

"They have a right to know," he said finally.

"No. They don't. They aren't the ones who will be living with the consequences."

Zadie nodded in agreement.

"Besides, we don't really have anything concrete to tell them," I said, unsure of who I was trying to convince.

"Then it's insane for us to even be thinking about this option. Have you had any other brilliant ideas on a different course of action?" he asked, voice almost pleading.

I chose to ignore his first comment.

"No. Not yet, but I'm working on it. I swear it. I haven't exactly had time in the twenty-four hours since the vow was made."

"I'll regret telling you what I found for the rest of my days if you don't find another way," he hissed.

"I know," I said, smiling softly. "But you'll have the rest of your very long immortal life to get over it."

They waited outside my room while I grabbed my bow and the regular arrows. I secured them to my back quickly.

"Please let this work," I whispered to the stars, wishing on them with the heart of a child.

"Sometimes the stars talk back, Zoe Eferhild."

The words Elvy had spoken to me when I was still mortal rang through me. A sense of true hope flickered in my chest, and I tried to stoke the flames there, wanting to believe in it more than anything.

It wasn't much, but a smaller gleam of hope seemed to tuck itself deep within me, and I let my eyes glaze back to black.

Embracing.

30

Rigil is Rigid
ZOE

I stood before the grassy plain that was lush with colorful fauna that seemed to always be in bloom.

The bioluminescent flowers glowed blue and green as Hesperia and her forces approached. I did one last check of my weapons and gave a silent nod to Finn and Zadie. Jelly was morphed into her true simargl form at my side.

"No room for error," I whispered, holding the shield tight around every soul on this battlefield.

Shields from Rigil were at the front, creating a powerful barrier between us and Hesperia, but I knew it would not hold against Elvy's magic for very long.

Hesperia's forces came directly for us, as we'd intended for them to.

Terran and Sierra were both astride their horses. I smiled at Damek, who Sierra rode now. He was as full of majesty as he'd been the last time I'd ridden him.

This would go smoothly. It had to.

My heart shattered and healed all at the same time the moment my eyes locked onto Elvy's. His black eyes mirrored my own, and my shadows called to him, desperate to claim him. My flame screamed, needing to reignite the hearth within. I knew Elvy felt the same as his gaze lingered on me. I did my best to quiet the torment within me, but my bonds were furious.

Hesperia's wild eyes traced over the force that had come to greet her. She grinned when she saw me and purposefully trailed her hand up and down my flame.

Death. Only death would do for her.

"That's close enough," I said, not pitching my voice too high. I wove a casual air about my tone, seemingly unbothered.

"I'll decide that, little sister," Hesperia said.

I hated her. Abhorred her. My shadows wanted to bathe in her blood, and I promised them they would get the chance when the time was right. I just had to make sure we actually killed her. A simple blade would not do, unfortunately. I'd considered beheading, but I needed her soul to die. Not just her body. Her entire essence needed to be wiped from this universe with zero chance of resurrection.

"Here," I said, holding out the vial containing the star seed. "Take what you've come for and leave."

Hesperia turned her head in curiosity at the ease of this interaction.

"And the bow," she said, as if that was actually in the realm of possibility.

I removed the bow from my back and held it in the hand that did not hold the star seed for Rigil. The bow thrummed with power. I turned to look at Hesperia. I realized why the songs of fate wanted me to bring this here. A distraction and confirmation of what I suspected.

I sent my magic towards her, looking for a weakness in her mental shield. Her hold on my husband was my entry point. My shadows blended within his, and I asked the question that would prompt her future intent.

"Are you so desperate for a connection with our father? Is that why you want this?" I asked, holding it up.

A flash of my sight flooded through me as I saw her burning the bow to stardust. She had no use for the bow itself. She only feared its power when I wielded it. I slipped from Elvy's shadows without her noticing.

"I have no need for the one who created me," she said, baring her teeth towards me. "Keep your precious bow. It won't make a difference in the end."

She planned to render me useless before I could do anything with it.

"We have no need to waste innocent lives," Sierra said, voice regal. "Be gone from our realm."

Hesperia's laughter flooded through the quiet space. The birds and frogs had smartly tucked themselves away from the vile creature, creating an eerie silence.

"I thought we could have a bit of fun?" she asked, unbuttoning the top few buttons on Elvy's shirt, caressing his chest.

I saw red, but I didn't flinch.

"Last chance, Hesperia," I said, looking into the eyes of my flame. "Take the star seed and go."

I threw the vial past the ground shields, and Hesperia stepped away from Elvy to unleash her shadow magic to catch the vial before it shattered, rendering it quite useless to her.

Simultaneously, I sent my magic pulsing through the ground, alerting Blaz and Imelda that it was go time while sending them Elvy's exact location.

Just as Hesperia reached the vial with her magic, Elvy shouted as he fell through a cavern beneath him.

By the time she turned around, her death weapon had been taken from her.

"What was that? Ten seconds, Finn?" I asked, smirking at Hesperia.

"I'd say seven," he said, grinning back.

"You witch," Hesperia said, pointing a death promise at me. "You aren't going to stop what's coming, sister."

She stepped closer, nose right up against the ground shield.

"Enjoy what little time you have left."

I stepped closer to her, raising my chin up at her, despite the fact that she was several inches taller than me.

"I'll see you in hell, sister," I vowed.

She raised a brow at me curiously, but I refused to give anything away.

"So you will. I have more innocent lives to claim," she said, and my heart mourned for those in Canopus. We may have prevented the annihilation of Rigil, but with Hesperia's magic no longer consumed by holding Elvy, she now held enough power to increase her legion through unwilling victims.

Hesperia and her forces turned away, disappearing into the shadows.

Cheers erupted all around us from the Court of Rigil, but I could not meet their enthusiasm. I had to get back to Elvy. My mask was so close to faltering, and I couldn't let it fall. Not here.

Terran and Sierra trotted their horses next to us.

"We thank you for this victory," Sierra said, eyes serious. "Call on us when it is time for the final battle in Vega. We will be there."

"I know," I said, gratitude real. "Celebrate tonight. We need to get home."

I unfurled my wings, along with Zadie and Finnian. Jelly already hovered in the air, ready to fly.

"You're not alone, Zoe Eferhild," Sierra called, just as the cosmos flooded my vision, taking me home to Vega—to Elvy.

***

I landed on the rooftop of the manor with the moon and cosmos seeming to guide me home.

Zadie and Finnian flanked either side, with Jelly alongside us.

I didn't ask where my flame was. I didn't have to. Our bond led me like a moth to its death light. No force imaginable would keep me from him.

I was only half aware that Zadie and Finnian had disappeared from behind me, with Jelly following them. Perhaps it was the frenzy in my eyes or the magic pulsing all around me, but they scattered swiftly as I started sprinting to our bedroom.

My heart stilled as I threw open the door and laid eyes on him for the first time in so very long without the threat of death wavering around us.

Elvy sat on our bed, hair pulled back into a bun, and his silver-brown curls circled his face. His gray eyes lifted to meet mine.

I slumped to my knees with the full force of the power that erupted between us. Our bond. Our flames. Our shadows.

Our love that would cross realms and shatter mountains to nothing but dust. A love that would obliterate all who threatened it.

"My starlight," he said, with a half-dimpled smile.

I wasn't sure if I crawled or floated on the stars themselves, who seemed to sing a song of triumph, but I was on my knees before him, eyes heating with tears.

"Elvy," I breathed, almost scared to touch him. I didn't know where he was broken or in what way she may have tortured him.

He scooted down to the floor, and my magic flooded out, examining every atom that made up Elvy and found nothing of consequence. Physically, he was fine, but...

"Come here," he said, opening his tattooed arms, and I collapsed into them.

I didn't care that I was angry at him for blocking me out. I didn't care that we still had one last battle to face to end this war. I didn't care about anything except this very moment.

I broke. Mask gone. One I would never have to wear in front of Elvy.

He stroked my hair, taking time to undo my tight braid, massaging my scalp gingerly.

"I love you," he whispered over and over again. "I'm here. We're here."

I held out a hand, unleashing a strand of my shadows, and his answered, intertwining themselves with each other like lovers.

The air seemed to buzz around us, and I let the rest of the universe fade from my mind.

"I love you, Elvy," I said, nestling into his chest.

My heart screamed with fire, demanding it reunite with its flame.

Elvy crooked a finger under my chin, tilting my gaze to meet his.

His eyes glanced down at my full lips, and I pressed upwards, needing to close the distance. He took only one second to pause before crushing his lips against mine, and my very soul groaned in pleasure at the rightness of him—of us.

He sucked my bottom lip into his, biting gently while gripping my hair just enough to create a pressure that had me wanting more.

I shifted to straddle his hips, already finding his desire for me there.

I broke away, breathless, and took him in.

"You truly are stunning," he said, and I laughed, as I'd been thinking the same about him.

Pressing my forehead against his, I breathed in his scent, reminding myself that this was real. I was safe in this moment.

"So painfully lovely," he said, brushing a stray hair from my eyes.

I ground myself against him, but was afraid to go further. What if he were tired? What if she'd hurt him?

"I need you," he whispered against my ear. "Remind me this is real."

A shiver ran down my spine, coating my skin in goosebumps.

He unbuckled the knives from across my chest, and I gasped, forgetting that I had them on. He laughed.

"Believe me, these are even more of a turn-on," he assured me, and my cheeks turned pink.

Slowly, much too slowly, he unzipped my leathers, exposing the simargl brand seared across my heart.

His eyes heated with desire, and my core was already aching to have him inside me.

He expertly slipped my arms out of the uniform, leaving me exposed in my black bra.

The low growl in his throat had me wanting to rip the rest of our clothes off, but I'd be patient.

He took the zipper on the front of my bra and tossed it to the side before I had time to blink.

He brought my lips back down to his, flicking his tongue against mine, and I moved against him, wanting more of him—all of him.

"I'm real," I said, pulling back. "Every bit of this moment is real."

I felt his smile against me as his mouth explored my bare body. I leaned my head back, groaning with pleasure.

"Elvy," I breathed, and he began working the rest of my uniform off without breaking the rhythm of his touch. "I've missed you."

"I've needed you, starlight," he said, laying me down on the floor, uniform thoroughly removed.

"You could have let me be there with you," I growled, chest flaring with anger.

"I had to protect you," he said, trailing his lips down my stomach and ripping my black panties off with his teeth.

"Bull," I said, not wanting to be reasoned with.

"Don't pout," he said, and his gray eyes flared to black, and my shadows called out to his.

Before I could come up with a response, Elvy's mouth found my center. I gasped as he took in the evidence of just how badly I needed him.

I gripped his hair tightly, still a little pissed at him, but the unreleased tension building in my core took precedence.

Elvy's shadows played with my sensitive skin, and the sensations were all too much.

He pressed his other hand along my pelvic bone, and I held my breath as he continued to find new ways to give my body and soul all the pleasure it craved.

The bundle of nerves combusted, and I cried out in the strongest bliss of my life, and he continued stroking, guiding me through the waves of euphoria.

I opened my eyes to find him staring at me as his own arousal grew in his hand.

"Mine," I said, with a desire to lay claim to him.

"Yours," he said, lining himself up with me, and I moved, wanting all of him.

He didn't make me wait a second longer as he shifted into me, and tears brimmed my eyes at the pure joy I experienced at being fully reunited with him.

"I've missed you," he said, moving inside me.

Without breaking his rhythm, he rolled me on top of him, and I sank even further onto him as I moved with him at his pace.

I let my anger fade away, knowing he did everything to protect me, but I didn't have to agree with it to radically accept him and his love. I was certainly no saint. Neither one of us could be when we were fighting evil incarnate.

I laced my fingers with his and used his palms to press against as we continued moving with each other, letting our fears and anger melt away and be replaced with a love that conquered all.

My release was building again, and he flipped me onto my back again while still using his fingers to bring out even more sensations from my body.

I bit his shoulder, sweat drenching us both at this point, but neither of us seemed to care.

Elvy's shadows sent cool waves around us, and I broke again for him—for us.

He grabbed both of my hips as he roared his very own release with me.

He collapsed onto my chest, just above my heart.

Our limbs were intertwined, and I couldn't tell where he ended and I began.

My mate in every way.

"I never want to be parted from you again," he said, as I stroked his curls. "Not even in death."

I stilled for only a fraction of a second, but he caught it.

"What is it?"

"Death is inevitable," I countered, but my voice betrayed me. He knew I was hiding something.

"What are you not telling me, Zoe Eferhild?" he asked, shifting so that he pulled out, and I was no longer in his lap.

"I guess we couldn't use our bodies to hide from reality forever, right?" I said, eyes down, and I hated the break in my voice.

"Oh, I'm not done with you, Zoe. Not by a long shot," he promised. "But I can't stand to see you like that."

He crushed his lips to mine, and I gave in to his power.

"We're not done talking about this," he said, pulling back. "But right now, I need you. And you need me."

He hardened beneath me, showing how true his words were.

"Let's forget the rest. Just for this moment," he murmured, knowing I was not ready to release my secrets to him just yet.

I nodded, kissing him back, and I let Elvy have his way with me... until it was my turn to have my way with him. We were a mess of limbs the rest of the night, working through our fears and frustrations with each other, but through all of that was our love.

31

She's My Always

CLODOVEA

Nearly every fiber of my being wanted to fly to Rigil to protect Elvy and Zoe.

My heart was another matter.

"She'll be arriving in Vega shortly after us," Tiergan said, as the cosmos flew by us.

"I know," I said, heart sinking at the thought of anything happening to her, but Delmira needed our backup if anything went wrong in Rigil. So, I'd go where I was called.

It wasn't long before the portal to Vega moved into our line of sight, and we both dove through the transport zone.

The night air was crisp as we crossed the border with Evander and a squadron of Shadowed greeting us on arrival.

"Clodovea," he said, nodding his head in respect to my position.

"Any word?" I asked as we continued flying towards the manor.

"Last communications support that things are going as planned. It won't be long before the Lady Astral makes her move."

"Good. And Imelda is with Blaz?"

"Yes, she and Blaz are on Elvy duty."

I didn't ask anymore questions, and we flew in silence the rest of the way.

Delmira waited for us on the rooftop, arms crossed, looking pissed as ever. She may outrank me, but I was far older than her and didn't feel like taking her crap tonight.

"Don't start, Delm," I said pointedly.

"I have half a mind to rip you a new one, Clove," she answered.

"You could try, *girl*. And you would fail," I said, emphasizing just how young she was to me.

"I'll leave it to Imelda then," she said, turning to acknowledge Tiergan.

"Aura is okay?" she asked with a hint of compassion in her voice, hidden beneath the business-like tone.

"Aura is safe and where she is meant to be," Tiergan said. "She will come when called by Vega."

Delm nodded and turned on her heels to the secure meeting room, and we followed behind her. Evander and his squad resumed their posts near the transport zones.

"Where's Finn?" I asked. "Back in the archives?"

"No. He's become Zoe's lapdog."

"Finn's in Rigil?"

"Yes," she said, brows furrowed in concern.

"What's going on?" I asked, and Tiergan raised an eyebrow.

"I don't know," she admitted, and Delm hated that more than anything. "But I plan to find out."

"Finn wouldn't do anything he shouldn't."

"Lines get blurred in war, Clove."

I stood by what I said. Whatever Zoe and Finn had going on would be for the greater good. Zoe was too much of a bleeding heart to let anything bad happen on her account.

Delmira's iris glowed on her desk, and a message came through loud and clear: "Mission success. We're coming home."

That was it. No frills or further explanation.

I braced myself, sweat breaking out beneath my arms, and my gut sank like a schoolgirl with her first crush. I was desperate to see Imelda again.

"I'll be right back," I said, racing towards our bedroom in the residential wing of the manor. I placed my immortal mark against the lock, using my magic as a key.

I threw open the too-heavy door and knelt next to the bed, tossing aside the gold rug. My breath quickened as I pried open the loose floorboard and picked up the little black box I'd hidden away there for years.

My palms were much too sweaty, and I could have used a shower. I'd wasted enough time, though, and began running back up to the rooftop where Imelda would be arriving soon.

I'd just crossed the threshold to the roof when Elvy, Blaz, and Imelda landed.

Duty called me to bow to my Lord Astral, but my eyes were set on Imelda as hers were on mine.

"Thank the stars you're safe," I said, and I was only briefly aware of the low chuckle of Elvy as he patted me on the shoulder before making his way into the manor. Delmira and Blaz were caught in their own stuff, and they faded from view, leaving just Imelda and me.

And she was pissed.

"Imelda," I began, but she shushed me.

"We're a team, Clove. Always. Our jobs are dangerous, but we don't go running off into known enemy territory without at least telling the other."

"I know," I said, apologies on my lips, but she wanted none of it.

"What's that?" she asked, pointing to the black box I'd gloriously forgotten to stow away.

My cheeks turned red as I tried to think of any reason I'd be holding a black box. I'd been foolish to do this now, of all places and of all times.

"Nothing," I said, turning my head, but Imelda placed a finger under my chin to bring my eyes to hers.

"Clodovea, what is that?" she asked softly. Gone was any trace of anger. She was giving me the opportunity to be just as vulnerable. To have a sense of belonging between us. I forgot how we were both dressed for battle, skin caked in sweat and dirt. I let go of the questions I had about the timing. It was just Imelda and me. Right here. In this moment.

"I've loved you for many mortal lifetimes now. I want to love you for many more. As your wife," I said, grasping her hand, as I kneeled on the rooftop. There were a billion brilliant stars in the sky tonight, but they all paled in comparison to the beauty of my beloved. "Will you marry me, Imelda? With whatever time we've got left?"

Tears were in both our eyes, and she nodded her head while pulling me up.

"Of course I will," she said, placing a kiss on my lips and pulling me ever closer to her.

"I'm just sorry it took me so long to ask," I said, and we both laughed, and I kissed her, pulling her forehead against mine.

"Let's do this thing," she said, smiling widely.

"Right now?" I asked, and she nodded.

"Why wait? As soon as Zoe gets back with Finn and we've all rested. Let's get married."

"Let's get married," I repeated, testing the words on my lips and smiling. I kissed her cheek and laced her fingers through mine. I slipped the simple silver band with a single teardrop diamond onto her left ring finger, then kissed her palm.

"It's beautiful," she said, letting the diamond glow in the light of the cosmos above.

I led her back to our room, and smiles were plastered on both our faces.

We took our time undressing each other before stepping into the shower to scrub the grime of battle off our bodies.

"I love you," she said, washing my back.

"I love you, Imelda," I said, turning to face her so the suds rinsed off my skin.

I crushed my mouth to hers, sucking in her lower lip. She gripped my hair with her hands, pulling me flush against her curvy body. She was breathtaking, and I took pleasure in the groan that escaped her as I moved my fingers against her.

"Clove," she gasped, as I knelt before her, flicking and teasing.

I glanced up at her to find her using her own hands to her advantage, and I let out a moan, sending vibrations against her. She fisted my hair as she cried out my name, and I tasted her desire on my tongue.

I shut off the water, wrapping us both in towels as we made our way to the bedroom, and I smiled every time the gleam of her diamond caught my eye.

Imelda pushed me onto the bed, nudging my legs open with her own.

"Wife," she purred. "I sure love the sound of that," she said, before causing me to grip the sheets of the bed as she trailed her tongue all the way up my torso, then higher.

"It's about time," I said, voice breathy.

She laughed, and it was a lovely melody that I would never tire of.

Imelda and I were a tangle of limbs the rest of the night as we made love until fatigue eventually required us to rest, much under protest from us. I wrapped her naked body against me, smiling as if everything was right in the world. Maybe in the realms, it wasn't, but in my heart… everything was finally *right*.

32

Isn't it Lovely
FREYJA

It's a shame we don't remember our first breath when we come into this world.

I had the unique privilege of knowing what that felt like as an Emerging immortal.

I gasped, breathing in the air of Algol for the first time as an immortal.

My eyes fluttered open to find a pair of sea-blue eyes staring back at me. Ander. My soul soared when his face lit up with a grin that only a few ever got to see.

"Freyja?" he asked, already holding my hand in his. "I had a feeling you would wake soon. Call it fate."

I stared back at him, taking in the surroundings with my immortal eyes. He had moved me to my bedroom. The room looked much the same, but everything was brighter, as if I had been looking through hazy eyes when I was mortal. The moon and stars cast more than enough light to see comfortably with, and the glow softly lit the room through the open door that led to the balcony.

My gaze returned to him.

"Ander," I said, smiling fondly.

"You did it," he said, adjusting so that his back was flush against the pillow next to the headboard. He pulled me into his arms, soothing me.

"You know, this is the second time you've been there when I came back from the dead," I pointed out, wrapping my arms around his muscled torso.

"You weren't dead this time. I had no doubt you'd make it back," he said, voice as confident as his words.

I tried to remember the trials, but found nothing. Only a lingering sense of... not doom. I couldn't quite place the feeling. Urgency, maybe?

And... there was something I did remember.

"I came to you... while I was gone?" I asked, a little unsure.

"Yes," he said. "An astral projection. I wasn't sure you would remember," he admitted.

"I can't remember anything else, but that," I said, smiling as I held my arms up to examine them, trying to find the magic beneath the surface.

"Maybe because you weren't in the realm of Nova during that moment," he said. "I'm just glad you are here, Freyja."

"At least I'm not a sobbing mess this time," I said, and he placed a kiss in my hair, breathing in my scent.

"I'd be fine with that, sweetheart. As long as I have you," he said seriously.

My back was suddenly on fire, and I shot up from his embrace, trying to reach the area to scratch it.

"What is it?" he asked, eyes frantic.

I leaped out of bed and went into the massive bathroom, flicking on the shower in one swift motion.

"Freyja?" he asked.

"Get it off!" I screamed and pulled on the simple black cotton dress that I was wearing.

Without question, Ander ripped the thing off me, and I slipped under the cool water, trying to soothe my back.

"Talk to me," he said, standing naked in the shower with me.

"My back is burning," I said, voice breaking as I panted through the pain.

He turned my back gently, examining the area with a gentle touch. My skin prickled where he trailed his fingers, and I rolled my shoulders back, trying to dispel the pressure.

Wings burst through my back, and I screamed as they made their entrance.

I'd never given birth before, but if it was even half as painful as bringing my wings into the world, I was never having kids.

"What the hell," I panted, as the pain finally ebbed. "I don't remember Zoe saying her wings hurt this bad."

"She had been remade," he said, turning my body so that I faced him now.

His eyes were slightly silvered as he took me in, and I felt my body wanting to shy away from his piercing gaze.

"You are incredible," he said, smiling widely. "Do you want to see?"

I nodded, curiosity getting the better of me. He led me to one of the large mirrors in the vast bathroom. My walk was a little awkward as I adjusted to the weight of the massive black wings sprouting from my back. They were lighter than they looked and mirrored Oleander's in an almost identical way. He sprouted his wings, morphing into his true Shadowed form with his tattoos spreading down his arms.

Both of our wings were a translucent black that seemed to have a glow about them. My wings had a bit more of a shimmer to them than Ander's, almost as if they had starlight in them.

"Oh my stars," I said, grabbing my chest.

A map of the Kingdom of Canis spread across my chest, taking up the entire area and moving between my breasts, marking me as a true Shadowed.

Oleander gently wove his fingers through mine, flipping my wrist over, and I gasped at the sight. My immortal mark, which glowed a deep black, twinkled back at us.

"Beautiful," he said, kissing the mark, which looked just like his.

He laced a finger through my hair, pulling a silver strand out, showing it to me.

"I'm Shadowed," I said, lips forming a small smile. "I can fly?"

"You can fly," he said, pulling me in close.

"No freaking way," I said, nearly bouncing with glee. "Can we go?"

"We can do whatever you want, sweetheart," he said, placing his lips against mine, and I sank into him.

I leaped into his arms, wrapping my legs around his waist, and our kiss turned into something much more fervent and hungry.

"Maybe we can wait on that," I said, laughing softly, and I felt him grin against me.

"As you wish," he said, moving his mouth lower, sending goosebumps across my skin.

"Ander," I said, leaning my head back against the bathroom wall that he'd at some point pushed me up against. He felt different as an immortal, or maybe it was just my senses. They were much more intense, and I groaned as he continued flicking and sucking.

Only holding me with one arm, he used the other to invoke pleasure from my apex, and he found me wanting. He groaned against my neck, sending vibrations through me.

"I need you," I said, pulling on his hair and digging into his back.

"You've got me," he said, continuing to find just the right spot that made my legs tremble.

With his thumb creating the perfect pressure, my release was nearly there.

"I love you," he said, nuzzling against my neck. "I have loved you from the moment you threatened to rip my throat out in Saint Andrews."

His blue eyes met mine, and I crushed my lips to his as he swallowed the cries of my bliss with his own moans of pleasure.

"I love you, Ander," I said, breathless and as serious as I ever was.

He shifted inside me as he kissed me gently while carrying me back to bed. He laid me on the edge, holding my hips up as he continued moving inside me.

I used my fingers to create more sensation as he continued his unforgiving rhythm. His gaze fell to the movement of my fingers, and his jaw clenched as his nostrils flared.

"You were made for me," he said, as his gaze held mine.

I shut my eyes as he took me over the edge again, and this time he came with me, holding onto my hips for dear life.

As the waves of the orgasm faded, he slowly pulled out of me, leaving me feeling empty. He swooped me into his arms, carrying me into the still-running shower.

He set me down gently, then began massaging my scalp with the now hot water before lathering it with shampoo.

"You love me?" he asked, eyes sheepish, as if he was a little scared he might not have heard me right the first time. Oh, this broken male. I loved him more than I could fathom.

I clasped each side of his face, making sure he was looking at me.

"I love you with all that I was, all that I am, and all that I will be. Always believe that. And if you ever doubt it, know that you are branded on my soul."

He stopped washing my hair and crushed his lips against mine.

"I don't know what I've done for the stars to bless me with you," he said, voice exposed, raw. He truly didn't know how special he was. I would spend the rest of my existence making sure he knew he was the whole realm to me.

I wrapped him in my arms and started swaying to the music I hummed from memory.

Ander wrapped his body around me and began moving with me, twirling me around beneath the spray of the water.

Before long, we were both laughing and smiling in this moment of joy and love.

These moments that made up who we were and where we would go.

33

Nothing Good Comes Easy

ELVY

Much to my dismay, we were no longer naked.

For quite possibly the first time since becoming immortal, I was so sore, moving felt like an impossibility. It was in all the best kinds of ways, but my body could use a rest, though my shadows and flame craved to be with her even still. They didn't seem satiated despite the amount of times Zoe and I had intertwined ourselves with each other over and over again.

She and Jelly were curled up at my side on the bed, and I couldn't stop myself from giving Jelly a good hour of much-earned pets for keeping our girl safe while I'd been away.

"We can't delay this conversation forever, Zo," I said, placing a kiss in her hair.

Her perfect cupid's bow lips pressed into a thin line as she shifted through the words she wanted to say. I was a patient male. The stars knew that by now. The scent of Hesperia had completely disappeared from me, replaced entirely by Zoe and the familiar comforts of Vega.

My eyes flashed to black briefly as I wished nothing more than to obliterate Hesperia to stardust, but something told me it was not my death to claim. It was the one who held my heart that would be her end, and I'd play whatever role was needed to see my flame through this.

Zoe entered the space of my mind that was always open to her… now when there was no chance of Hesperia getting to her through me. I winced at the pain I had caused her, despite my good intentions.

"Finn found something in the Hall of Memories. Something that he wouldn't have been able to find unless the celestials wanted him, too. Well, at least one of the celestials wanted us to find it. I can't imagine that Algol would have wanted us to discover this information, given their track record."

I'd been surprised to see Finn by her side when they'd rescued me, but I'd guessed it'd logistically made sense with Blaz and Imelda waiting to snatch me from below the ground. They'd crafted a genius plan, really. Hesperia would have only lapsed in her control for one thing only—that star seed. And they'd taken beautiful advantage of that.

"And?" I asked through our bond, voice level, letting her tell me in her own time and way.

"I hope it's meant to be a last resort," she admitted. *"But if the stars are showing us, then maybe they don't think there is any other way."*

My heartbeat kicked up a notch at her words. They were interlaced with fear, despite the confidence she was trying to present. I stroked my thumb in circles around the hand that I held, trying to offer whatever comfort I could.

"What did he find?"

"A way to create a new celestial… we think."

My muscles stilled for a fraction of a second as I let her words sink in. I continued trailing my fingers up and down her back, trying not to let my sudden, very real fear overcome me. I had so many questions about why this was relevant, but bombarding her with those wouldn't be fair.

"And what would that entail?"

She swallowed.

"We need to find Sirius. Talk to him."

"You want to talk to the creator of the celestials?" I asked in disbelief, though I don't know why anything Zoe did surprised me anymore. She'd threaten the life of a celestial. Why not talk to their creator, too?

"We need to find Sirius soon. To make the right provisions."

My chest sank.

"And why do we need to make a new celestial?"

"Maybe we don't need to," she said, pausing. *"But just in case."*

I tilted her chin to look into my eyes.

"There's something you're not telling me, flame."

"There is," she agreed. *"Promise you won't kill Finn… or Zadie."*

My lips pressed into a thin line as I clenched my jaw.

"What's going on, Zo?" I asked aloud, too on edge to use the bond.

"There's a surefire way to make sure Hesperia fails."

"We still don't know what she is after. Not really."

She held my gaze for a long time.

"I do," she said, voice breaking slightly. "Chaos. Death to the star realms. She has no interest in ruling the star realms or creating a new world in her name. She simply wants to end them. Killing everyone—and our father along with it, which would kill the celestials, too. Their powers are interchangeable within their realms… One goes, and they all do."

It was worse than anything we'd truly feared from her. She was actually crazy.

"We have to kill her," I said, though I wasn't sure how we'd do that, which pissed me off to no end.

"That's the ultimate plan, though I'm not sure how to do that yet."

"And what is this fail-safe of yours?" I nearly hissed out the last word.

"Kill Algol," she said, as if it were that simple.

"What do you mean, Zo?"

"Kill me, and Algol will die, rendering her plan quite useless. She can't complete the ritual unless she is tied to all five *ruling* celestials." She emphasized the word 'ruling.'

My body began to tremble at the thought of Zoe no longer being part of this world. It was an inconceivable thought. I absolutely would not stand for it in any way.

"Just hear me out," she said, voice desperate.

"No," I said quietly, and pulled her even closer to me. Jelly seemed to sense the tension in both of us and nuzzled closer, too.

"You must," she said, as if it were so easy. "You did not hesitate to take my place when Hesperia could have killed me then and there. You must hear what my life is truly worth to this realm."

"I don't care what it's worth to the realms. I care about you. Just you."

"Then listen to me now," she said, kissing my bare chest. "Just hear me out."

Despite my better judgement, I nodded, not trusting my words to let her speak her truth.

"The ritual calls for the five *ruling* celestials. Obviously, if Algol were killed now, that would kill every immortal of Algol, including Freyja. I would never agree to that."

I nodded for her to continue.

"If we create a new celestial and tied their essence to spirit instead… the only thing Algol will be tethered to is me. No one else would have to die."

"You're asking me to be okay with your death," I said, voice breaking. I struggled to keep my shadows at bay, sensing their bond was in some sort of danger. To me, it felt like she was.

"I'm asking you to be okay with saving the lives of those we are sworn to protect, Elvy. But this will only work if we've created a new celestial first, which I'm not entirely confident that we can do. I've already made the arrangements if it comes to that. I wouldn't ask you to be the one to…," she trailed off.

"To kill you?" I asked.

She nodded.

"Then who, pray tell, have you gotten to agree to end your existence?"

"Finn," she said, and my eyes flared with a rage I didn't think I was capable of. "You said you wouldn't be mad at him."

"I don't think I agreed to any such thing," I countered, standing up from the bed, pacing in front of the serene fireplace. I wish I felt the way it looked.

"He's made a blood oath, Elvy. He's dead if he doesn't fulfill it," she said.

"He's dead either way," I spat.

She folded into herself, shaking. Tears brimmed in her eyes, and my rage diffused just enough to let me hold her again.

"This isn't a choice I want to make," she said, leaning into me, and I couldn't help but try to soothe her. "If there were any other solution, I would take it. I don't want to die."

There was truth in her words. She didn't want this.

"What does your *sight* say?" I asked.

"It doesn't say much. Nothing concrete anyway. I hate this."

Her body rocked against me as she released this truth from her. Something she had been holding in all on her own for too long.

"And what about your fate to heal the realms, Zo? To bind the five elements back together?"

"I'd make sure it was done before I died. The realms would be safe from her after my death long enough for you all to find a way to end her once and for all."

"I can't say I am for this plan, Zo. I just can't."

"What if we don't have another solution to end her?"

"I'm going to find one," I vowed. I didn't care what it took. Hesperia bled so she could die. Granted, her blood was as black as the night sky, and we'd dealt her death blows to no avail in the past, but… she would be at her weakest when she came to Vega for the final star seed. That would be her time to perish. Somehow. Some way.

"And if you can't?"

"Then Finn will not need to fulfill his blood oath. I will be with you. Until the very end, Zoe Eferhild."

She pulled back to look into my eyes.

"No," she said, seeing through the intention of my words.

"There's no me without you, starlight," I said seriously.

"But our immortals need you," she argued.

"They have Delmira until the next Astral bloodline rises," he said.

Tears brimmed in both our eyes.

"War sucks," she said, laughing half-heartedly.

"Yeah, it does," I agreed, pulling her closer to me. "Just promise me one thing?"

She nodded.

"We try to find a way to kill her without either of us dying, okay?" I asked.

"Deal," she said, but I could see little hope remained in her for that, so I would be her hope—her starlight.

She started to speak again, but stopped herself.

I wove my fingers through hers, sending her my love and encouragement through our flame. "What is it, Zoe?"

"The Archer visited me in my dreams while you were away… he says he told me long ago how to end Hesperia," she murmured. "I've gone over our conversations a thousand times, but I can't think of anything that had anything to do with killing Hesperia. What if I'm leading us down the wrong path? What if I get someone hurt and Finn's fears come true? The Archer said this would only lead to grief, but I *see* no other option. He seemed so cryptic about death."

I absorbed her words before answering. It didn't bring me comfort to know of The Archer's warning, but I also knew we were all desperate to find an end to Hesperia by any means necessary. "If this path doesn't work out, then we will find the right one, Zoe. Did he tell you anything else?"

"Look to the beginning," she said, pressing her lips together.

I kissed her palm, then pressed it against my face. "Alright. We go to Sirius and explore that path. And we will look at the beginning."

"I just wish I knew the beginning of what," she said, green eyes gazing into mine.

"We will find it, Zo," I said, leaning into her more. "I believe in us."

"I think we should tell the others," I said, and her eyes met mine. "I know it's terrifying, and we'd rather be able to give them clear answers than potential empty hopes, but they are our family. They will help us."

Zoe looked away for a moment in consideration, then nodded. "Let's find a time to tell them."

The iris on her bedside table glowed in the hues of the rainbow, and she snatched it up, letting the message come through.

She nearly leaped out of bed as Freyja's voice came across realms, and full-on sobs rocked through her. There was a smile beneath all the tears as well.

"Freyja really did it," she said, wiping away the moisture from her eyes and coughing away the lingering emotions from her throat.

"See… good things can happen for us," I said, brushing a strand of hair out of her eyes.

I'd never been more thankful for some good news to instill us both with hope for the possibility of a good outcome when it felt like anything but that was possible.

"Can we invite them here? I don't think we should leave Vega right now," she said.

"You don't have to ever ask that, Zo," I said.

She nodded enthusiastically and sent her own message back to Freyja through the iris, inviting them to join us in Vega. The smile on her face solidified my vow. I would find a way to end Hesperia. There had to be a way. We had to be overlooking something, and I would find it.

Zoe's eyes met mine as she talked to her sister through the iris, and I took in this moment, committing it to memory. Her joy meant everything to me. She had given too much. We all had, and we all deserved to know peace. So, I would find it. I would find a way to bring her peace, the way she had brought it to me when I hadn't known at the time how broken I was.

My starlight.

34

Believe in Me
FREYJA

The cosmos flooded past us as Ander held me in his arms.

There had been exactly zero time to work on my flying, so he still had to carry me if we were traveling a great distance—especially to another realm.

We'd sent word to Zoe through the iris that I was back, and her scream of excitement on the other end had been nothing less than I expected. Within twenty-four hours, I was on my way to her.

It was too dangerous for any of them to leave Vega right now, so we came to them. Zadie had come back to Algol before we'd departed. She'd actually greeted me with a warm welcome, and the hug between us had felt less awkward than it had in some time.

Ander flew us close enough along the ocean of Vega that water sprayed softly against my face, making me laugh. Some kind of finned creature followed alongside us, but looked much too green and different to be dolphins. If I didn't know any better, I would have sworn I'd seen a horse swimming in the ocean.

Before I could examine them further, Oleander was gliding us to a large manor that seemed to be a beacon for the much empty city below, though the twinkle of city lights would fool anyone who was trying to pry, which I supposed was the point of it.

Oleander landed on the rooftop of the moonstone building where Tiergan, Elvy, Zoe, and the entirety of their Luminaries waited.

A welcoming party for me?

The moment my toes touched down, Zoe raced towards me, swinging me around with nothing but laughter and smiles emitting from her.

"I knew you'd do it," she said, pulling back so she could get a good look at me.

Her eyes flicked to my neckline, exposing the map of the Kingdom of Canis, and she twirled a strand of silver in her fingers.

"Shadowed," she breathed, smile growing impossibly wider.

"Yes," I said, closing my eyes to shift my wings into existence.

"Have you flown yet?" she asked excitedly, and I shook my head.

"No, not yet. I did just get back," I laughed softly.

"Right," she said, and Jelly nudged my thigh to draw my attention toward her. She shifted her wings, as if to say that we now matched.

"That's right, good girl," I said, giving her the obligatory head scratches.

Elvy came to me next, pulling me into a hug.

"We're glad to have you back," he said, voice serious.

"Thanks, Elvy," I said as he let me go.

Oleander moved to stand closer to me, and the rest of the Luminaries embraced me, with Tiergan greeting me last.

I didn't miss the tension underneath this happy moment. Zoe's face faltered the moment she thought I wasn't looking, and a twinge of pain radiated from my chest. I brushed my hair away to get a better look, and it felt like the pain was coming from where Algol was permanently marked near my collarbone.

"What is it?" Ander asked, noticing my movements.

"Something's wrong," I said, confusion running through me.

"Other than the looming war?" he asked, brows furrowed.

"I can't place it," I admitted. "Something just feels off."

The more I looked at Zoe, the more intense it became. I'd never been branded before, but this was what I imagined it to feel like.

"Hell, that hurts," I said, and my gaze flicked to Ander's blue eyes. The pain ebbed and went away. I looked back at Zoe, and the pain flared again.

"What's going on?" Zoe asked, a look of concern in her eyes.

I was a mess of confusion. This was my sister who would die protecting me. What the hell did Algol want?

"I'm not sure," I said honestly, but not wanting to give too much away until I knew what I was dealing with.

"Do you have a second gift?" she asked. "Like mine? Discernment? I used to get bad pains, too."

"Another?" Blaz asked, smiling as though he was greatly impressed.

I shook my head. "I already know what my gift is, and as far as I know, it is the only one I have."

The pain eased enough to a dull ache, and I kept Zoe out of my direct line of sight.

"What is it?" Delmira asked, stepping only slightly between Zoe and me. What was going on with them?

I looked at Oleander, and he nodded encouragingly.

"I can astral project," I said, smiling mischievously.

"No way," Blaz said. "That's sick."

Delmira nodded her head in approval, too, and relaxed her posture. Finn turned his head in curiosity, as if I were a test subject he found incredibly interesting. I wasn't sure whether to be flattered or disturbed.

Clodovea held Imelda's hand, and they both had smiles for each other, though they both nodded politely at my revelation. Their mind seemed to be somewhere else right now, and I wish I could escape with them. Tiergan stood discreetly behind Clove, seemingly lost in his own thoughts tonight, too.

"You know, we should celebrate," Zoe said, voice a little thicker than normal, as if she was straining not to cry.

"What did you have in mind?" Elvy asked, pulling her close.

"It's only fitting that my last mortal night was at a ball. I think it is only right to close the circle with one for Freyja's Emergence."

My sister had always hated things like that, but she knew I loved them. And the last ball I'd attended, no one had been able to see me. No one but Ander and Zoe. Tears brimmed in my eyes, and I leaned in to Ander.

"I think it's a brilliant idea," Ander said, and Elvy nodded his agreement.

"Hesperia could come at any moment," Delmira argued. "Is prancing around at a ball really the best idea?"

"I think it's exactly the right thing," Zoe said. "Hesperia wants us to live in fear, and we aren't going to give her that."

"Actually," Clodovea said, stepping forward with Imelda. "We have something to announce ourselves."

Zoe turned her head curiously, and she smiled before they spoke again. Her *sight* gave her the answer before they had time to speak.

Imelda raised her left hand to show the ring shining on her finger.

"Clodovea finally popped the question," Blaz said, grinning widely and pulling both ladies into a bear hug.

"Congratulations," Elvy said, kissing both on either cheek, followed by Zoe embracing them.

Delmira pursed her lips, but didn't protest the union. Finn hugged Imelda and Clodovea, seeming happy for the couple.

"We planned on inviting you all to a small ceremony. If you're going to the trouble of having a ball, we could do it just before?" Imelda asked. "If that's okay with you, Freyja?"

"Of course it is," I said, hugging them both. "We need more happiness in times like these. Isn't that right, Ander?"

"I completely agree," he said, squeezing my hand.

"It's settled then," Zoe said. "I'm glad we have two good things to celebrate. Despite it all."

There was something in Zoe's voice that seemed off, but I couldn't look at her too long without needing to avert my gaze from the throbbing pain coming from the star of Algol. It almost felt like a goodbye and an act of defiance all at the same time. I would corner my sister very soon to get my answers.

Elvy's clenched jaw said as much. Something was going on, and not everyone was privy to the information, but I couldn't tell who knew and who didn't.

If I knew my sister at all, she was planning on something that would be some sacrificial crap, and I wasn't accepting anymore of that in this lifetime.

"It's been a long day," Zoe said, giving me a powerful hug. "I'll show you and Oleander to your room."

There was a tightness in her eyes that hadn't been there when we'd arrived. Something was weighing on her soul.

"Alright. Lead the way," I said, looping my arm through hers.

I didn't ask questions. Not yet, when Ander was looming over us. Whatever was going on with Zoe, I had to get her alone to even have a chance of getting her to spill.

Zoe gave us both a goodbye before shutting the door behind her.

"What are you planning?" Ander asked, cornering me the moment the door clicked.

"Paranoid much?" I asked, rolling my eyes, and he raised a brow in response.

"No, sweetheart," he said, kissing my neck. "I just know you. Now, what's going on in that beautiful brain of yours?"

"I think Algol wants me to stop Zoe," I admitted. "The pain is coming from their star on my chest. Zoe's up to something."

"She always is," he said, sighing and pulling me onto his lap as he sat in a comfortable chair lined with gold velvet by the bed. "And you want to stop her?"

"I don't know that she needs to be stopped," I disagreed. "I just don't want her to carry whatever this is alone."

"She won't, Freyja. None of us will let that happen. Whatever Algol tasked you with, we'll figure it out."

I laid my head on his chest and knew he spoke the truth.

35
Vacillating
DELMIRA

I had never been one for pillow talk.

But here I was, yapping away about my problems to my *boyfriend*. I'd let the term slip before Blaz had left for Rigil, and he hadn't let me forget it.

"What's going on, Delm?" he asked, as his gigantic warm hand thumbed soothing strokes on my bare side. "I thought you'd be more relaxed after…"

"You screwed me sideways?"

"And all the other ways," he said, laughing heartily, and if we weren't careful, we'd be right back at each other in one fell swoop.

"I think my brother has gotten himself into something he can't get out of."

"Oh?" Blaz asked, brown eyes serious.

"Yeah," I answered, telling him everything I'd seen with Octavia.

"You don't really know what you saw, though," he countered. "And Octavia has no right to spy on our lady."

"Technically, I had been spying, too."

"That's different. You're sworn to serve and protect Zoe. Octavia is not."

"One could argue Octavia is bound by something even greater than that."

"This could all be solved if you'd just ask her, Delm," he said, sounding perfectly reasonable, which just made me irrationally angry.

I took a deep, steadying breath, trying not to let my short fuse get the better of me.

"I just don't see why she'd keep something like this from us."

"Maybe she's trying to protect us. Maybe it'll affect the outcome if we know before we should."

"We have a right to know," I countered.

"Not if it doesn't concern us," he said, pulling me flush with his body, and I tried to pay attention to every space our bodies connected. The logical part of my brain knew this, but the emotional part of my brain didn't care to listen to reason very often.

"Just talk to her before you do something you can't take back," he said, kissing my neck and sending shivers throughout my body.

"I hate it when you're right," I said, core aching with need.

"You love it," he said, moving lower and lower.

"Fine, I'll talk to her," I said, gasping on the last word as Blaz nipped at my inner thigh.

"Good girl," he said, and I felt the smile on his lips.

★★★

No amount of good sex and restful sleep would curb my appetite to confront Zoe, apparently.

Tonight was the night Zoe would meet her reckoning through me.

Whatever she was planning, she wasn't going to do it alone. I've believed in her crazy self throughout all of this. I'd trusted in her despite everything.

"Why right now, Delm?" Blaz asked, noting the promise in my eyes. "Tonight is for celebrating."

"She crossed a line when she involved Finn. She will answer me tonight."

"Finn got himself involved," he countered. "He's a grown male capable of deciding for himself."

"At her direction. At her order."

"You still don't know what it is, though, Delm. Can you at least try to enjoy tonight?"

I stopped dead in our tracks and faced him. His voice was soft, trying to quell the rage lurking within me.

"For me?" he pleaded, puppy-dog eyes gleaming at me.

"Okay," I agreed. "I will do my very best to enjoy tonight."

"We deserve a little happiness. All of us."

"I can agree with that," I said, letting him wrap me in his strong arms.

"We need to get ready," he said, and I glanced at the time to find that he was more than right.

I pulled open the black wardrobe adorned with lavender knobs and took out the lilac dress I'd had made a long time ago, but had never worn. I'd always felt the need to be dressed for battle, even at something as harmless as a ball. Getting caught off guard was not something I ever planned on experiencing.

But tonight… tonight I'd wear this dress. If nothing more than to spite Hesperia.

Blaz's eyes darkened as he took in the tight-fitting gown with a plunging neckline almost to my navel. The back was open, exposing the muscles there that I had honed to kill my enemies. The slit was daring, coming up all the way to my hip. One wrong move and onlookers would get more than they bargained for of their second, not that there would be any patrons of our city.

We'd opted to have the ball in the manor instead of Musterion in an effort to keep any wandering eyes away from the secret city. So, the only immortals in attendance would be the Luminaries, Tiergan, Oleander, Freyja, and a few select members of the Shadowed Legion. We wish we could offer them all a night off, but that wasn't our reality right now. When this was all over, we'd have a party big enough to host all of Vega and then some.

"We don't need to go, actually," Blaz said, placing both of his hands on either side of my hips as he gazed into the mirror that was in front of us. He looked handsome in his black suit, cut to fit him perfectly.

I kept my eyes on him as I strapped a blade to my thigh, and his eyes darkened further.

"And miss out on all the fun? I wouldn't dream of it," I said, cupping his cheek and placing a sultry kiss on his lips, brushing my body against him.

He let out a low growl, pulling me closer to him.

"I can't wait to undress you later," he whispered into my ear, sending shivers down my spine.

"Maybe I'll make you watch me instead," I said, winking.

"I don't care how it comes off, as long as it does," he said, jaw clenching.

I laced his hands in mine and led him towards the beach for Imelda and Clodovea's wedding.

The private beach in front of the manor had been transformed into a beautiful space for them. There was a small aisle adorned with bioluminescent plants that glowed in shades of green and blue. Strands of twinkle lights lined a wooden arch at the end of the aisle. It was simple and sweet. Something perfect for them.

Clodovea stood beneath the arch, wearing a silver A-line dress that hugged her in all the right places. Her braids were woven together to create a beautiful pattern down the length of her back, and she smiled when I caught her eye.

"You're really doing it," I said, giving her a fierce hug, genuinely happy for my friend, despite everything else that was going on around us.

"I'm only sorry I waited this long," she said, kissing me and then Blaz on the cheek. Her expression was softer than the usual warrior she always showed.

"I'm happy for you two," I said seriously, voice breaking only slightly. My eyes actually warmed with tears threatening to come out, and I sucked them right back up.

Clove gave me a knowing glance, but didn't comment. Blaz pulled me into our seat next to Finnian and Zoe.

"Your thoughts are everywhere tonight, sister," Finn murmured, and his brows furrowed as he tried to get a read on me.

I threw up a wall that I usually always had open for my twin, not wanting to reveal what I knew right now. No need for family drama on Imelda and Clodovea's wedding night. Well, at least not at the ceremony. The night was young, though.

Zoe gave me a small smile, but her eyes were in the stars tonight, as if she were searching for some answer there. Maybe in her father, or maybe she wished on the stars themselves. She glanced down at Jelly, scratching her ears, and I had an inkling they spoke to one another. I softened slightly towards her, knowing in my gut that she was struggling with what was coming. Whatever she was grappling with, it was weighing on her.

Oleander and Freyja were across the aisle, lost in each other, and the cynical part of me wanted to vomit, but she wasn't as loud tonight. Letting Blaz into my life had made me tender… and I wasn't entirely sure that was a bad thing. Not when it came to love, at least.

Tiergan sat behind them, but Clodovea motioned for the mustached man to join her at the arch. She whispered something in his ear, and he nodded, eyes gleaming silver as he moved to stand behind her.

"Who would have thought? The rebel leader being Clove's best man," Blaz whispered, laughing softly. "It makes you wonder what happened in Canopus."

"Clove hasn't shared that?"

"Not beyond what was mission-essential."

"Where is Elvy?" I asked no one in particular.

"With Imelda," Zoe answered, beckoning us to sit in her row. "She asked him to walk her down the aisle."

Soft music began playing as Elvy and Imelda made their way down the aisle from the manor. Imelda wore a mermaid-style dress with lace fitted over the bodice. Her hair was full and natural, with a flower pulling part of her hair back. Her best accessory was her smile, though, and her eyes were only for Clodovea.

We all rose as one as Elvy escorted Imelda down the glowing path of flowers. Heat threatened my eyes again, and this time… I let them fill. I embraced the happy tears that flowed down my face. Blaz wiped one of them away and squeezed my hand gently, placing a kiss on my cheek.

Maybe it was a hope that I would be capable of such love when I never thought that was something possible for me. Maybe it was because this moment was a good one out of the many bad ones lately. In all honesty, it didn't really matter why. It just was.

Imelda gave Elvy a kiss on the cheek as he handed her off to Clodovea and sat down beside his very own flame.

There was no priest or preacher like on Earth. It was just about them and declaring their vows underneath the stars and the heavens.

Their vows were filled with raw emotion and love. Not even the crash of waves could drown them out. In fact, the world seemed to pause for just a moment. The way it should have been at the joining of Elvy and Zoe. Before Hesperia blew it all to hell.

I glanced at Zoe, and there was no hint of resentment or that her thoughts had turned to a similar place. She just seemed happy for her friends, so I decided not to let Hesperia ruin this union, too.

We all shouted as they kissed each other, with Clodovea swooping Imelda into her arms. Zoe sent bursts of magic, and we followed suit to send the new couple out with a literal bang.

"Let's give them their moment," Tiergan said, face tear stroked as he blew into his handkerchief, sending his mustache blowing in the wind. "Please head into the ballroom in the manor."

If I had been told six months ago that the known rebel leader of the Sublunary would be attending this, I would have laughed.

Blaz held my hand as we followed behind Zoe and Freyja with their lovers attached to either side of them.

Jelly and Finnian trailed behind us, and I perked an eye at Jelly. She and Finn had never really bonded, and she seemed to raise an eyebrow at me, as if to remind me the same could be said about me.

Well, alrighty then.

The room was already buzzing with immortals who had not been present at the ceremony, and my stomach was filled with butterflies as I remembered this was the room Blaz and I had decided to do this thing for real. He kissed my cheek softly, as if I were something to be cherished.

"I remember it, too," he said, seeming to read my thoughts.

I squeezed his hand, eyes catching on Octavia, who wore a full brown dress, as if she was trying to make herself hide. She gave me a nod, as if we were conspirators together, so I glowered at her. I'd never betray Elvy or Zoe, and I still wasn't comfortable with the role she played against them. I shook the thought from my mind. All in due time. How much time remained to be seen.

Finn wore a tailored black suit, even though most of the males wore their Vega dress blues. He stood next to Zoe, who donned a beautiful emerald green dress with golden lace and beads on top of the silk. She truly was beautiful, but her eyes… they didn't quite meet her smile as she talked to Finn, as if something weighed heavily within her. Elvy rubbed soothing strokes down her back, and it was apparent that Zoe had a silencing shield around them.

I couldn't hear a thing, and Jelly stood at Zoe's back, having a complete stare-down with me.

Challenge accepted.

I pulled Blaz with me as I made a beeline for my Lady Astral. Blaz humphed beside me, but didn't protest.

"What are we talking about?" I asked, just as Oleander and Freyja joined the conversation.

"Nothing that needs to be discussed now," Zoe said, lips in a tight line.

"I'm afraid I'm going to have to insist, Lady Astral," I said, eyes hardening. I wanted to scream at her to trust me. Trust us. We had been through hell and back with her. Whatever she was doing, we would have her back.

"I've never been one to pull rank, Delmira," Elvy said, standing slightly in front of Zoe, which irritated me even further. I was not a danger to either of them, and they bloody well knew that. "But that is not your call."

Zoe pulled his arm back.

"What's going on, Zoe?" Freyja asked, wincing as if she were in pain. Oleander moved in even closer, and Jelly growled a low warning at all of us.

I seemed to be the only one who noticed Octavia creeping closer, but Zoe had extended the silencing shield around our party. She wouldn't be able to hear.

"Whatever we are assuming can't be worse than what is actually going on," I said, and Zoe's eyes glazed black for a moment.

She took a step back, and her expression seemed... *hurt*. Blaz moved by my side, seeming as conflicted as ever. He was Zoe and Elvy's general, but he was my... well, mine.

"You followed me," she said, her gift giving her discernment.

"Of course I did," I said, not ashamed of that fact. Not if it kept her and my twin safe.

Zoe's head whirled around to meet Octavia's eyes, and the betrayal there was tenfold to the look she'd given me. Octavia moved forward, bowing.

"It seems we have much to discuss," Zoe said. "And more than one of us has a truth to tell."

"It seems so, my lady," Octavia said, raising her chin, not shying away from the duty she felt to the Keepers.

Just then, the Shadowed Legion around us burst into applause, and Tiergan announced Clodovea and Imelda's arrival.

The tension broke between us all.

"Tomorrow," Zoe said stiffly. "We will give Clodovea and Imelda this night. As well as celebrate my sister's Emerging. Can we all agree on that?"

We nodded as if we had any other choice, and I internally kicked myself for bringing all of this up in the middle of what was supposed to be a night of merriment. I'd chosen not to be on a warpath tonight, and then in one fleeting moment, I'd gotten right back on it.

"Come on, Delm," Blaz said, pulling me into a dance without giving me a chance to protest.

"I'm an idiot," I said seriously.

"You're just… passionate," he said, smiling. "It's going to be okay. Whatever it is. We're a family. Families get a little dysfunctional at times."

I nodded, leaning my head against his chest. I wasn't paying attention to the music, but on the strength of him.

But we all kept our promise. We laughed. We loved. We embraced. At least for this moment.

36

Serum

ZOE

I sat in my bedroom, listening to the fire crackle as the flame turned from blue to green, then purple. It was like my private aurora borealis.

The bow felt heavy in my hand for the first time, as I sought answers I knew wouldn't come to me tonight. The metal of the arrows was cold against my skin, but they also held infinite power there.

I pulled from my essence, practicing stringing my light to the arrow as The Archer had taught me. It had become easier now, but I still had no idea how to end Hesperia, which seemed like the larger priority. The glowing gold orb hovered above me, and I gently coaxed a string of my essence forth. It stayed between my thumb and forefinger until I banished my spirit back inside me for now.

I knew I would get no more answers from The Archer, and I didn't know whether to love or hate him. The discernment within me knew I would not see him again until those final, critical moments. I had empathy for him, no doubt. The decision to kill my eldest sister lay before me as the choice had laid before him.

Only I would be the one to kill her. He would not.

Though stabbing her in the chest didn't seem to do much to her. So, maybe it was all a dream that I wished on the very stars who created this fate for me.

I thought back to his warning about this path being futile, but I had to try with no other leads. What had he meant by looking to the beginning? When I'd first encountered the prophecy while I'd still been mortal, he had led me towards learning the birthright I had as The Archer's daughter. Was this about my blood and Hesperia's? Did it have to do with my literal conception? That I was born, not created? Was he referencing when my path to the Emerging began when Elvy had come for me? There were so many possibilities, and I wanted to understand why he couldn't just tell me. Would that change the outcome of fate? Everything changed when Elvy had come to Saint Andrews. Maybe I'd start there.

I sighed, running a hand through my messy hair.

Strong hands massaged the back of my neck, and I startled, not realizing how tense I'd become sitting here in our bedroom. It had nothing to do with feeling unsafe, as it would have a year ago.

"Penny for your thoughts, flame?"

"It would take all the riches of Vega to sort them out, I'm afraid," I murmured, leaning into him.

Jelly laid her head on my lap, trying to give me any bit of comfort that only she could. My soul dog.

"We have to go to Sirius," I said, finally admitting that truth. Not only to myself, but to the universe.

"Yes," he agreed.

"King Aldrich and Queen Farron may not be happy about why we are there."

"That's true, too," he said, continuing to knead the rock-hard muscles of my neck. "Then again, they seemed to be on our side the last time we were there."

"Then they closed their borders to the High Astral Court and haven't returned a single missive."

"No, they haven't, but I understand their reasoning for closing off their borders in protection of the last defense to the mortal realms."

"I know," I admitted. "That doesn't make me resent it any less. Especially when we have no guarantee that will make a difference at all."

Elvy slipped over the couch so that I was sitting between his legs now.

"I think we are doing the right thing in telling the others what's going on. This isn't something we can do alone."

"But I'm the one who has to bear the fate of the choice," I said, sighing.

"And depending on which way fate swings for us, your choice will have an impact on more than just you. They have a right to know."

I didn't reply. He wasn't wrong, and I knew in my heart that I would do what I must to save my sister and the entire Court of Algol. They could spend the rest of their lives choosing to hate me if it brought them peace—if it meant they were alive to hate me.

Elvy laced his fingers through mine in both hands and gently kissed my neck.

"I still have faith we will find another way," he murmured, and I smiled at his resilience to be hopeful when all seemed lost.

"I love you," I whispered, letting myself feel my body pressed against his. I leaned my ear against his solid chest, listening to the beat of his heart. My gravity. My center that held eternally.

"I am your lover always," he replied.

The clock struck twelve, signaling that it was time to meet with the others. Even Octavia had been invited to this meeting. No more speculation or tiptoeing around what was to come. They would all have to live with the consequences of this knowledge, as I have.

"Let's go," I said, rising—like a phoenix from the ashes. Just one more time.

***

We sat in the familiar meeting room on top of the manor.

It felt as if a weight was pounding on my chest, trying to forge me into… well, I wasn't sure yet. A weapon, a leader, but maybe just a friend.

Elvy sat at my side, equal parties at the head of the table. Delmira sat to Elvy's right, and Clodovea sat to my left. Imelda sat next to her and, despite the severity of this meeting, their eyes still radiated with love. Finnian took his place by Delmira, and Blaz sat on the other side of him. Freyja and Oleander were at the other end of the table, and her eyes bore into mine.

I shifted my eyes quickly, passing over Tiergan, who sat by Imelda and Octavia, who sat by Blaz. Jelly lay peacefully at my feet, but her ears twitched, showing that she was very much listening. This was it. The immortals that I would unburden myself.

I glanced up towards the cosmos and found The Archer's constellation brighter than all the rest. Perhaps my father was here, waiting with bated breath. I felt the strings of destiny waiting to pluck their chord. They hesitated, unsure of which direction I would go. Hell, I still wasn't certain about anything.

"There is no part of me that wishes to cause you all pain," I started, taking in a deep breath. "But that is war. And the battle that decides the fate of this war is coming. And we are not ready."

I paused, looking each of them in the eye.

"We still have no weapon to kill Hesperia. With the star seeds consuming her, she is at her weakest physically, but her mortality remains the same. Mere weapons will not end her existence permanently."

I pressed my lips together. This was something they already knew.

"But she has found a way. We were wrong about her motives—about what she truly wants. The immortals I healed from her shadow magic learned of her endgame, and it won't leave anyone alive. Not one soul. Even Musterion will be lost. She has decided to become the thing my father feared—death."

No one breathed as they waited for me to explain, and the inner voice screamed at me to keep this from them. I could let them continue to have hope—to believe there was a future possible, but that would be a lie.

"What is she going to do, Zo?" Blaz asked, eyes calm, as if he was ready for the blow.

I looked at each of them. They all were braced for impact, sensing the severity of my words.

"You said it best, Tiergan. Hesperia is chaos. She is the definition of illogical," I said, taking a sip of water to calm my nerves. "The spell she is using to make herself a vessel for all five elemental realms is preparing to make herself into a celestial bomb. How do you kill a celestial? She found a way, and she plans to use it. The star courts will cease to exist, and the mortal realm along with it."

Everyone looked at each other, and then back to me, as if I might have said it wrong. I hadn't. Elvy gripped my thigh under the table in a show of solidarity.

"Why?" Freyja asked, blue eyes shining with tears and a fear I couldn't quell.

"This can't be just to get back at your father," Tiergan said, but his voice sounded unsure. We all knew what she was capable of.

"She was willing to sever the tethers of Algol just to prove a point. Just to get their attention, despite knowing what it would ultimately do to her and every immortal soul on Algol and Earth. Do you really think she is unwilling to die for what she believes to be just?"

We all stared back in silence, embracing the truth of my words. Hesperia was willing to go through with this. There would be no stopping her.

"So, all that stands between her and death to the star realms is us," Delmira said, voice a little softer than normal.

"Yes, we're it," I said.

Oleander spoke for the first time. "What's the strategy, Zoe?"

"While I believe in our Shadowed Legion, I do not want to leave the fate of the realms solely to our ability to defeat her in battle. She'll just keep coming back until she is obliterated to stardust herself. We can't keep constant guard over our star. That's no way to live, and it is unsustainable."

"But we don't know how to kill her… yet," Finnian said, pressing his lips together.

"We don't," I agreed. "But that is the ultimate goal. To end her existence… but there is another alternative."

I looked at the stars, letting my eyes glaze over to black, as I tried to *see* what the future held. Fate was quiet tonight. Perhaps it did not know the answer either.

Octavia's brows rose in curiosity. This was what she'd come for.

"I take it you and Delmira heard some interesting things in the Hall of Memories?" I prompted, and she nodded. Octavia didn't bother with excuses as to why she'd been keeping tabs on me. I could see in her heart that she was true. She had no ill will towards our court, and she would also do what it took to ensure there was a future for the star realms. Between that and dying, she'd take the first.

"You only saw half-truths," I swallowed, looking to Freyja. I hated the words that would soon be revealed. She looked pained as her eyes bored into mine, and I wondered if Algol plagued her still. I'd sensed his manipulation of her when she'd first arrived in Vega. The celestial had put her up to something, I was certain.

I looked to Finn and Elvy, and they nodded their encouragement. They'd wanted to tell everyone from the start. Luckily, they hadn't had to keep this secret long.

"Finnian found something truly ancient in the Hall of Memories. A way to make sure Hesperia fails and everyone lives."

"Not everyone," Finn corrected, and I glared at him to silence him further.

"What do you mean?" Oleander said, hands laced in Freyja's. My eyes softened at their embrace. If nothing else, they would be okay.

I paused for a moment before speaking my next words, knowing in my heart they could change everything.

"We create a new celestial."

Murmurs of disbelief and curiosity erupted around me, and I let the shock sink in.

"Go on," Clodovea said, eyes searching for hope, and I didn't blame her with her new bride at her side.

"We need to go to Sirius and talk to him. He is the creator of the celestials… only he can grant this, though I'm not sure how every detail works. Just the basics."

"But we'd be out of balance," Oleander argued. "We have five celestials with five elements already."

"We'd eliminate one," I said, feeling a little unhinged at the thought.

"What are you suggesting?" Octavia asked, and she did well in hiding what she truly felt. The secret purpose of the Keepers had trained her well.

"Hesperia needs all five ruling celestials alive to complete the ritual. Take out even one, and she won't succeed," Elvy said, jaw tightening. He still didn't like this solution. That wasn't enough. He loathed this outcome and would do everything in his power to ensure it didn't come to fruition. Despite all of that, he would not stop me. He would be there until the very end, and I would make sure he didn't follow me after.

"And what celestial is going to die?" Blaz asked, fists clenched.

"The only one we know how to kill. Algol," I said, voice unwavering, as I looked into both Oleander's and Freyja's eyes.

Oleander laughed lightly, but Freyja seemed ready for whatever was coming.

"Did you forget the little part where if you kill Algol, you kill everyone tied to that source of magic?" Oleander asked, voice threateningly calm.

"Do you really think I would let my sister die? After all I went through to bring her back? Your belief in me is heartwarming," I said, mocking the words he had thrown at me so many times. Granted, I had threatened Algol's life in exchange for my sister to be brought back to life, but I had been fairly certain Algol wouldn't call my bluff. I'd been right.

"Then what?" Octavia said. It was more of a demand than a request.

"If Sirius will create a new celestial with spirit, then I can tether that celestial to the other elementals. A shift of power, if you will."

"Has that ever been done before?" Imelda asked, looking at Finnian.

"I have no idea," he admitted. "I found exactly one passage about the creation of the celestials, and Zoe ran with it."

"I'm all about trailblazing," Zoe said. "Nova said I would burn. I'm just fulfilling that prophecy."

Freyja turned her eyes back on me, brows furrowing, trying to work out the puzzle—the underlying meaning.

"You intend to die," Freyja said—accusing. "That's how you plan to take out Algol."

Every eye turned to me. I knew Elvy hoped that they would talk me out of this, but my choice was final. It was beyond me.

"Yes. I do," I said, meeting each of their eyes. "I will for you and every soul in the star courts and on Earth. I will die so others may live."

Jelly whimpered her dislike of my words, and my heart grieved with her.

"I don't accept that," Delmira said, tears in her eyes. Whether they were from anger or sadness, I wasn't sure. Maybe both.

"You will accept it," I said.

"And you, Elvy? You're just going to let your mate die?" Oleander asked.

"Elvy does not speak for me. Nor do you," I said. "But let me make this clear. I do not want to die. I very much want to live. I hope beyond any hope you can possibly imagine that this does not come to fruition."

"So we need to figure out how to take Hesperia out," Blaz said.

"Yes, and in the meantime, we cover our bases. We come prepared to do what must be done during the final battle. Even if it means my death."

"But how do we make a celestial?" Clodovea asked. It was a fair question.

"I won't pretend to know the ins and outs of that process," I admitted. "That lies with Sirius."

"So we're splitting up again," Elvy said with the eyes of the Luminaries turning to him. "Hesperia is primed to come to Vega, though with me no longer under her control, she's going to take her time recouping her legion. We have time, but not much."

"My *sight* is set on her. I'll know when she makes the choice to move, but let's keep scouts at the ready."

"Aura will aid us in that," Clodovea said, and Tiergan nodded in agreement.

"Have the celestial courts ready to transport at a moment's notice. We'll need all of our allies if we're to win this."

"I'll see that it is done," Delmira vowed.

"The Keepers will support your efforts," Octavia said. "We do not wish to see the end just yet."

"How are we splitting?" Blaz asked, strategizing.

"Finnian will join Elvy and me," I said, voice clear. "The rest of you should stay in Vega."

"I'm with you," Jelly said through our bond, and I nodded slightly to her.

They wanted to protest. Blaz pressed his lips together to keep himself from arguing.

"I don't like leaving you that vulnerable, Zoe," he said.

"I don't need protecting, Blaz. What I need is our general readying our forces against Hesperia."

He nodded.

"You all have an important role to play. We trust the care of our immortals and the mortals of Earth to you," Elvy said, and I echoed the sentiment.

"I'm coming with you," Freyja said, rising from her seat along with Oleander.

"Correction. We will be coming with you," Oleander said. "The fate of this meeting with Sirius directly impacts me and those I star-vowed to protect. Do not fight with me on this, Zoe Eferhild."

I nodded. "Of course, Oleander. You and Freyja should come."

A song from the fates caught my ear, and I turned my head slightly, trying to understand the words they sang so softly to me. Yes, they would come. The stars were counting on it.

"What I don't understand is why Hesperia has immortals who are loyal to her when all she truly wants is to kill them," Finn mused.

"They believe her lies. That she will remake herself into a goddess. She is a cunning deceiver. Why would they believe for one minute she would kill herself?" Tiergan supplied, and I nodded my agreement.

"We leave at the setting of the evening moon," I said. "Remember, she will be at her weakest physically until she consumes the last star seed, which we do not want to happen under any circumstances."

"But her magic will be the strongest it's ever been now that she is not using the majority of it to hold me," Elvy said. "Plan accordingly with our allies."

"We don't know what will be waiting for us when we return," Elvy said, rising from his seat and looking each of our Luminaries in the eyes. "In case I don't have time then, know it has been an honor serving you—with you."

I rose next to my flame, raising a glass to the moon and the stars.

"For the heart of the new moon," I said, turning to Elvy.

"And the life in the starlight," he said, and we all drank from our goblets, unsure of what tomorrow held, but knowing that destiny would drive us forward—ever forward.

37

Rise Up

CLODOVEA

Imelda and I had exactly one night of bliss before reality decided to crush us all over again.

It had been such a lovely night, too. One filled with the love of my life in my arms until both of our bodies had given into exhaustion. It was as if our spirits knew that all we had was this one night.

In my heart, I'd known that to be true.

Imelda and I were in Musterion in the city center, observing the map hidden here long ago in the inner chambers of the capitol building. We were assessing the best transport zones for each court to use to create the strongest strategy against Hesperia's shadows. Aura hadn't given us much in her reports through the iris. Hesperia was buried deep within Canopus, but immortals had started disappearing again, which meant she likely had them enthralled to her. This ultimately meant that our hands would slaughter innocent lives. A collateral we would have to learn to live with.

Zadie and the immortals Zoe had healed had been working on finding a solution to help them come back to themselves without Zoe's magic, but there had been no update there. We certainly couldn't count on that moving forward, and Zoe would never be able to heal that many souls before the end of all this, no matter how deeply she might wish for that.

I sighed, bracing my body against the desk in front of me. My neck ached from the strain of the last twenty-four hours. Zoe, Elvy, Jelly, Finn, Oleander, and Freyja were on their way to Sirius right now.

Everything just felt *off*. Like we were on the cusp of something horrendous or truly great, but all these little pieces of the puzzle had to turn in our favor. We all were faced with the very real possibility that we would die soon, and the entire Kingdom of Canis along with it. King Aldrich and Queen Farron were fools to lock the borders to Sirius all this time. It would do nothing against the magic of Hesperia. They would perish along with the rest of us. Desperation sometimes breeds fruitless actions. Personally, I'd rather have action than be stagnant. We all found our own ways to cope, I suppose.

I sat down in one of the white leather chairs and stretched my arms over my head in a futile attempt to loosen the muscles locked up around my neck.

Imelda came up behind me and began massaging the knots out of my neck as if she was just that attuned to my needs, and I knew that she was.

"What are you thinking about?" she asked, and I let out a soft groan as my neck loosened at her magic touch.

"That I should have asked you to be my wife a long time ago," I said, and it was true.

"Better late than never," she said, kissing alongside my neck gently, and I shivered at the sensation. "Not until the very end."

I reached for her hand, kissing her palm softly. "I love you, Imelda."

"I know," she said, turning my chin so that she could place a deep kiss on my lips.

I leaned into her more, wanting to make this moment last just a little longer, but we had so much to do and no time to do it.

"Come on," she said. "We need to get these reports back to Delm and Blaz."

I sighed, knowing she was right.

I laced my fingers through hers and stowed the reports securely in my satchel.

"Let's take the long way at least," I said, and she grinned her response, nodding her head in agreement.

As we stepped out into the city center, I couldn't help the smile that graced my face. I would forever be in awe of this place, and my water magic seemed to sing whenever we were in Musterion.

"You'd never know there was a war going on with the way the city is bustling about," Imelda said, taking in all the immortals.

It was as if time truly stood still here. The immortals of Musterion knew, of course, why they had been evacuated here. They recognized the dangers that lurked beneath the surface, but they went on living, anyway. There was a part of me that admired them for that, and another beast inside of me who was envious that they had the choice to ignore the outside world.

"What are they supposed to do? Sit here and quake in fear about a future that may not come to pass?" Imelda asked. I hadn't realized I'd echoed my inner thoughts out loud.

"You have a point," I agreed as we moved along the edge of the city, closer to the forest. "I just want to be able to be as carefree as them."

"They aren't, though," she said. "They're keeping busy to distract themselves and their children from the looming death. Movement keeps the peace."

"You're right," I admitted.

"I usually am," she said, laughing, and I joined her.

I looked at each of them more closely, finding my wife to be correct. Hidden within the smiles and laughter was pain and worry in the eyes of the adults. Unwavering resilience in them, too. I wondered if they were content in this role… or if perhaps they wanted the option to fight with us. I shook the thought from my mind. For as long as I could remember, only the Shadowed immortals were warriors. In fact, they didn't really have much of a choice once they reached adulthood. It was simply the way of things, but maybe it shouldn't be? Isn't the freedom to choose the whole reason for Zoe's existence and enduring fight?

Now was not the time to bring this up, but after… I would advocate for this after.

As we made our way to the guarded exit of Musterion, I noticed a group of sea creatures following alongside us. The hippocampi and kelpie were a variety of shades of green, blue, and purple—perfect camouflage in these waters.

I halted our steps and turned to look at them curiously and *knowing*. I had no gift of discernment like Zoe, but my intuition was strong. Their numbers had grown significantly since we'd first discovered Musterion. In fact, all the sea creatures had seemed to migrate here at once. The populations were so dense that it was hard to tell where one beast ended and the other began.

One of the larger hippocampi stopped swimming the moment I stopped walking. I reminded myself of how it felt to fly on the back of a phoenix and of the might of the hippogriff. They wanted to fight for their Lady Astral. Maybe the hippocampi and kelpie simply wanted to do the same.

"Is that what you want?" I asked. "To fight for your realm—your element?"

The enormous hippocampi looked at me, and I swear it winked at me. The kelpie seemed much wilder than the hippocampi. They didn't seem particularly friendly, but that didn't mean they didn't want to fight.

"Did he just wink at you?" Imelda asked, shock in her voice.

"He?" I asked.

"Just a guess," she said. "I have no idea how to tell them apart."

An idea came to my mind as I pulled out a map of the reports. Maybe my inner ramblings a few moments ago hadn't been for naught.

"What are you thinking?" Imelda asked.

"Just a crazy idea," I said, looking between the map and the sea creatures, still staring at me with far too intelligent eyes. "Let's get back to Delmira and Blaz and see how insane I really am."

Imelda kissed me on the cheek before we sprinted down the exit tunnel and raced towards the lighthouse.

38

An Astral's Plea
FREYJA

I didn't know much about the High Astral Court other than what Oleander and Zoe had told me from their last visit there.

The monarchs seemed fair and just, but perhaps not as involved as they should have been in this fight. Sending the High Astral Shadowed forces to the other star courts would have been a decent start to their aid. Maybe they could have helped prevent Hesperia from obtaining the star seeds, but in my heart, I knew that wasn't true. They were trying to do what they could to prevent Hesperia's madness from reaching the mortals on Earth. Too bad their actions wouldn't be effective in the end.

Our entourage landed in the transport zone of the High Astral Court, and we were immediately surrounded by a variety of weapons and magical forces drawn on us the moment our toes touched down. Little did they know, there would be no getting through Zoe and Oleander's shield that protected us.

"We need to speak to the King and Queen. Immediately."

"You do not provide the orders, Lady Astral Zoe," one of the Shadowed responded. He must be a captain or some other leader.

"Time is not a luxury we have," Elvy said, stepping forward, and Oleander mirrored his movements.

"King Aldrich and Queen Farron have ordered these borders closed to everyone. No exceptions," the Shadowed responded.

"It'll be your death then," Zoe said, looking far more nonchalant than I knew she felt. Jelly growled low beside her, daring the Shadowed to step one little toe out of line.

"Are you threatening the High Astrals?" he asked, voice turning to an annoying pitch.

"No, no," Elvy laughed, darkness playing in his eyes but not going fully black. "But they will die nonetheless if you do not let us speak to them."

"Enough!" a feminine voice bellowed from the top of the stairs. Her braided blonde hair blew in the wind, and a dark gentleman with dreadlocks joined her. The crowns on top of their heads gave them away as Aldrich and Farron.

"You wear all five elemental courts on your crown," Zoe said, pitching her voice loud enough for them to hear. "Do not abandon them now."

"Zoe Eferhild, Realm-Healer—Emerging of Legends," Farron said, using some type of magic to carry her voice across to us without much effort. "Have you only come to give us a death notice?"

"No, Farron," she said, dropping the monarch's title. "I come to be your salvation."

Farron nodded, and the Shadowed instantly let us pass, but they followed closely behind us, eyes assessing our every breath. When we reached the top of the stairs, their eyes flickered to meet my own.

"And who is this?" Farron asked. "I assume she belongs with you, Oleander?"

Oleander's fingers were laced in mine. "Yes, Your Majesty. This is Freyja. Zoe's sister."

"I'd heard of this success, Zoe," Aldrich said, seeming earnest in his tone. I wanted to question exactly how he knew that sort of thing, but I decided against questioning his ability to spy. "But what did it cost you?"

Zoe looked to the stars, then back down to the King. "You might hold the answer to that more than I."

"What do you mean?" Farron asked, as she motioned for us to follow them into the grand moonstone halls that seemed to sparkle with starlight.

Farron and Aldrich sat on two thrones that were distinguished from the rest. As with their crowns, each star court was represented in the chair.

Zoe and Elvy sat on a small white couch with Jelly lying at Zoe's feet. Oleander and I sat on the matching set beside them. Finnian sat on the other side of Elvy, silent and watchful.

"Now, explain what is going on?" Farron asked, clasping her hands together in her lap. Her formal orange dress felt too stiff for this world—this moment. We were all wearing fighting leathers, though the Shadowed had taken our weapons upon entering the realm.

"We have need to commune with Sirius," Zoe stated. Way to get straight to the point there, sister.

"Only that?" Aldrich answered, looking aghast with disbelief.

"That is a privilege long held only by the monarchs currently in power. Even we have not been honored by his presence."

"So you've tried to speak with him?" I asked, catching the hint of rejection in her voice.

"Of course we have," Farron answered. "This is the worst war that has ever occurred in our history. We've begged the star's guidance."

"It's imperative that we speak with him," Zoe said again, voice more of a demand than a request.

"I cannot simply allow you into something so sacred," Farron argued.

Traditions and rules had a way of keeping us stunted from true growth. Surely they will see reason.

"You will die otherwise," my sister said. "Not only you, but every mortal and immortal soul you vowed to serve and protect will be obliterated to stardust. Is following *procedure* really worth that fate?"

"What are you implying Hesperia will do?"

"She's making herself into a celestial-killing bomb," Elvy said. "She's going to kill the celestials. Everything and everyone they are tied to will cease to exist."

"Meaning you, me, and everyone in this room," Oleander added. "Closing the borders to Sirius will not protect anyone."

Aldrich and Farron looked at each other, communicating silently in the way I sometimes saw Elvy and Zoe speak.

"We need to speak with the council," Farron finally spoke. "It is not only our decision to make."

Zoe wanted to argue, but she held her tongue.

"And how long will that take?" Elvy asked.

"We will speak with them immediately. It's late. I don't know how long the deliberations will last," Farron admitted.

Zoe's fists were clenched, and Jelly discreetly nuzzled her hand to get her to relax.

"Rooms have been arranged for you all," Aldrich said. "We will give you our decision when the council meeting adjourns."

I didn't miss the pointed look the monarchs gave my sister, and the turn of Zoe's head made me think she'd seen it as well.

"Thank you," Zoe said through gritted teeth, and we followed a guard to a suite of rooms that were all connected to a central parlour with plenty of space for us all.

As soon as the door slammed shut, Zoe and Oleander tossed up a silencing bubble.

"We don't have time for all this red tape," Zoe said, flopping down on the couch. Elvy and Jelly both joined her. "And something tells me Farron and Aldrich aren't keen to follow it either, but they are bound by laws in ways we are not…"

"I agree. We don't have the luxury to follow protocol," Oleander said, pacing around the room.

"Can you feel where it is? Your *sight*?" Finnian asked.

Zoe closed her eyes, focusing on the well of magic within her. A glow of white light flowed around her, but faded out just as quickly as it had begun.

"No, I can't get a read on it," she admitted, then turned to me. "But you… I felt something *good* when you and Oleander invited yourselves along on this journey. Maybe you're the key."

I shook my head at the thought, averting my gaze as my chest heated with pain again. I didn't know the first thing about finding Sirius.

"No, but you do have a unique power to move unseen," she countered, and Oleander paused his pacing.

"It could work," Finn admitted. "If we want to find this place before the High Astral Court has time to reject our request, this might be our only option. We don't even know if they will grant us the proper permissions."

"You realize going against them could be seen as high treason," Oleander stated. It was more of a fact than a way to deter us.

"We are due for a little rebellion, don't you think, Elvy?" Zoe asked.

"Better to commit high treason than to be dead," he agreed, and I realized that he would follow my sister into the nine hells if that's where they needed to go.

"Alright," I said, digging deep into my courage. "I've only done this like once or twice, but I can do it."

"I know you can, sweetheart," Oleander said, giving me a small kiss on the cheek.

I sprawled out on one of the empty couches and closed my eyes to focus on the task at hand. I've only ever accomplished this while sleeping, but I willed my magic to answer my call, and it obeyed.

My eyes flickered open to reveal a mirror image of me. She was translucent, but she was me.

"Did it work?" Zoe asked, trying to see what I did.

"It worked," I said, proud that I had conjured this perfect spymaster. "I need to concentrate."

I closed my eyes again, focusing on the connection between myself and the mirage. Suddenly, her eyes were my eyes, and the body I controlled was hers. I took a step forward and found that my mirror body answered. Everyone around me looked at my physical body. All except Ander, whose eyes bored into mine. I gave him a wink before darting off through the door without actually opening it.

If I were a super-powerful celestial creator thingy, where would I hide? Well, I guess he wasn't actually here, but his essence or connection was. I'd either be in the castle's heart like all the other star seeds, or I'd be at the highest point. Both had their advantages and disadvantages.

My gut said high, so I found my way outside, breezing past the Shadowed that were stationed around literally every corner. As much I wanted to eavesdrop on them, I focused on the mission. Who knew if any of them might have the gift of *sight* to see the invisible.

The crisp air flowed through me as I greeted the cosmos outside.

"I'm coming to find you, oh mighty one," I whispered to Sirius, and I swear I heard a chuckle in the surrounding air, but no one was there, so I kept pressing on. I scanned the horizon for the highest tower connected to the castle.

"Bingo," I said, trying to imagine myself floating upward to it.

Just like the time I'd visited Oleander, I began sailing up to the tower, but found I couldn't flow right into it like I could with the other walls. I moved to the bridge that connected the tower to the main castle and found the walls permeable. I glided through them and kept moving towards the massive doors at the end of the hall.

I tried again to flow through them, but found them resistant to my magic. I scoured the place, looking for any sign that the connection to Sirius was lurking in here somewhere.

Ever so subtly, I found a star pattern carved into the door, hidden by gems drilled into a seemingly random location. I was hopeless when it came to constellations and committed the map to my memory, reviewing it repeatedly until I had it down.

Instead of taking the easy way back down, I tried to find a way back through the castle, since that was the way we all would have to come.

The moment I crossed the threshold into the side of the bridge that was in the castle, two Shadowed guards waited for me. They couldn't see me, and I breathed a sigh of relief.

"How do I always get the terrible posts?" one of the males grumbled, crossing his arms, seeming utterly bored.

"We get paid the same whether we are standing in front of a door no one comes to or dying in battle, bro," the other one answered, shrugging.

I hoped that meant the way up would be relatively easy then. My sense of direction wasn't the best, but I moved in the direction I thought I needed to and after taking only two wrong turns, I finally made it back to our room.

Ander stood up at my arrival, and the others followed his line of sight. It was clear he was the only one who saw me, though.

"Did you get it?" he asked, and I nodded before melding my mirage with my own body again.

It was a little disorienting being back in my physical body. Every movement felt oddly heavy and sluggish.

"I think I found it," I admitted. "Toss me that pen and paper, Finnian."

He snatched them up and brought them to me. I sketched the star pattern I'd seen on the door and showed Oleander and Elvy.

"That's Sirius," Elvy said, and Oleander nodded his agreement.

"And how was the way up?" Zoe asked.

"Most of the Shadowed must be at the transport zones," I answered. "Once we get past the Shadowed on the main floor, we're golden. Only two guard the doors to Sirius."

"I can try to cloak us," Oleander said. "But I can only fully conceal two of us. Maybe three."

"Shadows?" Elvy asked, and Zo nodded.

"We can blend in well enough, I think." Zoe said. "And Finn, you stay here in case everything goes to hell?"

"I'll send an update to Delm and Zadie," he agreed.

"Deep breaths, everyone. We're about to meet the celestial maker," Zoe said, a fire in her eyes. The first I'd seen in her in quite some time. I didn't care how insane this mission was. I'd do it all over again just to see her have some life back in her.

"Let's go, sister," I said.

39

Wild Girl

DELMIRA

Blood coated my knuckles from the onslaught of punches I'd dealt to the punching bag.

Blaz held the other side steady for me, and a small smile played on my lips as I found him struggling to keep it from swinging too much.

I'd often wished that my star gifted magic would work to calm my nerves as much as it affected others, but then again, I hated the idea of not being fully in control of my emotions… no matter how difficult I found them to be.

We'd just gotten word through Finnian that they were moving in on Sirius.

"Why wouldn't the King and Queen be more amenable to them? I don't get it," I said, throwing another punch, sending a slice of pain through me.

I stepped back from the black bag, sizing up my next movements.

"I've always found Aldrich and Farron to be honorable," Blaz said, studying me. "Even when they were Lord and Lady Astral of Arcturus, they had a good reputation. Arcturus didn't really lose their honor until Kai and Seraphina."

I smoothly kicked the punching bag, followed by a flurry of blows from my fists.

"I get it. They don't want to overstep their powers. And the choices made in times of war matter, but we're on borrowed time as it is," I said, wiping a stray lilac hair from my brow.

"When we win this final battle," Blaz said, ignoring my pessimism. "You do realize our court will have to answer for this act."

I nodded. "And we will happily do so if that means we get to have a life afterwards."

Blaz moved from behind the punching bag and pulled my waist flush against him. A familiar, calloused palm tilted my chin to look into his brown eyes.

"Then let's make sure we have a fighting chance. Zoe and Elvy are doing their jobs. Let's do ours," he said, pulling me in for a deep kiss.

I let myself be present with him longer than I had in a while. I was tired of analyzing our troops and coordinating with the other courts, but we still needed the final touches. We had a solid ground battalion, and we had the air covered with the dragons, phoenixes, and hippogriffs. Ironically enough, it was our water attacks that were our weakest. Sure, we could wield the hell out of it, and some of our magic users were crafty in their lethal approach. It just felt unfinished, like we had this major vulnerability on our coastlines.

The doors to the private training room for the Luminaries flew open with Clodovea and Imelda sprinting towards us with a wild look about them.

"Do I even want to know what you two are thinking?" I asked, placing my hands on my hips.

"You're going to love this," Clove said, nodding enthusiastically. "Especially you, Blaz."

"We need to see the battle plans," Imelda said, and Blaz nodded.

"Let's go then," he said, not wasting anytime. He led us up to the secure meeting room on the roof and pulled up the hologram of our realm on top of the table so we could better see every vantage point.

"The circles are the points of entry into our realm, right?" Clodovea asked.

"Right," I said. "We plan to have each realm enter from these five main points, securing them from Hesperia. She's not going to breach where she knows a legion is waiting for her."

"And we will have our Shadowed Legion on these two," Blaz said, pointing to the next logical entry for Hesperia to try to come into our realm.

Clodovea's eyes narrowed on the biggest vulnerability of our defense. There was a small island off the coast in our bay that housed an entry zone.

"Let's force her to come in through there," she said, pointing to the island.

"Our water defense is lacking," Blaz said, shaking his head. "We could make the crossing difficult, but we can't hold it. Our boats are too fragile for war. They were made for fishing and transportation."

Imelda smiled at Clodovea in encouragement.

"What if our army had mounts in the water?"

Blaz and I both looked at her, puzzled.

"The hippocampi," Clodovea said. "They want to fight to defend our realm. Just like the phoenixes and the hippogriffs, and the dragons. They want to fight. I think the kelpies do, too."

Blaz furrowed his brows together and stroked his chin in thought. "It would give us a huge advantage. Especially for the water users who want to fight, but aren't Shadowed."

There had been many from Musterion who had volunteered to fight despite not having any combat experience or training. By the surprised look in Clodovea's eyes, she hadn't known this. The possibility of dying in no way deterred them from what they felt called to do.

"We have no time to train on the hippocampi," I said, running a hand through my hair, and I caught Clodovea's desire to argue with me. I held up my hand to silence her before words could pass her lips. "But that doesn't mean we won't try."

"It's a good idea, Clove," Blaz agreed. "We can help our immortals learn to ride the hippocampi as mounts. As for the kelpie…"

"They'll do whatever they please," Clodovea said, shrugging.

Imelda and Clodovea grinned at each other.

"Spread the word in Musterion," I said to both of them. "Anyone who wants to fight and isn't afraid to ride a creature we thought myth or extinct until a few months ago should report to the surface for placement."

They both nodded and hurried back out the door to Musterion.

"Will it give us an advantage?" I asked, looking back over the battle. We'd covered everything, thought of every possibility Hesperia could throw at us.

"It's one more edge than we had," Blaz nodded, circling his arms around me.

"How many riders do you think we'll have?" I asked.

"More than you think," he said, kissing my neck. "Our immortals want to defend the realm they call home, and we will let them answer."

"We will," I agreed, tapping on the screen to shut the hologram down, and Blaz picked me up, placing me on the table so that my legs straddled his waist.

"I'm going to tell you something, and I don't want you to argue with me," Blaz said, holding my gaze. My heart started pounding so heavily I thought it was going to leap out of my chest.

"Yes?" I asked, voice softer than my normal demanding tone.

"I love you," he said, kissing my lips, not giving me time to say anything else or to run.

When he pulled away from me, he smiled crookedly, but I was too stunned to say anything.

"I don't want you to say anything right now. I just wanted to tell you how I felt. And whatever you feel or don't feel is okay," he said, pressing his lips against my forehead.

I didn't know what to say, so I didn't say anything. I wrapped my arms around his torso and thanked the stars for giving him to me.

40

Sirius

ELVY

Zoe and I had our shadows tight around us while Oleander concealed himself and Freyja. Jelly hid easily within our protection, ears perked, listening for any movement.

We'd made it past the Shadowed stationed on the main floor and had slipped past the two guards standing in front of the door Freyja had pointed out as Sirius. I felt slightly guilty for getting past them so easily, but time was of the essence, and we had none to spare.

"How are we going to open the door?" Zoe asked through our bond, and I studied the encryption with little success in deciphering what it meant.

"I would venture to say this has everything to do with you and your sister," I replied, pointing to the two marks of the Northern Star that rested on each hand of the moonstone door.

Zoe moved in closer and motioned for Freyja to come beside her.

"The songs of fate smiled when I'd suggested Freyja come here," Zoe whispered through my mind.

I nodded, pulling the shadows over us, hoping the sound of the door would be muffled enough not to draw attention to it. Oleander gave me a nod, and he waved his hand in the air, expanding the silencing shield around us. We had no idea what magical protections would ignite the moment we opened the door. I had a feeling we would not be so lucky as to move in silence.

Freyja and Zoe nodded and placed their glowing immortal marks against the door handles, and the moonstone door filled with blue and black magic. No alarm blared, but even my shadows couldn't hide the light show the door was putting on. It unfortunately caught the eyes of the Shadowed standing guard. On instinct, Oleander and I moved in unison to shield our girls from the magic that was hurled our way.

The door was opening much too slowly, and the mere size of it must have cost the magic opening it significant effort.

"Silence them before they call for aid," Zoe said, eyes black with a future that was not yet written.

Oleander flew towards them, palms outstretched to their foreheads.

"Sleep," he commanded, sending his magic through them.

Without much fight, the two immortals fell to their knees in a slumber.

"Did we get them in time?" I asked, turning to Zoe.

Shouts from below us sent fear through me as my flame shook her head.

"Come on!" Freyja shouted as she and Zoe slipped through the door with Jelly right behind her charge. I followed behind them with Oleander on my tail.

The moment we crossed the threshold of the room, the moonstone door began groaning shut, moving at yet another glacial pace.

"Seriously?" Zoe said, eyeing the onslaught of Shadowed heading straight for us.

"Don't kill them," Freyja said, and Zoe agreed, though her shadows looked ready to shred them to ribbons.

My death magic was mostly still within me, not seeing them as much of a threat to my mate, but my shadows ached to meet their bond all the same.

Oleander sent out waves of his magic, and the Shadowed fell where they stood.

Mercifully, the gargantuan door finally sealed shut, casting us into an almost uncomfortable silence.

Zoe's eyes remained black as she leaned into her magic.

A half-smile crept over her as she saw the future.

"It seems Aldrich and Farron meant for us to do this," she said, voice echoing loudly in the vastness of the hall. "They are doing their best to keep the High Astral Council at bay. It seems they anticipated our movements and have gathered them at their behest. We don't have a lot of time."

That fact was somewhat of a relief, though whether they would admit their part in this was nothing I had time to worry about right now.

I turned to face the room, finding it covered in moonstone and crystals of all colors. It reminded me of the iris we now all held. In the center of the room, a large, glowing orb took up most of the space.

Freyja looked at Zoe with a confused expression.

"Why does this feel so familiar?" Freyja asked, and Zoe smiled in understanding.

"Because it would be. For any Emerging," my mate answered.

"What do we do?" I asked, circling the greatest source of power in all the star realms. Greater than even the celestials.

"We have to touch it. Embrace it," Zoe said, and a flicker of a memory seemed to cross Freyja's eyes.

"Is it safe?" Oleander asked, moving closer to Freyja.

"I have no guarantee of that, of course, but if it works like the trials…" she trailed off.

"Together," I said, and they all nodded in agreement. "On three."

"One," Oleander said.

"Two," Freyja echoed.

Zoe latched a hand around Jelly. "Wouldn't leave you behind," she assured.

"Three," Zoe said, and we simultaneously placed our hands on the orb of Sirius.

We didn't fly through the cosmos like we would in between realms. Instead, we landed in a realm of existence I struggled to make sense of. Galaxies of stars shone above us, so bright that I had to squint when looking into the night sky. Moonstone and crystals lay at my feet, and a throne that appeared to be made of diamonds was the only structure around us.

I laced my fingers through Zoe's, and Oleander and Freyja moved in closer to us as we all took in this strange world.

"Zoe Eferhild, Realm-Healer—Emerging of Legends," a voice spoke from nowhere and everywhere.

My wife turned back to the throne that had been empty just a second ago, but was now occupied by a figure that gave off a larger-than-life energy.

Zoe approached the throne, raising her chin to the male who sat there, and we all stood just behind her with Jelly and me on either side of her.

"I've been waiting a long time for this moment," Sirius said, smiling down kindly.

He was a pale young male, almost scarily so. He had silver hair that almost looked like a light purple, and his eyes were a piercing green… just like Zoe's when her flame was activated.

"You look so… *normal*," Zoe said, squinting at the creator of our celestials and kingdom. I tensed, hoping he didn't see that as an insult.

"Do I?" he asked, shrugging.

"In comparison to the celestials, I would say so," she answered.

"Mmmmm, my children have really made a mess of things, haven't they?"

"I would like to say no, but I'd be lying," she said, and he laughed softly.

"And we wouldn't want that, would we?"

He seemed to enjoy ending every sentence with a question.

"No matter. I've come to finish this," she said, taking a step closer, and we all moved with her.

"I cannot give you what you seek," he said, frowning. "It seems Vega was misguided in leading you to me. Algol won't take kindly to this, despite Vega's good intentions."

"It is the only way to guarantee Hesperia is not successful," Zoe argued, voice raising slightly.

"No. It is not," he said with a knowing smile that angered me, since I had a feeling he would not be direct about this at all.

"We have to stop Hesperia," Freyja said, moving closer to Zoe. "We need your help."

"You do not need my help, girl. Zoe has every tool needed to defeat her. I ensured your father guided you on the correct path after the mess his haste made of things. I owed him that much after my child's actions. Don't tell me I've made a mistake in choosing your Emerging gifts?"

"You decided that?" Zoe asked.

"I do," he said, smiling warmly. "And you were chosen with purpose, Zoe. You were chosen to be a *healer*. Not a *destroyer, life-bringer*."

"Destroying Hesperia is necessary for there to be any healing," she argued, and I was proud as hell of her, but also feared he would smite her where she stood.

"That is why you were gifted the shadows," he said, folding his arms in his lap, speaking with the patience of a saint.

"But my shadows can't kill her. I've tried," she said.

"No, they can't," he agreed, and I saw her internally curse him. I was pretty certain we all wanted to join her in that.

"But if you agree to make another celestial tied to spirit, this can all be over," Zoe said.

"I did not grant you the Emerging so that you could die, Zoe Eferhild. I granted you the Emerging so you could live. Are you so ready to give up everything because the answer has not fallen into your lap? Are you so willing to throw it all away because you're terrified of what Hesperia plans to do? Because you cannot control chaos?" he asked, and I was somewhat touched that Sirius was on our side. He wanted Zoe to live, perhaps as badly as I needed her to.

"But you could," Zoe started, but Sirius raised his hand.

"Yes, I could create another celestial, but it would cost you more than you know."

"More than the sacrifice of my own life?" Zoe asked, voice filled with sarcasm. It would be my wife who dealt out heavy sarcasm to the ultimate creator.

"Yes," he said, motioning her to come closer to him.

She took a hesitant step forward, and Jelly moved with her. Oleander placed a hand on my shoulder, holding me back, and I nodded, letting Zoe grow into this moment.

"May I?" he asked, holding palms to either side of her temple, and Zoe nodded, giving him permission to touch her.

The moment his hands made contact with her skin, Zoe's eyes went black and her expression was panicked as tears fell down her face. I tried to see what she saw through our flame, but whatever magic Sirius was using, it blocked me from her.

It took every bit of resolve I possessed not to snatch her away from him, but moments later, he released her.

"I do not wish for this future, do you?" he asked, eyes kind towards my mate. "A future that would come to pass from your desperation, Zoe. Not from your love. Do not repeat the same mistakes as your father."

She shook her head and wiped the tears from her eyes. I slipped an arm around her as she moved back to the rest of us.

"Look to the beginning, child. Every aspect of your Emerging was created with intention. Look within," he said, and Zoe nodded. The look of frustration was well hidden, but I knew my flame well.

"Despite the mistakes my child has made, I do wish for Algol to be redeemed. Being separated from the other elementals has

Algol twisted into something they are not. The spirit element is designed to bring happiness, curiosity, empathy, and compassion to my immortals and mortals alike. It was never meant to be corrupted into something so vile. This separation has caused dissent among my children and their children for far too long. Restore what your father created, Zoe Eferhild, and all will be right again."

His eyes softened with the love of a… father. Algol was his child, and he did not wish to see them perish.

"I have given you the means to cleanse Hesperia from these realms and restore peace to the star courts and Earth. Fate demands fairness and free will in times of war, as death is hungry and must be fed. You are perhaps my favorite creation, and I hope death remains famished for a good while longer."

"Thank you," Zoe said, bowing on one knee to Sirius, and we all followed suit.

"I hope I don't see any of you in my realm for many, many centuries," he said, smiling and sending waves of hope into us all. "Darkness and light go well together, don't you think?"

In the blink of an eye, we were back in the crystal cavern of Sirius, and my central nervous system startled at the incessant pounding on the door after so much quiet.

There were a million questions I wanted to ask my wife, but it would have to wait until we either escaped the irritation of the High Astral Council or turned them to our side.

Politics had always been the bane of my existence.

41

One Last Night
FREYJA

Zoe and I let our magic flow through the entrance, allowing the forces to surround us in the cavern.

I tried to keep my gaze away from Zoe as the uncomfortable pain in my chest had only grown since we'd spoken to Sirius.

Farron and Aldrich stood before us with unreadable expressions. I couldn't tell if they were pissed or impressed or neither of those emotions.

"You seem to have a habit of doing whatever you please," Farron said, speaking directly to Zoe.

"I was called here by Sirius himself. Are you suggesting I ignore my fate?" my sister asked, oh so brilliantly.

Farron's lips twitched in amusement for a flash of a second before her unreadable expression resumed its place.

"You were expressly told to wait until the High Astral Council had made its formal decree," Aldrich said, but I read between the lines. I felt like they hoped we did, too. They hadn't been able to let us into the building because of who they were… but they had no control over Sirius.

"How did they get through our guards?" Farron asked, directing the question to the less than friendly Shadowed who had escorted us to them when we'd arrived.

"I advised you against lessening the guards around Sirius, your grace. I thought it unwise to only have two on this floor once the Astrals showed interest in the star," he answered with a subtle hint of blame towards his sovereigns.

"You dare blame me for your failure?" Farron asked, and Zoe quickly hid her smug expression from revealing what we all four had realized. They had done what they could to let us get to Sirius as quickly as possible. They were undoubtedly on our side.

The Shadowed was quiet, which was the smartest decision he's made since walking into this room, probably.

"Escort them to their rooms, then to the nearest transport zone," Aldrich said, motioning everyone out of the cavern.

Farron pulled Zoe back slightly, and I couldn't hear the question she asked. Jelly exercised a patience I didn't feel as they conversed briefly. Zoe nodded, and Farron left her side to speak with her husband, or at least, I assumed they spoke through their bond with the looks they were giving each other.

"What was that about?" I asked, as Oleander threw up a shield around us again, concealing our conversation as best he could.

The Shadowed looked royally pissed off, and I couldn't help the smirk that crossed my face. A long-forgotten childish part of me really wanted to stick my tongue out at him, but I swallowed down a laugh instead.

"They promised they would send their aid when the final battle comes," she answered. "She also asked if I got what I needed."

"And did you?" I asked, looping her arm through mine, ignoring the pain in my chest.

"We'll discuss it later," she said, giving me a half-smile that let me know she was struggling with something.

"Promise?" I asked, feeling silly in asking her to promise something so monumental.

"As soon as we get to Vega," she agreed.

The grumpy pants guard opened the door in front of us, which led to our suite of rooms, and said, "Hurry up."

"Such a gentleman," I said, smiling widely at him.

He rolled his eyes, and Finnian seemed to nearly burst with questions. Zoe held up a finger, giving him the same answer that she'd given me.

"I packed your bags, so we are ready to go," he said, as both Elvy and Oleander helped him collect everything for transport.

Jelly circled around my sister, wings twitching with an urge to fly out of here.

I was getting much better at flying between realms, but I didn't quite glide as effortlessly as the others.

We followed the Shadowed guard to the outskirts of the High Astral Court and spread our wings, sights aimed for Vega.

★★★

I laced my fingers through Oleander's beneath the table that we all sat around in Vega.

All the Luminaries were here, along with Octavia, who said she was mostly here to ensure fate remained in the balance for the

Keepers. Tiergan was also in attendance with his rebel army already moved to Vega.

The room grew quiet as Zoe's eyes darkened, as she gazed into a future we couldn't see.

Moments later, her eyes were green once again, and both she and Elvy looked grim. Even Jelly's expression looked worried. She nuzzled my sister's hand before laying down again at her feet.

"Hesperia will make her move at evening, moonset tomorrow," she said, voice steady.

We now had a countdown to pull this off. In twenty-four hours, we would all either be alive or obliterated from existence.

"Were you successful in your mission?" Delmira asked, eyes searching for a hope she wouldn't find in my sister tonight. Not with that question, at least.

"We spoke with Sirius," Zoe said, shaking her head. "Creating a new celestial is off the table."

"It can't be done?" Blaz asked.

"It's not an option," Zoe said, voice firm, but I knew my sister. There was something she was leaving out—something she did not want the others to know. Something she *was* going to tell me before this night was over.

"So we kill her," Blaz said, lips pursing together as if it were just another night in the star realms, but there was a heavy fear in the air for us all. We'd done all we could do to ensure we would win this fight. We'd recruited all five elemental courts, the rebel leaders, and the High Astral Shadowed Legion. Farron and Aldrich had sworn their aid when the time came.

"We have an answer to everything except that," she said, defeat evident in her voice.

"You haven't let us down," I said, not caring what anyone else thought. "We haven't lost."

"We will if I can't kill her," Zoe said, fists clenching. Both Elvy and Jelly nudged her palms, forcing her to relax.

"Sirius said we have the tools to succeed in this fight, which means we have the means to kill her. There's something we're missing," Oleander said. I'd never seen him this stressed before. He had always possessed an air of 'I don't care' around him. Ander had this smooth, unwavering confidence that endeared me to him. He'd only ever shown his vulnerability to me, but now? He showed it to everyone.

Zoe stood from the table, pacing around the battle map.

"You said you had new recruits?" she asked, turning to Clodovea and Imelda.

They nodded enthusiastically. "Some powerful immortals who aren't Shadowed have volunteered to fight."

"Shouldn't we protect them?" Zoe asked.

"And deny them their right to fight for their loved ones and their star realm?" Delmira asked.

"The hippocampi and kelpie have proven their loyalty to our cause. The wingless immortals have bonded with them quickly. They will be a great help in this final battle," Clodovea said, and I couldn't help but have the hope of the stars at the light in her eyes.

"I'll contact the other Astrals. Let them know the moment to arrive," Zoe said.

"Send them to these specific zones," Blaz said, pointing to five different points on the map that would allow entry into Vega. "This should force Hesperia to enter on the island. We hadn't planned for the High Astral Shadowed to come. They can reinforce where needed."

"It's a good plan," Elvy said, nodding his approval.

"We'll buy you every second that we can," Delmira swore. "You'll figure this out, Zoe."

"We'll have a feast in Musterion tonight," Zoe said, ignoring Delmira's words because she didn't have the answer she wished she could give them. "Then everyone needs to rest. Even the patrols. We know when she's coming. We need everyone at their best."

We all nodded and rose from our seats to go our separate ways, but I caught hold of my sister before she could escape into herself.

"What aren't you telling everyone?" I asked, pulling her to the side away from both Elvy and Oleander, though I couldn't keep Jelly from following us.

"I don't know what you're talking about," she said, amusingly trying to lie to me.

"Tell me, Zo," I said, pleading with her to share the burden. "This pain in my chest is demanding that you tell me."

"Can you just trust that I'm protecting you?" she asked, eyes begging me to drop the issue.

"It's not your call to make if it concerns me," I said seriously. "No more sacrificing. No more bargaining. You and I have given enough, and we both get to make decisions *together*. As a team, Zo."

She sighed, biting her lip in defeat.

"That very reason is why I hesitate to tell you, Freyja," she said, pinching the skin between her eyes. "But you are right… I cannot make this choice for you. In order for Sirius to make a new celestial, there has to be a vessel—a sacrifice. An immortal of that realm has to ascend—become what the celestials are now."

My heart stilled for a moment as I took in her words.

"And you, my dear sister, are the perfect vessel to ascend," Zoe said, voice nearly a whisper.

"What?" I asked, and I swear I could hear the rage coming from Algol in whatever realm they were in now. Memories from my trials flooded through me—of Algol asking me to say no to this. And I'd promised I would do what was right.

"But you wouldn't be Freyja anymore," she said. "You'd give up your identity to become something wholly different. No more Oleander. No more anything. At least not in the same capacity that you experience life now."

"My stars," I said, terrified of the thought.

"No wonder Algol had been so against granting your Emergence," she said. "They'd resisted until the bitter end. I wonder if they knew your potential."

"I would say so. Algol all but begged me to say no to you in my last trial. They'd tried to make it seem like you were going to hurt me," I said, rolling my eyes. "I told them to get lost, in a manner of speaking."

She smiled at the image, then turned more serious.

"Thank you for never doubting me," she said. "If I had known that this crazy quest would involve this sacrifice from you… I could never ask that of you. I never would have pursued this. I've wasted so much time going down this fruitless avenue."

"I know, Zo. You saw a glimmer of hope and followed through on that. No one can blame you for it."

"What are you going to do?" she asked with a hint of fear.

"Even if I ascended, you would die, anyway," I said, and she nodded.

"Is our legacy to be the sisters who died and sacrificed everything that they were to save the mortal and star realms?" she mused, and I wanted to agree with her.

"I say we write a new legacy," I said, unwilling to believe that fate was the way we would be remembered. Such sorrow and pain for those we loved… no, we would find another path written in the stars. The pain in my chest was completely gone with the power of my words.

I told Algol I'd do what was right. And for once in my life… it was the easiest 'no' I'd ever blindly agreed to, though a cynical part of me hated to concur with him. If they hadn't been so cynical in the trial, this could all have been avoided. I'd never choose a destiny in which my sister would have to die. They should have known that, but Algol's fear had been too great, so they had yet again chosen hatred. They had tried to spread their sickness even further in a desperate plea to cling to their very own life. I longed for a future in which Algol's spirit element was all that Sirius had intended.

As the decision formed in my soul, the pain in my chest ebbed until it vanished. I suppose I passed Algol's final test.

"I just need time, sister," Zoe said, pulling me from my thoughts. "Time to figure out how to cure the poison of Hesperia."

"And we will make sure you have it," I said.

I embraced my sister, holding her close to me, vowing we would have many more moments like this in the future.

"I'll see you soon," Zoe said, kissing my cheek and taking Elvy's hand.

Ander's arm circled around my waist as he placed a gentle kiss on my lips.

"What was that about?" he asked.

"Just two sisters having a chat," I answered, and he didn't seem to believe me, though he didn't press for more information.

"Let's go freshen up before we go down to Musterion. I need to speak with Zadie, too."

I nodded, letting him guide me to our rooms in the manor as I let my thoughts drift to the dreams I prayed the stars would answer.

42

Feasts of the Future
ZOE

Musterion had only grown in its mysterious beauty since I'd last visited the secret city.

The immortals living here had decorated the entire city center with glowing starlights, twinkling lights, and beautiful water magic danced within the fountain. Someone with stunning magic had created a light show with different creatures made of water, and I smiled at both the children and adults, laughing at the story told. Even I found the little animals adorable. So did Jelly, who turned her head in wonder.

The city was filled with laughter, and it was refreshing to hear that song on the eve of battle.

This could be our last night of existence. We could choose to fret or…

We could choose to *live*.

And wasn't that the very choice that had gotten me right here in the first place?

My desire and plea to the universe to live with my dying breath.

And I would honor younger me now.

I would live tonight. I would be present for every moment with my friends and family.

For a healed world.

I took a sip of some fruity concoction and found Elvy smiling back at me, seeming to have read my mind.

He wrapped me in his arms, placing a kiss on my lips.

"My starlight," he said, swinging me around to some music that had started up.

The Luminaries joined around us, following in on the group dance. Freyja dragged Oleander into the fray, too, and I pretended not to see the smile across his face as Blaz challenged him to the most ridiculous dance battle.

The pair had us all roaring with deep belly laughs, and I found myself embracing every silly little moment despite the initial desire to hide behind my fingers in embarrassment for them both. Even Tiergan danced with us, moving smoothly for an elder immortal.

The immortal controlling the music eventually had mercy on us all and changed the melody to something slow and romantic. Elvy swept me into his arms, pulling me close, and I couldn't help but steal glances around me, seeing those I love loving each other.

For a moment, it was easy to see the future I could have with my family. And if I closed my eyes, listening to the chants of the world beyond, I knew my mother was with me. I felt her smiling at the life Freyja and I had created for ourselves—despite it all.

A murmur came rumbling through the crowd, pulling me from the visions of my mother, and a familiar presence graced us.

She was hidden behind Evander, who had escorted her here. I'd previously given him clearance should this soul ever cross our borders to bring her to me. She was family after all.

"June," I said, lips cracking into a smile.

"You didn't think I'd let you go to war alone now, did you, kid?" she asked, holding out her arms, and I raced towards her, letting her soothe me like her own child.

"What are you doing here?" I asked.

"I've fought for the star realms before, and I will happily do so again," she said, more serious than I'd ever heard her.

"Is my father…" I trailed off, not sure what to ask. He'd been more absent than ever, abandoning this fight to me.

"Your father is making peace with where he is now, but he will come. At the right moment, child. But not one second before then. Just as he promised," June said, tucking a stray hair from my braid behind my ear. My heart sank, wondering what my father could be preparing for.

"But how will I know when that it is?" I asked, desperately wanting my father to come for me. To be there in what could be my final moments.

"Lean into your gifts, Zo. He's given you everything you need. Stop searching. It's all within you," she said, placing a kiss on my forehead, and I shut my eyes, thinking through every conversation I'd had with my father. "It's all in the stars, kid."

I'd heard that so many times before. There was a part of me that believed the stars had chosen me with intent. Sirius had confirmed as much. But did I truly believe I possessed the power to kill Hesperia without sacrificing myself or someone I loved?

The inner child in me ewanted to believe my father had provided a way through this.

Elvy came to stand beside us, likely feeling the internal struggle I felt.

"We're glad to have another ally," Elvy said, holding his hand out to June, which she shook firmly.

"Will Phoebe be coming as well?" I asked, and she smiled, nodding towards Octavia.

"You should know better than I," June said pointedly, and Octavia's cheeks flushed pink with yet another secret she'd kept from us.

"The secrets of the Keepers are not mine to share," she said simply, and I again felt no malice in her. Everything she did, she did for the good of the star realms and the mortals of Earth. "Phoebe will do what all Keepers do... observe and record."

"And get involved when things are turning against fate," June added with a knowing smile.

Octavia nodded. "If we must."

"And must you?" I asked.

Octavia's lips pressed into a thin line as she considered.

"Fate hangs in the balance, both sides holding equal ground. I am not sure which way the weight will fall," she admitted.

"It sucks not having the answer, doesn't it? To not know what move to make?"

She nodded, not giving voice to that sentiment.

The surrounding immortals had continued partying around us, dancing to music that sent their bodies into carnal motions and their voices yelling widely.

"Come on," June said. "This is a party, after all. Let's have some fun."

I agreed, knowing the Keepers held no more answers for me than I had for them. I let the music guide my body as I danced against Elvy, and he moved fluidly with me. I caught my sister's eyes as she danced with Oleander, and we both laughed at each other, each deciding to embrace the joy that this moment brought us—brought everyone.

We all danced until our feet ached and our hearts were full of love and hope for tomorrow. As they danced around me, I gifted Freyja, Oleander, June, and Tiergan their very own charms, infused with my healing magic. I also replenished the magic infused with the Luminaries' charms.

"Here," I mumbled to Oleander, as I slipped an additional charm into his hand. "For Zadie."

He gave me a kiss on the cheek before twirling away with Freyja in his arms.

"Let's go," Elvy whispered in my ear, and I nodded.

Elvy swept me into his arms with Jelly trailing behind us discreetly. His gray eyes glimmered with love and perhaps a little lust as he carried me all the way out of Musterion and into our ocean-side manor. The city was quieter than normal, and the stars seemed to shine even brighter on this eve of battle.

Once we crossed the threshold, he set me down gently, and the only sounds we heard were our breaths, Jelly's paws padding behind us, and the crash of the ocean along the shoreline. This was real. Every bit of it. And I wanted to fight to make it safe again.

I paused at the library before slipping in, comforted by the familiar smell of the books.

"It's sad to think the written word here will be forgotten if we lose tomorrow," I said, brushing my fingers along the spines of books far older than I was. "That so many moments in time led to this point where we are one wrong move away from annihilation. Our choices now have an impact on the future."

He circled his arms around me from behind, resting his chin gently on my shoulder.

"I believed in you before I knew you," Elvy murmured. "That has never wavered."

I turned my neck so I could place a soft kiss against his lips, and he sucked in my bottom lip, deepening the kiss.

"I feel like my soul has always known you, Elvy," I said, laughing softly at how embarrassing it sounded, but his eyes were serious.

"I burned for you the moment my eyes found yours. And tomorrow, we fight for that love we found in Saint Andrews because it—we—are not insignificant."

He turned my body so that it was flush against him, and the pitter-patter of paws growing further away indicated Jelly had made her exit.

Elvy threw up some kind of shield to keep anyone else from coming in, as he simultaneously ripped my black dress off, leaving me exposed in a matching black lacy bra and thong.

My shadows purred as his gaze went up and down my body, and I embraced them, letting them come to the surface as my flame burned brighter than the fear in my heart. Elvy's eyes were a mixture of black and gray as he balanced his shadows as I did mine.

I unbuttoned his slate-gray shirt, exposing his broad, tattooed chest, trailing my fingers down his muscled arms, covered in star tattoos. The bulge in his pants mirrored the want in my own body, and I unbuckled his belt to unzip his pants.

He grabbed my wrists, kissing me with a groan, then placed my hands against his chest as he unclasped my bra from the front, baring myself to him with the warmth of the roaring blue-green fire beside us.

It took no time at all for his mouth and fingers to elicit a gasp from me as my head leaned against the bookshelves. My fingers gripped his silver-brown curls, needing him closer to me. He obliged, nipping and flicking until my legs grew weak with need, and he became my strength in that moment as I let myself go completely.

"I love you, Zoe," he said, against my chest, and I held my breath as I came for him—for us.

He saw me through the waves of pleasure, then I pushed him to the couch, wanting to straddle him. He rolled me over instead, so that he was on his knees in front of me.

"I wasn't finished," he said, ripping my thong the rest of the way off. His eyes looked as if he intended on devouring me, and I would happily let him.

He trailed kisses down my thigh until he reached my bundle of nerves. I gasped, knowing that his fingers and mouth found me more than wanting. I made use of my own hands, creating more friction as he flicked his tongue and moved his fingers into my very own oblivion. I let my worries go and all my doubts left with them, as Elvy forced me to be present in my body—in our moment with each other.

I came for him again, moaning out his name, and I felt his smile against me.

"Elvy," I said, smiling, and I opened my eyes to find him completely nude, arousal straining with need.

"I need you, Zoe," he said, voice low, and I got on my knees for him and took control of him, letting him fill me.

He gently curled his fingers in my hair, but let me be in control of the movements as I used my hands and tongue to bring out the wilder side of Elvy. I enjoyed knowing I was the one responsible for his groans.

He pulled out of my grasp and placed me on top of him as he leaned back against the couch. He stretched me to my breaking point, but I wanted him—all of him. Elvy's eyes were full of love as he shifted inside me. I pulled his lips to mine as he cupped each side of my face, then pressed his forehead against mine.

"I love you," he murmured again, like a prayer as he continued to move inside of me, and I believed every word he said.

"I know," I said, meeting his movements.

I used his round shoulders to lift myself with him as his rhythm increased, and the sensations building could not be denied as we both cried out our pleasure, holding each other close. I listened to the beat of his heart and knew that this moment was real and that I was safe. In his arms, I always would be.

43

The Future

FREYJA

Elvy and Zoe had snuck off from the party not long ago, but we would all see each other again before the battle began, so I wouldn't go interrupt whatever they were doing.

Oleander twirled me in his arms as the music continued. It was as if no one had wanted this moment to end, and I didn't mind prolonging it either. Delmira and Blaz looked cozy in the corner, and I wouldn't be surprised if they wandered off soon by the looks they were giving each other. Clodovea and Imelda had left not long after Elvy and Zoe. Finnian stood a little stiffly next to Octavia, and I felt a little guilty that Zadie couldn't be here yet.

"Zadie and Algol's Shadowed are ready to come?" I asked, heart beating a little faster knowing how close we were to facing the battle, and I wasn't exactly a battle expert. Oleander had trained me tirelessly, but I'd never had the opportunity to really put it into practice.

"Where is that mind of yours, Freyja?" he asked, holding me close against his firm body, and I let my head lean on his chest.

"Just thinking about tomorrow," I admitted.

"Tomorrow will come. Worry about it then," he said softly, but my uncertainties did not ease.

He tried again. "Other than our impending doom, what are you thinking about?"

"That I'm a liability tomorrow," I said, voicing my fear, but maybe it didn't have to be my truth.

Ander stopped moving, tilting my chin to look into his beautiful blue eyes.

"You are not a burden, Freyja," he said firmly.

I sighed, letting him pull me from the dance floor as we began our ascent to the surface.

"I logically know that… I think," I said. "I just… things could be different. If I were strong enough… if I were selfless enough."

"What do you mean?" he asked, brows raised, and I knew I'd eventually have to tell him what Zoe had learned from Sirius.

"That I'm the answer to creating a new celestial for Algol. I'm the perfect vessel, apparently," I said, and his rigid body showed just what he thought of that idea.

"And you are considering this?"

I shook my head. "No. Though I'm glad Zoe did give me the choice… after some coaxing, of course."

I smiled at the thought, and Oleander's laugh was strained.

"I can only imagine what your sister would have done with that information."

"Totally against it, if you can believe it," I said sarcastically, then turned more serious. "I considered it for a second, maybe, but Zoe would still have to die. And… I couldn't be with you. Not like this, anyway."

I pointed to our interlaced hands just in case he wasn't sure what I was referring to, and he kissed the back of my hand gently.

"If that's what you wanted…" he said, trailing off, and I could tell he would honor my choice, but that was unacceptable to me.

"To hell with that," I said. "No more sacrificing for any of us. If we die tomorrow because we fought our best and lost, I can live with that until she claims our lives. But I can't live with knowing my sister's dead."

"As you wish, my lady," he said seriously. "And you will fight and fight well."

"I hope you're right," I said, wishing on the stars that they would lend me strength to get through tomorrow.

"You've barely scratched the surface of your gift, Freyja. Magic has a way of coming in tenfold when we need it most. You might surprise yourself tomorrow."

"I do like surprises," I said as we reached the manor and made our way to our room for what could be the end of the beginning for us or our very last night in this world.

He tightened our interlaced fingers as he led me to our room, and I couldn't help the butterflies filling my core all the way to my chest.

We were silent as we breathed each other in, as if each moment was precious and purposeful.

The moment he shut our door behind us, he swept me into his arms and sat me on the bed, kneeling before me. I didn't ask questions as he unstrapped my shoes from my aching feet.

"Rise," he said, holding a hand out for me as he stood. I obeyed.

"Turn around," he murmured, voice tight, and goosebumps filled my flesh as I did what was asked.

He brushed gentle fingers across my neck to move my hair out of the way of his target—my zipper.

Oleander ever so slowly unzipped my dress, growling in approval at the knowledge I was wearing nothing underneath.

"You are perfect, Freyja," he said, sliding his fingers down my bare back as he pulled the straps of my dress down my shoulders.

The shiver was involuntary as my body seemed to hum with pleasure.

With my dress carelessly on the floor at my feet, he turned my shoulders around to face him, and he found my body aching for him at his gaze alone. I knew if he slipped a finger down my center, he'd find out just how badly I wanted him.

I smirked at the strained bulge in his pants, knowing he very much felt the same.

He placed a soft kiss against my lips, and I arched my back into his arms as I began unbuttoning his shirt, far less gracefully than he had undressed me. It was a miracle that I could find the buttons in the first place. Eventually, I managed to get the black fabric off the statue that was his body, and he breathed a laugh against my lips.

"I love you," he said, picking me up and then setting me on the bed.

"Show me how much," I said, leaning back on my elbows, and he unbuckled his black belt with a devious smile playing on his lips.

"For the rest of my existence," he said, pulling the rest of his clothes off.

Without so much as a warning, his tongue found the most sensitive part of me, causing me to fall all the way down on the bed, but there was no way a laugh was coming out of me, as he made me feel things with those fingers and his tongue.

He slipped another finger into my drenched core, flicking in just the right spot, that I swear the room was suddenly decorated with stars. I let go of my fears of inadequacy as he worshipped me like his own personal goddess.

As pleasure built up in my core, it felt like my body was filled with ice and my skin would surely explode as he made me come for him repeatedly. On the fourth explosion of bliss in a row, my magic stirred and swirled within me, and it felt like my soul was going to burst from the very depths of me.

The moment I climaxed, I felt my projection come out of me, almost like it was a second skin instead of something separate from me.

Ander pulled back, smiling at me as if I were the most magnificent thing he'd ever seen.

"Woah," he said, hovering his hand above my skin and touching my astral form that coated me. Gently, he placed his hand along the layer of astral magic, and I felt pleasure like I'd never felt before from his touch alone.

"What the hell is that?" I asked, panting, as he continued to feel every inch of me.

"I have no idea," he admitted, but his smile was very smug about it. For once, I didn't want to bite back at him. I just needed to feel him.

He slid up against me, lining himself up so that we could be joined, and his eyes found mine. I held his blue eyes as he slid all the way in with one shift forward, and I cried out at the sensation. He laced his fingers through mine and held them against the bed as his lips explored my body while keeping his pace a torturous song I never wanted to be free from.

My astral form coated every inch of my body, and where Ander touched me felt like a vibrating explosion of pleasure. I shifted my hips, taking him even deeper as I clawed at his back, trying to adjust to the sensation of this magic.

Just as I thought I would become atomic, Ander roared his release, and I fell into euphoria with him as my spirit settled around us.

I opened my eyes to find my astral form still glittering around me, and his eyes were on mine.

"You're glowing," he said, placing a gentle kiss on my lips. "I'd like to say it's all me, but this is some part of your magic."

He slowly lifted off me, and I sat up, looking into the mirror to find the second skin coating me still.

"What do you think this is?" I asked, holding up my hand, and he circled his arms around me from behind.

Again, wherever our bodies connected, felt like a thousand lightning bolts surging through me.

"I'm not sure, sweetheart."

"Do you feel anything? When you touch me?"

"Other than the obvious, no," he admitted, kissing my neck.

"Maybe it can't hurt you because I love you," I said, and he grinned widely.

"I don't think I'll ever tire of you saying that."

"Good," I said, turning to kiss his cheek.

I closed my eyes, trying to settle my soul—my magic—and when I felt like it'd answered my call, I opened my eyes to find that it had disappeared.

"See?" Oleander mused. "You'll surprise yourself tomorrow."

I smiled, believing that to be true.

"And the day after that, too," I said, willing my heart to believe in that hope.

44

Belonging
DELMIRA

"Well, it seems like our fearless leaders have gone off to have one last good time in the sheets before we all die," I said, shrugging my shoulders.

Blaz laughed deeply, rubbing his forehead with his fingers.

"I guess you're right," he said, and much to my surprise, he didn't deliver one of his familiar lines that usually ended with us losing ourselves in the physical pleasures of life.

Instead, Blaz laced his fingers through mine, not giving one crap what I had to say about it as the rest of our legions partied the night away.

"Get some sleep!" I called, and I was met with a few noncommittal responses.

"Come on, Delm. They know what to do," Blaz said, dragging me through the city center and through the exit tunnel of Musterion.

"So, you couldn't resist one last night in my bed, huh?" I teased, bumping his shoulder once we'd cleared the lighthouse that hid Musterion from the rest of the world.

"I will always say yes to you, Delmira," he admitted, but his tone was much more serious than the typical banter between us.

"Where are you going? The manor is that way," I said, pointing to the very obvious home of ours.

"We're not going to the manor," he said evasively, and I did my best to keep my mouth shut as he led me deeper into the abandoned city. I hated how empty it felt, and it seemed even lonelier after the hustle and bustle of Musterion.

Blaz was silent, but the flutter of his eyes told me he was thinking very seriously about something. Silence had always been uncomfortable for me. I often felt the need to fill it with noise, which was usually my running mouth, but I was working on that—whatever that meant.

I wasn't ashamed of who I was. I'd kept myself and my twin alive when the worst kinds of humanity wanted nothing but our sorrow. Reminding my brain that I didn't have to be in survival mode all the time was something I was learning to do.

Aura had told me how much Zoe had helped her heal from the hell Abel had done to her. A part of me had considered asking Zoe to help me sift through some of the stuff in my head, but I hated to ask her to see the worst parts of my life while we were dealing with all this life and death. Maybe I could ask for one of those charms. She'd already given me a bracelet with her physical healing magic stored in it. She'd probably be willing to give me one for… whatever this *feeling* was that made my chest tight.

I hadn't even noticed we'd stopped walking. I was so lost in my thoughts. Blaz raised an eyebrow at me curiously and turned his head.

"What are you thinking about?" he asked, but I countered.

"Where are we?" I asked, trying to get my bearings. We were in one of the newer districts, not far from the Shadowed Legion's headquarters. It was one of the tallest buildings in Vega, and certainly one of the sleekest.

"Come on," he said, and I clearly trusted him with my life because I followed right behind him with no questions asked, though I certainly had a few dozen that I wanted to interrogate him on.

Blaz pressed his immortal mark into the building's entrance, then pressed his mark against the elevator. It pinged open for us, and he pressed it one more time, then selected the penthouse floor.

I looked at him curiously, but I think I was a little too stunned to ask anything.

The elevator dinged our arrival, and Blaz used his mark as a key one more time, and the doors opened into a phenomenal suite.

He took my hand, leading me into the modern condo with hints of lilac interwoven into the black marble stone that lined the floors and walls. The moonlight coming in through the floor to ceiling windows that faced the ocean made the stone glimmer like starlight.

The furniture was mostly black, but again, there were hints of shades of purple throughout with throw blankets, pillows, and even some kitchen appliances.

"What is this?" I asked, doing my best not to be accusatory or suspicious.

His olive skin flushed red as he scratched the back of his head.

"Well?" I asked, a smidge too forcefully.

"I want us to live here. Together," he said. "I know you like staying at the manor, but I want us to grow together, and I think a good place to start is to share our lives with each other. You know, have our own space."

I felt like a deer caught in headlights. A flurry of emotions raced through my body, and they were moving too fast for my mind to discern what they were. My mouth opened and closed over and over again like an illiterate fish.

"Delm," Blaz said. "I'm sorry. I shouldn't have sprung this on you," he said, pulling on my arm to lead me out of the beautiful condo.

"Just give me a minute," I said, planting my feet firmly in place. Blaz dropped my arm, doing as I asked.

I walked over to the window, looking out at the ocean. It was a beautiful view of the city and the bay. The twinkle of the moonstone manor seemed to wink at me against the darkness surrounding it. The lighthouse was just beyond it, and I couldn't help but smile at both of those buildings that represented some of the most important people and moments of my life.

"You decorated this place for us?" I asked.

Blaz circled his arms around me, leaning his head against my shoulder.

"I did," he admitted. "The immortal who lived here has decided to stay in Musterion after the battle."

"And it came custom with my signature colors?" I prompted.

"I may or may not have been working on getting it renovated," he said, kissing my neck.

He twirled me around, pressing me up against the glass.

"So what do you say?" he asked, voice cracking slightly. Hell, it was a vulnerable question to ask, and it certainly did him favors that he had the balls to ask it.

"Okay," I said, smiling. "If we don't die tomorrow, I'll move in with you."

His face broke into the biggest grin I'd ever seen on him, as he pulled me into a dance to a song that only he could hear. He hauled me into his lap as he sat us on the couch, and I felt… peace as I embraced the surrounding quiet in this moment.

"Can I ask you another question?" Blaz asked, turning my chin so that I would meet his gaze.

"If you're going to ask me to marry you, let's slow the hell down," I joked, though it wouldn't be totally out of the question later on down the road.

Blaz laughed heartily, and I relaxed, knowing he saw the humor in it, too.

"What were you thinking about out there? Before we came into the building. You seemed to really have something on your mind."

"We have a lot going on," I said, the deflection coming so quickly and naturally that I didn't have time to decide whether I wanted to be truthful or not.

"You don't have to tell me if you don't want to, Delm," he said, holding me closer. "But I want to be a partner to you. In all things. If you want me to."

I nodded my head because I wanted that. I just didn't know the ins and outs of how the hell that was supposed to look.

"I was thinking about Aura," I admitted, and the surprise on his face almost made me laugh.

"In what way?" he asked, and I could tell he was desperately trying to remain open-minded.

"I was thinking that Zoe has helped her with the stuff she's been through. You know, with Abel. And I was thinking that maybe Zoe could help me, too."

By some act of the stars, I didn't hide from Blaz. I didn't make myself small in embarrassment, and he did not meet me with sympathy but with a deep understanding.

"Have you talked to her about it?" he asked.

"Not yet," I admitted. "I hadn't really thought about it much with everything going on."

"I'm sure she would help you right now if you asked her," he encouraged.

"I'm sure our Lord and Lady Astral are otherwise occupied at the moment," I said, laughing, and he joined in, too. "But I will ask her, I think. When this is all over."

"I can go with you if you want," he said, tucking my head underneath his chin, sending soothing touches to my very soul as he trailed his fingers down my back.

"I think I'd like that."

We stayed like that until our bodies grew stiff, and he spread us along the black couch, sinking into the luxurious cushion that felt like it had been formed for every ache my body usually felt when lying down. To my surprise, we didn't jump each other, but the moment felt intimate all on its own.

We held each other all night until we eventually lulled ourselves into a deep sleep with the cosmos shining down on us in one last night of peaceful dreams.

45

No Regrets
CLODOVEA

My wife led me away from the rest of Musterion and into our secret garden, hidden within the forest of the secret city.

The fairy lights were lit, and pillows and blankets were sprawled out, as if ready to welcome us.

I lay down on the cushions, pulling Imelda close to me as we both gazed at the cosmos shining through the ocean waters. Every now and then, I'd catch a glimpse of a hippocampus or other varying sea creature. The marine life seemed to prepare for their very own battle, and I wouldn't mind seeing a few sharks go to town on some of Hesperia's followers.

I trailed a hand down Imelda's arm, humming a song that had gotten stuck in my head recently.

"I love it when you sing," she said, pulling me from my thoughts.

"I'm not singing," I said, laughing and kissing the top of her head. "But thank you."

"Tiergan seems very affectionate towards you," she said, as we continued to watch our own personal aquarium.

"And I am fond of him," I admitted. "And my heart breaks for him all the same. You know… he's lost everything. His star. His lover…"

"And he's gained a new family, too," Imelda said seriously. "He's one of us now."

I smiled, believing that with every bit of my being.

"Think he'll find his happiness in the end?"

"I do," she said firmly, wrapping both arms around my waist.

"We've lived a lot of life, you and I," I said, twirling one of her curls in my fingers.

"We have."

"Any regrets?" I asked.

She paused, truly thinking about the question, and I pondered the thought myself, knowing we were on the cusp of life and death. We could go on living after tomorrow, or we could not, depending on which way fate swung in our favor. But now I could go into the future, knowing that I would have Imelda as my wife—in this life or the next.

"No regrets," she said after taking stock of the life she's lived. "Not one. Not to say I haven't made mistakes. Hell, we all have. But every choice we make leads us into the next moment of our lives, you know? Changing even one of those moments could change the overall outcome of who we are and where we go. So, no. I wouldn't change a single thing, in all honesty."

I held her closer, forming our bodies together, just embracing each other in this moment.

"I choose you every moment from now until death claims us," I said. "If we die tomorrow, I die with no regrets about that."

I had chosen love over fear, and I believed that had to count for something.

"Would it be crazy if we built a little house out here in the woods?" Imelda asked, sitting up to survey our surroundings better.

She pointed to a clearing surrounded by wildflowers that honestly seemed to beg for a small home. I'd always loved the magic of Rigil and would enjoy a home that had some of their beautiful magic.

"I'm sure Elvy and Zoe would approve," I said, beaming at the future that could be. Smiling children around us and Imelda by my side. I kept the thoughts to myself, but I knew in my heart Imelda would be a wonderful mother. I craved more than anything to raise a family with her.

This was a future that deserved my fight, and I would honor that.

Imelda and I spent the next few hours talking about our hopes and dreams for the future, choosing to believe there would be those things to look forward to after tomorrow. I refused to let Hesperia have authority over what I gave power to.

Tomorrow, we will send her ashes back to the stars, and Zoe will restore harmony to the star realms.

I choose to believe in that.

46

Song of Hope
ZOE

The coffee cup was almost too hot to hold, but I welcomed the sensation of feeling alive.

The warm liquid warmed my core, and I sighed with contentment on the balcony attached to our suite.

Jelly sat next to me, gazing out across the ocean with me.

"I will protect you today," she murmured through our simargl brand.

"And I've got your back, my good girl," I said, kneeling next to her so that we were at eye level. "Thank you. For all that you have done for me."

"It has been an honor," she answered, leaning into my palm.

Seeing her perish was not a future I would accept. I leaned my forehead against hers as I let her ground me to the here and now. The battle would be here within a few hours, and I had no idea if we'd have another quiet moment in this life.

So I embraced her, and the weight of her head on my shoulder filled me with the warmth and comfort of a companion that has been by my side through my darkest times. She was my light when I couldn't find the will to ignite the hearth within me.

"Until the end," I swore, as tears pricked my eyes. "We will fight for and with each other, little dragon."

And I knew in my heart that was true. If one of us met death today, neither of our hearts could bear it.

"What a beautiful view," Elvy said, and we both turned to find him leaning against the doorway with a cup of tea in his hand. "My girls."

I motioned for him to come sit with us on the lounger, and he encircled us both in his arms. This little family of mine was precious to me, and my heart ached at the evil that threatened to take it away from me. This all felt so needless. Yet, as I hoped for things to be different, I knew that was frivolous. They weren't different now, but when this was over, I would make sure immortals and mortals alike had a place to heal. Be it from this war or other things in life… we all had something hidden within us that needed a little light.

And I would burn for them.

I shook my thoughts away, tucking them elsewhere for safekeeping when I could afford to dream again.

"It'd be nice if we could use your death magic. Just end them all with a nod of your head," I mused, sipping another deep gulp of coffee. Nothing like a little death to go with this brew.

He kissed the top of my forehead, amused.

"Unfortunately, all of my training from my family has been about hiding this power. Not honing it. To let it loose around all of you… too unpredictable. I wouldn't be able to control who I killed or who I saved."

Of course, I knew that already, but a girl could still dream.

"We'll win this," I said. "And when it's all said and done, no more hiding who we are."

Elvy responded by pulling us both closer, as we sat in silence, listening to the waves crash along the shoreline.

This was real. And we would make it safe again.

***

Elvy zipped up my fighting leathers, and I double-checked that his were secure, too.

I fixed my knives across my chest, counting each hilt to make sure they were all there. Then, my flame attached my bow across my back, along with a large supply of arrows.

"Do we need any of these?" he asked, motioning towards the arrows The Archer had given me.

I leaned into my *sight,* trying to find the answer, only to be greeted with blurry visions and intentions I couldn't read. However, my gut seemed to scream at me, and I listened to its call. I wanted my father with me today, so I would adorn both his bow and the first arrow he'd led me to in Algol. They were proof that the stars believed in me, and I wanted to believe in them, too. Healing Algol had been my first mission in healing the realms. It was only fitting to come full circle.

We'd finally come to the end of the beginning.

"That one," I said, and he nodded, sliding it securely in with the rest of the arrows. I tossed my magic around them to ensure they stayed in place.

I examined my reflection in the mirror, scrutinizing myself. My hair was in a tight braid to keep it out of the way. I looked strong and ready for anything, though internally, I didn't quite match that feeling. However, what was coming was coming, and I would face my big sister for the last time. One of us was going to die tonight. No more running. No more sacrificing.

Elvy joined me in the mirror. His hair was pulled back in a tight bun, though his curls didn't let it smooth down much. His sword was across his back, and his hidden knives were fixed in place with his uniform.

"Ready?" he asked, and I took one beat to breathe deeply.

"I'm ready," I said, closing my eyes, meaning it. "She'll be here in exactly one hour."

Elvy nodded, sending the message to Delmira and then to the other Luminaries through the iris. Everyone had their place, and the other courts would be joining us at just the right moment.

Jelly joined us in the mirror, wings out but not lit with her simargl flames yet.

"Together," she said through our bond.

"Together," I agreed, patting her on the head. I just prayed I wasn't leading her to her death.

"Come on," Elvy said. "We've got to meet the others."

I nodded, letting him lace his fingers in mine as I mentally said goodbye to the four walls that had become my safe space in a realm that had once felt foreign. In this room, I'd shattered. I'd healed here, too. Perhaps more importantly, I'd embraced my destiny here. Now it was time to go meet it head-on.

★★★

We made our way to the beach that was connected to the manor as the rest of the Luminaries joined us, along with Tiergan, Oleander, and Freyja. I cared about every soul that stood around me, and I prayed to the cosmos that we would prevail today. We'd earned it.

"Report," Elvy said, nodding towards Delm.

"With Zoe's knowledge, we are confident in saying that Hesperia will use the transport zone on the island across the bay," she said, pointing to the small spit of land that would hopefully give us a slight advantage against Hesperia. "It won't hold her long, but with the mounts, we should be able to take out many of her legion. We have a feeling the kelpie without riders will drag them down to depths we don't even know about."

"Effective," I commented, and she nodded.

"Their disadvantage in the water is too great," Blaz confirmed. "But this won't give us much of an advantage against those who can fly."

"Which is the majority of her legion," Clodovea added. "Aura sent in the final report this morning."

Delmira nodded, having already received them from her. "It will be ideal if we can force their flying legion down and within range of our fighters positioned in the water."

"I will be on the front here," Blaz said, motioning to the beach around us.

"Oleander and Tiergan, we'd like you to be in the city when your legion arrives with Zadie. She doesn't know about Musterion. We anticipate she'll send shadows into the city at the very least."

"Be prepared that her shadows will seek more unwilling victims. She'll search for them in the city first," Elvy said.

Oleander nodded, not arguing in the slightest.

"The dragons will keep them busy in the air," Blaz added.

"Along with the phoenixes and hippogriff riders," Clodovea nodded.

"The air will mean their death," Delmira said, smiling viciously. "They will be forced to move the fight to land fairly quickly."

"And Rigil will enter through this transport zone, giving us an advantage here at the front," Blaz said, pointing off into the distance.

"And where will you be?" I asked.

"Where I'm needed," Delmira said. "Making adjustments where called for."

I nodded. Elvy and I knew our job already. End Hesperia.

"Imelda and I will be defending the entrance to Musterion. We won't let anyone get close," Clodovea said.

Imelda nodded her agreement.

"And where do you need me?" Freyja asked.

My *sight* flooded me as our decisions solidified more. I was able to *see* more clearly.

"You're with Oleander," I said. I didn't know her exact role, but I knew that it was vital that she was with him.

"And I'll be with you," June said, armed to the teeth with weapons stuffed in every spot available to her. It was still odd to see past the visual image of her being a sweet old lady.

"And me," Finn said, and I leaned into my gift more, trying to *see* the outcome, but the fates were not so generous as to tell me which side of the war would be won this night.

"Sure you can keep up, kid?" June asked, smirking towards Finnian.

"We'll see who is keeping up with whom," he said, giving her a quick squeeze.

I bowed, looking around at each of those I loved, then surveyed the playing field around us.

"This is it," I said. "The moment we have fought and bled for so that I could fulfill the prophecy I did not ask for. But none of us asked for this, yet each of us answered the impossible call the stars demanded of us. You all came to find me that day in Saint Andrews. Every moment since then has led us to right here. Right now. I've lived an entire lifetime since that day. And I fight for the lifetime waiting for each of us after this battle has been won and our victory has been claimed. You are my family. And I choose to believe in us. I choose each of you over fear, doubt, and any 'what if.' And I know you choose me, too."

I laced my fingers through Elvy's and Freyja's hands.

"I love you all," I said. "And I'm so thankful I chose to embrace this remarkable life as Realm-Healer—Emerging of Legends. More importantly, I am grateful for the family I have found in each of you. It's greater than I could have ever dreamed. What I know to be true is that this moment will pass. And I pray to see each of you on the other side of it."

My eyes heated with tears that I let fall. I wasn't trying to hide how I felt about any of them, and I was not ashamed for them to know I cared about them.

"We love you, too," Freyja said, squeezing my hand as she reached out to Oleander.

He grabbed hers and my heart warmed as he reached out to Tiergan's, who welcomed him.

One by one, we all embraced each other until we formed a circle around the beach that would soon be stained red with the blood of our enemies—with the hue of death. I didn't want to lose a soul who was part of this family now, but there was no guarantee we would all make it out of here alive. Each of us was willing to take that chance. For the good of the many.

I bowed my head, casting my healing magic into each of their pendants, sending them what help I could in their fights to come. I had given Freyja, Oleander, June, and Tiergan their own charms last night in an effort to keep them as safe as I possibly could.

"For the heart of the new moon," I said, peering at the moon and then at each of them.

"And the life in the starlight," Elvy said, and the rest echoed the sentiment.

"Get into your positions," I said, taking a deep breath. "She's coming."

They bowed, and I watched the backs of those I would not be fighting alongside. I prayed to the stars that they were quick-thinking, present-focused, and trusted their instincts to do what they had been trained to do. Worrying about them would not serve them in this moment. I could only worry about my big sister, whose time in these realms had come to an end.

Sirius had told me that I was meant to bring life into this world, but I knew I'd have to kill the poison first for life to flourish. I would have to become her death-bringer in whatever way fate called me to be.

47

Clockwork
DELMIRA

Calm. That was the only emotion I allowed to enter my mind. Embracing any other feeling would be futile and result in my or someone else's death.

I couldn't question whether Blaz would make it out of this final battle alive. I had to trust him and our legion to fight ruthlessly and without mercy. The way Blaz had trained us.

My eyes focused on the island where Hesperia's legion would enter to wreak hell on Vega. The stars and moon provided enough light that I could make out the bobbing heads of the hippocampi and some of the kelpie with their riders. Any who dared to cross via water would swiftly meet their end. The kelpie were a little more difficult to see with a darker green skin, but occasionally I caught a glance of their cruel red eyes. Still, their desire to fight for Vega was evident now.

Swirling lights of green formed on the beach, indicating that Rigil was entering their designated transport zone. They would be on the front lines with Blaz. Behind me, I could barely make out an unnatural darkness coming from the city, which should be Tiergan's forces arriving, along with Oleander's Shadowed.

I grinned, my spirit ready to spill blood.

The dragons of Arcturus and the phoenixes and hippogriffs of Canopus would arrive at the opportune moment. We'd wait to give the signal until Hesperia's Shadowed took flight across the ocean. We did not know how large their numbers were for certain, but with her magic no longer holding Elvy, we feared the worst.

This also meant we'd be spilling innocent blood this night. There would be citizens of Canopus who were fighting for Hesperia against their will, yet they would die anyway. I tried to take solace in the fact that their sacrifice would not be in vain. We would honor their deaths by ensuring their puppet master met her end.

A swirl of the cosmos glowed brightly at the center of the island.

She was here, and my immortal eyes grew wide as I took in the sheer number of her forces. She had hidden them well.

"Steady," I whispered, eyes glancing at Blaz below me. He was moving his battalions into position.

It was so quiet, as we collectively held our breath as one.

One.

Two.

Three.

Hesperia's winged legion took flight, and I was on the balls of my feet as I waited for our flying legions to descend upon them.

"Just a bit longer," I breathed, eyes narrowing. We didn't want to give them the opportunity to escape. They all needed to be out on the open water so we could attack them from below and above.

"Now," I whispered, and though they could not hear me, I heard a dragon's roar.

Like a flaming moon goddess astride a midnight dragon, Seraphina descended on Hesperia's legion, burning all in her path. Kai was right behind her on his massive brown beast with another six dragons in tow.

I took a little joy in the screams that followed their dragon's breath.

Hesperia's legion startled only for a moment before one section turned their focus on the dragons and the rest flew faster towards us. I gripped my sword, ready to strike true.

"Now," I mumbled again, and Aura entered through the swirling cosmos, leading her hidden army of phoenixes and hippogriffs, screeching their battle cry.

It was chaos, and I relished the cries.

Air users controlled the wind, slowing down those trying to escape the air assault.

The flying mounts forced Hesperia's legion to fly closer to the water, which proved just as lethal as Vega water magic erupted. Wild kelpie latched onto their victims and disappeared beneath the surface long enough to drown their victims before reappearing to take down another.

The riders of the hippocampi were more creative with their magic, using their gift to create walls of the ocean to block them in their path. Other wielders sent spears of ice into the hearts of their enemies, effectively ending them. One Vega rider and one mount from Canopus created a vortex of wind and water, sucking away Hesperia's flying legion to the depths of the ocean.

It was a beautiful sight, and I wished I could watch the brilliance all night.

But my hand was feeling a little twitchy to shed some blood.

Despite the incredible efforts of our court and our allies, many of Hesperia's legions got through and were moments away from breaching the beach where Blaz, Zoe, Jelly, June, Finnian, and Elvy waited, along with Sierra and Terran of Rigil.

The moment our enemies set foot on the beach, the legions of Rigil and Vega moved to the offense.

Hesperia was nowhere in sight, and I prayed that would not distract Zoe. Silver gleamed through the air as Zoe fatally flung her knives into those stupid enough to attack her, but I could tell she held back only slightly, trying to reserve her strength for Hesperia.

She was efficient in picking up the arrows she shot and the knives she threw from the corpses that met their death at her hands. What a warrior she had become.

Jelly's flames surrounded her, effectively distracting our enemies to make easy prey for the blade of Elvy's sword.

It was a smart tactic on Hesperia's part. Send her forces first to tire us out while she remained strong, though I hoped her use of the shadows on those of Canopus weakened her some.

I hovered above, trying to find our opponent's strategy as they moved in further up the beach. There didn't seem to be much of a rhyme or reason to their formation. There was no trident formation or some semblance of a plan to attack us. It was utter chaos. Hesperia's favorite flavor. It had its pros and cons.

Blaz was at the very front of the line, which was in no way a surprise. He fought gracefully with a skill that only centuries of mastery could convey in the way that he did. He used his water magic to drown his victims as he simultaneously sliced into their necks—his favored lethal blow.

My twin may have preferred books over the blade, but that did not mean he didn't know how to wield a weapon with as much perfection as myself. He and June worked together, swiftly felling foes with quick moves and glorious magic. Finn was an excellent strategist, using his gift to read the moves of his opponents before they made them. Perhaps that's why he didn't care for battle. He found it too mundane.

It was time to join the fight.

I was about to descend to the beach when I noticed a scattering of enemies heading towards the city center. Some diverted to the lighthouse, others to the heart of the city with shadows following them.

Oleander, Freyja, and Tiergan could handle the city, so I hastened to the lighthouse to back up Clodovea and Imelda.

Evander and his squad were stationed there with them, and I trusted the captain with my life. However, letting anyone get through to Musterion was unacceptable.

I flew hard and fast, eyes promising death to all who waited there.

48

Beyond

FREYJA

Oleander perked up, a sign that his magical tripwire had been activated.

He nodded to Tiergan and Zadie, and they all readied themselves for a fight. Ander cast out his magic, getting a feel for what was coming.

"At least five hundred by my count," Oleander said, and Tiergan nodded.

"I was hoping for an actual challenge," Tiergan said, grinning, mustache and all. I'd never seen him look so… cruel. He'd proven to be a kind male with a heart of gold. I was certain he took no pleasure in taking life, but perhaps today he did so with justice for Janus in mind. Today would be his late lover's victory, just as much as ours.

"Let them come," Oleander breathed.

Zadie stood beside a male I'd come to know as James. Ander had told me what had happened between him and Zoe, and my heart had broken for the male. It seemed no ill will had been with James towards my sister, though Oleander said they hadn't had a chance to mend their bridges yet.

It tugged at the heartstrings to know that he was ready to fight again after all he'd already endured. He was the definition of resilience.

We did not hide inside the buildings. We made our presence known in the city center. Whether Hesperia's legion questioned that was not our concern. We only needed to keep their eyes away from the lighthouse. Providing a distraction was the least of the sacrifices we were all willing to give to keep Hesperia away from Musterion.

My nerves were surprisingly calm, despite never having been in battle. I believed in what we fought for, and as much as I wanted to live… I wasn't afraid to die for someone I loved. I'd done it before, and I would do it again if that's what the fates demanded of me.

Sirius was on our side, and I took comfort in knowing that. He desired to see his child saved despite the wretched thing Algol had become without their connection to the balance of having all five stars commune as one. I feared that the other celestials would become just as corrupted if Zoe never gets the chance to bind them all back together again. Hesperia had sped up the process for Algol, and a small part of me recognized that they were not entirely themselves.

I had been chosen by Algol with the help of Vega. I had to believe that the spirit element and its celestial could be purified to what Sirius had always intended with his child. Hell, I was the perfect vessel for a celestial, which couldn't be possible without Sirius. I felt the swell of power lurking within me. This battle was my chance to harness it… I just had to figure out how to embrace the potential my magic held.

"Sixty seconds," Oleander called, and the muscles in my gut and calves tensed, ready to pounce.

I squeezed Ander's hand. "I love you. Beyond the end."

He looked at me with so much love in his eyes that I knew he understood what I meant. In this lifetime or the next, he was the one my soul would always find. Beyond the end.

And really… did the end exist? I had my doubts that the end was something so finite. No, souls—love—was much more complicated than that.

"I love you, too, Freyja," he whispered, then turned his icy blue eyes on our target.

A storm of winged Shadowed Legion descended on us, with Hesperia's shadows following them.

Oleander cast out his shield, but he made certain sections of it permeable with the intention of controlling the flow of the legion, making it easier to pick them off one by one.

Snarls of anger met us as our enemies hit the wall of magic, and the shadows crawled over the barrier, trying to find its weakness. It didn't take long for Hesperia's magic to find the three entry points Oleander had delicately crafted.

The Sublunary unsheathed their weapons in unison and followed Tiergan into our battle front, viciously tearing away at those who would dare cross. Hesperia was nowhere to be found, despite her shadows slithering in every crevice they could find.

They were searching…

"What are they looking for?" I asked, as Oleander continued to hold the shield for his legion and Tiergan's to slaughter any who were brave enough to breach it.

"I'd imagine she is looking for innocents to slay or control to fight for her."

"And if she doesn't find some?"

"Then there's a chance she'll go searching where we don't want her to,"

"Not good," I said, running a hand down my braid.

I looked around at the carnage, and the shadows seemed to get more frantic—desperate—in their search.

"I swore there would be no more sacrificing," I said, a sudden anger overtaking me, and I embraced it, letting the feeling guide me.

Ander was drenched in sweat at the control he wielded over our strategic barrier and the shield protecting us.

I refused to be useless.

"What's in that head of yours, sweetheart?" he asked through labored breaths.

"That I'll give the shadows something to find," I said,

"We can't beat the shadows," he said, eyes going a little wild at what fresh hell I was about to put him through.

"We don't need to beat them. We need to distract Hesperia. Let's make her think she's caught something worth stopping this maddening search."

I eyed our surroundings as I dove deeper into the well of my gift, trying to understand the power of spirit.

Closing my eyes, I called my astral projection forth, conjuring her to my will. She manifested beside me, and I willed her to take my form in this moment, becoming as real as I felt.

"This is a very bad idea," Ander said, still casting his magic against all odds.

"This will stop the shadows from finding Musterion. They'll take my projection."

"I don't like it," he admitted. "But it's your call."

"This will work, and it will save more of us from becoming her spawn."

He pressed his lips into a thin line, but nodded.

"Just keep silent," I whispered to my projection form, and she seemed to nod in understanding. I felt a little guilty sending her off on this mission, but I knew she'd return to me. I'd never sent her off like this before. In the past, I'd embraced her form, and I was a little worried about controlling her without doing that.

She raised her hand to touch my temple, and I heard her words in my mind.

"It's your magic. We answer to you. You need only ask."

It took everything that I possessed not to startle at my magic *talking* to me. I quickly shook the thought from me, unable to process that just now.

"Let the shadows take you. Make her think you're really me."

The projection nodded, answering the demand of my gift.

Perhaps my magic wanted to fight for justice just as badly as I did.

I nodded to Oleander, and he slowly removed the protective magic around my projection. It took only seconds for the shadows to envelop her before she was completely consumed in the chaos of Hesperia's magic.

When I opened my eyes again, the shadows and my projection were gone, but the battle still raged on.

I quickly sent a missive to Zoe, but I had no idea if she'd get it. I prayed to the stars to let her *sight* see true.

49

The Last Stand
CLODOVEA

They'd found us a little too quickly for comfort, but thankfully, Hesperia's shadows had gone into the city. For the sake of all those in Musterion, I prayed they did not come this way. I wasn't entirely sure what kind of defense we would be able to hold against that kind of magic.

We hadn't anticipated they would attack us so soon, yet Hesperia's legion came swiftly and efficiently towards us.

I glanced towards Imelda, and no words passed between us. They didn't need to. We fought for what was, who we were, and who we would be tomorrow.

"No one gets past us," I said, voice steady as I raised my sword.

"Agreed," she said, lifting her double blades.

Evander and his squad readied themselves beside us. I was happy to have them by my side. He'd always been an honorable male with skills nearly as lethal as my own, though I had a couple of centuries on him. I wouldn't be surprised if he surpassed me in the years to come.

And they would come.

My sword slashed through the first of Hesperia's legion like butter. I barely registered the cries of the wounded. My mind was solely focused on the enemy in front of me.

Being in Vega allowed our magic to flow easily to us, and my magic hummed to unleash itself on those who threatened our sacred star.

I called upon my water magic to freeze the oncoming flying legion's wings, forcing them to the ground. Unfortunately, merely falling from the sky did not prove fatal to immortals, but it still hurt like hell.

Imelda cast her water magic along the ground, and I called on my gift to freeze it over, making the terrain far more difficult to navigate for those unaccustomed to the ways of water magic.

Evander used the ice already on the ground to call spikes forth, impaling some of the immortals who fell for the trap.

Those fighting for Vega easily crossed the icy barrier, beheading Hesperia's fighters with a stroke of their swords.

I kicked a knife from one of our enemies, catching the soaring weapon in my hand with a gleam in my eye.

He paled at the grin that spread across my face as I sent his very own blade through his eye socket.

"Novice," I muttered, snatching the knife from his very dead corpse and slung it into my next victim as Imelda distracted her.

We made a killer team—quite literally.

A shout of pain came from behind me, and I whirled around to find Evander on the wrong end of a sword. The soldier holding the hilt twisted in viciously, making Evander's mouth spill blood.

Before I had time to end him myself, one of Evander's Shadowed killed him swiftly.

Imelda and I were both the best healers here, though we paled in comparison to Zoe, but we had to try.

"Keep them busy!" I shouted, and Evander's squad needed no further command from me to begin their onslaught of killing again.

I cradled him in my arms, pulsing my Vega's given healing magic through him. My skills weren't much better than a standard Shadowed medic, but Imelda sent her gift into him as well, doing what she could.

"Fuck," he murmured, clutching his side, eyes going wide.

"I've got you," I said, but I saw the light fading from him.

"I don't think you do," he said, and I jostled him to keep him from closing his eyes.

His wound had stitched together some, but it definitely wasn't in good shape.

Through the blood on my hands, I noticed the gleam of Zoe's pendant glowing beneath the light of the moon.

Perhaps life really was in the stars.

I ripped it from my wrist without a second thought and placed it in Evander's hand, holding his fist for him.

"Live," I demanded, and he breathed a sigh of relief as he took his first unlabored breath as Zoe's magic flooded through him.

"Hell, that hurts," he mumbled, sitting upright.

"You'll live," Imelda said, laughing softly, and we all looked at each other in a bit of disbelief.

"Thanks to you," Evander said, but I shook my head.

"Thanks to Zoe," I corrected, motioning to the pendant that had saved his life.

Imelda seemed relieved that Evander would be okay, but her eyes widened at the realization that I no longer had Zoe's protection. I prayed I wouldn't need it or Zoe could replenish the magic before we'd need it again.

"Are you okay?" shouted one of Evander's fighters as he ran towards us.

A brief glance around the battlefield indicated they had killed the immediate threat, but more were flying our way in the distance.

"I'll be alright," he said, standing on shaky feet.

"There are more coming. What are our orders?"

"We continuing protecting Musterion until we are told otherwise," I said, wiping the blood from my sword.

50

Time

ZOE

Blood coated my midnight-blue leathers, turning them a shade of deep purple.

Most of my knives were gone, and the few that remained sliced their way through the heart of the victim or follower of Hesperia. I didn't have time to wonder if this immortal had accepted Hesperia willingly or if she'd forced their bodies into this battle against their will. I simply had to keep going until she was ready to face me. Because I would be ready. No matter when that time came.

I glanced towards the island she took refuge in as dragon fire and the flames of the phoenix lit up the night sky. Though the screams of victory and sorrow filled the air around me, I could not hear them. It was as if there was something drowning it all out.

In the span of a few seconds, but after what felt like an hour, I took in that Elvy was bleeding from a cut on his brow. Jelly's snout was stained red, and Blaz was just to the right of my line of sight. Finn and June stayed close to my back, working in tandem with each other.

I'd noticed Hesperia's shadows heading towards the heart of the city as we'd predicted, but they'd disappeared not long after. My stomach swelled with discernment, and I leaned into my gift, trying to listen to the songs of fate once more.

I received flashes of Freyja and Oleander, but couldn't make out what was going on. No sense of dread came with the *sight*, and I had to trust in that. I pulled out the broken iris from one of the larger pockets strapped around my waist. It must have cracked in battle, leaving my communication vulnerable with the others.

I refocused on the battle, committed to concentrating on what I had control over—my magic and my weapons.

For every enemy we took down, two more seemed to take their place.

How many more lives were we to take before Hesperia showed herself? The transport zones had been locked down. She would not escape Vega. She would either leave this realm as stardust or as the victor. There was no other option.

An opening in the cosmos caught my attention, and fear initially entered my heart that Hesperia had summoned even more rein-forcements. A grin spread across my face as I saw familiar faces and Jelly howled as a pack of simargls soared across the sky with death in their eyes and flames in their wings. Tala and Skoll led them with King Aldrich and Queen Farron flying behind them with a legion of the High Astral Shadowed.

They'd come.

I felt the spirits of those fighting with me lift as the simargls touched down and our monarchs fought with lethal precision.

Tala and Skoll fought their way to us, and Jelly bowed her head in reverence to them.

"You've fought well, sister," Skoll said, black eyes on Jelly.

"Not a pup," she said, and the gore covering her fur was certainly evidence of that.

"Where do you need us?" Tala asked.

I quickly thought through our most vulnerable points.

"The lighthouse. Clodovea and Imelda will tell you what to do."

They bowed and howled for their pack to follow them. Aldrich and Farron had swiftly moved into fighting on the front with ease. They saw where the biggest threat lay and set their blades upon it.

My eyes glanced back to the island, and my heart stilled when I finally saw her.

Her eyes were completely black and wild as ever. Power radiated from her, like the swells of a tsunami.

"Come out, little mouse," I said, finding her eyes in the storm of blood and death.

She grinned.

The songs of fate sang their crescendo, knowing that the course of the universe would be changed forever by what came next. Time stood still as I beckoned her to me, and she swirled her shadows around her, and I braced for impact.

In what felt like three seconds, she stood before me, hair flailing around as if electricity were all around her.

I pointed a death promise at her, and she nodded slightly as if she was ready for this fight as much as I was.

The Archer's constellation grew so bright in the sky, I couldn't help but look at it. As did everyone else, apparently, as I became aware of the true silence that surrounded me. The legions had stopped fighting as Hesperia and I faced each other.

My heart sank at the dead immortals around me. So much death. So many innocent lives who had died fighting for the cause they believed in. Even more immortals who perished fighting for something they did not believe in—Hesperia. I grieved to see the amount of Vega's and Rigil's fighting leathers lying around me.

Sierra and Terran stood close by, just as covered in blood as the rest of us. They both rode astride their horses. Damek shimmered in the starlight with the amount of blood on his midnight coat.

Rage clouded my eyes, but I knew anger was nothing more than an emotion to hide behind. Elvy had seen my grief at a time I could only see my rage. Now... my heart overflowed with grief. Would I let it forge my fury or my grace?

I turned to Hesperia.

"You don't have to go through with this, sister," I said, not pitching my voice any higher than what she needed to hear me by.

I stretched out my hand, letting my well of power build. Oleander had once said my magic could pause the hearts of those with ill intent, but that didn't mean I could control what they chose to do with it.

And there was only a minuscule part of me that thought my big sister was capable of being saved. This moment was nothing more than a distraction.

Because I had a secret. One even Elvy did not know.

"Don't tell me you beg for my mercy here at the end, little sister," she purred. "I didn't mark you as weak."

I smiled, laughing softly. A metallic taste entered my mouth with the amount of blood covering me. I spat it out at her feet.

"I am not the one who has been hiding behind my forces," I said, motioning to the death around me.

I clenched my right hand, calling on the source of power that attached me to Algol. I would not give the celestial much of a choice in giving me every ounce of magic I required for the insanity I was about to pull.

Farron and Aldrich now stood to the side of me, fresh bruises already forming across their exposed skin. They were diplomats, yes. But they would do what was right for the good of those they served, even when they disagreed with the laws that made that difficult at times. The fact that they were here at all was evidence of that.

"The High Astral Council finally gave in?" I murmured, smirking at them.

"Not exactly," Farron said, eyes twinkling with battle lust. "But Aldrich and I refused to be on the wrong side of history this day. We are happy to fight under your command."

I nodded in understanding. This was our turf—our battle. They would follow where necessary. I turned back to Hesperia.

"Hail, the true sovereigns of the star realms," I said. "Leaders who are just and serve those under their command without hate in their hearts."

Hesperia sneered at my call out.

"My legion is happy to sacrifice on my behalf. It is a shame yours would not do the same," Hesperia said.

I snorted again.

"Yet, so many of your legion are here against their will. Like lambs gone to an unwilling slaughter. For a god they don't even believe in."

Hesperia scoffed.

"That is why I am here to guide them. Sheep don't know who should be their shepherd."

"You're still preaching that delusion?" I asked quietly. "I'm impressed with the way your tongue spouts such pretty lies."

I kept descending into my power, knowing I would need it all to do what I must. It would not kill Hesperia, but it would buy me time—and a diversion. But more than that, it would give those who had fallen justice. And I was happy to grant them this last gift.

"Enough talking," she said, raising her hands, making the shadows slither towards us.

"You're right," I said, leaning into the shadows that lived within me, embracing the cruel creature they could mold me into.

I knelt down to the ground, and Hesperia perked an eyebrow, almost seeming pleased. Did she actually think that I would bow to her? She truly was delusional.

I sent my magic out to those who had fallen, calling their spirits back to me—to this plane of existence.

Because I was of both Algol and Vega, and the only immortal in existence with the power to call death forward to the realm beyond the *inbetween.*

I knew only those with the gift of seeing spirits from Algol could understand what was happening, and I enjoyed the horror that filled their eyes as they saw hundreds of spirits rise from their corpses.

"Rise!" I shouted, amplifying my voice, and I saw a hint of nerves shining through Hesperia's wild smile. Those she had forced to die for her glared at her with a vehemence I couldn't hope to replicate. "Fight for the peace of the star realms. Fight for those who would perish under Hesperia. Fight so that others may live to see the rising of the morning moon!"

Their war-cry answered my call. They would fight. One. Last. Time.

Liam came into my view and gave me a low bow. It was because of him that I learned to wield this power, and I was glad to give him this gift. Liam's life had mattered, but his death would have meaning, too.

As one, the spirits of those who had fallen in battle descended on the legions of Hesperia like a swarm of vengeance.

"Now the fight really begins," I said, shooting an arrow into the next victim.

Hesperia's smile faltered only slightly, as if she had one last card to pull from her sleeve.

Perhaps she did. Perhaps she didn't.

Either way, she would meet her end this night.

51

I refuse

DELMIRA

All I could see was the surprise on Blaz's face as the sword sliced through his abdomen.

Nothing else mattered.

I raced towards Blaz with fire in my heart. Not him. Not Blaz. This world was so much better with his light.

My soul pleaded with the stars as I landed next to him and swiftly decapitated the immortal who had tried to take him from me.

"May you rot in the deepest pits of hell," I said, not bothering to wipe my sword clean as I whirled around, trying to find Zoe in the midst of all this chaos.

Zoe was already next to me, with Jelly and Elvy guarding our backs. June and Finnian were doing their best to keep our circle protected. I sent out my magic, trying to help Blaz be as calm as possible to not exacerbate the wound.

"Not good," Zoe said, assessing the damage as best she could.

I held my hand over the guts that seemed to spill out of Blaz. I would hold him together. Blaz muttered something, but his breathing was so labored, I couldn't understand what he said. I hesitated to look into his eyes, fearful of what I would find there.

Seeing the life fade out of those honey-brown eyes would end me. I couldn't do it.

"Delmira, I need you to move," Zoe said, gently but with finality in her voice. "If you want me to save his life, I need you to keep him calm while I work."

I nodded and gritted my teeth as I caught his gaze. In those eyes, I found a fight. He wouldn't leave me. Not while there was still breath in his lungs. I sent even more calm into him, trying to hold him steady.

"Stay with me, you stubborn immortal," I said, and he nodded. He would. We both had to leave his fate in Zoe's hands, and I trusted her. On the stars, I trusted her not to let him die.

I kept my eyes on Blaz as Zoe summoned the healing magic within her. She seemed to murmur a prayer as she sent her magic into the worst of his injuries.

I was barely aware of the snarls of Jelly and the clang of Elvy's sword. They were working furiously to give us the space we needed. The army of the dead and the reinforcements of King Aldrich and Queen Farron had certainly aided us in this fight, even though I could not see those who had passed.

A deep sigh of relief escaped Blaz as Zoe's magic poured into him, healing what would have been a life-ending wound.

Before I could think better of it, I crushed his lips to mine. He would not leave me, and I would not leave him. We would fight and die together, or live together. I accepted nothing else.

"That should take care of it," Zoe said, her hands shaking slightly. Her eyes flipped rapidly between green and black.

I slapped a hand on her shoulder. "Zoe, are you good?"

She nodded, but something was off about her response. She took the pendant dangling from Blaz's wrist and sent another wave of healing magic through it.

"That should keep you out of pain… for a while," she murmured, fatigue evident on her face.

"Elvy!" I shouted, pivoting around to find him fighting off three of Hesperia's vile followers. I swung right into battle, shoving him towards Zo. "Your flame is fading. Heal her!"

He didn't need to be told twice, and I let my body feel the battle as my Lord Astral went to lend his flame the strength only he possessed. I felt Blaz join me in the fight before I saw him, and he fought as if he had never been injured.

"Don't scare me like that again!" I growled at him.

"Just had to make sure you loved me!" he yelled, grinning back as he pierced the heart of our enemy.

"Screw you!" I screamed as we worked fluidly together once more.

"Later!" he said, downing another.

I couldn't help the laugh that escaped my lips. Blaz and I had always been good at this when nothing else seemed to work. Losing ourselves to the lust of battle was easy—effortless. And maybe we both secretly enjoyed what that meant.

52

Spirits

FREYJA

Hesperia's shadows had stolen away my projection form, but her legion kept coming.

But we were not alone. The hair on the back of my neck stood up as I watched the spirits of the fallen Shadowed around me rise from their felled bodies.

"What the…" I asked as Oleander continued to put his entire energy into the shield formation.

His back was drenched in sweat, and I knew his energy waned despite how strong his magical abilities were.

Ander took in the sight of the spirits around us, and understanding seemed to overtake him, which was good since I had no idea what was going on.

"Who called you?" he asked one spirit that had suddenly appeared.

"Life-bringer," the ghost whispered. "Let down your shield. Let us end this."

"Are you sure?" Ander asked, and the spirit nodded. "Wait… Liam?"

"In the flesh," the spirit named Liam grinned. "Only figuratively."

"Your brother—" Oleander began, but Liam held up a hand to silence him.

"I am here to fight with him. Let down the shield."

"Alright," Ander nodded.

He clenched his fists and pulled them to his side, and the shield evaporated around them. Our enemies took that as a sign of weakness, which was unfortunate for them.

"Ready to bite, viper?" Ander asked, drawing his own sword.

"We can't let anyone report back to Hesperia that I'm still around," I said, stepping back, trying to do what was best for the battle. "I don't want to hide away from this, but we can't let her have the advantage now that you're no longer shielding us."

I wasn't sure what fate demanded of me in this moment. I checked in with my projection, and she was still in the clutches of Hesperia's shadows—silent and waiting to see what Hesperia intended to do with her. My intuition bargained that she would pull her out at the very last moment. When she had no other cards to play.

I'd never received word back on the iris, so I had no idea if Zoe knew that the projection wasn't really me. I just had to embrace a hell of a lot of hope that she could see the truth.

He pulled his cloak from around his shoulders and placed it around me.

"No one will see you while you wear this without my permission," he swore, lighting up the cloak with the magic of his shield and shadows. "You're hidden as long as you wear this. You can choose to fight if you wish, but whatever you choose, I will be with you, Freyja."

I nodded, letting my nerves settle. His magic may keep me hidden, but it wouldn't make me invincible.

"Then we fight," I said, and he grinned widely.

I closed my eyes, and a fresh wave of magic surfaced over my body, like a second skin from before. Only this time, my body seemed to be blurred, as if it was hard to focus on.

"What is this?" I asked, holding up my hand in wonder.

"I think it's protection," he said, swiping a hand over my skin. I barely registered it. "Incredible. I've never seen spirit work this way."

I grinned, thanking my magic for showing up for me. "Let's not question a good thing."

He nodded. "Let's go."

Ander and I both joined the fray beside Zadie and Tiergan, who were both bruised and slashed from the battle, but their hearts were still high. With the spirits of the dead joining us in this fight, their energy seemed to be renewed with a sense of hope and wonder.

My blade slashed into my first victim. It was tougher to do than in training, but I kept going, trusting in my strength to see me through.

With Ander by my side, I was capable of anything.

I swiped again, surprised at how steady my muscles felt. I wasn't as graceful as the warriors around me, but I held my own.

Zadie was particularly lovely in battle, and I could see the allure she held for Finnian as she easily took on three enemies at once.

Ander's back was to me as we worked in a pairing formation, as our opponents circled around us, trying to see through Ander's illusion, but they would be hard-pressed to get through his magic.

I plunged into the heart of another enemy, but I took no satisfaction in his death as I moved to the next.

Liam and James had reunited, and they brought swift death to all who crossed their paths. Even in death, Liam was a force to be reckoned with. My heart grieved, knowing the brothers would not be reunited beyond this moment unless death claimed James tonight, and that was not something I wished for. I vowed to make sure James had a friend in me should we survive this war.

"Tiergan!" Ander called, and I turned to find Ander slicing an enemy down.

My heart stilled as my eyes followed the path down from Tiergan's look of shock to the blade piercing his chest.

I shuffled my way closer to him as he collapsed to his knees. Oleander joined me on the ground, trying to figure out the best way to remove the blade without killing him.

"Hold on, Tiergan," I said, eyes burning with tears I tried not to shed.

"Where's Zoe's pendant?" Ander asked.

"The magic is depleted," he answered, barely able to keep himself upright.

"Use mine," Ander said, moving to unclasp his bracelet, but Tiergan stopped him with his hand.

"No," Tiergan said, and I was briefly aware that our forces were keeping us protected in this moment. "It's too late."

His voice was labored, and blood covered his mouth from the internal bleeding, staining his brown mustache red.

"I can go find Zoe," Oleander said, but Tiergan shook his head. He seemed to struggle to speak.

"I will be at peace soon," he murmured, and his words sounded wet.

I squeezed his hand, letting him know he was not alone.

"It's my time," he said, smiling as he took one more labored breath before he collapsed into Ander's arms.

"Tiergan?" he asked, moving his body gently to the ground after removing the blade from his back that had dealt his death blow.

Nothing but the sounds of battle answered for a few seconds.

"Yes?" The answer had not come from Tiergan's body, but from above us. He stood as a spirit, ready to fight once again.

"I'm so sorry," Ander said, standing.

"We all have a time to die," Tiergan said, placing a hand on his shoulder. "It was mine."

Tiergan whirled around, looking somewhere in the distance that we could not see.

"I'm needed elsewhere," he said, taking off without another word.

I didn't know how to feel about any of this, but I closed Tiergan's eyes and looked at Oleander.

"Do you need a minute?" he asked.

I shook my head. Part of me wanted to break at the reality of knowing that Tiergan was gone, but that would serve no one right now.

"We fight," I said, rising once again.

53

Winged Friends
CLODOVEA

"Are those… simargls?" Imelda asked. "Wait, that's Skoll and Tala."

I'd heard of the alphas of the simargl pack in Arcturus, but had never had the pleasure of formally meeting them.

I pulled my sword from the gut of another faceless pawn and turned to greet the pair. Their fur was already bloodied and their wings were lit with their simargl flames.

"We can't let anyone breach the lighthouse," I said, no time for any other pleasantries.

The tide had turned in this battle, and I found fewer enemies to pierce my blade through. I feared to hope that this war could be over soon. We'd received no intelligence that Hesperia would be calling on any other reinforcements, but that knowledge only left me feeling unsettled.

I let the ocean of Vega revive my magic as I continued to strategically make the terrain more difficult for our enemies to cross.

Musterion and its purity would be saved above all else.

Skoll and Tala led the pack with as much effectiveness as a trained squad of Shadowed. They were beautifully lethal as they hunted as one in their pack.

We fought alongside each other. Arcturus and Vega. A year ago, I would have scoffed at the idea of such a truce, but now I couldn't imagine not having the other courts peacefully in our lives.

A call sounded from the front-lines, and our foes turned around at the noise, heading towards the reverberations in the air.

I wasn't sure what this meant, but I felt it in my gut that something pivotal was about to happen.

I turned to Imelda, and this moment of distraction nearly cost me.

"Clove!" Imelda screamed as I turned to find an enemy's blade poised to pierce my heart.

Out of nowhere, some force knocked the sword from my enemy, and a look of horror crossed their face. I couldn't understand what happened, but I took the advantage, swiftly killing them.

Imelda was by my side in an instant.

"That should have killed me," I whispered as a shiver ran over my body. I looked around, trying to find the source of my savior, but couldn't see anything out of the ordinary. A sense of familiarity surrounded me, but I didn't have time to analyze it now.

"We have to go," Imelda said, pulling on my arm.

"Right," I said, still feeling uneasy, as if my heart was breaking, but I didn't know why.

"We'll stay here," Evander said. "Musterion will stay protected. No matter what."

Skoll and Tala nodded their agreement, and they created a crescent moon formation around the lighthouse.

They would defend it with their lives.

"Let's go," Imelda said, taking my hand in hers as we flew to the front.

54

Reckoning

ZOE

Elvy used our flame to heal my fatigue, reigniting the fight and magic within me.

I'd exerted more magic than I ever had, and I knew I wasn't done. I feared burning out, but it was a fear I could not welcome.

"Just felt like raising the dead?" he whispered as he held me close, trying to distract me, even if it was just for a moment.

"They aren't really back," I said, though I wish I had that kind of power. In my heart, I knew no being alive should wield that kind of magic. "I called on their spirits to fulfill their unfinished business. They will go back to the realm of the dead when this is over."

"Still brilliant," he said, and I stretched my arms as the last of my fatigue was erased. "And we should thank the stars for that kind of magic."

I nodded, sitting up as the battle continued around us, but it seemed to dissipate some.

Clodovea and Imelda ran up to us then, with confusion in their eyes.

"What is it?" I asked.

"We felt a *call*. Did you not feel it?" she asked, and I shook my head. "It was like an irresistible summons to the front. We thought it was you."

Clodovea brushed a hand through her hair, exposing her bracelet that was covered in stained blood.

"What happened?" I asked, motioning towards the pendant. I reached out with my magic to find it completely drained. "Are you alright?"

"She saved Evander with it," Imelda said.

"And thank the stars for your healing magic and those bracelets, too," Elvy said, still reeling from the spirit magic I'd wielded.

"I wish had the strength to infuse every one of our Shadowed with one," I admitted, as I sent more healing magic back into Clodovea's pendant.

Elvy encircled me in his arms, sending his magic through our flame to replenish my stores.

I stilled.

I ran a hand through my hair, heart racing in double time.

"Say that again," I said, lurching away from Elvy.

My discernment swelled within me as I held my bow in front of me, rubbing the familiar groove with my thumb.

"The bracelets were a smart choice," Elvy repeated, brow raised.

Could it be that simple? The songs of fate seemed to cry louder, knowing that death could be on the horizon of the rising moon.

I unsheathed the single arrow my gifts had led me to bring. My memories flashed briefly to the moment I'd decided to steal it away. Fate had refused to let me leave the arrow behind in Algol. For this moment. I'd thought about using it at least a dozen times since the battle began, but every time I'd reached for it, I hadn't been able to bring myself to use it.

Not yet, my father had seemed to whisper to me, though I hadn't seen or heard from him since he'd given me the arrows. Just as he promised. He wouldn't be here until the right moment. My father had sent me after the arrow that he named the destroyer. He had ensured from the very beginning that I would have the means to see this fate fulfilled. The arrow that he'd been forced to use to unbind the star realms would be the one to propel us into peace. But it needed a little something after its magic had been depleted.

"What is it, Zoe?" Elvy asked, keeping a watchful eye around us.

"We're a perfect mated pair," I muttered, as a flood of memories circled around me, and I let Elvy see what I felt. The Archer and Sirius had both claimed I already had what I needed to end Hesperia. My mate and I were the perfect balance of life and death. Elvy had been chosen for me by something greater than our flesh and bone. We had been chosen flames by the stars themselves.

He was a part of me as much as I was a part of him. We were bound by the bonds of shadows and the magic of the flame.

Elvy was the beginning, and I'd fallen for him so instantly. This was the reason I'd been longing for our time in Saint Andrews. That had been fate speaking to me.

He was the death-bringer. I was the life-bringer. Together, we would end a life to bring in a new one.

"Infuse the arrow," I whispered. "With death."

I would not be the death-bringer. My mate would be.

Elvy's storm-gray eyes met mine as the battle raged on around us, but cries of fate seemed to slow time around us as we embraced this moment. We had the weapon all along.

He didn't have enough control to unleash his power on the masses without killing our own, but a concentrated transfer of power… that he could do with ease in the same way I made the pendants of healing.

Only a handful of seconds passed as Elvy clutched the arrow in his hand, and he embraced the death magic that he had been so ashamed of—the part of him that he had lived in fear of. It had followed his family's bloodline for generations for this one single moment in time. His family had carried this burden, hiding it away in the shadows, just so we could be right here, and they hadn't even known it.

Elvy's eyes were black as he infused the arrow with a lethal blow.

When it was finished, he handed the arrow back to me, and I nodded back to him. The arrow pulsed with dark magic. One I was intimately familiar with.

"We can kill her now," I whispered, eyes widening at the power that I held.

Elvy rose from the ground, holding his hand out to me.

"Let's finish this, Zoe Eferhild, Realm-Healer—Emerging of Legends."

"For a healed world," I said, clasping his hand in mine.

I turned to face the battle once more, unbothered by the spirits that surrounded me and with eyes narrowed on my prey. Calmly, I walked towards Hesperia, and the battle seemed to spread like the sea before me, as if fate had made it so. Perhaps the stars wanted a front-row seat to the show.

Hesperia pulled her shadow blade from one of my Shadowed, and my heart grieved for a moment, but my eyes never left my sister.

"Enough, Hesperia," I said, pitching my voice loudly as the clangs of swords around me ceased, and the spirits of the fallen paused in their own terrifying destruction. Note to self—don't make an enemy of the dead.

"Have you had enough, little sister?" she asked, sneering at me with false victory.

We had many more living forces than she, but it wasn't about that. We could never have peace while she still lived.

"I've had enough bloodshed, yes," I admitted. "It didn't have to be this way."

"But it did," she said, her shadows rising to guide me into death.

I wasn't ready to go with them yet.

I held my bow firmly in my left hand, with my right hand poised to snatch the arrow from where I kept it hidden, praying to the stars she would not sense the magic that lurked there.

"Our father tried to kill me, Zoe. He deserves to die."

"And all of us with him?" I asked, hoping even still that she would see reason.

"War has collateral damage," she said, shrugging.

I knew for certain that nothing but her death would stop her. She was too far gone and lost to her hatred of what my father had made her. A small part of me loved the exiled part of her that was hidden deep within the trenches of sorrow that made her who she was.

But not enough to spare her life for the lives of every immortal here.

"You seem to be missing one of your own," she smiled a too-wide grin.

I turned to the side, taking stock of all who stood around me.

The flying legions had landed, and I quickly found Aura, Rai, Seraphina, and Kai standing beside Sierra and Terran, who all looked battle-worn and fatigued. Farron and Aldrich were drenched in blood, but they were alive as well. I even saw Octavia way off in the distance with Phoebe, keeping a record of this pivotal moment. They were all alive, though. That's what counted.

They were covered in gore, but I found the faces of those I loved. Elvy, Blaz, Delm, Clodovea, Imelda, Finn, and June. All the Luminaries were accounted for. Behind Clodovea, I found Tiergan's spirit form, and my eyes burned with unshed tears. He smiled a mustache grin at me, and there were so many things I wanted to say to him. An unfamiliar male stood beside him, and I turned my head in wonder. Could it be? A single tear escaped me as I continued on.

On my other side, with the city in the background, I found Zadie, Oleander, and… *where was Freyja?*

A storm of shadows descended upon the beach in a swirling vortex of death.

When the shadows cleared, Freyja stood in Hesperia's clutches. I hadn't *seen* this coming. I tried to remember what I'd *seen* in the discernment I'd been given about Oleander and Freyja, but it hadn't been clear.

Something just didn't *feel* right.

Freyja stood silently, and I turned to Oleander, looking for some kind of confirmation, but Hesperia called my attention back to her.

"It's really simple, Zoe," she said, holding her shadow blade to the living artery in Freyja's neck.

"Give me Vega's star seed, and I'll let you all live your last moments in peace before I finish my spell."

Turn over the star seed and save my sister for what? A few moments. That would not do.

I looked to Freyja again and glanced back at Oleander. He was much too calm.

Recognition filled me. I knew this magic. I did not turn back to Oleander in fear that he or I would give something away.

In my periphery, June nodded to The Archer's constellation, and before I had a second to register, my father stood before me. His green eyes met their match in mine, and he smiled at me before turning to Hesperia.

"Daughter," he said, holding his hands out to her like a feral animal.

Hesperia hid her surprise well, only letting it flash in her eyes for a moment before she masked it with disgust, but I saw through her facade. I saw longing in there. I knew it because it matched what I'd seen of myself so often in the mirror. The longing to have a purpose—to be loved. To be enough. To be accepted.

My heart broke for her, but I knew she would never let us all walk away from this alive.

And I loved my father. Despite it all. I would not let her take him from me.

"How dare you speak to me," she said, eyes focused on him and not on me, though her shadows were dangerously close to where I stood, encircling our father, who stood between us. She still had Freyja in her clutches, her magic too wild to see what was obvious to me.

"It's my death you want, right?" he asked, voice calm. "I'm right here, Hesperia. Take me. You don't need to do this."

Her brows narrowed, and I tried to force my *sight* into submission. I begged—pleaded—for my gift to show me the outcome of this, to no avail, much to my dismay. I was as blind as the rest of them to this moment. Fate would turn this very night.

"You will die either way, father," she spat, and I made the mistake of stepping closer to him, and she averted her gaze to find me, which seemed to enrage her even more. "Of course, you protect your precious second daughter."

Blood leaked from a small wound on Freyja's neck, and I took a breath to settle my nerves.

The sound of the ocean reminded me of what was real and what was not. I couldn't lose sight of that.

Elvy stood to my right. If I were going to die, he planned to follow right after me. Jelly stood to my left, expression so much more wise and resolute than that of a mere dog.

"To the end," she murmured through our brand.

I glanced around the battlefield, meeting the faces of those I loved. Clodovea and Imelda clung to each other. Tiergan and the unfamiliar male stood behind them, with Farron and Aldrich just behind him. Blaz and Delmira's hands were threaded together. Zadie and Finnian embraced each other in a tight hold. Oleander stood hidden behind them, and I saw the truth of who stood behind him, cloaked from everyone else.

Everyone of them knew this could mean the end. Hesperia hadn't gotten our star seed yet, but if I failed right now, we were as good as dead.

"I forgive you, Hesperia," The Archer said. "And I am so sorry for the ways that I failed you. It is my failure that has caused all of this—that has created this hate and grief in your heart."

He stepped closer, and I kept my eyes on the footprints in the sand left behind with every step he took towards his first daughter. The daughter he had created out of desperation, not love. Hesperia could have been me.

I pulled the arrow from its sheath, notching it in the string of my father's bow. I let my magic flow into the bow as The Archer continued to move closer. He stood only a few steps away from her, as her shadows all but consumed them.

"One more step, and your precious second daughter's sister will meet her end," Hesperia taunted.

I'd have one shot. One moment. I had to make it count.

I raised my bow, pulling the string tight with the notched arrow ready to release.

Their fingertips brushed, and the shadows became more enraged and chaotic.

"I love you, Hesperia. I have always loved you," he said, and Hesperia's eyes went wide with confusion.

The Archer spun around her, so that he was behind her, holding her against his body.

The projection of Freyja disappeared, exposing Hesperia's chest to me.

I let the arrow fly.

I held my breath as I watched the death blow strike true.

Hesperia's eyes met mine as I stepped closer to her.

Where the arrow struck, black veins crept from its center, spreading throughout her pale body. Black blood spewed from her lips as she choked, gasping for breath. My father, still holding her, sat them both down gently on the sand.

I sank to my knees before her, threading one of her hands in mine.

"I am sorry I could not help you," I whispered as the light faded from her eyes and her heart slowed. Despite what she'd done, I would not let her die, seeing hate in my heart. I would not meet hate with hate. Not in this realm or the next. That did not mean I excused her actions or wished to spare her.

I glanced at my father, and my heart screamed as I saw the same black veins of death crawling up his neck.

I tried to pull Hesperia from him, but he held onto her tightly.

"I will not let her die alone," he whispered, and she glanced up weakly at him. "I wasn't there for her in the beginning, but I will be with her in the end."

"You knew it would come to this," I accused, the selfish part of me wanting my father to stay with me. I'd already known the grief of losing my parents. To lose another...

"I could not let you do this alone, little bear," he said, holding Hesperia as he held me with his gaze.

Tears heated my eyes as reality forced me to recognize it, despite my desire to wake from this dream.

He placed his hand on top of mine and Hesperia's joined hands.

"Death is peace," my father whispered as Hesperia closed her eyes. Her breath was barely audible. "I will always be with you, little bear, as I have always been."

He took one more deep breath, and I knew it would be his last.

A terrible jolt of electricity flooded my body, as if I were carrying the pain of Algol and heard their wails of irrefutable grief through me. They were losing their only son. I was losing my father. My body felt as if it were on fire, and it took my willpower alone to stifle my cries.

"You will burn, Zoe Eferhild," Nova whispered through me, and by the stars, I was burning.

"Just look to the stars," Elvy murmured, and my body heaved with a conjoined relief that this was over—and somehow I still felt like I'd lost. Maybe no one really wins in war.

I held onto their hands as their bodies turned to mist, as was Elvy's death magic.

All that was left was the glow of the four star seeds, each of the four courts Hesperia had stolen from.

A gentle hand touched my shoulder, and I let Elvy's strong arms envelop me in him.

"It's done," I whispered, as the tears rolled down my pinked cheeks.

Elvy sank into the sand beside me as I set my eyes on the cosmos, watching two orbs of light dance around each other, and I hoped beyond hope that Hesperia had found what she'd always wanted beneath all the hate—love.

55

Bittersweet

ELVY

I held my wife—my flame—my perfect mate as she grieved the loss of her father and what she'd had to do to save us all.

The stench of death no longer permeated the air as the evil of Hesperia dissipated from our realm.

I winced at the dead immortals that lay around me. So many of them had not deserved the fate they'd received.

"They got to fight in the end," Zoe muttered, reading me through our flame. "It is time for them to go."

Zoe sat up gingerly, wiping the remnants of her tears away. Blood coated her skin, and I itched to wash it away from her. However, I understood the statement she—we—bore in still wearing the hue of death. To ever forget what happened here this night would be a grievous disrespect to all who had died for it.

"Your sacrifice will not be forgotten. In this realm or the next. I vow this," Zoe said, speaking to the souls I could not see. "Peace is waiting for you. We will ensure the peace that you have fought for tonight lasts."

Zoe paused for a moment, covering her mouth with a sob, rocking her body.

"Tiergan," she cried. "I'm. I'm so sorry," she said, and my soul stilled. Tiergan had perished. I would give anything to see him right now. I turned to find Clodovea crying against Imelda at the news.

A sharp wail behind them had me turning to find Aura clinging to Rai. Tiergan had meant so much to her.

Oleander and Freyja moved closer to us, nodding their heads in confirmation as the rest of the Luminaries surrounded us.

"Janus is with him," Oleander said. "They are happy."

I nodded, looking past Zoe, trying to see what they did, to no avail.

Another male from Algol approached Zoe, and she turned to him next.

"James," she said, nodding slightly. "Liam."

The brothers she had told me about. I wanted to protect her, but knew that was something I could not offer her in this moment.

James wrapped his arms around her as she shed more tears. "I forgive you," he said, and my muscles relaxed.

She pulled away.

"I'm sorry I cannot bring you back, Liam," she said. "I can't hold this magic much longer."

James nodded, then turned to his brother, whom I could not see. "We'll see each other again."

I laced my fingers through hers, sending her my strength.

Zoe nodded at something the brothers said. "I know."

Oleander, Freyja, and Zadie all had tears in their eyes.

Though I couldn't see the spirits leaving, I felt in my soul they were gone.

Jelly nuzzled Zoe's palm, and my flame returned the affection.

"We have much work to do yet," she said, as our Luminaries and family encircled us.

There were no cheers of celebration at our so-called win. Yes, we'd preserved the Kingdom of Canis, but at what cost? We had to do better—be better—than our predecessors.

Fatigue filled my very essence, and I could see the same in every eye around me.

Freyja encircled my wife, and I nudged Blaz on the shoulder, pressing my lips into a thin line. There was so much to say, yet the words would not come. He'd nearly died in the defense of our realm.

"Take time," Oleander said from behind Freyja, but his words were directed at Zoe. "We can take time to honor the fallen. To embrace this."

Zoe nodded, then turned to me, fear in her eyes. She'd fought for this moment for what felt like an eternity. To think of what came after… I wasn't sure any of us had really hoped for what came after it.

"Come," I said, lacing my fingers through my flames. I knew what I needed to do.

I briefly glanced at Farron and Aldrich, and they nodded their approval for what I was about to do.

I led Zoe up onto an elevated rock formation on the beach and sent her comfort through our flame.

"We are the stars and the stars are us," I said, pitching my voice as loud as I could muster after such a strenuous battle. "As we come from the stars, so we will return to them when our starlight fades into the darkness. Take time. Say goodbye to your loved ones.

With the rising morning moon, we will return them to the stars, where they will shine on us until it is our turn to join them."

I was met with a mixture of prayers, sobs, and wails of grief. There were just too many to burn in the way we usually practiced. I would talk to Kai and Seraphina to see if I could get the aid of dragon fire for this passing.

I turned to our Luminaries and the family we'd chosen. "Do whatever you need. We'll meet you at the passing."

They all murmured their goodbyes, and I swept my flame into my arms, taking flight for our home. Jelly flew behind us, refusing to let Zoe be far from her after what they'd gone through together.

I didn't allow myself to take stock of the damage to our city. Not tonight. We would begin to rebuild when we'd honored our dead and Zoe had restored the star realms. Tonight, I would hold nothing but love for the one to whom the stars mated me. She deserved my undivided devotion. Nothing less.

My feet barely grazed the rooftop as I made my way into our bedroom suite. Jelly plopped down by the fireplace as I carried Zoe into our bathroom. I pulled off my leathers, then hers. No words passed between us, but where our hands met on our bodies, we both sent the healing magic of the flame between us.

My eyes did not leave the worst of her wounds until I saw them thread together, whole once again. Goosebumps covered her flesh, and my eyes trailed the mark of her tattoos up her arms, and stayed on her brand of the simargl. I hated to admit the fear of meeting her gaze, not knowing what I would see in her eyes. I wasn't sure my soul could handle seeing the brilliant green flame of her eyes dulled to a lifeless mourning.

It'd taken me centuries to recover from the death of my parents. To do what Zoe had done… to be the one to extinguish the life of her father and to know the tumultuous relationship they'd had to the very end. But in the end, he was there, and I prayed she found some solace in that.

I cast aside my feelings, refusing to let fear dictate my actions.

Delicate fingers grazed my chin, tilting my eyes to meet my wife's.

Brilliant green met me.

I trailed a finger down her cheek, committing this moment to memory. Such beauty despite the lethal power that was at the core of my wife—and I did not mean her gift from Algol. Zoe was life.

Zoe's touch left me shivering at her very energy.

My jaw clenched with tension as I held myself back from losing myself in her—with her—for her.

Heat filled the room, despite the showers not being on. This force was the magnitude between us. Not flames. Just us and the way we loved each other.

I pressed my lips against hers, gently at first, as I cupped her chin in my hand, tugging on her braid, dried blood making it stiff. Her body responded to me, leaning into the kiss, and I sucked her bottom lip in mine, and the soft groan coming from her was like finding water after weeks in the desert.

"I love you," I murmured, over and over again as I traced every curve of her body and settled on her hips. She leaned her forehead against mine as we listened to each other's breathing slow and become one.

"I love you, Elvy," she whispered. "Somehow, I'm so scared of what's coming. In finding purpose now that I've nearly fulfilled what my father began so long ago. No one ever talks about coming home. After," she paused, taking a deep breath. "After the killing is done. Is life really supposed to go back to how it was? This is what I Emerged for. For a healed world."

"And so we will heal it," I promised. "Together. With every choice—every moment—we will figure it out together."

I wrapped Zoe in my arms, embracing everywhere our bodies met.

"You decide what happens next, Zo. You get to choose for yourself, not me, not for the good of others, just you."

Her jade-green eyes burned through me, and I could not wait to see what she chose to do next. Not just in the next sixty seconds, but without the fates pressing down on her… I could not wait to be by her side as she chose herself for herself. Not out of defiance to the stars. Not out of tragedy. But out of joy and a thrill for life.

"What are you thinking, Elvy?"

I grinned.

"Thinking of all you have yet to embrace about this life," I answered, kissing the back of her hand. "And how excited I am to see you live it."

Her eyes glazed over to a deep black, and I was not afraid as my shadows answered the call of their bond.

"What do you *see*?" I asked.

She smiled secretly, blocking me out from her visions, something so rare between us, but I was not upset. I didn't want to know. I wanted to experience each moment fresh and new. No spoilers for me.

"Are you happy there?" I asked, heart beating in time with my flame.

She nodded, shifting her eyes back to green.

"We're going to be very happy, Elvy," she said, wrapping her arms around me, and I embraced her.

I kissed her softly, loving the way her lips felt against mine.

"It's time we started living. Maybe for the first time."

I reached over to turn on the heat of the shower. We'd survived. Now it was time to start living. Whatever that looked like for us. In a healed world. A better one.

"First things first," I said, pulling her into the shower. "Let's wash the past off us."

We'd step out of this, ready to embrace our future. No matter how unsure it might feel. We would find our way together.

56

Presence

FREYJA

"What now?" I asked, brushing my still wet hair from the shower Ander and I had just gotten out of.

"We attend the passing, and then we can do whatever you desire," he said, taking the brush gently from my hand and continuing to work the tangles out of my hair.

"But what do I do? You're the Lord Astral of Algol. Zadie is your second. What am I supposed to… do?"

His blue eyes met mine in the mirror in front of me, brows scrunched in thought. A smirk played on his lips.

"Would it interest you to be the Lady Astral of Algol?" he asked, and I could tell he was desperately trying to hide his smile, and I refused to give him the satisfaction of looking shocked, no matter what my heart might feel.

"That had better not be a marriage proposal, Ander," I chastised. "I expect far more flair than that."

He kissed the top of my hair, laughing softly.

"Oh, what fun this will be, sweetheart," he said, braiding my hair loosely down my back now that the tangles had vanished under the delicate but thorough touch of his hand. "An immortal life without the bite of your ice would simply be unacceptable."

I bit my lip, face flushing against my ivory skin.

"Teasing aside… was there anything you were keen on as a mortal? Something you wanted to do? Did young Freyja have any dreams of being a veterinarian or something like that?" he asked.

I turned my head, looking at my reflection in the mirror, trying to remember a time I'd wanted to be something other than who I was.

"All I can remember from my life is wanting to… *live*. I wanted to travel and see the world. The thought of a job—in the traditional sense—never crossed my mind other than what would get me by until my next trip."

And that was true. I'd worked at hostels, bars, or anywhere that would pay in cash. Aspiring for anything else had never been the dream for me.

"Living for the present is all that really mattered to me," I admitted, shrugging.

He bent down, kissing my neck tenderly, and I shivered at the feel of him against me. This *male*.

"I do like the sound of that," I mumbled, more vulnerable than perhaps I'd ever been.

"The sound of what, exactly?" he murmured, a breath away from my lips, and I turned to face him.

I'd come back from the actual dead. I could stand to tell him what I was feeling.

"The thought of being by your side… in that way… for the rest of our existence. I would like that."

His eyes softened at my admission.

"Then you shall have it, sweetheart," he said, cupping my flushed face in his strong embrace, kissing me gently. "I'd marry you this very moment if you'd let me."

I couldn't help the smile and roar of laughter that came from me.

"Now, now, Ander. Let's not get ahead of ourselves."

He nibbled my neck with his teeth, and my laughter quickly turned into a groan.

"If convincing is what you need, I have no problem showing you how good it will be to spend forever with me."

And I believed him.

57

Anti-Warrior

DELMIRA

"Have you ever thought about doing something… else?" I asked, slipping on some clean fighting leathers.

The thought of putting on civilian clothes just didn't sit right with my central nervous system. It wasn't yet convinced that the fight was really over. I wasn't sure that it ever would be.

"What do you mean?" Blaz asked, fussing with his hair in the full-length mirror in my room in Elvy and Zoe's manor. We didn't want to bring the blood and grime of the fight to what would be our future home.

"Like all of this," I said, pointing to our uniforms. "You know, just something less… stabby."

He paused, thinking for a moment.

"No, not really. But I was born in the star realms, Delm. We all get to have a little fun before life gets serious."

I nodded, jealously surging through me. Most immortals have decades to *find themselves* before committing to their future. Hell, I'd had to fight for my life ever since my mortal parents dropped us off at the orphanage at the ripe age of three years old. Fighting was a talent that had helped me survive… but I wasn't sure I wanted to fight for the rest of my life.

"What if I don't want to do this anymore?" I asked, testing the words out. They felt a little unnatural, but right all the same.

"You don't want to be second anymore?" he asked, folding my hands in his.

I met his eyes, pressing my lips into a thin line, truly trying to sit with the question. Did I?

"I'm not sure," I said honestly, averting my eyes to the floor, too afraid to see his reaction to my impending vulnerability. "I've been tearing out throats my entire life. Finn has his books and research. He's coped with all our stuff better than I ever have. I know I've hidden behind the duty of the second. But if I'm being honest with myself… I think it's finally caught up to me. I'm afraid once the dust clears after all of this, I'll break. When everyone else is moving on, I'm going to be stuck in fight-or-flight mode. And I don't want to run."

A gentle warrior's hand caressed mine.

"Delm, I will support you in every way," he said, tilting my chin up to meet his eyes. "Until you feel safe, I will stand by your side in all things. And even past then."

I circled my arms around his waist, and the tension in my shoulders loosened some at his admission. The road to recovery would probably be paved with so many obstacles, and to have him by my side through it all meant everything to me.

I pulled back so I could look him in the eyes.

"I love you, Blaz," I said, voice steady.

His eyes lit up at the most vulnerable thing I'll ever utter to him.

"Say it again," he whispered, cupping my cheek in his rough palm.

"I love you," I repeated, and he closed his eyes, laughing softly as he breathed us in.

"I love you, Delm," he said, picking me up and twirling me around the room.

After setting me back down on my own two feet, he fastened his hands in mine.

"We will figure this out together. We could move to the outland villages and become farmers. Anything you want," he said seriously.

"Blaz, I want to be here in the city with our family," I promised, and I meant it. "I just don't know what I want my role to be now."

"And that's okay," he said, kissing me softly.

"Thank you," I whispered. "For holding space with me and for not giving up on me."

"Never," he said, sealing that vow with a kiss that I found myself leaning into.

I protested when he started pulling away, but I couldn't help but join in his laughter.

"Come on, Delm. The passing will start soon," he said, face grim with the ceremony that was to come.

I nodded my head and let him take his hand in mine as he led us away from this blissful bubble between us and into the grief that would feel suffocating the moment I crossed the threshold.

I took a deep breath and closed the door behind me.

58

And then there was...
CLODOVEA

Imelda and I stood outside the doors of Musterion, ready to tell them that we'd won, but it didn't feel like a victory when not all of their loved ones would be returning with us.

A fraction of the riders who had so bravely volunteered for this battle survived.

They stood behind us now with looks of defeat and *longing*.

Longing to hold their loved ones close and tell them they no longer had to fear tomorrow.

I hesitated to open the door and turned back to the crowd.

They nodded their encouragement, and the look in their eyes solidified their promise that we all mourned as one.

We'd fought as one. Died as one. And we would rise as one.

I swallowed down the rest of my fears and opened the massive gate to Musterion that had kept our immortals safe for so long.

Now this city could be so much more than a secret safe harbor. It could be for anyone who dared to embrace all that life could be, and I knew Imelda and I would find our home here among them. I only wished Tiergan could be here to see it.

A breeze floated around me, and a sense of peace washed through me. He would watch over us and this place.

As we made our way down the tunnel and the light from the city became brighter, our footsteps moved a little quicker and the chatter around me grew with anticipation of reunification.

When we stepped out into the light of the city, there was no one to be found at first.

Slowly, a few heads peeped out of windows and cracked doors. Shouts rang through the air as the immortals hiding here realized that we were not an invading army, but their loved ones returning home to them.

There was some confusion at first as people shouted names and cries of joy as they realized their family members were alive.

What I was not prepared for were the sobs of sorrow that filled the air, as some immortals realized their loved ones had not made it home. My heart sank at their pain, and I vowed to help them find healing in whatever way I could.

For now, all I could do was hold their pain with them.

So that's what I did with Imelda by my side. I let them know that they were not alone. I didn't offer empty condolences or a promise that things would be better. How could I do that?

But I offered them my strength and my ear.

Their burden would never be theirs to bear alone.

Not as long as there was breath in my lungs. And I knew that Zoe and Elvy would do all they could to see that promise through.

Healing was on all of us, and no one would walk this journey alone.

59

The Passing

ELVY

We'd gathered our dead on the beach as delicately as possible, taking care to treat their bodies with the respect they deserved.

Many water wielders of Vega took care to cleanse the bodies and kept them cooled while we worked to get the passing in order.

Zoe stood off in the distance, communing with Seraphina and Kai, along with Aldrich and Farron, to work with the dragons and simargls to complete the passing. It was time our immortals were returned to the stars, as it was our custom.

Octavia fluttered around with her magical notepad, recording history. I despised that this day existed, but it was important that we remembered it, so I let her be.

"We would like to contribute to the fallen," Sierra said, with Terran by her side.

"Of course," I said, knowing their numbers were just as great as ours. "This is for all of us."

Sierra and Terran both nodded and held out their hands, casting their beautiful ground magic that was truly an art form.

They covered each slain immortal's head with a flower wreath and used moss and wildflowers to create memorials for each of them.

By the time they were finished, if I hadn't known the immortals lying on the beach were dead, I would assume they were sleeping in a beautiful garden.

"Thank you," I said, trying to memorize the faces of all who had died during this battle. I prayed that peace would find them in their next life, and that they would guide us true in the years to come amongst the stars. I prayed their sacrifice was never forgotten in the cosmos above.

I knelt next to Tiergan's body and squeezed his hand.

"Thank you. For all that you sacrificed to ensure a peace that could never be broken again."

I could have sworn I felt a hand on my shoulder, but it was gone just as quickly as it'd come.

I rose as Zoe slid her hand into mine as she took in the sight.

"Beautiful," she murmured, and her voice sounded thick with an emotion I felt deeply with her.

Clodovea and Imelda approached the beach that had become a mass memorial, leading those of Musterion to the surface for the first time since this all began. My heart flinched as I watched a female kneel beside one of the deceased and cling to his chest with wails echoing across the ocean.

She wasn't alone in her grief.

A swirling portal of stars opened in the night sky, and my instinct was to go on the attack, but I relaxed, knowing that all five realms had been invited here to pay their respects and see their loved ones through the passing.

Immortals from all star courts had perished during this fight, and they all deserved the right to say goodbye to those who paid the ultimate sacrifice.

A flood of immortals came down from the night sky, landing on the beach. Some immortals reunited with shouts of joy and prayers to the heavens that their loved one had made it through this. Others joined the mourning, and the air felt heavy with grief.

To recover from this seemed impossible, but we would.

Because we lived.

And we would not let their deaths be in vain.

Zoe's hand twitched in mine, and I felt a longing within her at the pain surrounding her. Jelly nudged her leg, feeling her discomfort.

"I need to help them," she said through our bond. *"To heal them."*

"I know," I answered. *"But today, let them grieve. Let them feel. There's far too many for even your magic, Zoe. This will take time."*

"My magic calls to them," she said, but not in disagreement with me. *"But I know it is not for me to fix. When they are ready, I will be there."*

We didn't rush anyone with their goodbyes, as our magic kept the area as a safe space for them to take their time.

The rest of the Luminaries made their way over to us, with June, Oleander, Freyja, and Zadie following behind them. Aura and Rai approached us as well. Their hands were laced together, and she radiated more confidence than I'd ever seen in the female.

"I can't believe Tiergan is gone," Clodovea said as Imelda wrapped her arms around her.

"His first act in death was to save you," Oleander said, pressing his lips into a thin line. "I just hadn't realized it at the time, but when you told us of your phantom savior… it had to be him."

Clove let out a fresh wave of tears, and Aura wrapped her arms around her friend. I didn't know all that had happened in Canopus, but I knew Tiergan, Aura, and Clodovea had all grown closer while there.

June stepped up, encircling them on instinct. "I didn't know the male well, but I'm here for you in whatever way you need me."

Blaz and Imelda squeezed June's shoulder. "I think he would approve," Blaz said, and Zo nodded her agreement.

"He's with Janus now. They can finally have their peace," Zoe said, voice breaking a few times. "I just wish it could have been different. That they could have lived out their days here together."

We all circled around Tiergan, sharing our favorite moments with him. It was strange to laugh at a time like this, but I felt like this was how he would have wanted it. He would want to be remembered for the life he lived, not for his death. He was so much more than that one moment.

It was hard to pull away from each other, but we all knew it was time to send their bodies back to the stars. The crowd had grown quieter, and we took our places to perform the rites of the passing.

"The time has come to send our immortals through their passing to the stars," I said, standing with Zoe by my side. The other Astrals and King Aldrich and Queen Farron stood around us—a united front and a promise of peace for the future. "Seraphina and Kai, along with their dragons, have agreed to send them back to the stars with their dragon's breath."

I paused, turning to Zoe.

"May we never forget this moment, and may it create lasting peace in the star realms. It has been an honor fighting alongside you all to purge the evil from these realms. May we love deeply and embrace the good that lives in the light and the dark. We are the stars, and the stars are us. We come from them and so must we return," I said. "May peace be with you all."

I stepped back and nodded to the Lord and Lady Astrals of Arcturus.

The dragon riders communed with their mounts, and as one, their dragons burned our slain brothers and sisters until there was nothing but ash left to return to the stars. The simargls surrounded the memorial gardens, offering their bodies protection in a way only the simargls—life protectors—could.

Aura and Rai, along with their loyal followers in Canopus, used their air magic to lift the ashes of the fallen into the cosmos to complete the passing of this life.

"You are all welcome to stay in our realm for as long as you wish. My mate will be departing soon to fulfill the rest of her fate as the realm-healer, which will reunite the tethers to our realms once more. We will remember the ways of old and how we used to live in harmony."

King Aldrich and Queen Farron stood beside me, ready to address their subjects.

"We invite you all to Sirius in a month's time to mark the end of Hesperia's reign of terror. Let us join together in bringing in a new age where we embrace all that we are. No longer divided, but unified in our peace and belonging with each other," Farron said with a steady voice interwoven with heavy grief.

There were no cheers at either of our words, and I hadn't expected any. This wasn't the time to celebrate, but I felt the essence of resilience permeating the air. They would come to Sirius to fulfill what the fallen had died for. To see the prophecy come to fruition.

60

Restoration

ZOE

This was the first breath of air in Algol that didn't make me feel like I was suffocating.

Hesperia's sickness was truly gone from this realm, and it was time to tether Algol back to Sirius—back to their father.

Part of me was scared to lose this well of power—this connection—to Algol. I wouldn't be as strong, and I'd lose any leverage I had over the celestial.

In my heart, I knew the time of bargains, threats, and maiming was over. This was a time for peace, and for peace to be with us, I had to repair what my sister had broken.

Elvy and Jelly stood beside me in the cavern within Oleander's castle. A swirling mass of black liquid stared back at me—the link to Algol. Freyja, Oleander, Zadie, and Finnian stood behind me—waiting.

Oleander had watched me heal Algol in this very room. What a monumental moment that had been? It felt so long ago.

It had been my instinct, though. My magic from Vega longing to heal its celestial sibling, no matter how corrupt and sick they had become. A feeling I could certainly relate to. Only Algol would heal… Hesperia would not. She was gone for good.

Not that I wished her to be here. I wasn't that much of a saint. I guess I wished she would have chosen differently and that our father would have created her from a heart of love instead of hate. She had been doomed from the start.

I pulled out one of the arrows my father had given me and notched it securely in the bow we had sacrificed so much of ourselves to get. No more blood payments or oaths.

Closing my eyes, I focused on my center, listening to the steady rhythm of Elvy's heart. This was real. I was safe.

When I opened my eyes, the glowing orb of my essence hovered above me, and I easily pinched off a string, securing it to the bow. I was a true Daughter of Algol. I had the sole right to do this sort of magic. Spirit was what connected us all more than anything else.

With my essence securely attached, I then pulled out Algol's life force, which was connected to me, securing its tether to my bow. The moment it was linked, it felt like an entire universe was off my shoulders. To say I felt lighter was a grievous understatement.

I pulled the bowstring taut, aiming straight for Sirius through the glowing orb that was also a portal. Though I was sure no one else could see it, I clearly saw the glow of Sirius at the other end, waiting to welcome not only the connection of my essence, but also to embrace Algol back home.

I let the arrow fly.

It struck true.

My body lit up with the glow of life.

"Life-bringer. Realm-healer. You will burn," Nova said, whispering through my mind.

I'd always thought it a dooming thing to know I would burn, but this fire—it made me feel alive.

I turned to my flame to find his gray eyes staring back at me. He wasn't afraid, and neither was I. This was my destiny. I'd found my way to this moment, and it was important that I lived it.

"One down. Four to go," I said, spreading my wings, ready to fly to Vega.

"It already feels… different," Oleander muttered, nodding his head in thanks to me. Freyja laced her fingers through his, leaning her head on his shoulder.

"I'll see you both soon," I said, smiling at the future that I knew was now possible.

To love freely and never have to choose which parts of ourselves to love over the other.

I gave them a brief wink as I took off into the cosmos with Jelly and Elvy right behind me.

***

It didn't take long for us to reach Vega and our court's connection to the star.

The Luminaries minus Finnian stood around me as I faced the cosmic portal that connected the star realms together.

June squeezed my shoulder as I took a deep breath to ready myself.

"You kept bloomin', Zo," she said, smiling. "Your father and mother are so proud of you."

"I know," I said, gripping her hand in thanks. She let go, and I called my essence forth, repeating the same process I had in Algol.

Once I had the string of my soul attached to the arrow, I took a steadying breath and aimed.

I let the arrow soar until it hit its mark.

Just like last time, my body was engulfed in a brilliant burning light that not even my shadows had a prayer of dulling.

"Arcturus next," I said, embracing the pulse of magic flowing through me. I thought I'd feel empty after releasing my connection to Algol, but this kind of magic that I wielded now felt even more infinite in an entirely different way. This magic came from the universe that gifted me this soul.

Elvy and Jelly stood on either side of me as we all three unfurled our wings to fly to Arcturus, where Kai and Seraphina waited for us.

"We love you all," I nodded to our family, and they waved their goodbyes as we lifted off into the stars.

***

Seraphina and Kai stood beside us as I gazed into the portal that held the link to their celestial.

"Are you ready?" I asked, and they both nodded.

Their dragons wouldn't fit in this smaller cavern, but Skoll and Tala had made the journey here to see this moment in history unfold.

Kai and Seraphina both gasped when they saw my body glow with the power of life within me. I quickly took aim, finding my target through the cosmic portal.

I let the arrow find its mark before re-attaching the bow to my back.

"That's it?" Kai asked, and I wanted to roll my eyes at him.

"That's it," I said, smiling, unwilling to let even Kai dampen my spirits.

"Thank you," Seraphina said, bowing in reverence to the power I'd just wielded.

"We'll see you in Sirius?" I asked.

"Of course," she answered, and I turned to Skoll and Tala.

"Thank you for the protection the simargls offered my immortals during the fight," I said, bowing deeply to them.

"We are with you, Realm-Healer," they said, and Jelly howled with them as all three threw their heads back at the moon.

I gave Jelly ear scratches and kissed her snout.

"Two more to go, girl," I said, and she nodded, spreading her wings.

Elvy and I unfolded our wings again to journey to Rigil, and we took off into the galaxies above once more.

★★★

Sierra and Terran were quick to greet us in their familiar realm that felt like a second home to me in the realm of the stars.

They led us quickly to their sacred connection to Rigil, hidden and protected beneath their home.

"Tell us what you need," Sierra said, silver hair shining in the bioluminescent glow of creatures crawling on the ceiling of the caverns, making it look like the stars above.

"I don't need anything from you," I said, eyeing the glowing orb that held the portal. "You've done your duty. It is time for me to fulfill mine."

My essence came to me naturally now, and I had no hesitation in attaching a string of my soul to the arrow.

I found my target easily through the portal that held the cosmos.

I took a deep breath and released my arrow, watching it pierce its mark.

I re-attached my bow, smiling that my task was nearly complete. One more tether to go.

"Thank you," Sierra said, bowing slightly.

"May the peace you have brought last for the ages to come," Terran said, lowering his head.

"That we have brought," I said, threading my fingers through Elvy's. "Thank you for your willingness to help rebuild what has been damaged in Vega."

"It was the least we could offer," Terran said, squeezing Elvy's shoulders.

"Take care," Elvy said, as we three lifted into the cosmos to our final destination.

★★★

Canopus had been ravaged worse than every other court except Vega.

Hesperia's sickness had corrupted the very air here. Fortunately, the power wielded by those of Canopus was purging it quickly.

Elvy and I landed in the city center with Jelly by our side, where Rai and Aura waited for us.

Aura immediately wrapped me in her arms, and I smiled at my friend.

"It's good to see you happy," I said, motioning towards the male next to her. "You must be Rai. I've heard good things."

My heart dropped for a moment. So many of those good things had come from the words of Tiergan. Aura seemed to recognize this, too.

"Tiergan was a good male," she said. "I'm glad Rai got to meet him."

"Though I only knew him briefly, what he did for Aura will never be forgotten," Rai said.

"No, he never will be," I said seriously, and Elvy squeezed my hand.

"Come on, let me show you the way," Aura said, pulling us through the hidden tunnels beneath the archives.

Elvy tensed the moment we went below the surface, and I rubbed my thumb subtly in circles on his hand, reminding him that he was here and safe with me.

Aura held her mark against a large gateway, and we all stepped into the cavern to find the cosmic portal staring back at us.

"Do you need anything?" Aura asked, stepping to the side with Rai.

Elvy was still rigid, but he had relaxed somewhat. He hadn't told me everything he'd endured in these tunnels, and by the looks of it, he had a healing journey of his own to take. One that I would walk in him with, as he had done for me so many times before.

"No," I said, repeating the process for the last time.

As the last arrow found its mark, I glowed brighter than I ever had before. It wasn't painful. Quite the contrary. It felt exhilarating and full of life. My mission was now complete. In the grand scheme of it, anyway. I knew healing was far from over.

"Let's go home," I said, smiling at Elvy and Jelly.

Aura and Rai thanked us and quickly led us back to the surface. Elvy was instantly looser once we could breathe fresher air.

"See you on Sirius," I said, nodding to our hosts.

"Please send a missive if you should need any healers," Elvy said, finding his voice again.

"Thank you for your unyielding kindness," Aura said, bowing back as we took off into the galaxies above, sights set on our home.

61

The Power of Five
ZOE

One Month Later

The city of Vega was beautiful at twilight.

My hands were laced in Elvy's as we walked the familiar streets of Vega. Jelly trotted silently behind us, lost in her own thoughts, it seemed.

I'd always admired Vega's ability to interweave different textures together with a sense of cohesiveness. Musterion was evidence of the beauty of our combined magic.

Crafters from Rigil had assisted us in repairing our city from the final battle with Hesperia. Their work healed the scars on our buildings with delicate care. Wood and clay intertwined together with brilliant gems against the stone structures that had been ravaged during the battle. Their craftsmanship would never let us forget what happened in this city only a month ago, but it would also forever show that healing was possible.

We passed the Hall of Memories, and I bowed slightly at the mysterious building that still held many secrets. Octavia and other Keepers under her direction worked tirelessly in there and other archives in Musterion to bring light to our history. I hadn't seen

Phoebe, but I assumed she aided Octavia in whatever way the stars deemed.

We had all hoped that the restoration of our bonds to the celestials would resurface memories that had been stolen from the immortals who had lived during that time. This hadn't happened, but slowly—painfully so—immortals were experiencing new magic within themselves. Magic that had been dormant for some time. This was especially true for the younger immortals who had not sworn fealty to a star yet.

There was a lot of confusion and fear despite the peace that we all universally felt with Hesperia's sickness gone from this world. Tonight we had the opportunity to reunite in Sirius. The entire realms was invited, not just the Lord and Lady Astrals.

This victory wasn't just ours to celebrate. It had been earned by the blood of every immortal soul here, and I was happy to share in this joy with them all.

Elvy squeezed my hand, and I glanced towards him, heart stilling at the beauty of his gray eyes and brilliant smile.

"Your thoughts are loud tonight," he said, kissing my palm. "And I share them with you."

We stood outside our moonstone manor, and he placed his hands on my hips, pressing his lips to mine. The ocean sounded in the background, and the night sky was a display of colorful lights and stars.

"This is real, Zoe Eferhild," he said, dipping me low and my hair cascaded towards the ground. Jelly yipped and jumped excitedly in our periphery, and I couldn't help the laughter that escaped my lips as he placed a gentle trail of kisses down my neck.

He pulled back, and I looked into his gray eyes. A few of his curls hung around his face, and I brushed them out of his eyes.

"I love you," I said, pulling him to me, and he crushed his lips against mine.

"I love you, Zo. Even when we are both nothing more than starlight."

He lifted me into his arms, and cheers erupted from the door of the manor, which was crammed with our Luminaries. Blaz whooped and hooked his arm around Delmira's head, and she promptly punched him in the gut. Clodovea and Imelda were both smiling softly at us, with Finnian off to the side. He had informed us that he would be moving to Algol permanently in the near future. While I would miss him greatly—we all would—I was thrilled that he could have a real love with Zadie.

They were also all dressed in formal court attire.

"Is it that late?" I asked, realizing it was almost time to head to Sirius.

"You've still got some time," Clodovea said, motioning us both in. "But I'd hurry."

Elvy swept me into his arms, running us up the steps to our room.

"Dont get distracted!" Blaz called, and Elvy and I both laughed.

★★★

The High Astral Court was as stunning as ever, and for the first time in my immortal existence, I could truly appreciate it without having some nefarious reason for being here. It felt close to blissful.

Despite running late, Elvy and I had slipped into the archives to complete the registration of my magic as the Lady Astral of Vega. I had expected some huge thing, but it had taken all of five minutes and we were back out with the rest of the crowd.

King Aldrich and Queen Farron hosted the entire star realms in the courtyard. After closing their borders for so long, I was afraid that immortals would not come. I was happy to see that my fear was unwarranted. Somehow, they'd managed the space to be big enough to hold whomever wished to come, and it seemed like the majority of the five realms were present.

One soul who would not be here this night was June. She had gone back to Saint Andrews with promises to stay connected in our efforts on the mortal plane. We would be working together with Octavia and the other Keepers to rectify what had been done to humanity. Octavia had gone to Earth with June to begin preliminary data collection on the state of affairs, so we would have a good baseline to start with. I'd given her the keys to my bungalow in Saint Andrews with a promise never to keep things from us again. She had agreed all too willingly, and I held no ill feelings in my heart for her. This was a time of peace for everyone.

I exhaled a deep breath, letting go of tomorrow's worries and refocused on the present.

I sipped my lemon water and popped some mango into my mouth, savoring the sweetness of the fruit. Elvy, Jelly, and the rest of the Luminaries surrounded me as I scanned the crowd for familiar faces.

Our monarchs had not formally addressed us yet. It seemed they desired to mingle with everyone first to make it feel less formal to have them there. I appreciated the notion.

It didn't take long for me to find Freyja and Oleander, and I waved them over as her blue eyes found me. The grin that spread across her face reminded me that all of this pain had been worth it in the end.

Because she was here with me, getting to live a full life.

"Freyja," I said, pulling her into a strong hug. "How are things?"

"I'm finding my place," she said, turning around looking for someone. She waved her hand when she found him—James.

"Zoe," he said, bowing briefly. "It's so good to see you."

"Likewise," I said, leaning my head against Elvy, who was talking to Oleander about the stars only knew what. My heart warmed as I saw Liam's eyes in the eyes of his brother.

"James and I are working with the former Sublunary," Freyja said excitedly.

"Former?" I asked, turning to James.

"Their mission has been accomplished. No need for a rebel alliance now that we are free to choose," he said simply. "They are working together with those of us who were under Hesperia's control."

"And how are you aiding them, exactly?" I asked Freyja.

"We're helping immortals get housing and placement in their chosen star realm. We're promoting education on wielding multiple star's magic. Some immortals are still a little timid about it."

"But accepting," James added. "We're teaching immortals harmony."

"You both should talk with the King and Queen about this. I'm sure this project would be beneficial across the realms."

Freyja nodded enthusiastically. "We plan to tonight."

"Elvy and I would love to help in any way we can," I said, and Elvy drew his attention back to us from Oleander.

"Whatever my wife has volunteered me for, I am certainly happy to do for you, Freyja," he said, smiling sincerely.

Oleander placed a hand on his shoulder. "Be careful what you promise, brother."

My heart stopped and brow raised at the word brother coming from Oleander. They'd needlessly hated each other for so long… it was healing to see them growing together.

Before I had time to psychoanalyze that comment, a few others joined us.

"Hey, Zo," Aura said, holding her pregnant belly with one hand. Rai stood protectively beside her. His eyes constantly flickered around us, seeming to find it difficult to relax. Living in isolation and fear for so long had likely made it hard for him to adjust.

"It's good to see you two happy," I said.

"The same could be said for you two," he said, and his grin was genuine. "Thank you again for sending us healers. We should find Sierra and Terran as well. Their crafters were a huge help in the rebuilding of Canopus."

"As they were for us, too," Elvy said, nodding his agreement.

"I hope the charms are helping?" I asked Aura. Vega had sent healers and my spirit-healing magic to help them repair the damage wrought by Hesperia.

"They are, and we can't thank you enough," she admitted. "We hope to have you and Elvy in our realm soon."

"Of course," I said, turning to Elvy, who smiled his approval.

"We'd be honored," Elvy said, shaking Rai's hand.

"We would love to show you how kind the way of wind can be after your treatment there," Aura said quietly.

Elvy's jaw clenched only slightly, as he still dealt with the torture Hesperia had put him through in Canopus. He'd woken up several nights screaming, and I'd stayed with him until he'd fallen back to sleep. I'd been helping him with my magic as much as I could, and that he would allow.

"I would love to create new memories there," he said, smiling kindly towards them.

Aura and Rai both bowed as a few other immortals joined us.

"Sierra, Terran," Clodovea said, hugging her friend tightly. Sierra embraced Imelda next, while Elvy and Terran moved into an easy conversation.

"Your crafters are brilliant," I said to Sierra. "Vega has never looked more beautiful."

"And Canopus. Thank you for your resources," Aura said, leaning into Rai.

"We're in this together," she said, then turned to me. "Damek sends his well wishes."

Before Damek, I'd never considered myself a lover of horses, and maybe I still wasn't. However, Damek and I had a bond. One I loved.

"Elvy and I will have to visit sometime. I'd love to see him."

"Our doors are always open to you all," she said, bowing slightly. Her head lifted, and she winked after noticing that I still wore the ring of Rigil that she'd given to me when we'd first set out on our mission to find the bow. "I'm glad it proved useful to you."

"As am I," I said, turning my head curiously. If there had ever been a doubt in my mind that she had Algol running through her veins, those doubts were gone now.

Before I could venture down that rabbit hole, Kai and Seraphina joined us. All the Lord and Lady Astrals were now complete.

"How is Arcturus?" I asked, and the murmurs of side conversations grew quiet, with interests piqued.

"It is how it was always meant to be," Seraphina said, smiling shyly. "The simargls have restored the land. We are growing our first crops in centuries. Life is flourishing."

"We are glad to hear of it," Queen Farron said, approaching us from behind. "May it continue to grow."

We all bowed low at the monarch's arrival.

King Aldrich laced his fingers through Farron's. It was oddly affectionate for them, but I think we all wanted a sense of that closeness.

"Each of you deserves a personal thanks for protecting and defending our star realms. May we continue to learn and grow together as one unified kingdom," Aldrich said, nodding to all of us.

"It is time to address our immortals," Farron said, pulling her husband onto a slightly elevated platform.

It took only seconds for conversations to die out as they waited patiently for everyone to quiet down.

Farron spoke.

"We won't take up too much of your time, as there is still much merriment to be made. For the first time in our reign, we know true peace without the lurking threat of evil. The prophecy of the Realm-Healer has come to pass, and our bonds have been reunited once more, as The Archer intended. We all now possess the unequivocal right to embrace who we truly are."

"Farron and I wish to make our stance clear on this. You all have the entire support of the High Astral Council and our own authority to be united in whatever way you choose. We are excited about the future of the star realms and all that we have to learn from each other," Aldrich said.

"Eat. Drink. Embrace this moment. For there are many more to come," Farron said, raising her glass to the stars.

We all followed suit as she drank her fill, and applause and shouts of glee filled the night sky.

For a moment, time stood still, as if the universe paused just for me. I looked around, trying to find the source of this magic, and found the cosmic eyes of Nova staring back at me.

"Zoe Eferhild, Realm-Healer—Emerging of Legends," Nova said, bowing to me deeply. A gesture she had never offered before.

"Nova?" I asked, confusion likely clear on my face.

"I have come to pay my respects to the life-bringer," she said, smiling. "You burned."

"So I did," I acknowledged. "All those times you told me I would burn… you spoke life over me. Not death."

"I hoped," she said, smiling softly.

"Thank you," I said, a hint of silver in my eyes.

"Be at peace, child of the cosmos."

Before I could even attempt to ask anymore questions, time resumed and Elvy swung me around, pointing to the stars in the sky.

I peered up to find The Archer's constellation shining brilliantly in the night sky. A glowing light display of green, blue, pink, and purple shimmered so low to the ground that I thought I could reach up and touch it. Shooting stars filled the sky, and there was a collective gasp of silence around us as the celestials seemed to be offering their very own display of love for all of us.

I pulled Elvy's lips to mine, embracing this moment.

62

Healing

ZOE

O*ne Year Later*

"It has a nice ring to it," Freyja said, threading her fingers through mine as she turned her head to get a different angle.

"You sure?" I asked, smiling again at the onyx engagement ring Oleander had surprised her with a month ago. "I wasn't sure about the name, to be honest."

"I think it's perfect," Elvy said, snaking an arm around my waist.

"What are we looking at?" Blaz asked, approaching hand-in-hand with Delmira.

"The sign," Delmira said, rolling her eyes and pointing.

"Tiv's Healing," Finnian said with Zadie's arm looped through his. Finnian and Zadie had decided to split their time between Vega and Algol, but with Zadie's position in Algol, they lived there on a more permanent basis. "I like it."

"A combination of Tiergan and Vivian. I wanted to find a way to honor them," I said.

"We couldn't be prouder," Clodovea said, grinning widely with Imelda by her side.

"It reminds me so much of Saint Andrews," Imelda commented, and I smiled at the recognition.

That had been my intention with this place. Jelly barked, wagging her tail at the arrival of her friends. I was only sad that June was not here to share this moment with me. She'd gone back to Earth not long after the passing, with plans to return to the rescue for the time being and aid Octavia in data collection. Unsurprisingly, she had kept her promise to do whatever she could in the mortal realm as spirit healed itself. Octavia had also gotten a lesson from June in what true hard work looked like. I did not envy her.

I snickered, biting my lip at the times I'd found June so exasperating as a mortal.

I bent down to pet Jelly and glanced back at my family.

"You act like you didn't see them last night at dinner, little dragon," I said, laughing, but Blaz obliged her request to be the center of attention.

The outside was the same color as my beach bungalow and had the same beachy vibes, though it was made of much sturdier material.

"Want to see the inside?" I asked, and they all nodded.

I placed my immortal mark against the lock and swung the heavy white door open.

The inside housed a small waiting room with a fully stocked coffee bar.

"Of course, you already have a pot made," Oleander said, laughing.

"What's a little healing without liquid caffeine?" I asked, pouring the liquid nectar into a mug with sea turtles that I picked up from a local artisan market in Musterion. I'd bought ten different mugs, all with a unique story to tell, to keep here. I thought it was fitting in a place designed for people to tell their stories.

Just off the waiting room was a shop of sorts that housed a variety of charms to be worn on one of the bracelets or necklaces on the other rack. If those weren't appealing, there was also an assortment of rings.

"You're going to do some great work here, Zo," Elvy murmured from behind me, kissing my cheek.

"I just hope they will come," I whispered.

"They will," Freyja encouraged, and for some reason, I believed her.

The war had been won, but so many were still fighting battles no one else could see. And I intended to help them. If they'd let me. Elvy had agreed to give me extra healing through our flames on days I worked with others, refusing to let me burn out needlessly.

I was more grateful for him and in love with my star-chosen mate every single day.

He'd helped me create this little slice of a safe haven. It was next to the lighthouse, so immortals from both the above city of Vega and those in Musterion would have easy access to my practice.

I was happy to have a purpose outside of being the Lady Astral or Elvy's wife, or even Zoe Eferhild, Realm-Healer—Emerging of Legends. I was just Zoe.

And that was enough.

63

Epilogue
ZOE

ive Years Later

It had been some time since I'd felt the sand of Saint Andrews between my toes.

It had been even longer since I'd felt the warmth of the sun on my skin, and I lifted my head to embrace as much as I safely could.

I'd swung by my former home expecting to be filled with longing, but those walls no longer brought me the same sense of joy and peace they once had. Octavia and the rest of our court used the bungalow as they wished, and I was happy to share it with them.

Soft fur brushed against my shoulder, and I opened my eyes to find Jelly situating herself between Elvy and me.

"Throw the ball," she said, eyes glowing a slight orange in the rays of the sunset. The sky was painted with purple, orange, and yellow. The air smelled of saltwater and felt fresh against my skin.

"No flying this time," I said, laughing. "You'll freak out the humans."

Jelly turned her head, looking at me expectantly and not promising a single thing. I glanced at Elvy, who shrugged. He always gave in to what she wanted.

I laughed, pulling her favorite tennis ball from my satchel and throwing it towards Blaz, who seemed to be waiting for her. She deserved to have some fun after the work she puts into the healing practice. Unsurprisingly, Jelly had taken well to being the resident therapy dog, so attuned to other's emotions. I was happy that we had both found our places in this life.

Jelly took off at a speed that would rival even the most elite mortal dogs, and I raised a brow at Elvy.

"Seems Blaz and Jelly were in cahoots," I said, leaning my head on his shoulder.

"They always are," he agreed, laughing as Jelly leaped onto Blaz's chest while catching the ball midair.

Delmira roared with laughter as Blaz landed hard on the sand. The glitter of her engagement ring glistened with the catch of the sunlight, and I couldn't keep the smile from my face.

Delmira hadn't officially resigned as our second, but she had been on a five-year sabbatical and neither Elvy nor I wanted to rush her. Clodovea had moved into the second position in her absence and was doing a phenomenal job. With true peace in the star realms, Delm was free to take as much time as she needed to heal. I'd seen her for about two years for spirit healing treatments, and she rarely wore any of my charms these days, which made my heart glow with her happiness. She'd faced her trauma and had come out the victor.

Not long after our sessions had ended, she and Blaz had taken off to travel everywhere she'd wanted to visit and beyond. Blaz had popped the question in New Zealand a year ago, and as far as we all knew, no date had been set.

"Aunt Zo!" a tiny voice called, and a beautiful five-year-old girl with dimples and curly hair stumbled her way over to us.

"Charlie!" I squealed back, opening my arms for her to fall into. I wrapped her in my arms and brushed her nose, which was covered in sand. "What do you think?"

"Sand is fun!" she laughed, pointing at her mothers.

Clodovea and Imelda kneeled down in the sand and motioned for Charlie to come help them build a sand castle. Charlie screeched in excitement and ran as fast as her little legs would take her to her parents.

Imelda and Clodovea had adopted Charlie about a year after the war with Hesperia had ended. Her biological mother had lost her husband in the war, and I believe her grief overcame her. No matter her reasons, Charlie was well-loved and wanted for nothing.

Elvy and I had talked about children, and neither of us had any particular interest in bringing life into this world right now. Loving Charlie was enough for us, and she was reaping the spoils of that from all the Luminaries.

"Hey sis," Freyja said, sitting beside me, and Oleander plopped down on the sand next to her.

"I still hate sand," Oleander said, but there was a smirk on his lips and love in his eyes for my sister.

"Did Zadie and Finn come?" I asked, ignoring his snide remark.

"They did," Freyja said, nodding towards where Blaz and Delmira were playing with Jelly.

"I think that's the first time I've seen Zadie in another color besides black," I said, admiring the blue of her romper.

"Algol continues to… shift," Freyja answered. "For the better."

I laced my fingers through hers. "I'm glad."

"I'm glad you both could come," Elvy said, eyes flicking just past them. Delmira had Finn pinned, and I did not want to be on the end of whatever that chastising was. "Should I intervene?"

We all laughed as Finn got the upper hand. It didn't take long before they were laughing with each other good-naturedly.

I sensed a familiar presence behind me, and I grinned in recognition.

"Hey, June," I said as she took a seat around the fire pit.

"It's good to see you, kiddo," she said, stretching her hands near the fire to warm them. It was only October, but as the sun faded away, revealing the night sky, there was a coolness in the air.

"How's the rescue?"

"Slow," she said, smiling. "And that's not a bad thing."

"No," I agreed. "How are the other operations down here?" I asked.

We knew mending Algol back to the Kingdom of Canis was only the beginning of helping the mortals of Earth. Their spirit had been damaged so deeply by what Hesperia and the celestials had done. We'd accomplished what we could to aid them without intervening too much or taking away their free will.

"Excellent," she said, smiling so widely that the lines by her eyes deepened. "But I'll let the numbers girl tell you the stats."

Octavia appeared beside her and flipped open a notebook with rows upon rows of data across the page. I'd offer to get her something more technical, but she'd declined, stating that it was the Keeper's way. I feared Phoebe had a lot to do with that notion, but it wasn't for me to question.

"Crime rates are down globally," Octavia began. "Carbon emissions have decreased by forty percent, and new laws are being passed to help sustain this planet for future generations. Substance use is down so much that a significant percentage of treatment facilities have closed. People seem… happier."

I prayed for a world where someone could walk down the street and not fear for their safety, and humanity took collective responsibility for their mortal realm.

It seems our diligence has had a lasting impact, but our work here would likely never be finished.

"What's next?"

"Men still hunger for power. There are seeds of unrest. Getting a global compact for peace is still the goal, though I fear we are decades away from that coming to fruition."

"Then we keep hope alive for them, and we continue our duty," I said, meeting the eyes of those around me.

Oleander and Freyja nodded in agreement with me, and her cheeks flushed pink as his gaze lingered on hers. There was a lightness to Oleander that I'd never seen in him before Hesperia's demise. She laced her fingers through his, uniting their wedding band tattoos together, though she still wore her onyx engagement ring.

The spirit of Algol was shifting into what Sirius had always wanted for this realm. It was taking more time than any of us liked, but it was happening. That was all that mattered.

I glanced up at the night sky to find The Archer's constellation shining down upon us, as if to give us his blessing.

Elvy squeezed my arm, sending me a warm embrace through our flame. I missed my father and what could have been. I hoped he was at peace.

I'd read through the records that Octavia and Phoebe had kept of the final battle and what had happened since. Despite the deceit initially, Octavia had proven nothing but loyal to the Court of Vega and the mission to protect and serve immortals and mortals alike.

"Come on!" Blaz called and waved his hands wildly for us to join them on the beach volleyball court.

"I don't know if I can take Blaz sulking for a month if I beat him again," I said, laughing as I took Elvy's outstretched hand to help me up.

"Well, I certainly will take amusement in it," Oleander said, smiling.

It didn't take us long to ignite his wild antics, and Charlie seemed to find Uncle Blaz as amusing as the rest of us.

I looked into the eyes of everyone around me—my family. We'd all found each other when our souls needed to. We'd fought beside each other and were willing to die together.

Through it all, we'd grown together when evil had tempted us to give up.

I'd chosen them. And they'd chosen me.

I bent down to scratch Jelly's ears as I took in this moment.

I'd never been more grateful for choosing to embrace this life.

For moments like these.

I rose, staring at Blaz. "Girls against guys."

"You're on," he answered.

I smiled.

I'd emerged, refusing to let the darkness eclipse the light that lived within us all, so that I could embrace this moment in time.

Because it was not insignificant.

Acknowledgements

We did it. The Zoe Eferhild Chronicles has come to an end, but these characters will stay with me always, as I hope they will always stay with you. I am so humbled by the love and support I have felt across the globe. To imagine people reading this from all walks of life is a shock I will never recover from.

To my Heavenly Father for all the ways He has made the stars and moon comfort my soul. For the conviction to write this story.

To you, the reader, this entire series was a love letter to you. I hope you have felt seen by these characters and that you felt loved through these pages. I value your existence endlessly. I hope you fully embrace this life and all it has to give.

To my Mimi and Mom, who are always the first to read my books and listen to my ideas. Neither one of them has ever made me believe that any dream of mine was too large. I am grateful to have you both in my life.

To my husband, who is not a reader, but is still my number one fan in this life. I cherish you. You have never made me feel like I couldn't accomplish something. You are easy to dream big with.

Thank you to my long list of friends who have cheered me on from the beginning of this adventure. Special thank you's to Lisbeth and Kelby, who are my number one hype women for anything

I write. You two have kept me grounded when my headspace threatened to send me spiraling into doubt.

To my four dogs, whom I could always count on to snuggle beside me when writing. While you think you are lapdogs at eighty pounds, you are not, but I am so happy you kept my toes warm.

To the entire Indie Author community and the readers who support Indie Authors, you are the reason being an Indie Author is an amazing journey. Thank you.

About the author

E.C. Lawton is the author of The Zoe Eferhild Chronicles, which is her debut series. She writes books about mental health with a magical twist in an easy-to-read fantasy world. E.C. is also a psychology adjunct professor and therapist. When not writing, she can be found nose-deep in a book, adventuring outdoors with her husband, drinking too much coffee, listening to true crime podcasts, and hanging out with her wolf pack.

Make sure you subscribe to E.C.'s newsletter at her website, authoreclawton.com to stay up to date with new projects. E.C. is releasing a six-book contemporary romance series in 2027. Stay tuned!

Connect with E.C. on her socials at ec_lawton or via the QR code.

Also by

E.C. is currently developing a new high fantasy series, anticipated to come out in 2028! E.C. also has a six book small town romance series in the works for 2027. Make sure you are following her on all social media at ec_lawton to stay up to date. Subscribe to her newsletter at authoreclawton.com to learn about ARC and Street Team opportunities.

The Zoe Eferhild Chronicles is a completed trilogy in ebook, paperback, and hardback.